SEVEN SPRINGS

Lindsay Shayne

SEVEN SPRINGS

A Novel

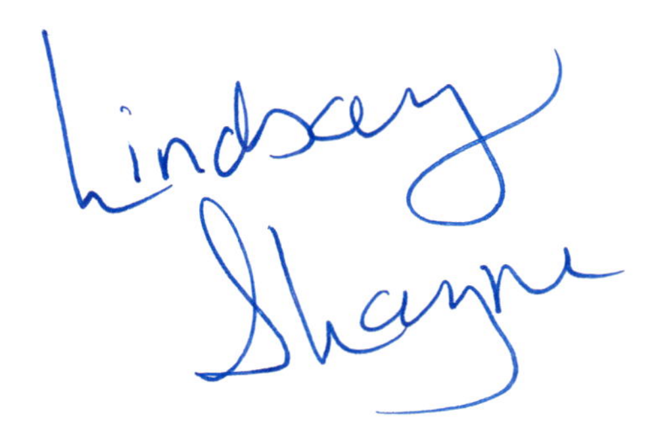

2017 Songbird Publishing Paperback Edition

Songbird Publishing
Edmonton, Alberta, Canada

Printed in the U.S.A.

ISBN-13: 978-1981177042
ISBN-10: 1981177043

Author's Note:

This novel is a work of fiction, and while many of the towns, corporations and individuals within are fictional, they represent the turmoil of the formative years of the District of Alberta and illustrate the struggle of those affected by the interprovincial and transcontinental rail lines.

Lindsay Shayne

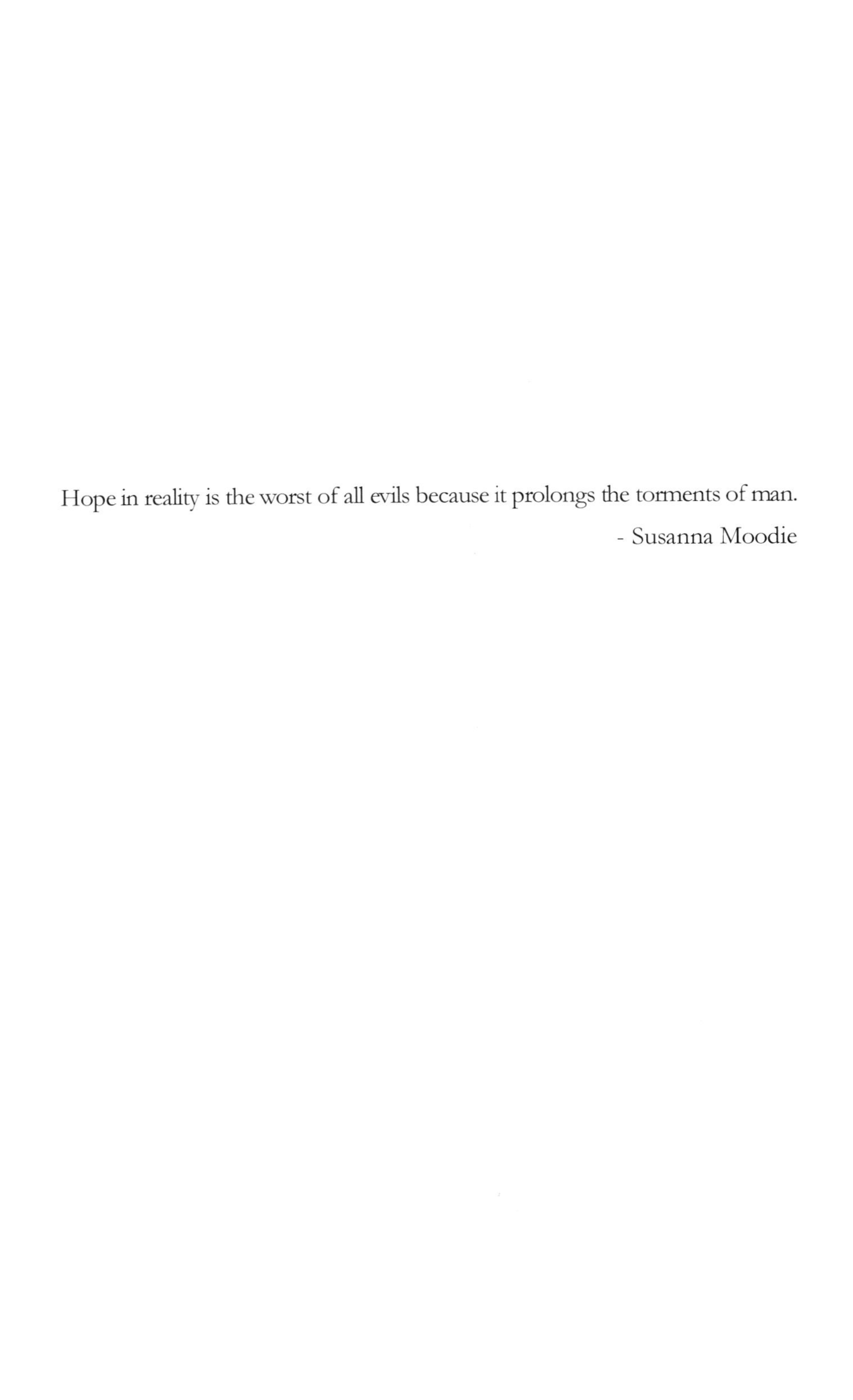

Hope in reality is the worst of all evils because it prolongs the torments of man.

- Susanna Moodie

Table of Contents

Spring, 1882

Spring, 1902

Spring, 1903

Spring, 1904

Spring, 1905

Spring, 1898

Chapter One

The reading of the will was scheduled to begin after tea and prior to the evening's dinner service. Charles had cleared out the lounge and arranged seating facing the large desk at the back of the room. No immediate family were expected to attend as Mr. Danbury was a bachelor, but Charles knew there were always those who descended upon the executors, waiting to peck at their share of the breadcrumbs.

The lawyer situated himself at the head of the room, organizing documents in front of him as citizens filed in. Charles ushered in the last of the patrons and seated himself in the first row. The anticipation of each person in attendance created a tension that was broken only by muffled whispers and the occasional sob. He peered behind his shoulder and scanned the crowd for any familiar faces; aside from a regular guest or two, he was unacquainted with the society around him. He turned back around in his chair and nodded to the lawyer who coughed briefly and thumbed the bridge of his spectacles before speaking.

"We are gathered here today regarding the disbursements of the estate of Knox Samuel Danbury, this day, April 3rd, 1898. As to his last will and testament, he bequeaths the following: fifty dollars to Seamus McCann, gardener and caretaker of his estate; fifty dollars to Eliza Potter, housekeeper; and five hundred dollars to Charles Prescott, general manager of this hotel. The remainder is hereby left to Angus Martin Danbury, his relation in Exeter. Disbursements of the funds shall be forthcoming within the week with the deed to the estate being transferred concurrently."

The lawyer spoke without emotion, and the party left the room as quickly as they had entered it. The shuffle of their footsteps pounded through Charles' ears, and he wished he could cover them to block out the sound. He stood for a moment alone, staring at the hurried pattern of the red damask rug underfoot. The snap of a closing portfolio brought him out of his reverie, and he rushed to stop the lawyer before he left.

"Beg pardon, sir," he said, touching the man on the shoulder. "What is to become of...?"

"Your cheque will be posted shortly, as I said. All in good time, lad," the lawyer said without stopping his exit.

"No, I mean...I am referring to the hotel, to my position as manager of this hotel," he said as he moved in front of the lawyer to halt him.

"That would depend on the owner. I suppose your fate is in his hands now," he said, pushing past Charles and continuing on his way. "I would expect him to sell, however. They always sell."

Charles felt the cold sweat begin to bead upon his skin; the dark hair at his temples became damp. He hurried into the lobby, turning and jostling as each guest passed by in their turn. The hectic pace nauseated him, and so he made his way out of the foyer to keep from fainting.

"Mr. Prescott, could you help me for a moment?" the front desk clerk asked as he struggled to organize the patrons who were waiting to check in.

"One moment, Andrew. I need a moment." Charles rushed past the front desk and barrelled through the swinging door to the kitchen. Andrew stood still with confusion, for his manager had never been one to leave guests waiting.

"Good day, Mr. Prescott," rang out from all corners of the kitchen as staff paused their duties to greet him.

"Yes," he said, as it was the only reply he could manage. He could feel the tension building in his chest - a rapid pounding progressing from his heart to his head. The smell of stewing rabbit caused a churn in his stomach and intense salivation at the back of his mouth. He moved through the array of cooks and servers, around the banquet supplies, chafing dishes, crystal and china and into the adjacent laundry room. The drastic change in temperature and the intense moisture that hung in the air caused him to sweat profusely. His eyes darted back and forth as he searched the perimeter for the exit. He bumped into passing staff and bins of starched white linens as he tried to escape.

"Beg pardon," he said, turning in apology to a hanging sack of laundry. He tried to orient himself but the room was now spinning, and the loosening of his collar and ascot did little to revive his senses. He lifted the cool iron latch on the back door and leaned his entire weight forward to open it.

The brisk morning air of the alley struck him instantly, causing him to lose his balance and fall into an apple crate seat next to a burgeoning family of rats. He closed his eyes and breathed deeply. Now faced with the reek of the garbage pile, he longed for the scent of the stew. The embroidered handkerchief he removed from his breast pocket was now drenched, and would do little to draw up his sorrow. With elbows on knees and head in hands, Charles' entire body began to quiver as the tears sprang forth.

Heaving sobs were reserved for private, often in instances of a close family death or bankruptcy. For Charles, however, the life he had envisioned for himself and the comfortable existence he had afforded his wife and daughter were all but lost. The pittance would not allow for any luxury or continuance of their current status. It would throw his family into poverty in short order. He had incurred a large amount of debt over the years in an attempt to provide a place in society for his wife. Although Abigail was not excessively wealthy, she was accustomed to her status as a merchant's daughter. Charles' mismanagement of her inheritance and thoughtless spending had rendered her small fortune to almost nothing, save for a hundred dollar dowry set aside for their daughter. As he wiped down his short beard with his sweaty palm, he ran through the numbers in his head. The debts to be paid and the funds available danced in his mind like an innocent young lady and an unwanted suitor.

"How do I explain this to Abigail?" he asked himself, wringing his hands together so tightly that his knuckles burned white. He swallowed hard in an attempt to rid his throat of the solid lump that was lodged there and shook his head as if trying to rearrange the figures back into the black. He stood quickly and steadied himself on the brick wall when he heard the latch lift on the heavy door.

"Mr. Prescott. Whatever are you doing out here?" the young porter asked, removing his pillbox hat and taking up the seat that his superior had abandoned. He pulled a cigarette out of his pocket and offered it to Charles who stood motionless against the wall beside him.

"No thank you, Timothy, I am feeling quite out of sorts today."

"You just need some tea and biscuits, sir. Give you the strength to face the day."

"I shall heed that advice. Thank you, lad." Charles straightened his sack coat and returned inside the hotel. He entered the lobby and was drawn to the front desk by the Morse Code of Andrew's pencil tapping repeatedly on the booking ledger.

"All the reservations have been checked in, sir. The empty rooms are prepared and lay in wait."

"I am afraid I must depart, Andrew. I am feeling unwell. Please see that the guests are well taken care of. Mr. Dupuis can give you a hand. I ask that you do not contact me unless it is an absolute emergency."

"Very good, sir," Andrew said while trying to ascertain in Charles' looks any cause for alarm. He had never known Mr. Prescott to be ill in the eight years under his employ.

* * *

Abigail's bedchamber was empty that morning, as it had been in the early hours of nearly every morning since her marriage. Now, nearly twelve years later, she fully understood that the long hours Charles spent at the hotel were for their family's benefit. The birds outside of her window sung a familiar tune, a bright melody that would raise even the most weary. She stretched and sighed as she ambled to the open panes. The breeze flitted her thin cotton nightgown with a breath of lilac fresh off the bloom.

The side garden was an area full of activity amongst the first dew drops of spring. The songbirds were gathered in the large willow tree. Abigail often sang to the birds, and it pleased her when they answered her call, an orchestra of chirps and coos prompting her to continue. She rested her hands on the windowsill and leaned forward, extending into the cool morning air. She released a melody that could be heard out to the lane on the other side of the house, greeting passersby and rousing the household as it resonated through the walls.

Emma was already awake. Now roused by the sound of her mother's voice, she pulled her ashen curls into a low ponytail and secured it loosely with a ribbon. She hurried to the master bedroom for a closer audience. She paused for a second at the tall wooden doors before her soft rap elicited a response from within.

"Come in, my love," Abigail said, maintaining her position at the window.

"Do not stop, Mama," Emma said, pushing the door open and rushing to her mother's side.

"Perhaps the birds would like to revel in their own song," Abigail said, stroking her daughter's face and taking a place beside her in the window seat.

"Why would they want that? I think they see you as their big mama bird! Please, sing some more."

As Abigail began to sing, Emma rested her cheek against her mother's bosom, rising and gently falling with each breath she took. She could feel the vibrations of sound moving up through the depths of her mother's chest, past her lips and into the wind. The tunes were English folk songs, many of which Abigail learned from her own mother. Simple songs, yet true in meaning and melody. Although Emma was too young to discern the deep lyric meaning of those songs, the haunting emotions in each phrase impacted her as though she had lived through those feelings herself. As she sang, Abigail rocked her daughter gently and closed her eyes to concentrate on the rhythm of her heart.

"Which birds are those, Mama?" Emma asked, distracted by the smaller birds flying between the trees.

"Sparrows, I believe."

"They are lovely, but they do not sing nearly as well as you."

"Each creature is unique and each voice is their own."

"But some voices, like the crows, do not have beauty. They have squawk."

"Other crows recognize that voice as one of their own and welcome it. To them, it's beautiful."

Abigail was busy with preparations for the supper she had planned to celebrate Charles' good fortune. The party of six was to include the Dorchesters and the Becks. Josephine Dorchester was a childhood friend of Abigail's, but the infrequency of their visits frayed the close bond they had shared in their youth. They enjoyed each other's company, but the nature of their husbands' work and their obligations in society left little chance for an intimate friendship. The Becks were more acquainted with Charles and owned a fine hotel in the city's Inner Harbour.

The windows on the main floor of the house had been opened to allow the crisp spring air to freshen the dining room. Emma was seated in her favourite corner of the library with her prized volume of *Audubon's Birds* resting heavily on her lap. She carefully turned the pages of the fine gift from her mother, given to her the previous fall for her eleventh birthday. She ran her plump fingers over the colourful lithographs and explored the nature of the continent through its illustrations. She glanced up occasionally to watch her mother scuttle about in the adjacent room.

"Over here please, Margaret," Abigail called out to the housekeeper who was weighed down with a large bouquet of white lilacs. Every few moments, she would pass by the door giving orders or carrying an object to put in its place. Emma knew to keep her distance during these types of preparations, as her mother was meticulous in how she liked things arranged.

Margaret grabbed the edge of the freshly pressed table cloth and tossed it out in front of her. The air caught it and waved it outwards, so it billowed and fell into place on the large cherry wood surface. Abigail helped to situate it symmetrically and insisted on setting her own table. The gold-leafed chargers were placed down first, followed by the china, crystal and silver. She inspected each piece individually, careful that her society guests would not be affronted by a dirty knife or goblet. She retrieved the vase of lilacs from the sideboard and cautiously placed it in the middle of the spread. She carefully inspected each place setting, making small adjustments if they were at all out of line.

"Everything looks splendid, Mama," Emma said from the doorway, swishing her periwinkle dress as she stood.

"Thank you, my love. I want everything to be well when your father arrives. Today is an important day, and I know his mind will be much occupied in dealing with his new role as owner of the hotel."

Emma followed her mother into the kitchen. Abigail placed the apron's linen band over her head and turned to prompt Emma to tie the straps at the small of her back with a giant bow.

"May I not dine with you all tonight? I would so much like to attend Papa's party."

"Not tonight, my love. There are many things that Papa and I would like to discuss with our guests. Matters that do not concern young ladies," she said, leading Emma through the house to the side garden.

"I should so very much like a party," she said in a huff as she sat down on the bench under the willow tree. Abigail smiled, embraced her and gave her a kiss on the forehead.

"Tomorrow, when the excitement has died down, what would you say to having our own party? Just the three of us. We could have roasted pork."

"And whipped potatoes?"

"And long green beans."

"And lemon curd tartlets?"

"With raspberry cream," said Abigail, smiling.

"I can hardly wait until tomorrow, Mama. So much to look forward to!"

"There now, would you like to help me gather some more flowers? Margaret was quite right. We need more colour."

Chapter Two

Charles left the hotel and turned down Barrie Street towards the park in the centre of town. He had removed the keys from the small box under his office desk and opened his safe before leaving, taking with him a thin stack of Northern York Railway stocks. He held the parchment in his hands and carried on through the park, greeting passersby with a nod of his head and abbreviated smile.

The offices of Brookworth and Wade were situated on King Street near the wharf. The smell of industry hung low in the city's mercantile region and Charles hastened his pace into the building to escape the stench. The tiny office was full and the speculators were packed tighter than the kippers from the shoreline factories. Investment houses had become commonplace with interests ranging from local importers to the search for a northwest passage. Charles pushed through the crowd and made his way to the reception desk. The clerk peered over his spectacles and set down his pencil.

"How can I help, sir," he said as the impatience strained his voice.

"I am looking to discuss my stocks here. I need to know their value. I may need to sell."

The clerk moved quickly and swiped the stocks from his hand. He opened the folded papers and scanned the heading for the company name. *Northern York Railway* was imprinted across the top, with the number of shares listed below. He thumbed each slip, recording in his mind the figure in each corner. The clerk could not move his eyes from the documents and quietly excused himself. He moved to the room in the rear and knocked on the door just below the brass plate embossed with the senior partner's name.

"Yes, yes. Come in," the voice said. The clerk motioned for Charles to come forward. He snaked through the melee towards the open door. A plump man was seated behind a long mahogany desk piled high with files and forms. Charles seated himself opposite the man and looked around at the mounds of paper piled upon any available surface in the room. Cigar smoke floated from Mr. Wade's mouth and encircled his stout face before exiting through the nearest window.

"I see you have some shares in the Northern York. You purchased them in the summer of '87, I see."

"Yes, I purchased them upon marriage. Now that I am in need of funds, I am thankful I had the foresight to invest."

"I have some sad news about your stocks, young man. The Northern York has long since been abolished. It was taken over by the bankrupt Eastern Atlantic some years ago. The stock has no value, I'm afraid. I am sorry to be the bearer of this news, but we would not be willing to offer you anything."

Mr. Wade watched as Charles' demeanour altered. He had entered the room hopeful, but with each second he sat in the hazy room, his situation became more dire. The tick of the hands on the grandfather clock strained with impatience as Charles extended his own to thank the gentleman for his assistance.

The sting of the wrought iron railing on the street-side stairs caused his heart to jump, and so he thumped down on his bottom and closed his eyes to quell the nausea. He had purchased the stock with most of Abigail's dowry and had not informed her of the expenditure. He was told previously by Mr. Danbury that stocks were the only sound and secure investment; his steadfast mentorship meant his advice was law. Charles paused for a moment and drew his breath, unable to shake the feeling that he would soon be forced to divulge his shortcomings to his beloved wife. He wondered for a moment how he would break the news to her that the home they lived in would go to the inheritor, and within a week he would have no income to speak of.

He pulled at the chain that hung from his vest pocket and pulled out his watch. The afternoon was dwindling, but there were still a good many hours before he was expected home for supper. He gathered the strength to stand and brushed the dust from his backside. He scanned the shopfronts for a familiar sign to establish the direction to Shelby House. He hurried along the avenue towards his home knowing that no matter the speed of his stride, he would never outpace his debtors. The money he would receive from Mr. Danbury's estate would cover his outstanding debts, but he would be left with little more than half to live on.

The garden wrapped around Shelby House like a horseshoe, embracing the brick façade with flowers and foliage. The yard extended out the back and was separated from the neighbour's property by a waist-high fence. The ornate filigree barrier continued around the perimeter and flanked the house to the front gate. Charles stood on the opposite side of Johnson Street, camouflaged by the bustle of neighbours walking the boulevard that afternoon. He walked several steps in one direction, craned his head towards his garden, and then turned around fully to retrace his steps. As he paced, he watched Abigail and Emma through those perfunctory glances, unsure of how to approach them.

"Whatever will we do?" Charles repeated to himself under his breath, unconcerned with how he would be perceived by his neighbours as he engaged in solitary conversation. He stopped for a moment to face the house directly. The carriages charged past in both directions, preventing him from crossing and providing him more time to gather his thoughts and breath.

The bundle of fresh flowers grew in Emma's arms; bluebells, violets and begonias created a colourful tapestry against her pale skin.

"Shall we pick some roses? This is a special event tonight," she said.

"That is a splendid idea, my love," Abigail said as she moved to the large yellow rose bush on the right side of the house. As she leaned down to cut a few stems for her bouquet, she caught sight of Charles standing motionless across the street.

"Charles!" she said with a wave and smile, a motion echoed by Emma who skipped up behind her.

"Why is Papa not at the hotel?"

"I am curious to learn the reason myself."

Charles waited a moment before crossing the busy thoroughfare, not only to ensure his safety but to give him more time to prepare for the interrogation.

"Why are you home so early? This is a lovely surprise," Abigail said, leaning over to kiss his cheek when he arrived at the gate.

"It is a beautiful day. It is the perfect time to spend with my ladies."

"Look at all of the flowers we have gathered for your party, Papa," Emma said as she thrust the bouquet in her father's direction. Charles resisted the panic that was creeping back into his thoughts as he realized he had forgotten about the evening's event.

"How nice, petty. They will do very well," he said with a forced calmness, bending down to give her a kiss on the cheek. "May I have some daisies too?"

"Daisies? They are too plain, Papa. Perhaps some lilies?"

"That would be perfect," he said as he took Abigail's hand in his.

"I will find you the biggest and most colourful lilies in our garden," she said, exchanging the bundle of flowers for the scissors in her mother's hand and dashing to the lily patch on the other side of the house.

"I wondered if you'd come home when you heard the news. How wonderful, Charles. It is all turning out as we planned."

"I must speak with you, Abigail. There have been some rather unfortunate developments in regards to the inheritance," he said as they ambled to the bench in the shade.

"Whatever is the matter, Charles?" she said, searching his eyes for answers. She understood that excision from the will was a possibility, but Charles had never considered it, for he fervently trusted Mr. Danbury's word.

"It will come as a great shock, and I fear telling you for all of the implications this news brings."

"Have you been cut out?" she asked as she squeezed his hand firmly. Charles released a deep sigh as if her intuitive questioning had relieved him of the burden of telling her.

"I was left five hundred, but half of that is already accounted for."

"What is to become of the hotel?" she asked calmly.

"I am not entirely certain. The lawyer informed us that the estate was bequeathed to an English relation."

"Oh, Charles."

"While there is a possibility that I may be retained to run The Danbury, the lawyer stressed that the new owner will likely sell. If that is the case, I doubt I will ever meet the man who is responsible for extinguishing my livelihood. I am so very sorry, my dear. I never imagined fate would deal me so unlucky a hand."

Charles looked at his wife with pain and regret and averted his eyes when the same feelings became visible in hers. Abigail thought immediately of Emma. She rose from her seat and broke the bond of reassurance that Charles tried to provide through his touch.

"Abby," he said as he rose to follow her quick strides along the side of the house. She stopped at the corner and braced herself against the rough brick, her yellow dress flapping against the stone and dampening the sound of his approaching footsteps. She watched her daughter as she hunched over the lily patch, shearing the stems close to the root.

"What are we to do?" Abigail asked as Charles embraced her around the waist from behind. He buried his face in her hair and inhaled deeply. The scent of almonds was intoxicating and for a moment he was unable to comprehend the question she was asking. She turned to face him and asked again.

"I can hardly think, let alone determine the next course of action."

"Can we not just pay the monthly dues to his relation and stay on here? It would be cruel to move Emma from her friends and school."

"This home was a provision from Mr. Danbury while I managed the hotel. We cannot afford to stay here on our own."

Chapter Three

The smells emanating from the kitchen were savoury intermingled with the subtle sweetness of Abigail's famous raisin pudding. The scent of roasted lamb hung in the air and filled the house with a sense of occasion and welcome. The party was expected to arrive any moment, and with Emma in her nursery and Margaret putting the final touches on the main course, Charles and Abigail found they had but a few moments to collect themselves before their guests' arrival.

"I hardly know what I will say to Edwin. He will certainly ask about the hotel. How do I spare myself from the humiliation?" Charles poured himself a glass of sherry. "Perhaps they have already heard, and I will be saved from relaying the news."

"That could very well be. So, we can either acknowledge our misgivings honestly or put it off knowing that they may see through our avoidance of the subject." Abigail softly kissed his cheek and gave his arm a squeeze. "I think we should opt for the former."

"Yes, you are right. It will be more difficult to bear the truth if we try to hide it."

The brass bell beside the doorway echoed through the foyer, followed by three hearty raps in succession. Herbert, the man Charles hired specifically for the occasion, greeted the Becks as they entered. They were from one of the most prominent hotelier families in the region, speculating in real estate and charging themselves with the running of The Charlotte, the most prestigious hotel in the city. While they could be viewed as rivals of old Mr. Danbury, Edwin Beck and Charles found much common ground and had formed a fast friendship in the early days of his apprenticeship.

"How do you do, Charles? Looking well, I see," Edwin said, handing his overcoat and hat to Herbert. Abigail stood demurely next to her husband, waiting to greet the wives.

"Jean, you look lovely this evening. Emerald green is so becoming on you," she said, offering the compliment with a sincerity rarely found amongst women in competition for the most admired in the room.

The Dorchesters arrived soon after. Abigail fidgeted with her ring as Josephine and her husband Francis ascended the steps. Before learning Charles' news, she was excited for them to share in her family's good fortune. Now she yearned to cower behind the brocade drapes for fear of their reactions.

"So lovely to see you, Abigail," Josephine said, taking her friend's hands.

"Yes, it has been far too long," Abigail said as she ushered her guests into the drawing room.

The feeling amongst the guests was electric in anticipation of Charles' announcement. The attitudes of the hosts were more subdued, however, with their painted smiles and forced joviality. The party picked up on their feelings shortly after their arrival, with Edwin drawing the room's attention to Charles.

"Why the long face, my boy? Surely the world is not quite so heavy," he said with a slap to his friend's back.

"My apologies. I have many things on my mind at present. I think the most pressing is that lamb," Charles said in a weak attempt at deflection.

"It was very busy at the hotel today, was it not my dear? Charles sometimes has difficulty relaxing in the evenings," Abigail said, suddenly in support of her husband's suggestion to conceal the truth.

"That is understandable," Francis said. "It is often difficult to break the ties of our employ when we return home each night. I spent far too much time at the office in my youth, but I have learned that family comes first."

Abigail resented the implication that Charles' main priority was not his family. She knew full well that the time and effort he dedicated to his business was a direct correlation to the dedication he had to his family.

"Yes of course," Charles said as he cast his eyes downward to his feet. "I suppose we are all entitled to our bad days, Frank. But enough of this gloom. How are you all getting along?"

The party was seated in the dining room and the first course was well under way when Edwin brought forth the question that Charles had been dreading since their arrival.

"So Charles, any grand plans for The Danbury now that you're at the helm? Perhaps you will sell and move to the continent? It must be thrilling to be young with so many opportunities available to you. What I wouldn't give to have my youth again," he said, turning to his wife with a smile.

The question was consistent with the expectant looks from most everyone around the table. Charles shuffled uncomfortably in his chair and searched for an excuse. He glanced at Abigail beside him and her kind eyes reminded him that the truth might be the easiest way to bear these tidings. He swallowed hard, cleared his throat and closed his eyes tight in an attempt to organize his thoughts. All eyes were focused on him and he returned each one of their looks in turn as he spoke.

"Travelling to the continent would be fine, indeed, but…" Charles paused for a moment and felt Abigail's hand rest gently on his arm. "There have been some developments. I am afraid the hotel is not mine after all."

Gasps were heard from the ladies and the gentlemen's confusion contorted their faces.

"Whatever do you mean? Was it not understood that The Danbury would pass to you?" Francis asked.

"I see now that I may have been naive in that assumption. It has been two years since Mr. Danbury made that assertion. I did not feel it would be right to address the issue with him while he was ill. I have been left but a small sum. The remainder of the estate has been left to a relation." Charles stared down at his plate and poked the jiggling aspic with his fork.

"It is all so shocking," Josephine said as she turned to her friend to offer her condolences. "Whatever shall you do? Will Charles remain on as manager?"

"I should imagine not," Charles interjected. "I should think you would be very well pleased, Edwin. I doubt you will have much competition in the city when the hotel closes."

"He means to close? Perhaps some good will come of this after all," Jean said, being more direct in her enthusiasm than her husband.

"Hold your tongue, Jeanie. There is little joy in profiting from another's misfortune," Edwin said.

"Perhaps we can take you on, Charles," Jean said in an attempt to soften her hasty response.

Charles could feel the colour in his face redden at the suggestion that he might be employed under a man who was considered his equal just moments before.

"That is very kind, but since the news just came forth today, we need some time to discuss our options and determine the best course of action. This may be our last party at Shelby House, so please, let us enjoy our supper."

After the last of the celebratory champagne was drunk, the men moved to the study for brandy while the ladies moved to the drawing room for port and conversation. Abigail seated herself on the large sofa while her two guests sat in the high backed chairs on either side. The mood was sombre as Jean made an effort to condole with her hostess.

"I am sorry if I offended you and Charles earlier, Abigail. Sometimes my mouth speaks before my mind understands what I am saying. I truly meant no disrespect," she said, taking a long, slow sip from her glass. Abigail smiled and shook her head. She understood Mrs. Beck's feelings, as it was a natural impulse to seek out personal benefit in any situation.

"Please do not worry yourself, Jean. In all honesty, when we learned of Mr. Danbury's illness, it was impossible not to think of the financial implications. It was foolhardy to have planned our future on the verbal promise of inheritance.

"You would not be the first," Josephine said, moving from her chair to claim a seat beside Abigail. "I cannot bear to think of you leaving this lovely home. Where will you go?"

"That I am unsure of. I doubt it will be in Sydenham, though. Mr. Danbury was more than generous to let us this house, but without a large income, we simply cannot afford it."

"Surely there is no need to fear," Jean said. "Charles will have no trouble securing employment in any number of hotels in town."

Abigail held back her tears at Jean's remark. Her friends were kind, but they were naive in their belief that Charles would be willing to engage in employment below the station he was trained for. He had navigated the ranks for close to twenty years, first as an apprentice to Mr. Le Mont in Toronto and then to Mr. Danbury upon marriage. He was a master of his trade, and Abigail knew he would be reluctant to accept a position below his current role.

"Do not fret, my dear. Charles can begin to make inquiries in the morning," Josephine said. "There's always The Welly or The Brock. Perhaps he could be a dormitory master at Queen's."

Abigail did not hold her company in reproach for their suggestions, although the thought of Charles commanding a dormitory full of young men was nearly enough to make her smile.

"I wonder if I should start making inquiries as well."

"Charles should have ample time to seek out work and secure a new home. That is not your responsibility," Jean said.

"I mean inquires for myself. If we are to have a change in status, perhaps it is only appropriate that I look for work as well," Abigail said, unable to comprehend the words that came forth from her own mouth.

"You, work? Whatever for? Come now, Abigail, be reasonable. I understand that today's events have come as a shock to you, but certainly things will never be so dire that you would have to work," Josephine said.

"Maybe if I could secure a little extra income, we would be able to stay in the neighbourhood."

"Even if you were to entertain such an idea, what on earth would you think of doing? Do you have any skills beyond your ability to set a lovely table?"

"I can bake a little," Abigail said sheepishly.

"And I suppose you can embroider shawls and festoon your own hats. Well then, a tradeswoman you shall be," Josephine said with a laugh. "Honestly, Abigail. Your occupation is to ensure that Charles has everything he needs to do his. The rest is up to him."

Upstairs, the men had gathered in the study. Surrounded by dark wood and the deep orange flicker of the fire, Charles poured out the brandy and passed an overly full glass to both of his friends.

"Drink will only dull the pain, my boy," Edwin said as he inspected his glass in the firelight before sitting down near the hearth.

"It is rather nice," Francis said, as he took a sip from his glass and took the seat opposite. Charles remained standing, teetering about with an agitated stance. He never really moved anywhere, but rather shifted his weight from one foot to another.

"Come now, Charles. Do sit down and join us. It does little good to fret about it now," Edwin said.

"How does one not fret?" Charles said, taking the last seat in the semi-circle. "I cannot escape from thoughts of ruination, poverty and harm coming to my family."

"Now is the time to start weighing your options. Have you anything in mind?" Francis asked.

"I have been mulling around the prospect of a café or perhaps a shop. We could live above stairs with Emma."

"What do you know of running a shop?" Edwin asked. "A café might be a better prospect, but you are not a restauranteur. Besides, you know the money is not made on the food, it's made on the lodgings. Why not start a place of your own?"

"Of course, a hotel of our own. We could move out of Sydenham altogether and take over one of the manors in Alwington. It should only cost twenty or thirty thousand, but it will put me in direct competition with you, so perhaps it would be worth the expenditure." Charles chuckled at the absurdity of the proposal.

"Who said anything about Kingston?"

"Where then, Toronto? Montreal? The quickest way to dwindle funds is to relocate."

"Have you considered one of the districts? There are seemingly endless opportunities for young men who are willing to work hard."

"I am hardly young, Edwin."

"Younger than the two of us," he said, spurring one of the few laughs shared by anyone that evening.

"The railway has cut through the districts, and will likely open up the whole region," Francis said.

"Yes, I have heard talk from some of the guests passing through the hotel, and in *The Whig*, of course. It seems they are desperate to expand."

"Desperate times?" Charles said.

"Perhaps this is the sort of opportunity that could benefit you," Edwin said.

"Surely you do not mean for me to homestead."

"There must be a need for hoteliers in those areas, what with the transients and settlers," Francis said.

"That could very well be, but we hardly have the means to build a hotel."

"What about foreclosures? You know as well as I do how difficult it is to make a hotel a success. With your experience and Abigail's help, you could make a go of it, certainly," Edwin said.

Charles was at once flattered and sceptical of their assurances. "If others have failed, what makes them so sure that I will be different?" he wondered. He had experience on his side, but that did him little good without the funds to support it. He leaned back in his chair and took a long, slow draw from his cigar. As he sat, flanked by two men with more money than he could spend in two lifetimes, he wondered if it was possible to make a living out of virtually nothing. He had read numerous accounts of men taking their chances on the frontier and making a fortune, but he had also heard of men who thought they could farm without proper equipment or who trudged up to the Yukon without so much as a pair of boots. As he watched the log crackle and burn from charcoal to ashen white, he pondered his options.

"'The Prescott' has a nice ring to it, does it not?" Francis said, encouragingly.

"You're a steady chap. You can take on a challenge," Edwin said.

"A challenge," Charles said. "Yes, I believe that from this day forward my life will be a challenge, indeed."

The conversation with the ladies had lifted Abigail's spirits, but by the time the party left just after midnight, both she and Charles were left mentally fatigued.

"I am sorry, my dear. Our situation is not playing out in the way I had planned," Charles said, pulling back the lace coverlet and settling into bed. Abigail moved in close and rested her head upon his chest. She moved her hand across his belly in small circles, in an attempt to soothe him.

"All is not so bad," she said. "The ladies were quite supportive, even when I brought forward some possibilities for my occupation."

"Your occupation? Whatever do you mean?" Charles said as he sat up in bed.

"Well, it is not improbable that I will be required to work in order to provide a little extra income. As I said earlier, I will not starve in order to feed my pride."

"I doubt we will ever be in so dire a situation that you will be required to work. Your main task is the rearing of Emma. Since our status will change, we will have to dismiss Margaret. I suppose you will be charged with running the household as well."

"I cannot help but worry about how we will manage. Did Edwin happen to offer you employment? I know I should not expect him to bail us out, but is that not the purpose of rich friends?"

"He made no offer other than his advice."

Charles hesitated for a moment and examined Abigail's face in the lamplight. The soft amber glow highlighted the fine lines around her mouth which always grew deeper as she smiled. Although she was merely smirking at the snobbery of his friend, Charles wondered if she would ever know joy again.

"Have you thought about the possibility of relocating?" he said.

"I have hardly had the chance to think at all, Charles. Where do you have in mind?"

"Edwin suggested moving out west, perhaps to start our own hotel."

The shock of the proposal was evident in the wideness of Abigail's eyes. She repositioned herself on the bed in order to face him directly.

"How far west?" she asked, praying that he meant only as far as Toronto or Windsor.

"To the frontier."

She took a deep breath and leaned back on her pillow. She gazed up at the moulded ceiling, the shadows increasing the depth and detail of the pattern. As her eyes ran over the filigreed maze, she wondered if the tracks that crisscrossed the lands west of Ontario swirled to into each other or if they ran in rigid lines towards a finite destination.

"Edwin suggested one of the districts," Charles said cautiously. "They are offering land cheaply and he informed me that there may be an opportunity to purchase a small hotel or other existing building for a reasonable rate. It seems like a solid idea."

Abigail said nothing for a moment as the idea of leaving her hometown played out in her mind. With her parents passed on and no other family, there was little keeping her in Kingston other than her daughter's comfort and her friendship with Josephine.

"What will become of Emma? It seems a punishment to remove her from the only home she has known."

"Kingston is all any of us have known for so long. But we cannot let fear or uncertainty prevent us from making a life for ourselves."

"Perhaps we can stay in Ontario. Surely there has to be work available somewhere?"

Charles felt her trepidation burn into him. While he was also uncertain, he expected to be trusted with bringing forth an option that was in the best interest of his family.

"You have heard about the developments in the area, have you not? With the expansion of the railway, there will certainly be no shortage of visitors."

"Do we have enough funds to make the move?" she asked as she brought the covers in close under her chin.

"After my debts are paid and we book a passage, we should have enough to purchase a small hotel on a decent portion of land. That is why Edwin's suggestion seems reasonable. I simply cannot beat the rates. I would still be a hotel owner, just in a different location."

"Are there hotels available in the region?" she asked, wondering how they expected to make a living if the previous owners were unable to make it a success.

"He assured me that there must be. I believe the key is that I have a great deal of experience in this field, where others may have not. It is easy enough to throw money at a venture, but without the knowledge gained from previous failings and successes, it is no wonder that some were unable to make a go of it. If you are not opposed to the idea, I shall start making inquiries tomorrow."

Abigail fell silent for a moment as she considered the words the ladies had spoken earlier that evening. There was no better time to offer her love and support; she would do what she could to ensure he maintained confidence in his decisions about their future.

"I am not opposed, Charles. I would follow you anywhere, as you are well aware," she said as she nestled into a comfortable repose with Charles' arms wrapped around her. "Will you be returning to the hotel in the morning?"

"I expect I must. It would be prudent to have a definitive answer about my fate and the future of the hotel."

"Try to find some sleep, my love. Tomorrow will come soon enough."

Chapter Four

Word came through the hotel's telegraph just after nine o'clock that morning. Charles had spent the majority of the previous night wondering about the man who would take over the hotel and if he held any remorse for so negatively affecting the lives of so many. He moved through his duties in a subdued sort of trance and his staff could sense his taciturn disposition.

The wire was simple, yet direct:

-- *Reservations to stop immediately. Last guests to leave within the week. Hotel will cease operations. Letter to follow. A. Danbury.* --

The contents of the telegram left little room for interpretation. After his staff were informed of the change in ownership and the plan to close The Danbury, Charles was confronted with the reality of the situation. A part of him had hoped that the hotel would remain open and he would keep his position. A fleeting sense of gratitude soon followed as he was removed from the unfavourable dynamic of working under a man whose ideas and processes would be unfamiliar and contrary to his own. He understood that a man's success is not so much defined by the amount of money he can earn, but in the amount of control he maintains over his own life.

Charles left the hotel just before luncheon and moved through the Inner Harbour at a distracted pace. He settled in at City Park with a view of the cricket fields across the lane. He wagered that a copy of *The Whig* and a quiet bench would be the ideal way to get a better understanding of his prospects.

The paper was thick and dense with stories and details of the many trials surrounding the railway and the transcontinental expansion to the west. The tales were interspersed with politics and provided lofty accounts of the rampant prosperity and fistfuls of money to be earned in the region. Charles knew better than to believe wholeheartedly the accounts inked on those pages, for it was common knowledge that only the most sensational reports were printed. Good stories sold newspapers, and he was not going to allow himself to be blinded by empty promises.

The middle section of the paper was dedicated to advertisements. They ran the gamut from small, local sales inquiries to full page postings with etchings of railway cars, grand mountain ranges and vast expanses of open water. One of the more prominent announcements featured a beaver chomping through the words, "Be a busy beaver! Claim 64 acres for only $10." Charles dismissed those deals for he had neither the experience nor inclination to transform a forested lot into an area fit for farming. He turned the page and his eyes darted to an advertisement for a real estate broker out of Calgary.

Foreclosed buildings and properties for sale.

Cash up front. Immediate possession.

Lots available in d. of Assiniboia, d. of Alberta,

d. of Saskatchewan and the Northern Territories.

Be a part of the growth of our great nation.

Contact K. Pedersen. Inglewood Holdings.

Charles studied the remainder of the paper but nothing piqued his interest like the notice from Mr. Pedersen. He removed a small notepad from his breast pocket and detached the stubby pencil from its leather loop. He licked the tip of the graphite and jotted down his thoughts before closing the worn cover and returning it to the pouch against his breast. He folded the newspaper and placed it under his arm as he walked quickly from the park down to King Street and straight to the telegraph office.

"Good day, sir. How can I help you?" The clerk said from behind the counter.

"I would like to send a telegraph to this gentleman in Calgary," he said as he handed the clerk his newspaper and the note to accompany it. Although he had access to a machine at the hotel, he thought better of using it for a such sensitive correspondence.

"Certainly, sir."

He watched as the clerk pressed the black and white keys for each letter scribed, followed by a turn of the rotary dial to send the message. Charles felt nausea and excitement at the prospect of leaving Kingston. He knew that if they were going to make such a drastic change, he had limited time to secure a property and move.

"The message has been sent, sir. Will that be all?"

"Yes, thank you. If a response comes in, please send it directly to my residence."

The mood was sombre when Charles arrived back at The Danbury shortly after the luncheon service. The conversations amongst the staff were centred on the unfortunate news they had all received just a few hours prior.

"Firein' us all. Can you imagine? I thought for sure Prescott had it in the bag," one of the housekeepers uttered.

"It's a real shame," was heard commiserated from one of the busboys to another.

"We're all going to be out of work by week's end. Sure don't give you much time to tidy up your affairs. Don't know what's going to happen to us all," said another.

Charles heard versions of the same chatter repeated around him for the full duration of his shift. Despite their thinly veiled pleas for empathy, he could say little to comfort them for his mind was occupied by his own hardship. Although the loss of work had thrust him towards the precipice of what could well be the grandest experience of his life, he could not help but blame the late Mr. Danbury for his current lot. Although he was afforded the opportunity to learn the hotelier craft from a master, he now wondered if the grooming and preparations for him to take over were tactics used to make him more dedicated and hardworking. Try as he might, he was unable to feel gratitude for his years of employment and the use of Shelby House. He was unable to feel compassion for a man who had reneged on his guarantee of a livelihood and had trounced upon the promise of a comfortable existence for his family.

When Charles left the hotel after the tea service, he made inquiries as to the exact totals outstanding on his accounts. With his sparse savings and the money owed, he had less than four hundred dollars remaining. He was careful not to put forth a figure to Mr. Pedersen that was outside of his price range; he wanted to ensure they had enough funds to move and keep them well until the hotel became profitable. He reckoned there would be a limit to the number of items they could afford to transport, and since the furniture of Shelby House now belonged to the young Mr. Danbury, Charles believed a furnished residence would be most practical. With their clothing and personal items, he would relocate his family with little more than two trunks each.

When Charles arrived home, he opened the back door to find the ladies in the garden enjoying the bright afternoon. Emma lay under the large elm, consumed by the colourful displays of plumage in her *Audubon's Birds* while Abigail watched her from the bench beside. She was pondering the wisdom her father proffered on her wedding day: "All can be mended with love and communication." She did not doubt the romantic portion of the anecdote and even considered her ignorance of their finances to be care on Charles' part to save her from the mundanity of accounting. She knew that her dowry was used in some way to supplement their income, but was unsure of what those investments were.

"Good day, ladies," he said as he moved towards the blanket set out on the grass and took a seat beside his daughter.

"Hello, my love. Would you care to join us for some refreshments?" Abigail said as she motioned to a small tray of aged Balderson and sliced tart apples.

"Have some cheese, Papa. It is your favourite," Emma said, lifting the tray towards him. Charles accepted the offering and reached over to tear a piece of rye from the loaf.

"How did you both enjoy your day?"

"It was very nice, Papa. Mama has been showing me some of the birds from my book that we have right here in Ontario," she said, snuggling up to her father.

"Right here in our own garden, in fact. She seems to have found her first passion."

"One she shares with you," he said with a smile. "Which of the birds do you prefer, petty?"

"The Northern Cardinal, of course. They must be such an important bird due to their bright colour." Emma loved every picture and every bird within, although she had not yet seen most of them in person. She thumbed through the volume until she found her favourite.

"You see, Papa? Look at their lovely red plumage. That means the feathers. So many other birds look so plain compared to the cardinal."

"Perhaps they are plain so that their costumes do not distract from their voices," Abigail said.

"That could well be, Mama. Do you see these ugly ones? I wager their songs are the sweetest of all," Emma said as she pointed to a wild turkey and caused her parents to laugh. Abigail smiled at her husband, for she could see that his mood had markedly improved. Her own mood had turned towards fear and apprehension.

"What would you think about travelling to see some new varieties of your beloved birds, petty?"

"That would be splendid, Papa! Are we going abroad? Stacy Chapman and her family are leaving for Paris next week. I should so very much like go to Paris, too. Would that not be lovely, Mama?" she said as she shoved her book to the side and stood up in front of them. "Stacy said that when they travelled there last year, she went to the opera house three times! She showed me the big lavender dress that her father bought specially. La-da-

da," she said as she danced and twirled before them. "If we go to the opera, perhaps they will ask Mama to sing with them. They will pluck her from the audience and pull her right on stage." She reached for her mother's hands and pulled her up to stand beside her. As Abigail stood, she curtsied at the imagined applause.

"I too would love to travel to Paris, my love, but we are not to make that journey this year," Abigail said as she brushed Emma's hair from her face.

"Where are we to go then?" she asked as she ceased her dance.

"Your mother and I have come to the decision that we will be moving our family to a new home," he said as he examined the growing confusion on his daughter's face. Her expression transitioned from jovial and excited to drawn and morose. Charles could feel her distress at the prospect of leaving her comfortable home. She sat down on the blanket in a huff as the tears ran down her cheeks.

"I do not understand, Papa. Are we no longer to live at Shelby House?" she said, as she nuzzled into her father's side. He had no definitive answer but proceeded nonetheless.

"Do you remember those stories from the paper about the West? The big mountains and the prospectors with their gold pans and pick-axes?"

"We are going to the Klondike?" she exclaimed. "Mama, are we going to try to strike it rich? Bonanza! Bonanza!"

"We are not going to the Klondike, my love. Your father meant to say that we are planning to move to one of the western districts," Abigail said, throwing a scolding glance at Charles for filling her head with nonsense.

"How wonderful! When are we leaving, Papa? Are we to take the train? May I bring my dolls along? Oh, Papa!" she said as she dried her tears with the back of her hand.

Abigail sat down on the other side of the blanket and looked at Emma incredulously. She could not believe the sudden change in her disposition and the fervent willingness to relocate. When Abigail's mother died, around the same age as Emma, she and her father moved several times within Kingston. Clinging to memories of her mother and yearning for a sense of the familiar, each subsequent move was as painful and debilitating as uprooting a tree. Emma viewed the news with an unabashed optimism, eager for a new experience.

"We will have to be very discerning about what we bring on the voyage. This is a way for all of us to start anew and approach our lives with less focus on frivolities," Charles said, accusing himself of materialism more than his wife and daughter.

"Yes, Papa. I shall start sorting my things at once," Emma said as she leapt up and ran into the house. Charles and Abigail looked at each other and laughed.

"That went better than I had expected," Abigail said as she gathered up the trays and napkins. Charles folded the blanket and followed her inside.

"What were you expecting?" he asked as they took their places near the fire in the drawing room.

"I am not entirely certain. Some resistance, surely. When I was her age, I would have been perfectly content to stay in one place forever."

"You cannot view this from your own perspective. You moved numerous times, and so craved a home and consistency. Emma has been confined to one home, leaving little opportunity for change or diversity. Of course she would be eager."

"I wonder if it is too much change at once. I hope the journey will not be too hard on her. Fortunately, she cannot see beyond her excitement."

"After the day I have had, I am rather excited myself," Charles said as he retrieved the newspaper from the side table. He flipped to the page with Mr. Pedersen's advert and passed it to Abigail. "There are a number of foreclosed homes and properties for sale by this gentleman, Mr. Pedersen."

"You have certainly made some headway today. I have hardly had time understand the severity of our situation, let alone plan our departure and move."

"I can think of nothing other than finding a good prospect for you and Emma. I telegraphed him today to make an inquiry as to what he has available. The funds from Danbury should arrive by the end of the week. Mr. Pedersen should send more information in a day or two. If we find a suitable place, I will finalize the details and sign the deed in Calgary."

"When do you expect to leave?"

"A week from Friday."

Abigail's head spun with the details of their resettlement. Although she gave Charles credit for having the tenacity to arrange matters efficiently, she had little idea of how to prepare a house to move with so little notice; she soon realized that most of the items around her would be left behind.

The telegram arrived early the next evening just as Margaret was adding sprigs of rosemary and sage to the supper stew and Abigail was overseeing Emma's final piano lesson. Charles was in his study preparing the documents necessary to discharge his debts. He tore the sealed envelope open and withdrew the contents.

-- Several small hotels and land avail. in d. of Alberta. Send further info. regarding specific needs. – K.P. --

Charles knew there was not time enough to send a written correspondence; although it was expensive, telegrams would have to suffice. He took out a slip of paper from his desk drawer and carefully drafted the message.

Seeking affordable, furnished hotel in central d. of Alberta on several acres. Seeking foreclosed deed. Arrive in Calgary next week. Modest budget. C. Prescott.

Charles looked over the note to ensure that all of the major details were included. He did not want Mr. Pedersen to mistake him for a wealthy speculator, nor did he want to be cast aside because of his meagre savings. He wanted to make clear his intentions and what he could afford so there would not be any surprises when they arrived in Calgary.

Chapter Five

The telegram was waiting when Charles arrived home for afternoon tea. He saw little point of staying at The Danbury for the full extent of his regular hours, for his mind was now fully engaged elsewhere. He had waited outside the telegraph office that morning to ensure his message was the first transmitted when they opened for business. Abigail and Emma were seated in the drawing room and when Charles entered they could hardly wait for the news. They had both been eying the unopened response on the end table for the past hour and a half.

"Did we find a new home, Papa?"

"Hush now, Emma," Abigail said. "Give your father a chance to read."

"I do hope so, petty," he said as he cut the top of the envelope with his paperknife and read the message aloud.

-- Townsite of Bowlea. Large two story wood-framed boarding house. 64 acres. Mostly lake. Ample furnishings. Rail line to be completed in coming months. Solid opportunity. $200 for all. Payment upon transfer of deed. - K.P. --

"A lake? That sounds ideal," Emma said, unable to contain her enthusiasm.

"Is that within your price range?" Abigail asked, careful not to inquire too deeply into their finances.

"Yes, it is well within range. I know it is short notice, but we must leave as planned on Friday."

"That leaves very little time."

"We have but little choice, my dear. It will be some work, but Margaret can help," he said as he moved towards Abigail and took her hand. "All will be well, I assure you. All will be well."

The movement within the house was swift; under Abigail's direction, their collective belongings were funnelled into the guestroom for sorting. She had reserved one large trunk to hold the family's heirlooms including an ornate crocheted tablecloth made by her mother. Tucked within a tattered piece of fabric was the only photograph she had of her father, seated against a wall of books with his hands folded conservatively in his lap. She searched each drawer and cubby for any keepsakes and then searched them again to make sure nothing was forgotten. Emma conducted the same search of her own space, rifling through chests of toys and sorting through her large collection of books. *Audubon* would be the first item she packed, but it was reserved for the small carpet bag she would take with her into the passenger car.

"Shall you survey all of the species you see on the journey, my love?" Abigail asked as she entered the small, dishevelled room.

"Oh yes, Mama. I should think I will see every bird in my book at some point along the way. Look here. My trunk is filling up very quickly, Mama. I am not sure if there will be enough room for everything."

"I am facing the same dilemma myself. We must be discerning and pack only those items that we truly need or truly love," Abigail said moving to Emma's wardrobe and examining the garments that hung there.

"But I truly love everything, Mama. It seems unfair to make me choose. Why can we not bring what we like?" Abigail empathized with her daughter's annoyance but knew she had to be consistent in her message or they would never make it on the train.

"Do you recall the stories Papa read to you about the Nomads and the Roma who travel from one place to another, never able to stay in one place for long? Think of how little they are able to take with them. Oftentimes they move with only what they can carry," Abigail said, as she laid Emma's fine dresses into the trunk.

"I suppose I do get to bring a great deal more than that. I shall do as you say and only choose the most important items," she said as she flung a tattered doll into the discard pile.

As they packed up Emma's belongings, Abigail's mind was far off, thinking about the times she had packed up and moved households in her youth. She was curious whether her mother had concerned herself with her father's expenditures, and determined she must have, for his finances were far more unstable than Charles' and she could think of nothing else.

As she hunched over and attempted to lift Emma's trunk from the floor to the bed, she felt a sharp sting in her lower back. When she released the trunk and reached for the sore spot, she wondered if Charles would hire help when they arrived in Bowlea or if the burden would fall solely on her shoulders. She hummed a tune loudly as a form of distraction and left the luggage where it lay for the footman.

***

Helen Wallace recognized the tune as one of her favourites and began to hum along to the muted tones of her daughter's voice.

Young Abigail's voice was soft and fragile – gentle compared to her mother's strong soprano. Helen had never heard her daughter sing before and listened without offering comment or criticism. Abigail was singing for the pure delight of it, and as her mother looked on, she continued with an imperfect sweetness. As the harmony of Helen's humming came to an end, so too did her daughter's melody.

"You surprise me, Abigail. I had no idea you had such a lovely voice. Well done, darling."

"I do? But I sound nothing like you when I sing. I never dreamed I was any good at all," she said as she sat on her bed.

"Remember what I told you about all of the different bird calls? How each one is distinct but beautiful? It is the same with you and I. Our voices may be different – mine is an older trained voice and yours is young and raw – but both sound lovely in their own way."

"Sometimes I wish that I could open my mouth and those wonderful sounds would come out like they do for you. But then I sing and it just seems so plain."

"You must embrace the voice you were given, darling. I can teach you to sing properly through superior training and technique. But you must allow your voice to be its own. There is no need to emulate. You should embrace your natural gift."

"I have a gift?" Abigail asked. She was in awe that someone with so much talent would see the same in her.

"Yes, of course. I am only surprised that you did not reveal it sooner. Could you sing me something else?" Helen asked as she took a seat next to Abigail's overflowing trunk.

"What would you like?" she asked, fidgeting with her cold fingers.

"How about *Maggie Murphy's Home*? You know that tune, of that I am certain."

Abigail stood in front of her mother and studied the curves and contours of her face. She was soothed by her kind eyes and encouraged by her smile. She was anxious for her approval, for she had never performed before and usually sang quietly to herself. In that moment, her mother looked on as an active audience and Abigail's fear and inexperience instantly caused her lip to quiver and the colour of her face to grow red.

"Where do you usually sing, my darling?" Helen asked as she sensed her daughter's apprehension.

"I sometimes sing in my room when you are down taking tea with the ladies. I also like to sing in the garden behind the big oak. No one can hear me back there," she said quietly.

"I can see that you are nervous, my love. That is not only understandable but completely natural. When I first began performing, I was around your age. I remember feeling so alone in front of all those people."

"How would you calm yourself?"

"I would imagine I was in my favourite place, which at the time was my tree house in the back yard. I would spend hours there, peering out to the forest below. I would sing to the squirrels and birds and spiders and frogs. I knew they would listen without judgement. So before I was set to perform, I would close my eyes and imagine I was back in that tiny house with those woodland friends as my audience."

"Did it help you to sing?"

"Oh yes, my fear would wash away."

"I shall try, Mama," Abigail said. She closed her eyes and pictured a dozen porcelain dolls with set curls and embroidered gowns. She imagined they were her audience in a grand opera hall and that they had cast aside any other engagements just to hear her. She took a deep breath, opened her eyes and began to sing. The sound was soft and pure, with little effort behind it. There was a modest vibrato and gentle tone that Helen instantly appreciated. Abigail became flustered and stopped when her voice slightly cracked.

"Carry on, darling, please."

As Abigail sang, her body relaxed and her confidence built incrementally until she reached the song's climax. As the final notes rang out from her tiny body, the goosebumps peppered Helen's skin. The excitement of witnessing her daughter's immense talent caused her to stand and applaud.

"Oh, how lovely!" she exclaimed as she hurried to embrace her. "That was not so difficult, was it?"

"I was scared at first, but your trick helped. Teach me some more, Mama, please."

"We have a great deal to do right now, my darling. We are leaving in less than a week. We cannot start lessons until we are settled in our new home."

Abigail's head hung down and she stared at her feet. She was unsure of how to cope with feeling so jubilant one moment and so dejected the next.

"Fret not, my dear. I do not mean that you have to stop singing, but I will be unable to give your tuition my full attention. You must be patient," Helen said as she took her daughter's hand in hers.

"Where's Freddy, Mama?" Emma said, breaking Abigail out of her reflection. "Please help, Mama. I simply cannot leave without him."

Abigail reached behind her to retrieve the stuffed bear and tossed it high in the air, aiming for the target of pink taffeta in Emma's trunk.

***

The mood at The Danbury was sombre, for it was the last day of operations before it closed indefinitely. A number of staff had easily found new positions and Charles wondered if moving his family across the continent was the best strategy after all. He could not bear to man the front desk any longer, and so moved to his main floor office as the last guests trickled out through the lobby. He was tired of answering their inquiries and had grown even more weary of discussing his future plans with staff. Doubt invaded his mind further when Andrew remarked that his skills were transferrable to any number of roles in the service or mercantile fields. Charles, however, remained stoically vague; he told guests that the hotel had been sold, and staff that both he and his family welcomed the change. The prospect of admitting some degree of failure was not an option. He firmly believed that finding lesser work in Kingston would expose him to ridicule regarding his abilities as a manager.

Charles sifted through the side cabinets of his desk and removed a folded map he had purchased that morning when he booked their passage to Calgary. He wanted to show Emma the country outside of Ontario and the vast wilderness they were travelling into. He opened the leaves and laid it out flat on the desk, smoothing out the creases with the edge of his fist. He leaned over it to inspected it more closely.

The central section was roughly drawn and faint etchings of the borders were the only distinction between the districts. The drawings of the east and British Columbia held far more detail and signalled to Charles a marked difference in the levels of civilization. Calgary was noted by a small black dot, and Charles measured its distance from Kingston with the joints of his thumb. He fingered the route through Assiniboia to Alberta and stopped just below the line that separated it from Athabasca. He felt overwhelmed at the size of the districts and wondered where within that vast terrain the town of Bowlea would fall. He wondered if it would be nestled in a valley near the mountains or perched atop the banks of one of the region's great rivers. Charles knew only of this land from the newspapers which made it exceedingly difficult to determine which details were true. He had minor reservations about their safety but understood that a township would have at least some governance and sense of community. He studied the map for a few moments longer before placing the folded square into the breast pocket of his overcoat.

"The Rivards have checked out, sir. How would you like me to proceed?" Andrew asked from the doorway.

"Have one of the ladies clean the room and take the linens down to the laundry. The staff have already been paid and the expenditure noted on the account. They may leave after they have cleaned their work areas if they have not already done so. I will close up this evening, so you are free to go," Charles said as he began to gather up his personal effects.

"Very good, sir." Andrew stood in the doorway for a moment and could not help but notice the methodical way in which Charles packed his belongings. He thought it fitting that he was as diligent in his departure as he was in his everyday business.

"I wanted to thank you for taking on me and Emily, Mr. Prescott. I've learned a great deal," the young man said as he offered his hand in friendship. Charles smiled and returned the gesture with a deliberate grip.

"Thank you, Andrew. It was a pleasure to work alongside you. I am sure you will find much success at The Princess."

Andrew left the office and was followed thereafter by a steady procession of staff eager to bid their kind manager goodbye. As each one wished him well, Charles was grateful to have worked with such amiable people. They worked hard and made every effort to ease the burdens of his workday. Even on their last shift, they worked to ensure he would have little left to do but bolt the front door. As the last of them said their farewells, Charles left his office with only his satchel and a pewter-framed photograph of Abigail holding baby Emma. He was startled by a knock on the door and nearly dropped the portrait.

"Good evening, Charles," Edwin said as he removed his hat and entered the lobby.

"Edwin, I was not expecting to see you before I left. It is good of you to come by."

Edwin looked up at the large painting of the hotel's namesake that hung above the front desk.

"It has been a long road, has it not? Working your way up from porter to manager."

"Indeed," Charles said absently.

"You have a look of worry on your face, my boy. I understand that it is rarely easy to let go of one's passion, but…"

"That is not what concerns me, Eddie."

"What it is then?"

"Do you suppose the town will be set up in a civilized manner? Will the guests be in line with the type of patrons we are used to?"

"I would not expect that, my boy. These are new lands you are going into. The established families that we normally cater to are just that – established. It will take time before the ingrained civilities of our society become commonplace there. I am sure you will have your share of cattlemen."

"As long as they are not all cattlemen. I can adjust, but I do not know how the ladies will manage without at least a little cultivated society."

"Regardless of the status of your clientele, I can guarantee one thing: it will likely be more work than any of you have done before."

"I have worked hard for my successes, do not mistake that fact."

"No one is denying that, Charles."

"I know how it must look from an outsider's perspective. When I consider the advantages I have had, I wonder if perhaps Mr. Danbury did me a disservice by allowing me so many luxuries under his employ."

"I give my manager lodgings, Charles. It has been the thing for years. I think you will do well to start afresh. Trust me when I say that you will never feel more satisfied than when the money you earn is yours alone. Your success entirely correlates to how much effort you are willing to put in."

"I am a little scared, to tell the truth," Charles said, looking down at his hands.

"We all have fears in life, lad, but adventure cannot be one of them."

Charles looked at Edwin and returned his smile.

"An adventure. Yes, I suppose it is when you think about it."

"Embrace it. Any adventure one is willing to take must be deemed a success."

As Charles stood in The Danbury's doorway, he watched Edwin's carriage grow smaller as the distance between them increased. He wondered how altruistic his friend's intentions were; it made him uncomfortable to consider that he was being encouraged to leave in order to benefit Edwin's business. After his experience with Mr. Danbury, Charles now knew that people are not always honest, and may capitalize on one situation at the expense of another.

Charles shut the door and made a final tour of the hotel. The walls groaned and popped and he turned to look behind him when a creak of the floorboards startled him. He was acutely aware that he was alone in the hotel for the first time since he began his apprenticeship. He marvelled at how strange it felt to be enclosed by a building that once pulsated with vitality but now sat stagnant. He was unable to escape the feeling that part of him had died and he was mourning a time in his life that no longer existed. He fought back emotions as his future hung before him as if suspended over steel tracks, speeding towards the unknown.

As the last candle was extinguished, the only light came from the streetlamps outside. He stood for a moment in front of the mirror. He examined his face, highlighted in tones of copper and grey. The lines were cut deeply for a man of thirty-six years, his youth given to the walls around him. He unfurled a small black cloth he had retrieved from the laundry and hung it over the mirror.

Chapter Six

"Are you afraid at all?" Josephine asked, taking a bite of her vanilla cream tartlet.

"I am rather nervous, but I am sure that comes more from uncertainty than fear," Abigail said, as she filled her cup with more hot tea.

"Do not fret, Abby, all will be well. I know it seems like so much change at once, but with your strength, I know you will persevere."

Abigail brought the lip of her teacup close to her nose and inhaled deeply. The warmth and Ceylon aroma helped ease the tension in her neck.

"What if the hotel is not a success?"

"I would not let that concern you. Charles has given you details of the property, has he not?"

"To some extent, yes. It is a boarding house, but the property has been foreclosed. We are told there is a post office and a small church. The property is sixty-four acres on the edge of town, although most of that land is taken up by a lake. From Charles' communications with the broker it sounds like a thriving little community."

"That sounds rather lovely, save for the Indians and rogues!"

The pair broke into the hearty laughs of their youth, and Abigail felt embarrassed that in her naivety she presumed they would be in contact with only the most wholesome of settlers.

"I am going to be quite lost without you," Josephine said as she tried to regain her decorum.

"As will I. Write me often, Jo."

"You know I am an infrequent correspondent, but I will do my best. And how is Emma taking all of this change? I suspect she is rather distraught."

"I am proud to say she is taking the change in stride, but she does not carry with her the shackles of responsibility that we do."

"Children do have a far easier time of it. I wonder if she will have your impulsive spirit when she comes of age?"

"I am hardly impulsive, particularly in this case. Charles, on the other hand, has shown impulsivity to the point of foolishness."

"Is that truly how you feel?" Josephine asked, startled by Abigail's frankness.

"No. I beg your pardon, Jo. I applaud his efforts, but I still do not understand why we cannot simply stay in Kingston."

"Is that what you would prefer?"

"Why yes, of course."

"And why would you wish to stay in a place you have been your whole life? To me and perhaps to Charles as well, that seems dreadfully dull."

"I have travelled some if you recall."

"Taking a steam engine to Toronto on holiday is no comparison to having the chance to explore a place where so few have been. I would count myself privileged for that opportunity." She removed a slip of paper from her handbag and folded it in half, pressing the crease with her gloved hand as she passed it to Abigail.

"These are my particulars. You may write me as often as you like. I want to know that you are well, that all is well," she said as she restrained her tears.

"Dear Jo. I shall write you very often. I will so long to hear how you are keeping. Particularly news about your boys."

"When do you expect to leave?"

"On Friday."

"I say, Charles is rather impulsive," Josephine said with a smirk.

"We have but three days to sort out the final details. We are not quite packed, but I am sure we will be ready in time. Charles is closing the hotel today, so we will have a couple of days together with Emma before we depart. Will I see you before I go?"

"I am afraid I am engaged for the rest of the week. I will not be able to see you off. I hope you are not disappointed. If I had had more notice, I may have been able to rearrange my affairs."

Abigail followed close behind as her closest friend straightened her hat and prepared to leave Shelby House for what she expected to be forever.

"Do take care," Josephine said, giving her friend a tight embrace.

"I shall miss you a great deal."

"And I you," she said as she took Abigail's delicate hand. "What is life for any of us but an adventure?"

Abigail watched from the front porch as Josephine's carriage departed. She stood for some time, watching the traffic and passersby and wondering if the town of Bowlea would possess the same degree of energy and excitement.

"Perhaps it will be a great adventure," she thought, "and exciting enough to rival any magazine story."

Chapter Seven

"Come along, Emma, we must hurry. The train will depart without us, and then where will we be?" Abigail said as she rushed through the house in the final minutes before they left for the station.

"Have you seen my satchel?" Charles asked in a panicked tone, for it held all of his essential documentation and the whole of his financial resources.

"Yes, I have it here. You must be sure to keep that bag with you at all times, my dear. It will prove very difficult to buy property without any money."

Abigail put on her travelling gloves and adjusted her daughter's straw bonnet.

"Do I look like a world traveller?" Emma said as she twirled in place with her arms outstretched.

"Oh yes, quite the adventuress," Charles said as he playfully pinched her side. "Have you everything, petty?"

"Yes, Papa," she said as she grabbed the wooden handles of her carpet bag and hefted it up to rest on her hip.

"Abby?"

"Yes, I have everything."

The family moved down to the street to make way for the footmen who swiftly moved the trunks into the back of the flat-bottomed carriage.

Margaret stood on the front landing and watched her family depart. She looked about the main foyer of the house and wondered if her next family would be as kind and generous as the Prescotts.

"Walk on, hey, walk on," the coachman said as he flicked his wrist and snapped the reins against the backs of the horses charged with pulling the load.

The carriage lurched forward, and Emma turned in her seat to maintain her view of the neighbourhood homes as they drifted past.

"Will you miss Kingston, Mama?"

"There are some things I will miss, my love. The riverfront is one of my favourite places, and I will, of course, miss my friends," she said as she tried to focus on the hurried view from the opposite side of the carriage.

"I will miss my friends, too, but I will miss the garden most of all. And you, Papa? What will you miss?"

"I was quite fond of our home, and enjoyed our time there very much," he said, resisting the urge to say something pertaining to steady employment. "I formed many friendships over the years, but in many ways, I shall miss the hotel the most. It gave me such pleasure to be of service to new patrons every day," he said, smiling at his daughter.

"Just think of all the new people you will meet, Papa. I think the new hotel will be even busier than the old one."

Abigail squeezed her hands together in her lap, her white knuckles camouflaged by her tawny gloves. Her stomach was tense as were most of the muscles in her body. They were running late, and the train was already boarding, and she found it difficult to compose her thoughts.

"All aboard," the conductor called out as the smell of burning coal wafted through the air. The smoke stung Emma's nostrils and caused her eyes to water. She wiped her nose with her hand as her mother thrust a handkerchief towards her. The ladies stood in line to board the second class car while Charles ensured that all of the trunks had been portered to the baggage area.

"Destination, sir?" the attendant asked.

"Calgary."

"Very good, sir. The trunks will be offloaded when you arrive."

Abigail looked around at the snaking lines of travellers around her. She caught the eye of a young girl a few years younger than Emma who was frightened and had clearly been crying. In that moment, Abigail wished she could join her behind the heavy folds of her mother's dress. As the Prescotts arrived at the front of the line, the attendant reached for Emma's hand to help her aboard. She felt like a lady and took his gloved hand with her head raised as high as she could lift it while still being able to see the steps before her. Her mother guided her with a gentle hand into the passenger car, while Charles followed close behind until they were seated.

"How long will we stay in Calgary, Papa?" Emma said as she searched through her bag for a pencil.

"Only a day or two, petty. Mr. Pedersen is expecting me so it should not take long to finalize the details. Mr. Beck has arranged for us to stay at his friend's boarding house, so I trust you will be comfortable."

"Are you writing goodbye notes to your friends?" Abigail asked as Emma began to scribble in her notebook.

"No, Mama, we have already said our goodbyes. I am writing down everything I love about Kingston and everything I will miss."

Abigail mentally compiled a similar list as the train whistle blew and the engine began its slow acceleration to travelling speed. Each member of the family was buried deep in thought, and for the first few hours, nary a word was said between them. Charles and Abigail gazed ahead absentmindedly, while Emma had her nose pressed against the window, her eyes quickly scanning the landscape as the steamer barrelled through it.

The journey from Kingston to Calgary was to take six days. It was not difficult to maintain decorum and formality in the first hours of the trip, but boredom and mental fatigue eventually overtook every passenger on board.

"How long until we arrive, Mama?"

"Midday on Thursday, my love."

Emma did not welcome that response, and so let out an exaggerated sigh and slumped back in her chair, causing her chin to rest on her chest and her lips to slope into a frown. Abigail wished there was a way to assuage her daughter's boredom, but as she had no way to occupy her own mind, she simply returned her gaze to the blurred landscapes outside her window.

The days passed slowly. The rhythm of raindrops on the car's wooden shell matched the chug of the engine, and Charles' mood was made more heavy by the weight of the blustery sky. The clouds hung low in dark grey sheets, and the wind blew droplets hard against the windows. His gaze fixated on the hills in the distance that rolled like bales of hay spread out in endless rows towards the horizon. The grass grew high and covered sections of the track ahead, and train cut through the overgrowth as if to plow a new crop of settlers into the land.

Charles entertained the ladies during long stretches of track with stories from the *Royal Northwest Mounted Police Tales from the Klondyke*. Emma was particularly fond of them, and she often daydreamed about the men in red coming to her defense as she bashed down the Dawson River in a runaway rowboat. She imagined them fording the shallow banks on their sleek black steeds to keep her from tumbling over the jagged falls.

The corners of Emma's own book were starting to fray. Her index finger and thumb picked at the corners where the ivory canvas appeared dull and aged. The volume had been opened and closed countless times during the trip, particularly whenever the sight of an unknown bird warranted explanation. She had thumbed through its pages and inspected each feathered creature, but she could not keep her eyes from growing weary. She wrapped the book in her ivory shawl and set it on the seat beside her.

"May I take a walk, Mama? I need to stretch my legs. I will not venture far, I promise."

"I shall come with you," Abigail said as she put her hand through the satin loop of her handbag and started to rise.

"There is no need, Mama. I will not go far."

"Very well," she said as she looked to Charles for a more firm hand of caution. He simply smiled with a gentle nod and returned to his paper.

Emma wandered through the second class car and passed all manner of traveller. There was a young boy about her age who offered a smile as she walked by. She wondered if his family were to be homesteaders and perhaps have a farm near Bowlea. She continued towards the rear of the car where a group of men had gathered to play cards for money. Their loud jeers and the smell of whiskey and tobacco caused Emma to scurry past.

The thick iron door at the rear was secured with a heavy bolt. She stood on her toes to look through the high window into the observation car. There was a large platform and a railing and a few empty chairs. She looked behind her and could see the tiny figures of her parents distracted by conversation.

"Excuse me, miss," a young steward said from behind her. "Do you need help with the latch?"

"Oh yes, please," she said, stepping aside.

He lifted the bolt lock and pressed down on the lever. The door slid open. Emma watched as he performed the same smooth manoeuvre on the last car's latch. She held tight to the doorframe as he stood on the small metal plate that acted as a platform between the two cars. He held out his hand to help her balance as she crossed. She hesitated slightly and looked back at where her parents sat. She took the steward's hand and stepped over to the next car. As she crossed, the cars rattled and shook. She looked down at the quaking threshold; the ties passed so rapidly below her that they were merely streaks of rock and wood.

"Thank you, sir," she said as she stepped foot onto the deck.

"Very good, miss," he said as he tipped his hat and returned to the passenger car, shuttering the door behind him.

The car bobbed and heaved as it was pulled towards Calgary. Emma tightly held the railing with both hands, careful not to stand too close to the edge. The prairie extended out further than her eyes could see. She leaned forward slightly to watch the train glide forward with each tie surrendered beneath the car. The sound of steel on steel was deafening. A holler of "Hello!" was instantly consumed by the chug of the engine, but as she stood, she could hear something in the air akin to a quack. She looked overhead and found a gaggle of geese soaring in the sky; she was transfixed by their formation. She had watched geese waddle through the parks of Kingston many times, but had never before seen a perfect triangle formed by dozens of the giant birds.

Emma watched as their wings flapped in rhythmic strokes as they tried to keep pace with the train. She remembered reading once that geese were migratory birds who flew thousands of miles in search of safe lands to spend their winters. As the snow was almost completely melted, she assumed they were returning north now that the warmer seasons were upon them. She was encouraged by their strength to return to home each year and hoped her new community would also be worth the journey. She waved goodbye as they overtook the train and fell out of view.

Although the train moved swiftly, the minutes passed slowly, and Emma grew anxious to reach her new home. The quest for adventure had grown tiresome, and she could not wait to hear the thud of her boots on the station platform. As she leaned against the barrier, she began to wonder what it meant to settle on the frontier. She wondered about the families who lived in the shanties on the cliffs of the Assiniboia and if the children stood at the river's edge and shouted their names just to hear the echo. She wondered what her new home would look like and which birds would inhabit the lake lands. She hoped for a patisserie with eclairs and petit-fours, and tall, chilled glasses of milk. She laughed when she thought of their home being overrun with cows and horses and chickens. She wondered if their very own man in red would patrol the dirt streets on horseback and protect the townsfolk from harm. She thought about every unknown of that place called Bowlea but wished most of all for a garden and a school full of children.

Emma was startled and nearly lost her footing when the door opened abruptly behind her. She held tight to the railing and turned to find her father fraught with worry. Her head hung low as Charles reached out to grasp her shoulders.

"Emma! Whatever are you doing here? This is not a safe place for children. Come now, your mother and I have been worried to death about you. It is not safe here." Charles reached around Emma's waist and pulled her fingers one by one from the cold railing.

"I am sorry, Papa. I did not mean to."

He whisked her through gangway corridor and pulled her into the passenger car. He pulled her close and kissed the top of her head.

"Your mother is sick with worry. What if something had happened to you? What if the train had jerked and you lost your footing. You have been very foolish, Emma."

She was unable to meet his disapproving stare, for she knew she would cry instantly. Instead, she tightened her embrace and whimpered her apologies into the bristly wool of his waistcoat.

"You must surrender your book. You shall not look at it until I say so." He clasped her hand and led her back to their seats. She stumbled alongside him as she struggled to match his stride.

"But Papa, what about all the new birds? How will I know what I am seeing?"

"You will have to wait. You will learn to understand that you still need our guidance and permission."

By the time they reached Abigail at the front of the car, Emma's cheeks were damp. She was unaccustomed to discipline because he rarely had reason to reprimand her.

"Oh, my love, you had me so worried," Abigail said she took Emma's hands and knelt down before her. "Why did you run off? I thought you were going to stay close by."

"I am sorry, Mama. I was only seeking a breath of air that did not taste of cigars. I should not have gone outside. I am sorry." She returned to her seat and placed her book on her lap. "Papa said I must give up my birds. I cannot imagine being without them."

Abigail could feel Emma's distress as she took the book from her hands and tucked it into her travel bag. She disliked the feeling of being on bad terms with her daughter, but felt the punishment was not too severe.

Charles and Abigail singularly contemplated their destination and barely spoke for the rest of the journey. Abigail was preoccupied with the state of the hotel and the home they were to build therein. She wondered at the availability of help in the small settlement and the sheer volume of work it would take to keep things in order without her housekeeper. Charles pondered less the effort required to make the hotel rooms boardable, and more the frequency and consistency of those seeking to rent them. Meanwhile, Emma's whimpers had lulled her to sleep, and she did not wake until the train pulled into Calgary's station at half-past three.

The energy within the car was palpable. The excitement of this new place coursed through each passenger's blood, whether he was the patriarch of an established family or a young bachelor with nothing but the dirt under his feet. The Prescotts waited for the melee to subside, determined to move from their seats only once the aisle had cleared. Howling and cheering could be heard farther down in the car, with hungry men expounding plans for their prophesized influx of funds.

"Gold! I'll fill my saddlebags full. There'll be no picking and panning for me, no sir. As soon as I make my fortune on land specs, I'll walk into the broker's and buy mine." The scrappy young man brimmed with confidence and his new-found friends laughed and cheered.

"I'm going to buy me some cattle," another man said to the crowd. "Cattle as far as the eye can see. So many head on so much land, my family will never want for anything."

"And you'll eat beefsteak for breakfast, lunch and supper," a voice said as the men around him laughed.

"That's a fact," he said, nodding in agreement.

As Charles disembarked and shuffled along the platform, Abigail clung to his arm, terrified that they would find themselves separated and lost within the crowd. Emma could feel her mother's tight grip on her arm and took comfort in the twinge of pain. They were soon cast aside by other young families who seemed to know where to go and who to see without much inquiry. The porters heaved their trunks onto a trolley, and Charles inspected them closely to ensure there was no damage or missing items. With the ladies tagging closely behind, he pushed through the travellers and pulled the cart to a calmer corner of the platform.

"At last! Some reprieve," he said as the family nestled into the corner by the ticketing window and watched the river of people flow past. He wondered how anyone could find their way amongst the incessant cajoling of the prospectors.

"Spend a thousand, make ten!" they hollered. "Buy a house today, sell it tomorrow! Triple your money!" Tickets and pamphlets littered the deck like tiny pieces of hope, but they did little to reassure Abigail.

"What shall we do?" she asked.

"We make our way to the boarding house to catch our breath and settle in for the night."

The old, wearied driver of a cab and two waited beside the station holding aloft a small paper sign that read *'C. Prescott.'* Charles motioned for the man to meet him nearer the platform so he could assist him with loading the trunks. The fellow held out his hand to help the ladies aboard, then hoisted himself onto the driver's seat; once Charles was seated he gave a flick of the reins and set them on their way.

"Next stop Ol' 'Berta."

Calgary reeked of coal and manure. The roads and walkways were mere trodden paths as new as the settlers who cut them.

"Hi-yip," the driver said as he prompted the horses to trot up the narrow avenue and part the sea of people with his cab. The lanes were littered with waste, and as they rode through the young city, it felt as disposable as the instant incomes it created. Brokerages and land title agencies had taken over much of Eighth Avenue, and financiers loitered before their open office doors waiting to prey upon the settlers. As their carriage waited to turn the corner onto First Street, Abigail peered out from the window. She felt pangs of disgust as she observed men stumbling in the street, drenched in the sour smell of intoxication and moving on to the next brothel or tavern. She turned her back to the window to shield Emma from the degradation.

"Whoa," the driver said, as he came to a stop in front of The Alberta Hotel.

Charles was the first to step down upon the muddy earth. He stood in appreciation of the large structure for several moments before the clearance of Abigail's throat caused him to break from his reverie and usher his wife and daughter to the ground. The ladies were thankful for a night in a soft bed and a restful sleep, while Charles was taken by the size and quality of the structure itself.

"The stonework is marvellous. It looks to be a common material on the avenue, but the result is so elegant. Look at the intricacies of the arched windows there. Three levels occupying a full block. Their revenue must be extraordinary."

Charles led Emma towards the front entrance while Abigail lagged behind. She slowed to a halt when she took notice of several men gathered on the terrace. The group were giving their full attention to a grizzled old man who picked a ramshackle guitar and sung slightly out of tune. Emma doubled back to fetch her mother and tugged at her hand when she found her.

"Come along, Mama. I am ever so tired," she said as she prodded Abigail towards the lobby.

"It is one of my favourites. *Listen to the Mockingbird*," she said, remaining steadfast in her stance.

"Are they not all your favourites?" Charles said as he joined them.

"Hush now."

When the stony voice of the fellow faltered, the men rallied to hum along to the beat of his strums. Abigail's foot tapped the sandstone tiles as she began to sing the lyrics in harmony. The old man was struck by the tone of her sound, and quieted down to allow her to shine. As his voice faded away, he gave her a nod to continue on her own. Even the roar of the carts around them seemed to dampen as the gathering focused solely on her.

I'm dreaming now of Hally,
Sweet Hally, sweet Hally,
I'm dreaming now of Hally,
For the thought of her is one that never dies;
She's sleeping in the valley,
In the valley, in the valley,
She's sleeping in the valley,
And the mockingbird is singing where she lies.[1]

---

[1] Excerpt from *Listen to the Mockingbird*. Music by Richard Milburn. Lyrics by Septimus Winner. Published 1855.

Abigail's voice floated atop the chords like a butterfly bouncing from bud to bud. As the crowd grew, her passion touched each man independently, reminding them that even amongst new friends they were alone and far from home. As she drew air for the song's final phrase, her audience held their own breaths, hanging on to the longing and wonder she evoked. She smiled and bowed graciously before them as they erupted into rapturous applause and nodded at Charles with envy.

"You sing like an angel, my dear," a gentleman said as he greeted her with a firm handshake. "Mr. Lyle, owner of The Alberta. I daresay, we may have to bring you on board. A bit of entertainment for the lads. They have not listened to anything other than their own voices since they arrived."

"Not even the voice of reason," one young man said with his head hung low, and his hands rammed deep into his pockets.

"Thank you, sir," Abigail returned. "I rarely pass up a chance to sing."

"If you will excuse us, it has been a long trip," Charles said as he moved in closer to her.

"Yes, certainly, I will not keep you. Let's get you settled, shall we?"

He led Abigail and Emma into the hotel while Charles followed close behind. The flash of pride rose in Charles' face as men he had never met slapped him on the back and offered their praise at his landing such an accomplished wife.

"Please allow me to check you in," Mr. Lyle said as he took his place at the front desk. "You shall have plenty of respite in your room before supper. Name, please."

"Charles Prescott. I believe my colleague Edwin Beck…"

"Mr. Prescott, of course! Mr. Beck has made all of the arrangements. He insists on settling your bill."

"Oh, is that so?" Charles turned to his family and smiled, breathing a silent sigh of relief at the saving of a precious few dollars.

"Indeed. He meant it as a testament to your family's courage in settling in the district."

Abigail was also thankful for their friend's generosity, but was bemused that their stay in Calgary would cost him little more than a few glasses of fine brandy.

"That is very kind indeed, but not entirely unexpected. I would likely be quite entertained if one of our set was in the same position," Charles said with a chuckle.

"Well, you certainly deserve credit for taking the risk. Most people have no concept of what it's like building your life from the ground up. You can only truly have empathy when you have lived it yourself."

"You were a settler, then?" Abigail asked.

"One of the first. We were part of a caravan that came over from Winnipeg. Our plan was to settle in Fort McLeod, but when we heard tell of the promise of Fort Calgary, we headed north. That was a long time ago, now. Before the train was even a prospect. Enough of my rambling. Let me show you to your suite. Daniel, please take these trunks to room twenty-two."

A spunky young lad jumped to attention and hurried to load the brass trolley with the Prescott's luggage. He inched the cart towards the manual lift at the rear of the lobby by using the full weight of his body as leverage.

"And how did you find the journey, madam?" Mr. Lyle asked Abigail as he led the trio upstairs to the second floor.

"Exhausting, really," she said. "There is little rest in anticipation."

"There are a great many things to be excited about, aren't there? This city is bursting with opportunity, and it seems everyone wants to strike that iron straight out of the fire. Here we are," he said, opening the door to their bedchamber. "I know you're all anxious to get settled and rest, but I would like to extend an invitation to dine with my wife and I tonight. We are quite informal and eat in the main hall with the other boarders. Spending time in their company may lend you a bit of perspective. I would take their advice with caution, but I would listen all the same. The soup is served promptly at eight."

"That is very kind," Charles said. "We will see you then."

He shut the door to their room and was determined to get some rest, but the raucous sounds of both the lobby and street were barely dampened, and they could still hear the old man's guitar throb through the walls. The modest size of their quarters was complimented by simple yet elegant furnishings. The windows faced the avenue and helped to brighten the naturally dim space. The room was well appointed for a small family; Emma's bed was situated at the opposite end of the room, affording her parents the comfort of a small amount of privacy.

Abigail took off her hat, wiped her brow with a handkerchief and took a seat on the bed. Emma languidly took off her bonnet and overcoat and strewn them over her dressing chair. Although she had slept during the last hours of the trip, the weariness of relocation overcame her.

"How long will we be staying here, Papa?" Emma asked for she wanted them to leave before the sun rose the next morning.

"We should be able to leave the day after next. I only have a few errands to complete tomorrow, and we will be on our way."

She snapped the brass clasps of her trunk open, and lifted the top wide. She sunk to her knees and began to sift through the contents for her nightgown. Abigail glanced over and saw her daughter waist-deep in clothing and at risk of toppling head first into the sea of fabric.

"What are you looking for, my love?"

"I just want to go to bed, Mama. I need my bedclothes."

"But its still afternoon. There is no need to change. As worldly travellers, we must allow ourselves a few concessions."

Abigail moved in close to her daughter and lifted her away from the trunk. Emma laboured as she stood and extended her arms, an instant indication of Abigail's new duty as lady's maid. She tugged on the ribbon of Emma's dress and lifted the petticoat above her head. Emma's fatigued arms dropped back down against the layers of her chemise, and she sat down with a heavy thump on the bed. Abigail knelt down to unlace the boots that her small fingers were too tired to attempt.

"It is very fine country," Emma said through a yawn in an effort to diminish her earlier mishap.

"It is very much so," Abigail said with a forgiving tone. "While we were travelling, I imagined myself wandering through the fields and getting lost in the meadows."

"And being rescued by a handsome Mountie?"

"On his strong, black steed," she said with a kind smile. Emma grinned sheepishly and moved in close to embrace her mother.

"I am sorry, Mama. I do not know what came over me. I suppose I was growing tired of looking out the window."

"It was a foolish episode, but I do understand your need to move about. It has been a very long journey for us all." Abigail loosely folded the garments and placed the pile on Emma's trunk. "Once we arrive in our new home, we will feel like ourselves again."

Abigail pulled a plush bear from the carpet bag as Emma sought out warmth under the covers. The exhaustion was evident on her face as her eyes shut and she nestled into the pillows.

"Did you forget this passenger?" Abigail said as she tucked in the bear beside her.

"Freddy," Emma said in a muffled whisper as she drifted to sleep.

"A rest will do you good."

Charles had settled in and was seated at the small desk under the window. Scattered on the white spruce surface were numerous papers and banknotes along with a growing list of essential supplies to be purchased the following day. Abigail marvelled at his tirelessness and wondered if he would be able to rest even when he lay down for the night.

"Finally, some calm," she said in a low whisper as her hand moved in soothing circles upon his back. She could feel the tension in his shoulders and sensed his anxiety. She knew that the coming days of business dealings and travel would bring a great deal of stress.

"I had no idea Calgary would be so busy. This is not what I expected at all," he said as he left her comforting touch to look out the window.

"What were you expecting?" Abigail followed and stood with him as the glazed panes pulsed from the excitement outside.

"Order, I suppose. It seems to me there is little rhyme or reason whatsoever," he said as he scanned the traffic of ramshackle carriages, cabs, and covered wagons interspersed with travel-worn labourers and dapper businessmen. "I suppose some of these chaps have yet to learn the art of playing their hands close to their chests. I see just as many men down on their luck as there are triumphs."

"It is like any venture, my dear. There are always those who approach things methodically and those who barrel through without forethought at all. I wish we would have had more time to plan."

"But planning can only get you so far," Charles said. "One also has to balance it with intuition and a little bit of luck. Do not be distressed, my dear. With our savings, we have a bit more than chance on our side."

Abigail stood in front of the window for some time, tracing the paths of the people below with her finger on the glass. Charles noted a pained look on her face, but the reflection in the window helped to blur her trepidation.

"All will be well, Abby. We will be rebuilding our future soon enough."

"I am glad you feel certain, Charles," she said as she wiped the criss-crossed mist from the pane with the palm of her hand.

Chapter Eight

The dining hall contained a large main table for general boarders and a smaller table for the hotel owner and his more prominent guests. For the gentlemen, the ample dishes of stews and breads and were laid out on the sparsely set table and they were free to serve themselves until their bellies were warmed and satisfied. At the owner's table, each place setting included the finest china, silver and crystal with each course planned to arrive in succession. The Prescott's entered the hall and were hailed by a wave and a smile from Mr. Lyle. They would be the only other guests seated with him that evening.

"I hope you had time to settle in and rest," Mr. Lyle said as he pulled the chair out for Abigail.

"Yes, thank you. Emma is so tired that she could not be awoken," Abigail said. "She will be disappointed to have missed supper."

"Well then, I will send you back with a little something for her. She will be thankful for the rest in the morning, I assure you. Mr. and Mrs.

Prescott, may I introduce my wife, Violet," he said, motioning to the woman beside him. She was a splendid lady, out of place in such a harsh city. Her pale skin was set off by a burgundy dress and a pile of blond curls set at the crown of her head.

"It is a pleasure to meet you both," she said with a gentle bow. "Herbert has told me of your marvellous voice, Mrs. Prescott. It is refreshing to see a cultivated woman come through our doors. As of late, it is mostly young men who seek lodging."

"You are very kind, Mrs. Lyle. Singing is one of my greatest pleasures. Although, I have not performed in quite some time."

"I sometimes urge her to sing more in society. She coyly refuses, of course, only to spring into song when I least expect it," Charles said. Abigail could feel a reassuring squeeze on her knee under the table.

"What are your plans while you are in Calgary? Are you looking to buy property in the city?" Mr. Lyle asked.

"No, we are not planning to settle here. We are moving on to our new home east of Red Deer on Sunday. I thought it was best for my family to find some peace for a day or two, and a restful night's sleep," Charles said. The demeanour of Mr. Lyle changed in that instant, and a stern look came over his face.

"I offer you an unsolicited warning, my boy. Too many men have crossed the Bow River with expectations of a future that had no chance of succeeding. I implore you to be cautious. There are few men in this new world who are trustworthy and fewer still willing to give sage advice. Even some advisors are only in it for their own gain. There was a young chap on the north side who inherited a large amount of property from his father. One of those old homesteaders. Within days, investors weaseled the property out of him for a thousand dollars. The chap was rather pleased with the deal until he learned that the property was sold again eight days later for three times that amount."

"Thank you, Mr. Lyle; I will heed that warning. I was able to make arrangements with the broker before I left Kingston, so I am sure everything is in order. I meet with him tomorrow to finalize the details."

"Just be mindful," Mrs. Lyle said graciously. "It is not always prudent to take advice from those who receive payment for giving it. They offer promises of prosperity, but are inconsistent in their delivery."

Charles said nothing and simply stared at the basket of rolls on the sideboard.

"Thank you. We will take care," Abigail said as the worry returned to her face. She reached under the table discreetly and took Charles' hand in hers.

"We were young once too, and took a great risk to come to Calgary," Mr. Lyle said. "But look at us now."

"You must admit, dear, that the first few years were rather trying," Mrs. Lyle said. "Travellers coming to the fort were sporadic, and most visitors only stayed for a day or two. Things have improved, mind you. We have some guests now who stay for a month or more. For them, it is worth the expense to be the first in line for lots."

"Lots?" Abigail asked.

"Parcels of land. With the rail moving west, the land alongside the tracks is being sold for a pittance. There is a large upfront investment for equipment and horses and so forth. But for many, the dividends are well worth the risk."

"Oh, but we have no interest in farming. We are looking for something a bit more cosmopolitan," Charles said with a gentle laugh as he tried to appease his own doubts.

"Is that so? Then you had best stay in Calgary, for there is little society on the prairies, save for the gophers and geese," Mr. Lyle said with a chuckle.

The supper crowd had finished their meals, and some of the guests filed into the adjoining drawing room for brandy and cigars, while others took their whisky on the verandah. Mrs. Lyle led Abigail to a small sitting room and poured two crystal glasses of sherry.

"I forgot how nice it is to have time away from the men in the evenings," Abigail said as she settled into a cushioned chair near the fire. "I feel as though I have been surrounded by them for days."

"They can be trying, at times. The nature of the boom means that there are few ladies who come through. It is a welcome change to have your company."

"I have been on the train with rowdy men since we left Winnipeg. A calm, gentle voice is soothing to my ears."

"Yours is the voice that is most welcome. Herbert told me himself that he has rarely heard anything so beautiful."

"Singing is my one great passion."

"Have you only one? You must find more, particularly if you mean to survive the winters here. Days can be incredibly long and lonesome."

"We are a close family. I doubt any of us will be lonely."

"Loneliness descends upon us unwillingly, particularly when we are required to pass through the seasons with only the same few people for company. Relationships can crack when there is little room to grow."

The colour left Abigail's face as she listened to her host's reflections and considered her own future. When Mrs. Lyle looked over, she was startled by her ashen looks.

"My dear, do not fret. You do not realize how fortunate you are; to trust your partner implicitly and give your life to that person is quite something to behold. I did the same with Herbert in my youth and have never once regretted the decision, even when our only food was pemmican, and we had barely enough wood to warm our tents. Having a partner with the same ideals will guide you through many trials."

Abigail took a sip of her sherry and felt a sense of comfort as the liquor warmed her lips and tongue. She paused for a moment and took in her surroundings. The hotel's energy was vibrant and robust, and there was no indication that they wanted for visitors. The Lyles' situation had started out much like theirs, albeit decidedly more ambitious. Abigail felt deeply that if she and Charles approached this venture together, there was no reason why they should not succeed. Charles would be occupied with the running of the business, and she would avert loneliness by ensuring that their time spent together, doing any task laid before her, would be filled with joy and gratitude.

A wistful melody coaxed them to join the men in the drawing room. Abigail followed Mrs. Lyle's lead and seated herself next to Charles opposite the piano.

"This is what I want," Abigail said quietly as she placed Charles' hand in hers. "Look around you. These men are just like you. They are simply seeking an opportunity to be in control of their own destinies. Can you not feel the sense of community and camaraderie? Look at Mrs. Lyle. She seems content with the success of their business and well pleased to be in support of her husband. Having now seen how The Alberta is managed, I can more easily imagine the comings and goings of our own visitors. They will be transient little parts of our family."

"I am glad you are feeling better about our move, Abby. I have been keeping an eye on Mr. Lyle's operations, but have avoided inquiring about the finer details for fear of appearing like an inspector. This venture seems profitable, but we must keep in mind that this is a much larger hotel and there is no way to ensure this volume of visitors." As Charles looked around at the lively gathering, he silently hoped that he would host each one of them in his own boarding house.

"Mrs. Lyle informed me that the success of the hotel did not come without a great deal of sacrifice. They began their venture with just five rooms. Now they have over forty. That sort of expansion did not occur overnight."

"Considering they were also established as a boarding house before the boom struck, perhaps they are not the best models."

"Perhaps not, but it does give one hope."

The music of the piano stopped, and as Abigail turned towards the instrument, she noticed Mr. Lyle seeking her attention.

"Mrs. Prescott, as a welcomed guest, would you do us the honour of an entertainment? The magic of your voice would give us all such pleasure," he said as he motioned for her to approach the piano. Abigail was taken aback by the forwardness of the request, but understood that she had made a hurried acquaintance with Mrs. Lyle, who now looked upon her as a friend.

"Why of course, I should be delighted," she said with a friendly intonation that hid her hesitation. As she moved towards the instrument, the crowd drew closer so as not to miss a single note.

"Might you have *The Winter Woods*?" She asked Mrs. Lyle, who was now seated before the black and white keys.

"Indeed I do." She rustled through the large stack of sheets atop the piano, settled into position and began to play.

As Abigail began to sing the haunting melody, the mood in the room shifted; the tension in the muscles of the men seemed to fade with each phrase.

Grey skies float overhead

Scrawling thoughts in my mind with a thunderous pen

The story of my life will unfold

A thousand layers to be told

As the notes drifted around the room, they touched each man differently. Some stood in admiration of Abigail's soft, rounded frame which she draped in delicate silks and lace. Others stared at the carpet underfoot and remembered loved ones and the lives they had left behind. It was impossible to merely enjoy the music for she imbued each phrase with both melancholy and wonder.

Charles looked on from the corner of the drawing room. From his initial position in the front row, he had moved as far away from the stage as possible to give Abigail space to entertain without distraction. He watched her passion shine through as she sang, and could see in those moments that she was truly happy. When she sang in society, he was proud of her abilities and encouraged her. But he never quite accepted that she was popular for more than her grace and kindness.

The piano pounded out the crescendo. Abigail closed her eyes as she finished with a silent calm that left her audience pensive and in awe. A few moments passed before she took a breath and opened her eyes. As she stood, she could feel the men's emotion as they reflected upon the poetry she just sang. The room erupted into cheers and applause, with some guests moving towards the piano to offer their praise. Mrs. Lyle moved from her seat to stand with Abigail and provide modest deflection from the admiration.

"Well done!" One of the men exclaimed as he recalled how the unpredictability of the Milk River had taken his father's life.

"You should tour the camps, ma'am, or head up to the Klondyke," a younger boy said, as he gaped at the prettiest lady he had ever seen.

"Splendid, child," said Mr. Lyle, as he joined his wife at Abigail's side. "Wherever did you learn to sing with such emotion?"

"It comes naturally, I suppose," she said as Charles approached and gave her his arm. "I sing in society, of course, but they are a rather captive audience."

"You must have had the finest teachers," said Mrs. Lyle.

"No, not at all." The pangs of shyness tinted Abigail's cheeks a brighter shade of rose.

"But you must have learned somehow."

"When I was young I would sing in the great room of our house. My father would stomp the floor when I became too loud, as he spent a good deal of time in the study upstairs. For fear of annoying him too much, I would move out into the garden where my most dedicated tutors were the rabbits," she said with a laugh.

"And I suppose the squirrels were your audience?" Asked Mr. Lyle with a bemused grin.

"And the birds," Abigail said with a smile.

"That was until now," said Mrs. Lyle.

"Quite so, Mrs. Prescott. The whole town will be enamoured with you before long," Mr. Lyle said.

"Perhaps it is a good thing that we board the train soon. If I stayed in town much longer, my ego would no longer fit on the wagon."

Chapter Nine

Charles arrived at the firm of Pedersen and Lowe just prior to his scheduled appointment. The reception area was full of young men much like him, waiting with sporadic patience to purchase individual parcels of destiny. No man in the room looked older than twenty-five, and their conversations spoke to the naivety of their expectations.

"I wonder if the bank would secure a loan for ten thousand?" One of the men said as he rubbed his hands together.

"I wonder if Lowe will sell me as many acres?" said another.

Charles waded through the throng and queued up at reception. The line moved quickly as the clerk cross-referenced the names given with the appointments in the ledger. Charles glanced at the clock in the cabinet and back to the watch from his pocket. He expected to see Mr. Pedersen soon, as he was right on time.

"Name," the clerk said without looking up from his book.

"Charles Prescott. I have an appointment with Mr. Pedersen at eight-thirty," he said as he kneaded the brim of his hat in his hands.

"Here we are. Angus will take you in," he said in a flat tone as he motioned for his assistant to escort Charles to the adjacent office.

Four large tables were positioned in the centre of the room with several chairs arranged around them. The walls could nary be seen for the dozens of large maps of the western districts nailed to them. Flags and pins protruded from each chart, marking the most prominent and desirable locations. Some of the plans were more detailed and showed the topography of the region while others were lightly coloured and illustrated the variety of crops that could be grown in a specific area. On the tables were more large maps, some which showed the projected paths of the Grand Trunk Pacific and Canadian Pacific Rail lines.

"Mr. Prescott, I'm happy to see you. Are you looking forward to getting established, lad?" a voice said from behind a large desk at the rear of the room. Mr. Pedersen was dressed in a red waistcoat and resembled a ringmaster more than a property broker. His large belly protruded from above his belt line, and the rolls around his neck poured over his tight collar.

"I am excited to see the property and get my family settled. I have brought my particulars and the funds, of course," Charles said, as he rifled through his bag for the documents and Dominion bank notes.

"Yes, come have a seat. You are still interested in the property in Bowlea, then? We do have other properties that may suit your needs."

"We are looking for a hotel, preferably along the rail line. From what you described, the location and price of the property in Bowlea would be ideal."

"Yes, wonderful plan. This quarter-section here is only two hundred. You can hardly say no to a dollar and a quarter per acre. There is no land to clear, as a good two-thirds are taken up by the lake here. The previous owners cleared the sixty acres, and I believe the property is the envy of the whole township."

"How many people are there?" he asked as Mr. Pedersen unfurled a small map and splayed it on the desk before him. Charles scooted his chair forward and hunched over the large map to get a better view.

"Last I heard about eighty. It is a small community, but since it falls along the rail line, it offers a good opportunity for trade. See here," Mr. Pedersen said as he reached across the table to the east side of the district and fingered a thatched black line on the parchment. "With the rail comes many opportunities to help the traveller on their way. You should never want for business. The line is expected to branch east from Red Deer and pass through the township to Saskatoon to join the transcontinental. Construction is set to be completed within three months."

Charles listened intently as the broker spoke, and believed him when he affirmed that a boarding house along a new transportation route would be an ideal way to own property cheaply. He soon understood that there would be nothing but positive expansion in the region going forward.

"Bear in mind," Mr. Pedersen continued, "a road runs through town, and there will be opportunities to house executive workers of the line. There are several small towns and villages that follow along the route, so there are sure to be plenty of patrons passing through. See here," Mr. Pedersen said as he moved a small red block along the path.

"Yes, I see," Charles said as he looked at the scattered dots.

"This should be a very easy decision for you. The district has so many prospects. There is no way to go wrong."

"I understand your viewpoint, Mr. Pedersen. I just want to make sure it is a location that my wife and daughter would enjoy," Charles said. He studied the broker carefully during this exchange, and through his movements and the tone of his voice, could not detect any falsehood or malicious intent. He was not accustomed to hastily trusting any man, but felt that Mr. Pedersen was trustworthy and deserving of his business.

"Your wife and daughter! Well, do they enjoy lakes, rivers, meadows, forests, and vast open spaces?" Mr. Pedersen said as he grew more rushed and animated.

"Abigail is very fond of nature," Charles began with a smile.

"The eastern district is as fine as an English garden, and Bowlea is no exception. A damn fine spot, if there ever was one," he said, pointing to a small black dot on the map.

"Yes, I see it there. But not so many inhabitants?" Charles asked.

"Less than a hundred, but don't let that alarm you. Once the rail goes through there will be visitors aplenty."

"Why did the previous owners sell?"

"That's the thing with this business, son. We never really get into the particulars. But the boarding house is fully furnished and ready for possession."

"What is the sum of the parcel of land including the hotel and furnishings?" Charles asked.

"Three hundred dollars. Won't find a better deal anywhere in town," he said as he gathered the paperwork.

"In our correspondence, you quoted two hundred. I was expecting you to offer me a fair price. I assumed you were an honest man. See here? In your telegram you quoted two hundred dollars," Charles said, shaking his head.

"Oh yes. My apologies, Mr. Prescott. Two hundred. It has been so busy it's difficult to keep all of the quotes straight," he said as the colour rose in his face. Charles could see that while he was in many ways a respectable man, the opportunity to swindle young men was far too tempting to ignore. It was fortunate that Charles had the foresight to bring all of the documentation required to receive the stated price. "The area for sale is marked here," he said as he pointed to a series of outlined blocks south of the rail line. "The hotel is here, and a number of lots fall south."

Charles studied the map and the details of the Bowlea township. There were several lots scattered throughout the area with many properties along the main road.

"A quarter section with furnished boarding house, carriage and stables for two hundred dollars?"

"Yes, sir, a bargain for the taking. I will need the funds from you up front so my partner can prepare the land title and deed straight away. And I need to find the keys, of course."

Mr. Pedersen opened a large cabinet that hung on the wall and stared at dozens of rings of keys arranged on brass pegs. A little paper tag hung from each set, and Charles admired the skill required to so effectively keep track of which keys belonged to which property. The broker hovered his hand over the rows of keys and, as if by magic, plucked a set from the top row.

"Alphabetical, you see," he said, as he showed Charles the name *Bowlea* scrawled on the tag in thick, black ink. The ring held several keys for various rooms and locks on the property. "You're free to take possession immediately. The train only goes as far as Red Deer, but you can hire a coach there to take you the remainder of the way."

"Thank you for your assistance, Mr. Pedersen," Charles beamed. The pride of ownership was evident by his broad smile.

"Your wife will be pleased, sir," he said as he rang the bell and his lawyer entered the room.

"Mr. Prescott, Mr. Lowe will take care of you from here. Mitchell, please prepare this lot for purchase, including the building here. Mr. Prescott will be taking possession immediately as the amount has been paid in full."

The lawyer's office was small and sparse, and Charles sat in silence as Mr. Lowe filled out the deed to the property. Charles was transfixed by the scratching of the fountain pen as it scrawled his fate onto the vellum. Mr. Lowe placed the sheets one by one into the seal press and squeezed the lever to notarize them. Charles took the deed from his hands and held it tightly in his own.

"There you are, Mr. Prescott. You are now a landowner," Mr. Lowe said as he ushered Charles from his seat to the reception area.

"Thank you," Charles said as the door closed abruptly behind him.

"Mr. Pedersen will see you now," the clerk said to the room. The next young man sprang from his seat, eager to buy a piece of his future.

Abigail and Emma walked downstairs to see about some breakfast. The smell of the freshly baked treats filled the halls with the most welcoming aroma, and caused Emma to realize just how hungry she was.

"Three biscuits with butter, please. And two glasses of milk," Abigail said to the attendant.

"Might we have some cream puffs, Mama? Do you not see how perfectly scrumptious they look?" Emma said as she pointed to the tray of pastries on display before them. Abigail considered the small amount of pocket money she had, and was hesitant to splurge. Understanding that it was unlikely they would see such refined fare in their new town, she conceded and ordered two with lemon glaze. Once their selections were laid before them, Abigail generously buttered the third biscuit and wrapped it in her linen handkerchief. She hoped it would stay fresh long enough for Charles to enjoy it.

"Quickly, now," Abigail said as she urged her daughter to gulp down her milk. "We are to meet your father in the park at half past ten, and I want to take a look at some of the shops along the way."

Abigail took a larger bite of her biscuit than was considered ladylike and smirked at Emma as she chewed. Her daughter ate with the same lack of decorum but caught herself before she licked the bit of jam off her finger. As she wiped the residue off her hands with a napkin, she peered over her mother's shoulder to see a gentleman approaching the hotel's front desk.

"Look at that fellow, Mama," she said quietly with a tilt of her head. "He must have ten men. Look at all those trunks!"

Abigail's curiosity was piqued by her daughter's assertions, but her propriety urged her not to look. She considered dropping her butter knife and then retrieving it, but opted instead to take a moment in the powder room so she could see the spectacle for herself. She pushed her chair out from the table and stood, slowly pivoting on her heels to turn.

The man stood at the long wooden counter and gave instructions to Mr. Lyle and his assistant in a way that demonstrated that even though he was a guest, he was in charge. Abigail counted a series of eight porters who carried leather-bound chests into the lobby and piled the trolley high. The fluidity with which they arranged the travel-worn trunks suggested a routine that was often repeated.

Abigail walked in their direction, spying the gentleman from afar and admiring the fine quality of his Derby hat and top coat. She thought he would not have been out of place at The Danbury. She turned back towards Emma and flashed her a playful smile. As she swivelled back in the direction of the ladies room, she forcefully bumped into one of the chambermaids, sending the stack of wood she carried crashing to the floor. Nearly everyone in the lobby stopped to look in their direction.

"Oh my! Pardon me! I am so sorry, miss," Abigail said as she crouched down to help pick up the logs.

"No trouble at all, ma'am. I should have been more careful."

The maid fumbled as she tried to pile the wood on her arm with one hand while waving Abigail away from the mess with the other. As Abigail returned to her feet, she saw the gentleman look her way. The fellow was eager to get to his room, but found himself drawn to her natural beauty. He smirked to himself as he noticed her fine attire and he wondered how long she had been in that part of the country.

The manager of the hotel waved his arm in a quick circle above his head. The porters immediately stood at attention.

"This way lads. Up the stairs to the third floor."

They shuffled as they marched through the corridor, each one passing the gentleman in their turn. As Abigail stood in the middle of the lobby, smoothing down her wrinkled skirt, the gentleman paused to give her a final smile and tip of his hat. She felt an uneasiness at his admiration of her. Although she was flattered, she offered only a shallow nod and faint smile as she hurried past him to rejoin Emma at their breakfast table.

"Are you alright?"

"Yes, quite. You know as well as any why I never step foot in a china shop," she said as they giggled.

"Did you get a closer look at the fellow? Was he even more handsome up close? He must be very important to have all those boys waiting on him," Emma said with widening eyes.

"Yes, I imagine he might be." Abigail retrieved a cream puff from the silver tray between them. As she savoured the delicacy, she found herself going over the details of the gentleman's demeanour. He reminded her greatly of her own father, and she wondered what it must have been like for him to travel great distances with an entourage. She wondered at the man's occupation and family but was urged out of her reverie by Emma's reminder of their noon rendezvous.

Charles walked confidently as he made his way to the park. In the front pocket of his satchel held the future he had promised to his family. The transaction happened much as he expected, but his new responsibility thrust a heavier weight upon his shoulders than he envisioned. He found a moment of solitude under the shade of a birch tree; he closed his eyes as the wind brushed his skin and rustled the leaves overhead. He wondered how his family would fare on the frontier. He wondered how Abigail felt being guided by a decision that was ultimately his. He removed the deed from his pocket and slowly unfolded it. His fingertips grazed the raised details of the seal, an official confirmation of his choices. A small map of the area was included, as well as the detailed coordinates to the exact location of his property. The map was crude but showed a horseshoe-shaped lake curving through all but southeast edge of his land. Although his billfold felt markedly lighter, Charles was confident that his remaining funds would suffice to launch the venture and see them through until regular visitor tenancy became an assured source of income. He folded the map and placed it back in the pouch. He walked towards the courtyard to share his news with the ladies.

Abigail sat on the bench while Emma kneeled on the shawl she had laid upon the dewy grass. Under the fluttering leaves of a young poplar, Abigail spied a mother squirrel with her two miniature babies.

"Look, Emma," she said in a whisper, pointing to the small family. Rushing around them in frantic circles was a small beast that Abigail instantly knew was the father. He gathered nuts, twigs and leaves in his mouth and when his cheeks could hold no more, he would zip up the tree to unload his bounty. Emma lay down and outstretched her hands to rest atop the cool blades of grass. With a delicate flicker of her fingers, she enticed one of the babies to toddle over to investigate. As Charles approached he startled the rodents and sent them scampering in different directions.

"Papa!" Emma yelped as she pushed herself to her knees.

"I am sorry, petty, I did not notice your new friends," he said as he took a place beside Abigail. She was perched on the edge of the wrought iron seat and watched impatiently as Charles removed the deed from his pocket and handed it to her.

"A piece of property of our own."

"Oh, Charles, how wonderful," she said as she unfolded the crisp document and reviewed the fresh ink of his signature.

"You see, everything is working out as planned. Look here, this is a map of the township," he said, handing the map carefully to Emma. "See this mark here? This is where our new home stands, right on the edge of Aspen Street. The shaded area around it is the lake."

"It sounds delightful, Papa," she said as her cheeks began to ache under the strain of her enduring smile.

"The rail line runs just here, you see," he said, showing the map to Abigail. "Mr. Pedersen assured me that it would be completed in less than three months. He said there will be workers and transients in the area that will keep us turning a small profit until the line is fully operational. I expect we will leave tomorrow, now that everything is settled."

"May we leave today, Papa?" Emma asked.

"Not today, Emma, for I have yet to book a train."

"Well you had better head to the station," Abigail said. "Emma is nearly as excited as I am."

Chapter Ten

The train to Edmonton arrived in Red Deer just past nine o'clock the following morning. The items Charles needed were procured swiftly, and the family had him to thank for the expedience of the purchases. Ledger books, pens and ink, washing sodas, lamp oil, candles, pantry items and coal were piled into the coach he had hired outside of the Elk River Mercantile. The largest of his purchases was a mottled grey horse who followed closely alongside the four rented ponies. The journey over the rugged trail was scheduled to take twenty hours, and Charles was sure to buy Abigail and Emma each two wool blankets; one to break the bite of the cool prairie wind and the other to cushion their bottoms. As they passed through the abandoned Tail Creek settlement, the low dives of the vultures over a dying buffalo stood as a testament to the wildness of their destination. An overnight stay at Susannah's Stopping House, however, was a fleeting indication of civilisation. Their break was brief, but Charles thought her scones were enough to entice him back one day.

The lengthening spring days and increase in sunlight had given Charles the false promise of arriving and unloading the wagon before nightfall. The roads were mere trails, barely broken into the dense soil of the grassland. Heavy rains and a short burst of hail had made the mud thicker than sourdough and extended the second leg of their journey by nearly half a day.

The carriage was steady as it climbed the final hill to bring the Prescotts into the tiny settlement. The collection of buildings was sparse, and there seemed to be little consistency in their design or the materials used to construct them. Ramshackle shops with wooden facades stood alongside vacant lots and appeared as dim as fading lamps on an abandoned street. Each structure was designed as a potential business, dispensing in the necessities of life on the prairies. To accommodate each entrepreneur, they were outfitted with a sitting room and kitchen in the back and sleeping quarters above shop. The tinderboxes were interspersed amid the brick of the post office and the tents of men headed to the southern collieries.

As the horses trotted along the only lane through town, Charles was greeted by friendly nods from a few of the residents. Abigail craned her neck to see over his shoulder and could only make out blurred faces as the wagon passed by. She understood their curiosity, as the entrance of newcomers could arouse curiosity and scrutiny in any community. The townsfolk were no doubt aware that the previous hotel owners had left everything behind, and already held opinions of the Prescotts' intentions. Emma looked through the small opening in the canvas and tried to determine which building was her school. As she bumped along in the twilight and strained to see beyond each faint outline, she wondered if any town in the district had such charm.

At the end of Aspen Street, before it extended out of town, sat a red brick building. It rose two stories high, and with twelve windows visible on the upper story, Charles estimated the room count at twenty. A white wooden verandah wrapped around the perimeter of the main floor and was mirrored by balconies and railings on the second. The slate black roof was hidden in the evening sky, and the white shutters peered out from the flanks of each window. The stable was empty, and the carriage was locked tight to the well pump.

Charles' excitement resonated with Abigail and caused her to smile beamingly. Emma perked up in her seat as the wagon pulled up in front of The Olesky Boarding House. The sign was faded and cracked and showed a great deal of age, while the building it hung from did not. The driver loaded the trunks onto the drying mud and worked with Charles to offload the provisions. He left the goods in a pile at the front entrance and turned the wagon back in the direction of Red Deer.

"This looks promising, Charles," Abigail said as she walked along the perimeter of the building. Emma followed close behind and stopped every few yards to peek through the windows. Charles joined the ladies on the back porch and took each of them into the comfort of his arms. As they looked out into the night sky, they could not see beyond the moonlight dancing on the water's surface. An exploration of the surrounding fields would have to wait until morning.

"We have arrived, my dears. I know it was not the most pleasant journey, but I can assure you both that the possibilities here are very promising. The work will be hard, but honest, and everything we put into this venture, we will get back in personal satisfaction and accomplishment."

"I am not afraid to work hard, Papa," Emma said, returning her father's embrace. "I love digging in the garden."

"There now, I am glad to hear it!"

"I am not afraid either," Abigail said as she rested her head on Charles' shoulder. "Although I am not entirely sure how much help I will be. Josephine was not wrong when she said my duties should be relegated to sweeping and boiling water."

"You will be who I look to for that feminine touch. You will make this place our home, and fill it with laughter and memories. And, of course, clean laundry." Charles gently ribbed Abigail for he knew that dabbing a few droplets of rogue tea from her blouse was the extent of her experience as a laundress.

Abigail laughed with Emma and Charles as they walked the creaking planks to the front entrance. Charles had assured Abigail that her work in the hotel was necessary for only the first few weeks until they had enough business to warrant a housekeeper. Abigail had seen the maids at Shelby House struggle with the daily maintenance of the household, and was wholly unfamiliar with the grit required to undertake it for more than an hour or two.

Charles removed the heavy set of keys from his pocket and inserted the largest brass into the lock. In a brief moment of hesitation, he wondered if the door would open or if he was a victim of the type of fraud Mr. Lyle had warned him about. He turned the key hard and with a quick jerk, the latch clicked open.

The smell inside the hotel was musty, and dust particles floated like fireflies. Charles was thankful that the daylight was spent ensuring their safe arrival, but he so wished it was still afternoon.

"First thing, we must start a fire and light the lamps," he said as he moved about the lobby and gathered up the candlesticks he could see around them. "You two can gather firewood from outside. I noticed a stack on the back porch."

Abigail and Emma cautiously moved through the kitchen to the rear of the building and opened the door to the outside. The breeze off the water was crisp, and the fine mist delighted their faces with a cool tickle.

"I can hardly wait for morning, Mama. Do you suppose the lake is surrounded by those lovely high grasses? They are breeding grounds for all kinds of foul."

"It certainly could be. We saw enough of it along the way. Here, I will help you. Hold out your arms."

The light from the fireplace cast an amber tone over the covered furnishings. Charles was anxious to see what items were left behind and whether they would do his vision justice. His main task for now, however, was to find a place for them to sleep.

"I imagine all of the rooms are upstairs," he said as he held the lamp high and illuminated the stairwell. He was far too weary to locate the family's quarters and felt a guestroom would do for the night. "Come now, each of you bring a candle, and we shall prepare our beds."

Charles led his family into the hallway, and as the flicker from his candle tinted the walls around them, he could see the faint pattern of doors lined up like soldiers on either side. The first room at the top of the stairs held a large office that occupied the entire east side of the building. As he walked down the narrow corridor with the ladies following closely behind, he opened a few of the guest room doors in succession; he was greeted by the same small bed, desk, chair and wardrobe in each. There was a larger room at the far end whose only addition to the basic amenities was an iron tea stove. The room appeared to be specifically designated for families and would serve their purposes for the evening nicely. Their temporary lodgings held a wide brass bed and a stacking bunk near the window. Emma rushed in and hurriedly climbed the ladder to ensure the morning's first view of the lake.

"Wait, my love, let us shake out the sheets first," Abigail said. "I think it may be best for us to sleep in our clothes tonight." She was thankful it was so dark, for she could hardly bear the sight of dust at Shelby House and was confident there would be at least a half inch on every surface of their new home. She wondered how long the hotel had been vacant and how long it had been since a warm body had slept there.

The family settled into their beds and drew warmth from their thick wool blankets and the fire from the small stove in the corner. As Emma drifted off, she thought about her dolls and how they must have felt each time she put them to sleep in only their petticoats. Abigail felt ashamed that her daughter would be forced to sleep in such a setting, particularly since she had already endured the train bunks and the cots at Miss Susannah's. But her thoughts could not compete with the weight of her eyelids, and she conceded that this arrangement would only last the night.

As Charles tried to find comfort in the rigid flock bed, his stomach turned with uneasiness. His mind could not escape the thoughts of all the things to be done tomorrow and every day thereafter.

The faint sound of chirping awoke Emma just before dawn. As she stretched and released a heaving yawn, the sunrise slowly changed the colours in the room from pale brown to a light, warm ginger. She created a small porthole to the outside by wrapping the tip of her finger with her bed sheet and wiping it in small circles against the grimy pane. A sliver of sun peeked over the undulating grasslands, and the tones of rose and tangerine glinted off the still lakewater. Morning frost dusted the fortress of young reeds along the lake's perimeter and enticed Emma from the top bunk to explore the wetlands. She climbed down the ladder and opened the door with the guile of a field mouse.

As she crept down the stairs to the main level, she noticed two framed pictures lining the walls of the stairwell. One showed an image of a family gathered around a large tent in the forest. Beside it hung a more formal portrait of a husband and wife and their three children: two sons around her age and an infant daughter. She stared at the sepia photographs for a moment and wondered what had caused the old owners to leave so hastily that they would neglect to take such personal keepsakes. She continued her descent to the main level and ambled into the lobby. The interior looked much different in the early morning light and far more pleasant to her than the night before. The furnishings were covered with a variety of old bed sheets, and Emma resisted the urge to unveil what amounted to a room full of unopened gifts.

The hotel's design echoed the needs of the other businesses in town but their family quarters were separated from the rest of the main floor by a thick wall of brick. The lobby was simple and plain with a short front desk and small seating area. Adjacent to the entrance sat the lounge and dining room where guests would gather for communal meals. On the east side, guests could find comfort in the well-appointed drawing room and pass the long, rural evenings listening to songs from the upright piano.

Emma was coaxed into the drawing room by the sight of hundreds of books along the back wall. She quickly scanned the titles, hoping for some illustrated volumes, but the covering of dust masked the embossed titles along their spines. The logs her father had set alight in the fireplace the night before had burned down to embers, so she added another along with some kindling to keep her parents from waking with a chill. Layers of thick brocade and sheer linen draped the front windows, and Emma corded each panel back to brighten the room with more sunshine.

She wandered into the dining hall past the lounge and pushed through the swinging set of chest-high doors that led into the kitchen; they chirped with a desperate need for oil. A large wood burning stove and open-pit fireplace were nestled in the corner. Cast iron pots and kettles were stacked on the floor beside the hearth, and the blisters of rust on their surface spoke to the lapse since their last use. The pump at the sink was covered in cobwebs, but Emma's thirst prompted her to test its utility. A chip of red paint peeled from the heavy wood handle as she lifted the lever; with a few heavy strokes, a brown sludge was drawn up from the well. As she continued to pump, the brown liquid began to clear, and she cupped her hand to bring the water to her mouth. In the middle of the kitchen was a large wooden work surface. The light of dawn refracted through the trays of glassware and china that lay on nearly every flat surface of the room. A large iron ring inset into the floorboards led to the pantry. Emma's imagination coaxed her to the entrance of the secret lair, but no give from a hard tug of the ring indicated that no buried treasure would be found that day.

The windows above the basin faced the large field, and Emma could see blurred patches of jade and flax through the filthy glass. The door to the back porch was latched, and Emma pushed hard to force it open. The endless fingers of high grass beckoned her to run out and feel their soft fronds on her skin. The hills in the distance heaved slightly and formed dales and meadows around the shimmering water. She ran off the porch, each of her light footsteps cutting a path to the sandy shore. As she ran, dozens of small marsh birds were shaken from their repose by the rustling of the grass and grain around them. Hundreds of tiny creatures flew up and around her, only to sink back into their nests of intertwining stalks. She tried to catch them in her cupped palms as she ran, but their size and agility left them far out of reach.

The property was flanked on three sides by the lake. As Emma turned to look at her new home from the shoreline, she noticed how little land surrounded it. There was enough land for a good-sized garden, but it would only be enough to feed her own family. Her father was a hotelier, and she understood that they were not meant to be farmers. She ran along the edge of the lake as the water splashed against her unlaced boots and gurgles of water erupted from beneath each displaced pebble. As she kicked the water, her eyes caught sight of a wooden barrier erected at the far end of the property. She waded her way through the reeds to the shallow embankment in the northeast corner. The barrier was erected atop the unfinished irons of a rail line. A sign affixed to the front of the barrier read: Bowlea Terminus - END OF LINE.

Emma looked at the structure confusedly, and wondered why the railway had not continued through the meadow. From the conversations she had overheard between her parents, she understood that they expected the rail to come before fall. She wondered if perhaps this route was a part of another line, and the main line was being built through a different part of town.

"Emma!" she heard her mother call from the porch. She turned and ran back to the hotel, anxious to tell her about the serenity of their own personal lake.

"Mama, just look! Is it not splendid?" she asked as she rushed to her mother's side.

"It is quite beautiful," Abigail said as she took a moment to survey their surroundings.

"Come with me; I want to show you the lake!" Emma said with a tug on her mother's arm.

"Not right now, my love. There is a great deal of work to do. We are in no position to receive guests and your father wants the hotel up and running within the week. We are heading to the general store to post an advertisement. Would you like to see your new home in the daylight?"

Emma was disappointed that they would not be able to laze away the morning perched under a parasol on the lakeshore. She was excited to see the ducks and geese up close but wanted more than anything to see their new community.

"Yes, Mama. I will just take a moment to wash up."

Chapter Eleven

Bowlea was awake and a few of its residents were already milling about Aspen Street. They were occupied with their errands, and paid little mind to the newcomers.

"Look, Mama, there is the school," Emma said as she pointed to a newer structure in an area surrounded by large trees and an open play area. The schoolyard was empty, and Abigail assumed that the children were inside as their lessons would be in progress at that hour. The smell of fresh bread lured the family to the town's mercantile, where they stopped to procure breakfast.

"How do you do?" Charles asked the young man at the till.

"Hi-ya," he said as he shuffled the fresh baking to the front of the long counter. "How can I help you folks today?"

"We arrived last night and have not had time to get settled. We are in need of some breakfast. A half dozen rolls, please. And a half pound of smoked ham."

"Sure thing, sir. Where did y'all come from?" he asked as he began to cut thin slices from the large ham on the back table.

"We have just arrived from Ontario. Kingston. We have taken over the hotel at the end of the street," Charles said as he picked through the bushel of apples at the front of the store.

"The whole town's been wondering who took up the place ever since the broker's sign came down," the young man said, as he wrapped the ham in brown parchment and placed the rolls in a thin paper bag.

"Could we get some milk too, Papa?" Emma asked.

"The milk was brought in fresh from Jones this morning."

"Yes, that would be lovely," Abigail said.

"I'm James Coupland, Jr. My dad and me run this store. We're open daily at dawn and don't close until dark. If you need anything at all, we'll be here," he said as he handed the litre of milk to Abigail.

"Thank you, Mr. Coupland. We are the Prescotts. Charles, Abigail and Emma."

"Welcome to Bowlea."

"Thank you, that is very kind."

"Thank you, lad," Charles said. "May you point us in the direction of the post office?"

"It's two doors down on this side of the lane. Can't miss it."

"What a friendly young man, Charles," Abigail said as they strode the planked walkway to their next stop. "I hope the rest of the townsfolk are as affable as him."

As the Prescotts walked down the lane, they were greeted by passersby who tipped their hats and bid them good day. Their pleasantries lifted Abigail's spirits, and she grew confident that Charles had made the right choice. Charles was less certain as he noted the number of boarded windows and the ratio of people to buildings. The post office was situated in a small brick building. The sign above the porch was detailed in black and gold. and the lettering was as crisp as if it had been put up the day prior. The bell affixed to the door jingled when the family entered, and the face that greeted them from behind the counter was professional and personable.

"Good day, sir, ma'am, miss," she said, addressing each of them with a friendly smile.

"Good day. I was wondering if I might put up an advertisement. We are seeking two people for casual work at our hotel," Charles said.

"Certainly, sir," she said as she moved from behind the counter and pinned the advertisement to the community board.

"If you would be so kind as to mention our notice to anyone you think may be interested. I would like to hire as soon as possible."

"I'll pass the word along. Name's Doris Winters. I'm the postmistress here in Bowlea," she said, extending a hand for Charles to shake.

"Pleased to meet you, madam. I am Charles Prescott. This is my wife Abigail and daughter Emma."

"You are all very welcome. This is a small township, but the people are kind and god-fearing. We tend to look out for each other. I am sure you'll find it to your liking. My husband was the schoolmaster, but there isn't much need for a school nowadays. There used to be a couple dozen kids, but most everyone moved on because of the train. It's only us hearty folk that stayed behind. We make due well enough with the travellers that pass through and the settlers who like to keep in touch with their old lives."

Mrs. Winters looked to Emma whose head hung low at the prospect of being tutored at home.

"I'm sure you'll find activity enough, young lady," she said to her with a smile. "This is no big city, to be sure, but I tend to like the big skies and grasslands much more."

"Yes, it is quite lovely," Emma said as she raised her head and offered her a forced smile.

"I have a feeling we are going to be very happy here. I feel welcome already," Abigail said.

The Prescotts bid the postmistress good day and made their way towards their new home. As they walked from the south end, they passed a livery and stables, a small bank and the physician's office. A small outpost of the Northwest Mounted Police was located at the far end of the street, while a small graveyard was nestled beside the tiny church. They continued their walk around the town and within a half-hour found themselves back at the hotel. A young man stood on the front porch, nervously fiddling with the tattered cap in this hands. He smiled broadly and smoothed his hair with the palm of his hand as the Prescotts ascended the steps.

"I am afraid we are not quite ready to take guests, son," Charles said as he noticed that he carried no bag.

"I've come about the job, sir. Mrs. Winters said you're looking for a hand." He smiled sheepishly at Abigail and Emma who stood behind Charles.

"Already? But we only posted the advert a few minutes ago," Charles said in disbelief.

"There are few jobs in town, sir, and I would be happy for any work you could throw my way. I did some odd jobs for the Oleskys before they left, so I know the building well. I'm smart and fit, and honest, sir."

"I'm sure you are, young man. What is your name?"

"Tobias Boychuk, sir," he said as his nervousness died down.

"And you live with your parents here in town?"

"No, sir. I let a room from Mr. Winters. I have no family here." Tobias glanced at Abigail and quickly brought his view back down to the work-worn leather on his feet. She could see the boy was no more than fifteen and wondered how he found himself alone in that part of the country.

"I'm sure Mrs. Winters can vouch for me, sir. I'm a hard worker, and I keep to myself. I won't be a bother, promise."

"Do you require lodging, or would you prefer to stay on with the Winters?"

"I would like to stay there, sir. Mrs. Winters would miss me at cribbage if I wasn't around after dinner. And I expect I would appreciate the change of scenery at the end of the work day."

Charles smirked at his remark, not only because he had been a tenant of Mr. Danbury's but because he knew there would be little escape from the constancy of his own work.

"Have you much experience working the soil? We would like to get in a garden as soon as possible."

"Yessir, I can garden. I can fix most anything. I can work with wood," he said, as his face softened and showed signs of pride.

"Very well, the pay is fifty cents per day, and you will have lunch provided. The workday starts at six and ends at six with an hour for lunch and Sundays for yourself. I'll need you to start today. How does one o'clock sound?"

"Thank you, sir," Tobias said as he heartily shook Charles' hand and bounded back to the post office.

"He seems like a fine young man, Charles," Abigail said.

"Yes, he seems a good sort. We will find out soon enough how hard he is willing to work. Come, let us have breakfast," he said as he entered the hotel and closed the door behind him.

Abigail removed the overturned chairs from the small table in the kitchen and wiped the surface with a damp rag. She opened the packet of ham and set it in the middle of the table. She rarely dined so informally, save for picnics in the park, but Charles had warned of a period of adjustment. She rinsed out three short glasses, filled them with milk and set them on the table. She ripped the rolls open with a dull knife.

"I hope to have something more substantial for dinner," she said as her empty stomach called out with a grumble. She composed each sandwich with their few slices of ham and wished she was able to find the butter among their provisions.

"Tobias and I will get everything unloaded and then get started on the cleaning. Eat up; we have a great deal of work to do today."

"How do you like the town, Emma?" Abigail asked through hurried bites.

"It is a shame there is no school. I was so looking forward to meeting new friends," Emma said with a sad tinge to her voice.

"You shall make friends with the birds then," she said as she gave her daughter a playful wink.

Emma smiled as she set down the brief resentment she felt. She knew it was not her mother's fault the town was not as vibrant as she had hoped. Whatever her circumstance now, it was still a welcome change from the nursery.

"With it being so close to summer and with so much to do, perhaps it is best that we postpone your studies until September. I will teach you myself."

"You must see the library they left behind, Papa," Emma said. "There must be books on every topic."

"Is that so? Then you must have your pick when we finish setting up for business."

"Please, Papa, may I pick one today?"

"Not now, petty. We must focus on work before we can think of leisure."

"But Papa..." Emma said, as her plea was interrupted by a faint rap at the door. "Is that a guest already?"

"Hush now, finish your roll," Abigail said.

Charles moved quickly to the door and paused for a moment to brush the crumbs from his moustache. When he opened the door, he found a woman some years younger than Abigail standing on the landing.

"May I help you?" he asked.

"Beg pardon, sir. Are you the gentleman who is re-opening the hotel?" she asked. Her eyes were tired and matched the worn appearance of her clothes. As Charles introduced himself and shook her hand, the coldness of her skin surprised him considering the warmth of the air outside.

"What is your experience?"

"I have worked as a housemaid since my youth, sir. I worked for the Quinns for a spell, but they moved on when the work dried up. I've been staying with the Joneses. I helped out with their babies, but they're almost grown now. I'd like to stay on in Bowlea if I can."

Abigail could see the woman from her position in the kitchen and moved to the door for closer inspection. Emma set aside her breakfast and followed suit.

"How do you do, ma'am, I'm Laura Shaw."

"Good day, Laura."

"There will be a great deal of work to do," Charles said. "Laundry, cleaning, keeping house as well as cooking. The guest rooms will also need to be kept up, but my wife and daughter will be helping with that."

"Yes, sir. I'm no stranger to hard work. Taking care of a household and lodgings would be a fine bit easier than the babies. I welcome the change." She rocked back and forth on her heels as she waited for Charles to make his decision.

"The pay is thirty-five cents per day, including your room and board. We have just hired another employee, Tobias, who will tend the property and maintain the building."

"I've seen him at the Winters'," Laura said. "It all sounds very good, sir. I can start straight away."

Charles looked to Abigail who nodded her approval of the hire. She led Laura to the kitchen and through the laundry to the staff quarters. The rooms had not been prepared and were in the same state as the rest of the hotel.

"I believe the first order of business will be to prepare your sleeping quarters and our family suite. We will fare poorly if we do not have proper sleeping arrangements as soon as possible." Abigail ran Shelby House and was well acquainted with organizing the daily tasks of the household staff.

"Where would I find the cleaning cupboard, ma'am?" Laura said as she removed her coat and bonnet and lay them across the dusty desk chair.

"I am not sure. Let us see what we can find."

The provisions were piled in the lobby, and Abigail searched the heap for the sack of washing soap. The utility closet off the kitchen held a number of brooms and dustpans while the large laundry basins sat overturned on the back porch. Fallen clotheslines draped from tall wooden posts where laundry once hung. Laura opened the door to the family quarters which extended west from the kitchen. Their new home was made up of a small drawing room with fireplace, a master bedchamber and two smaller bedrooms. As Abigail quickly surveyed her surroundings, she thought the smallest room would do well as a study area for Emma; her bedroom next door was small and bright, and the window provided an ideal view of the lake. The master suite was sparsely furnished, and Abigail was thankful that their quarters lacked any personal traces of the previous owners; it served her better to think of her family as the first inhabitants.

"We shall tackle the house one room at a time," she said, handing a broom to Emma.

"But I want to go outside! Do you not see how lovely it is today, Mama?"

"Yes, I too would very much like to spend the day outdoors, but the main priority, as I have already asserted, is to make the hotel habitable for us and our guests. Now come here and give me a hand, if you please. Laura will do quite well with our quarters."

"Yes, Mama," Emma said begrudgingly as they moved into the hotel's drawing room. She was beginning to understand the sacrifices her father had spoken of.

Heavy cloth draped each piece of furniture and concealed the clocks and paintings. As Abigail lifted each sheet, in turn, she marvelled at the fine quality of the furnishings, and the amount of items that were left behind.

"Now, Emma, your job is to carefully gather up all of the linen and put them on the back porch. Try not to shake about too much on your way out. The more you shake, the more we sweep."

The cleaning and preparation of the hotel took nearly a week, and when the ladies at last found a moment's repose, they sat on the back steps and watched the sun hang above the hills. They each took pride in their efforts to make the lodgings look as fine as they did, but were more excited to welcome a few days rest than a drawing room full of guests.

Tobias had spent the bulk of his time preparing the garden for planting. He had roped off and tilled a scant acre between the main building and the stables. It was still mid-spring, and Charles wanted to complete the seeding within the next few days; with the rurality of their current location, it was essential to grow enough food to keep his family and staff in good health while stocking his pantry for the influx of guests.

The hotel was scheduled to open the following day. The daily wages of his staff had put a dent in Charles' funds, and boarders were needed to replenish the dwindling stack of dollars in his tobacco tin safe. The work had been gruelling, but when Charles toured the hotel and saw all they had accomplished, he knew any traveller would feel welcome to stay there.

Leisure time had been scarce since the Prescotts' arrival, leaving them little opportunity to meet their neighbours. The inquisitive gazes of passersby demonstrated some interest in their lives, but no one had yet come to call. Charles presumed that they stayed back for fear of troubling them while they were clearly occupied.

"Do we have time to go down to the lake now, Mama?" Emma asked as she eyed the shimmering pool in the distance.

"I do suppose we have done as much as we can for now. Let us all walk down. Laura, would you care to join us?" Abigail asked as she gathered the strength to lift her weary body from the comfort of the hard wooden steps.

"No thanks, ma'am. I'll just take some time to myself before I start supper," Laura said.

"Yes, of course. You deserve a bit of rest. And you, sir?" Abigail said as she moved towards Charles and placed her arms about his waist.

"I would like to get the sign repainted and hung today while it is still light. Perhaps tomorrow."

"Alright. In that case, I will have to beat Emma to the lake myself." Abigail ran past her daughter and gave her a playful pinch on the side. Emma was coaxed into following her mother's lead and left one corner of the sheet she was hanging droop down from the line like a wilted lily.

Tobias looked longingly at the lake and wiped the droplets of sweat from his brow. He wished that he could plunge headlong into the fresh waters and wipe away the layer of grime that clung to his skin. Charles pulled out his pocket watch and checked the time; he then stared up at the sky to examine the position of the sun.

"It is a quarter to four now, Tobias. Can you ensure me that you will be back in time to help me hang the sign?" Charles said with a smirk.

Tobias dropped the rake at the side of the garden and seemed to jump over the entire expanse of overturned soil. He turned back and yelled a gracious thanks while he ran as fast as he could towards the lake. The ladies stopped and turned only to see a dirty, sweaty blur approaching from the house. He ran past, unbuttoning his shirt as he moved. He reached the shore far before them and removed his shirt and boots, and peeled off his sweat-soaked socks. He ran into the lake, lifting his knees high as the water splashed and resisted his entry. He outstretched his arms and fell forward, becoming completely submerged by the cool water.

Charles could see Tobias' figure splashing around from the house, and was pleased that the boy was able to relieve some tension. He had worked him hard over the last week and understood that kindness and compassion went a long way in building trust and loyalty in an employee. He removed his hat and took a seat on the porch to rest for a moment. He had never been fond of being wet, and the idea of being fully submerged in pool larger than a washtub quickened his pulse and made his stomach uneasy.

Emma hastened her pace towards the lake, creating a gap between her mother that Abigail tried to regain with her long, steady strides. But Emma arrived at the shore first and called out to her new friend.

"Is the water warm?" she asked as she removed her boots and short stockings.

"It's perfect!" he said as he allowed the water to push him onto his back to bob on the surface.

Abigail reached the shore as Emma tested the water with her toes.

"Not too deep, my love. We must order you a proper suit if you wish to swim," she said as she followed Emma's lead and bared her feet.

Emma gathered up the layers of her dress and apron and bunched them in front of her, just above her knees. Her giggles came forth as each step took her deeper into the chilly water.

"It is so cold!" Emma called out to Tobias, as she felt the goose pimples emerge on her skin.

"You just need to get used to it! Come on, Mrs. Prescott. I'm sure you'll love it, too!"

"Come on, Mama, it really is lovely."

"I thought you said it was cold?" Abigail asked, teasingly.

She stood at the edge of the water for a moment and watched as the clouds floated low against the light blue sky. The water tickled her toes, and she curled and wiggled them between the sand and the frigid liquid. She flung the water off her feet in alternating kicks and taunted Emma with splashes of water against the back of her legs. Abigail smiled and laughed at the sight of Emma splashing Tobias in the same way and was thankful that she had a friend to enjoy her time with. As the party played, a strong, deep rumble could be heard in the sky.

"Look!" Tobias said as he pointed overhead.

Above them flew dozens of large white birds, the likes of which the ladies had never seen. Their massive bodies floated in the air, and Abigail wondered how they could possibly stay aloft. Emma's neck strained as she looked up, her mouth gaping wide at the spectacle of the giant birds. Their bugle call echoed across the water as they circled overhead and prepared to land. Their wings spanned a length that Emma herself could not mimic, even with her arms outstretched as far as they could go. They glided towards the surface and seemed to hover motionlessly before their plump bodies made contact with the water. Their wings flapped and spritzed the air around them as they settled into their positions near the northern shore.

"Look at all of the geese, Mama," Emma said as she pointed to a large number of birds bobbing on the surface.

"Those are unlike any geese I have seen before," Abigail said, as she squinted her eyes for a better focus.

"I believe they are swans, ma'am," Tobias said as he emerged from the water. "They come and stay in these parts during this time of year."

"Swans! My first new species, Mama," Emma exclaimed.

"We used to get them lots down in Fort Macleod. We used to sit on the trestle after the train passed and watch them sail down the river. There were so many that even in July the river looked like it was covered in snow. When I saw them the first spring I was here in Bowlea it felt like I was home."

As Emma listened to Tobias reminisce, she wondered at how such a tender soul had found himself alone in these harsh lands.

After the evening chores were completed, Emma was grateful for the opportunity to learn more about their earlier discovery. She pulled the book from her bag and unwrapped the shawl overlaying it. She moved to the back porch and sat on the steps, opening the book to the index. *Cygnus Buccinator* was listed amongst several other varieties of swans, and she thought their name related to the signal of their call quite well. As she carefully flipped the pages to view the plate, Tobias entered from the kitchen and took a seat beside her.

"Is that one of the books from the library?" he asked, as he lifted the front cover as it sat on her lap.

"No, I brought it with me. It was a gift from my mother. It is a picture book about the different birds of America. I remember seeing a picture of those swans."

"I've seen them on the lake before, but they never seem to stay long. I think it must be a sign of fall when they leave."

"We only get to enjoy them for a few months, then," she said with a frown as she traced the swan's painted image with her finger.

"There's still plenty of time to get your fill. After chores tomorrow, what do you say we walk to the northern shore to get a better look?"

"Yes, please!" Emma said as she smiled at her new friend. Tobias smiled back and admired her enthusiasm.

"How do you like Bowlea so far? Is it what you expected?" He plucked a piece of the tall grass that grew up against the railing and put it between his front teeth.

"I did not know what to expect, but I do like it here very much. One can hardly compare it to Kingston."

"Kingston, where is that?"

"In Ontario. It's on a lake, too. Lake Ontario is so big that when you look out from Morton's Wharf, you can hardly see where the water ends."

"That sounds like a sight to see. I've never seen anything outside of Alberta, myself. But I like it just fine."

"You were born here?"

"Down south in a place called Lethbridge. My pa worked all sorts of jobs. He worked in the mines for a while and then got on the crew building the Crow's Nest Line on the Pacific."

"What is the Pacific?" she asked, wondering if it had something to do with the ocean.

"The main rail line. I'm sure you must have travelled on it to get here," he said with a chuckle.

"Yes, of course," she said as she cast her eyes down on her book and blushed hard at his teasing. She wanted to appear cultured and educated, but there were evidently many aspects of district life she had yet to learn. "Where is your family now?"

Tobias looked out to the rye fields beyond the lake and paused for several moments before answering.

"My ma died three years ago from the fever. She just fell ill one day and never got better. She was so sick. It's a strange thing, having someone die in front of you." His gaze remained fixed on the spot in the distance.

"I am sorry, Tobias." Emma felt tears start to form in her eyes as she recalled the times her own mother had been only mildly ill; she could not imagine being without her now. "Where is your father?"

"It's been two years now since he passed. We were out by Pincher Creek doing some work for a rancher down there. We were trying to mate a bull with a cow, but the bull turned."

Emma watched Tobias as the colour left his face and his voice lowered to a whisper.

"He just started to charge. I jumped in the pen and tried to stop him before my pa got hurt, but the bull went mad and gored him. He gored him three times, right around here," he said as he motioned to the area around his stomach. "The lead hand tried to rope him, but it was too late. He got me a good one too, up here on my shoulder. I came out alright, though."

Emma was still and quiet. She did not know how to respond to such a tragic account. She thought of how brave he was to go through the world on his own and could not understand how he could speak of his losses so calmly. She placed her small hand atop his and gave it a squeeze. He looked at her with tears in his eyes and gave her an abbreviated smile. He was happy to have her hand to hold.

***

Charles opened the front doors of the hotel and placed a small sign on the floorboards of the porch. He had placed an advertisement in the *Calgary Herald* and hoped that word of the hotel's opening would spread through the nearby communities. He rearranged the wicker chairs and table on the front porch and seated himself down to wait for the first arrival.

"Good morning, Charles. How goes your opening day?" Mr. Winters called out from the lane.

"It has only just started, Louis," he said with a smile and a nod of his cap.

"Then, I wish you good day and good luck. The Oleskys never really had a good run of it," he said as he moved past the stairs.

Charles' ears perked up at this revelation, and he invited the postmaster to join him for a cup of tea. He was eager for friendship and had but little chance to learn more about the town or its inhabitants.

"Did you know the Oleskys well?" he asked as Mr. Winters obliged and sat down to some refreshment.

"Fairly well. Valeri moved here with his wife and children about five years ago, just after the C.P. linked out west. This place was built in the early seventies, long after most of the homesteaders had moved cross-country. There were some trappers and prospectors, but Bowlea didn't benefit from the rush as much as some towns on the route did. I suppose Val thought that when the rail came through it would open up the area like other parts of the district. He waited those five years, and the rail never did come through." Mr. Winters smiled unassumingly at Charles and dunked a vanilla wafer into his tea.

Charles could hardly accept what he was hearing. As he listened, he quietly grew ashamed of his own assumptions. He never once speculated that the reason for the Oleskys departure was a lack of visitors.

"I was told that the train would be completed shortly. Three months, at the latest," he said as he tried to steady his voice.

Mr. Winters let out a hearty laugh but soon checked himself, for it was Charles' livelihood that he was in fear of mocking. His laugh gently flowed into a sigh.

"I apologize for my reaction. It's just that we were all told the rail was coming, and on many occasions. Whenever we inquire as to the state of the rail, we're told it will be coming soon. We don't really know who to contact anymore since the line has changed hands so many times. Most of the residents left while they still had a little money to do so. Others, like Jones and me are able to make a modest living because of the essential services we provide. Times have been hard on our little town. There is no denying that."

Charles could hardly think, let alone speak a word. He could not get past the thought that he had been fooled. He shook his head and began a more direct line of questioning.

"Forgive me, but when did you and your family move here?"

"Going on ten years now."

"You have managed well," Charles said, with a glint of hope in his voice.

"Yes, but as I said, we are paid by Ottawa, and those cheques come every month like clockwork. Without those funds, we would have left some time ago. This town once had nearly three hundred residents. Now we have barely a hundred. If growth doesn't happen soon, I fear the remaining folks will move on to Red Deer or Edmonton."

"The broker assured me that the rail line would be completed by first snowfall. I can only hope that he was being truthful," Charles said as he stared at the reflection in his tea.

"Let us all hope so. Bowlea is a lovely place if only the railmen could see its potential."

"Good day, Mr. Winters, how do you do?" Abigail asked as she joined them and took a seat beside Charles.

"Fine, fine. I'm just off myself. Take care, Charles. Your family will do well in time," he said as he bid farewell and shuffled back to the post office.

Charles remained silent as Abigail poured herself a cup of tea. She studied him carefully as he sat in introspection.

"Is all well, Charles?"

He could not verbalize an answer but uttered only a low grunt. His eyes were transfixed on the lane as he quietly prayed for carriages full of weary travellers to pull up before them. He ran through the numbers and the amount of money he had remaining and attempted to stave off panic. His teacup shook and rattled the saucer as he put it down and Abigail placed her hand on his.

"Whatever is the matter, Charles?"

"What if no one comes?"

"Come now; we have only just opened our doors. One cannot expect to have patrons flood the halls within the first quarter-hour," she said with a kind laugh.

"No, what if no one ever comes? What if the train never passes through this little town?"

"That is nonsense. Mr. Pedersen assured you that the rail line would be completed, did he not?"

"Yes."

"Then that is the assertion we must cling to. You have told me yourself many times that there is no place in this business for doubt."

Charles nodded his head in agreement, although his thoughts did not match his movements. He was not at all comforted by Abigail's positivity. After she returned to the kitchen, he sat for hours in quiet reflection. The day passed in much the same manner with kind salutations from the occasional passersby. But as the darkness crept over the village, Charles was resigned that no visitors would come that day.

As the weeks passed, the Prescotts' daily rituals followed much the same pattern. Charles would wake, prepare one of his finer suits for wear, grease and comb down his hair and take his place in the wicker chair immediately after breakfast. After the completion of her chores, Emma would sit for hours poring over the books in the drawing room or spending time in the garden with Tobias. Circumstances were perhaps most difficult for Abigail, who had taken over the housekeeping after Laura was released from her duties the week prior.

Although she was familiar with how a household was run, Abigail was not accustomed to carrying out those duties herself. For the first time in her thirty-three years, she was responsible for the cleaning, the laundry and the preparation of food. Emma was a modest help, but her youth made her unreliable and stubborn. Tobias was well acquainted with the rigours of working life, but his enthusiasm for it waned when Charles reduced his workday and pay by half. He was reluctant to leave, however, for it was the first time since his father died that he felt like part of a family.

It was the first week of summer and the morning sun was already rising high. Abigail stood at the drawing room window and observed Charles' discontent. Her resentment towards him and their situation grew, and she was unsure of how to cope with her contrary feelings. It had been barely a month, but her ardent support of his decisions had grown tiresome.

"Is there anything I can get for you, my dear?" she asked as she moved outside and approached him from behind.

"No thank you."

Abigail was not surprised that he offered very little in the way of a response. The flow of conversation was barely a trickle, and she was anxious to pull him out of his melancholy state.

"Emma and I are heading down to the lake. Would you care to join us?"

Charles did not offer a response; he simply stared at the lane and waited.

Dawn had barely broken the next morning when a heavy knock was heard on the front door. The household was already awake and readying themselves for the day ahead. Tobias was at work sweeping the ash out of the kitchen hearth, and laid down the broom and hurried to the front door.

"Wait one moment, Toby," Charles said as he rushed to put on his waistcoat and smooth his hair back. He stumbled through the kitchen, bumping into the table and careening off any object that stood in his path. "I would like to be the first to greet them."

He moved as swiftly as he could towards the promise of a few dollars pay and unlatched the door. He swung it open and found a weary young man with a heavy pack slung over one shoulder.

"Good morning, lad," Charles said through his toothy grin.

"Do you have any rooms?" he asked, thumping the sack on the planks beneath his feet.

"Yes, certainly," he said as he picked up the bag and ushered the young man to the counter. "It is just upstairs. It has a single bed and offers a view of the lake."

"That's fine."

"Room ten please, Tobias."

"How much do I owe you?" the traveller asked, pulling a small leather pouch from his dungarees.

"The rate is two dollars per night and includes your breakfast. Supper is ten cents; a bath is five. Payment is due at checkout. How long do you plan to stay in Bowlea?" he asked, hoping the income would last more than one night.

"I'll push on tomorrow. I just need a good sleep and a hot meal. A bath would suit me fine, too."

Tobias led the young man up to his room, and Charles called for Abigail to boil the water and prepare the bath. The house was alive at their first source of revenue and Charles was beside himself with hope.

"Do you see? I knew they would come."

Abigail offered a smile and a tender grasp of his shoulder but neglected to point out that the man was their first tenant since their arrival five weeks prior. She well understood the importance of optimism and was determined the improve his spirits with her attitude.

"The first of many guests, surely. I will prepare the bath and ready some tea and breakfast for our guest."

"Thank you, my dear. You will see. Our luck will turn around soon enough."

Abigail gathered fresh towels to put in the bathhouse and solicited help from the others to complete the breakfast chores.

"Your father must be pleased," Tobias said as he and Emma took turns carrying buckets of well water to the large kettle.

"Oh, yes. But as Mama has said, one cannot pin their hopes on a single occupant."

Spring, 1902

Chapter Twelve

In the four years following, their little hotel had maintained a frequency of a few guests per month. A settler would pass through town on occasion, but their tenancy rarely lasted more than a day or two. The livery was forced to close, as Mr. Henry lacked sufficient business to buy hay to feed his team. The N.W.M.P. detachment was disbanded, and the officers relocated to New Stirling. Little was left in town, and even the Couplands were forced to abandon their shop. The Winters took on the role of merchant in the tight corners of the post office, but with so few customers, their requirements for stock were minimal.

In the early months as a hotelier on the frontier, Charles awoke each morning to the fresh promise of business. He would rise before dawn, make his own tea and set down to the task of reviewing his ledger. The funds going out contrasted with the funds incoming and he spent a good deal of the hours before breakfast ensuring that the figures remained in the black. When the weather was mild, he held his position on the front porch from the first chirp of the chickadee until the loons bellowed their evening calls. During the long winter months, he counted the seasoned logs in the back shed and portioned out lamp oil and coal. He arranged and re-arranged the dry goods, marking the amounts withdrawn and what remained to ensure they would have the means to survive.

The uncertainty and endless chores drove Charles and Abigail farther apart than they had ever been. The space between them stretched farther than the tract of land between Bowlea and Kingston; Charles now spent his nights on a converted bunk in his upstairs office. While the majority of his time was spent in quiet contemplation, when he did find the motivation to help with household tasks, he felled trees for firewood and kept a close watch on the garden. He was meticulous in his habit of collecting vegetable seeds, for he needed to perpetuate his resources into each subsequent year.

As each season passed, he further buried the regret he felt at the impact of frontier life on his family. There was neither a business need nor the money to keep hired staff, other than Tobias. Even when the young lad's wage was again reduced by half, he could not imagine leaving the Prescotts. He had moved into the staff quarters a year into his employment when it made better financial sense for him to save on the rent he was paying to Mrs. Winters. It was a better deal for Charles, as well, for the room was now included in his salary. The savings were only a minor benefit for Tobias, whose main motivation for staying was to maintain a close proximity to Emma. Each day he was in her company, his admiration for her grew. In the summer he would teach her to hold her breath underwater and go on deep-sea expeditions to find the *Nautilus*. When the temperature dipped below zero, they would hitch Winnie up to the sleigh and charge through inches of snow to cross the frozen Ashcroft Brook. The majority of his time, however, was occupied with earning money by any means he could. He knew that mucking pig pens and plowing rye fields helped grow the mound of money he kept in his old woollen stocking just as well as hauling sacks of flour for Mr. Winters.

Emma worked hard to help her mother in any way she could, but also made an effort to ensure she had some time for leisure at the end of each day. She spent her free time consumed with books and refining the techniques learned through her mother's dedicated tutorial of piano. Each morning for the two hours after breakfast, both she and Tobias were tutored in the fundamentals of math, nature, literature and music which did nothing to increase their wages or employability, but allowed them to maintain occupation during the frigid winters. In the summer, Emma reserved Sunday afternoons for herself. When she was not cavorting in the lake, she would wander the meadows around Bowlea with Tobias. They would chase each other up and down the hills, and hold hands and laugh when they became winded and fell into the bed of tall grasses. As they walked the fields, she would gather the petals of prickly roses, which she would later dry and bundle into fragrant muslin sachets. When he was out in the barn, she would slip them into the top drawer of his dresser so that each morning he would think of her.

Abigail yearned for her daughter's youth and often moved through her day in a perpetual state of weariness. She was nagged by incessant aches in her lower back and rough, chapped skin on her hands. She would end her work day unceremoniously with a tepid sponge-bath, and a whispered good night as Charles ascended the stairs to his office bedroom. Each morning she rose with the duty to complete the breakfast chores, and barely rested again until the last supper dish was placed back in the cupboard. With the burden of laundry, cooking and preserving vegetables, there was little energy left for activities that brought her joy. She found minor pleasure in the expansion of her culinary arts and looked forward to teaching Emma and Tobias each morning. But without Charles' interest, she developed an unwillingness to relay her experiences or feelings to him. She was often dismissed, and the feeling of being a bother taught her quickly to limit their interactions.

Over the last several months, Abigail's thoughts were consumed with the financial health of her family. Although it was not her habit to concern herself with Charles' private matters, she suspected that he was nearing insolvency. She had inquired throughout town for any occupation, but there was barely enough work to keep the business owners employed. Charles had few financial obligations other than fuel, food and sundry provisions and she assumed they were paid for by their guests. She knew better than to ask about money, but as they had not seen a visitor in nearly six weeks, she had no other choice but to inquire.

"Charles, may I have a word?" she asked as he sat at his desk and studied the ledgers before him.

"Yes, yes," he said dismissively as he failed to look up from his work.

"Charles, could you please give me your attention for a moment? I must speak with you."

Her tone had an assertiveness that Charles was not accustomed to; he laid down his fountain pen and gave her his full attention.

"I am sorry, my dear. What is it?"

"I am not entirely sure how to broach this subject, and I understand that you may find it rather brazen," she said with great trepidation.

"You are concerning me, Abigail. Whatever is the matter?"

"I am rather worried about the amount of funds we have remaining. I have considered the little amounts of income we have earned since our arrival and how much we spend just to survive. I fear we must be close to bankrupt," she said, speaking her thoughts as calmly as she could.

"That is nothing you should concern yourself with. Have we not managed thus far?" Charles asked as he shuffled his papers and resumed the calculation of his ledger.

"If you call barely surviving managing," she said in a raised voice that immediately refocused Charles' attention.

"Have I not always provided for you, cared for you, loved you? I do my best to provide a safe and stable home, do I not?" he asked as indignation strained his speech.

"Our home is fine, Charles, but what about the money?" she asked in a softened tone. "You must tell me what we have remaining." She was frightened by her own insistence and was anxious for his response. They had never spoken to each other in that manner before, and Charles' reaction was not what she expected. He sunk down further in his seat, placed his head in his hands and began to sob.

"This is not what I planned," he said, unable to meet Abigail's gaze. "Edwin assured me that the best option was for us to move out west. My research showed it to be a sound idea, but everything was done in such haste. I put the blame on no one but myself. I put all of my faith and hope into a venture that never had a chance of succeeding. I pulled you and Emma out of your home. I will never forgive myself for bringing you to this godforsaken place."

"How could you foresee this? The entire town pinned their hopes on a train that never appeared. That is hardly your doing."

"Of course it is my doing. If only I had swallowed my pride and stayed in Kingston, I could have had a steady salary as lead porter at The Charlotte. Our life would not have turned out so poorly."

Abigail pulled Charles out of the chair by his hands, fighting his desire to remain sunken under the weight of his discontent. Through his complaints, she led him through the lobby and out to the back porch.

"Is everything alright, Papa?" Emma asked as the couple moved quickly through the kitchen.

"Not now, my love," Abigail said as the screen door crashed shut behind her.

Emma stood motionless, wondering why her father had been so distraught. She moved near the sink and strained her ears to listen. Abigail sat Charles down in the heavy wooden rocker and pulled over another chair to sit beside him.

"Do you see this, Charles?" she asked as she motioned to the lavender glow that cascaded over the hills as the clouds bloomed from amber to crimson. The wind blew the grass in gentle waves across the back fields while the glass lake reflected the sunrise through thin surface ripples.

"This is ours," she said, squeezing his hand tightly in hers. "We own this outright, and no one can take it away from us. Think about what we had in Kingston. A house we did not own, furniture that was not ours, a lifestyle that in no way matched our means and friends in society who all but forgot us when we could no longer afford their acquaintance. How wonderful it is not to put on airs, or to dress only in a manner deemed socially acceptable. I would never give up the freedoms we have gained since relocating to Bowlea. I feel like myself here."

"I do not understand how you can be happy here. I have ruined life for both you and Emma. Do you not realize how much it pains me to see you in plain, cheap clothing? To watch as you both toil for hours each day to keep us all clean and fed? This is not what I would have wished for either of you. I thought guests would be frequent enough to allow us to maintain our status. But it is not to be," he said, wiping the tears from his eyes with the edge of his shirt sleeve. "I have failed you."

"I know it has not been easy, but you have not failed us. Please understand that."

"I have neglected you both. Emma as a father, and you as a husband. I am sorry, Abigail."

The pair embraced, and Charles was thankful that she held steady as he sniffled over her shoulder. She struggled with how to cope with his grief, and so held him tight and warmed his back with soothing strokes.

"All will be well, Charles. All will be well." She backed away and lifted his chin from his chest with a delicate touch and wiped a tear from his cheek with her fingertips. "We have managed thus far, have we not?"

"There is no more," he whispered through a shallow breath.

"Nothing?" Abigail felt the light pulse of her heart quicken into deep, heavy throbs. She repeated the phrase, as she was in disbelief of what he was saying.

"We have but a hundred dollars, barely enough to last through winter."

"There must be more than that," Abigail said, unable to comprehend the extent of their poverty. "Perhaps we can use the funds set aside for Emma?"

"I spent the sum of her dowry on our relocation to Bowlea."

"Not all of it, surely."

"All, and then some."

"Let us sell the stocks, then," she said with mounting distress.

"I learned on the day of Danbury's estate hearing that our stocks are worthless."

"Worthless," Abigail muttered. She was at once speechless and cross, and Charles could see that she felt deceived by his secrecy.

"I should have told you, but with all of the uncertainty after Danbury's death, I could not bear to burden you with further doubt."

"Papa said they were a sound investment. As good as gold," she said, incredulous that the absence of a rail line would again impact them so greatly. She gazed at Charles through bleary eyes and tried to regain her composure. "Nothing is insurmountable. We will just have to think of alternative ways to earn money. I could ask Josephine. She always has a surplus of funds."

"No, please. I cannot bear the thought of our friends being made aware of our situation."

Emma listened intently to their conversation and was consumed by thoughts of again being forced to abandon her home and her friendships. She immediately thought of the money she had saved in the small wooden box under her bed. She hurried to her room and emptied the contents onto her quilt. She counted the coins one-by-one and secured them back inside the box once she had determined the sum.

Abigail left Charles on the back porch to allow him time to calm himself. She moved to the kitchen to boil a kettle of hot tea and butter a few of his favourite honey biscuits.

"It's not much, but it may help," Emma said as she presented her mother with the offering. "There is twelve and a quarter."

"My love, this is unnecessary."

"I did not intend to listen to your conversation, but father was so distraught, I thought I must. I cannot offer you much in the way of help, but at least it is something."

She took the box and walked into the family drawing room with Emma tailing her so closely that she half-expected a tug on her apron strings.

"I truly do not know what we shall do," Abigail said as they both took a seat on the small sofa. "Jones has enough family to do all of his milking, and Tobias has taken the few hours a month that the Winters are willing to pay. I cannot think of any way we can make money other than selling the few items we have of value. I supposed there is always the piano, but I cannot imagine anyone in these parts is in need of such an instrument." Abigail lay the box in her lap and allowed her head to hang low, with an expression that matched her husband's. In that moment, Emma was brightened by an idea that caused her to start in her seat.

"What if you were to sing, Mama?"

"Perform? I doubt anyone in Bowlea would pay for an entertainment," she said with a slight laugh.

"I am not thinking of Bowlea."

"Where do you have in mind?"

"If we take Winnie up past Dormer, are there not small towns every ten miles or so? We could travel to a few different towns every weekend," Emma said with overflowing optimism.

"Your idea seems rather ambitious, my love. How would we possibly have the means to do such a thing? We cannot afford to stay in a hotel or even a stopping house, for that matter. Lodgings would surely negate any profits we made. And besides, where on earth would we perform? The church would be the only place I can think of with a piano. I refuse to sing in a saloon."

"You could perform in the hotels themselves, could you not? If we travel to one of the larger towns, there will surely be places that would host us for the weekend. If we leave early on Thursday morning, we could do shows on Friday and Saturday nights and then leave at dawn on Sunday," she said. "We would be away no more than five days at a time."

"How can we book a performance without anyone having heard me sing? I have no reputation."

"You have no reputation here," Emma said. "If the newspapers can tout the west as something it is not and regale their readers with stories of its greatness, who is to say we cannot use those same tactics in the promotion of your talents?"

"It is a rather shameful deceit."

"What is deception in the face of destitution? You are a brilliant singer, are you not? There is no deceit in that fact. 'Society Darling, Abigail Prescott – Alberta's Treasured Songbird!'"

Abigail blushed at her daughter's impression of P.T. Barnum and doubted if anyone would be willing to pay more than five cents to watch her perform. She wondered if the earnings would outweigh the effort of travel and the hardship of leaving Charles for any period of time.

"We could hardly travel alone," Abigail said. "Perhaps Tobias would be willing to accompany us."

"I am sure he would not mind. If we demand accommodation and ten dollars per show, it will be well worth our time."

"Ten dollars! Surely no one would pay such a sum. Your expectations are far too lofty," she said, shaking her head.

"Will you allow me to make some inquiries, Mama? We must tell them what you are worth. Once they hear you sing there will be no doubt of your value."

"Inquire at will, my love, but please understand that nothing at all may come of it."

* * *

The postal delivery arrived as scheduled just before the noon hour. Emma watched from the dining room as the carriage from Red Deer dropped off the mail to Mrs. Winters. She grabbed her shawl and hurried out the door to see if there was any word about her mother's employment.

"Good day, Mrs. Winters. How do you do? Is there anything for us today?"

"I haven't had a chance to sort the mail yet, dear," she said with a smile as she lifted the small canvas sack onto the worn wooden slab behind her. Emma had made the same inquiry for the last three weeks, and Mrs. Winters hoped the delivery would bring good news.

"That's fine; I can wait."

"Suit yourself," the postmistress said as she sifted through the letters in search of the Prescott name. "You've been anxious to receive a letter for some time now, Emma. Are you waiting to hear from a suitor?"

"No, ma'am, I am waiting to hear about work," she said as a slight blush rose to her face.

"Oh, are you planning to leave Bowlea? That would be such a shame."

"It would only be for a few days at a time. I could never imagine leaving for good."

"Neither could I. Well, here is something," Mrs. Winters said as she held up a small ivory envelope. She checked for a return address, but the back was merely stamped: The Regent Hotel. Emma sprang forward and snatched the letter from her hand.

"Oh, thank you Mrs. Winters! Thank you ever so much," she said as she bounded out the door and hurried back down the lane.

"Mama!" she shouted as she entered the lobby. "Mama, come quickly."

"What is it, my love?" Abigail asked as she appeared from the kitchen. Emma grabbed her hand and led her into the drawing room, closing the door behind her.

"Look here," she said as she flashed the letter before her. "It is a response from The Regent Hotel in Red Deer."

"I would not expect a proposal. They are most likely just being polite in their refusal," she said as Emma tore open the envelope. She pulled out the paper and read the message aloud.

"Dear Mrs. Prescott. We would be pleased to invite you for a trial at The Regent Hotel in Red Deer. Accommodations will be provided with five dollars pay for your initial performance. If you are well received, we will offer you weekly room and board and a ten dollar salary per week. Please make arrangements to arrive for your first performance on April 11th. Please respond as soon a possible to confirm. Reginald Smythe, General Manager, The Regent Hotel."

"What did you tell them, Emma?" Abigail asked as she took the letter and read it over again. "What could you have said to prompt them to make such an offer?"

"I simply told them that you were the finest singer in eastern Canada, renowned for your ability to take even the most simple folk song and turn it into a work of art," she said with a mischievous giggle.

"No wonder they are willing to pay such a sum! I have hardly sung a note in months. How can I possibly perform with enough skill to back up your praise of me? How will I uphold the expectation of being so well-regarded?"

"I don't think you realize how much practice you get on a daily basis. When you're sweeping the porch or the guest rooms, you are always in song. You sing out melodies when you are kneading bread or stacking wood. You rarely miss a morning's chance to sing for the blackbirds along the shore. I doubt you are even in need of rehearsal."

Abigail examined the black ink scrawled upon the ivory sheet and imagined the notes of her favourite songs spattered on a parchment page. She thought of the joy singing had always brought her, and the peace of mind it would bring her husband if she were able to supplement their income.

"I think we had better run through a few songs. The audience in Red Deer may be a bit more discerning than shorebirds."

"It would only be for three nights, and Tobias would ensure our safety," Abigail said when she, at last, had the courage to approach Charles on the subject. She had gone through the conversation in her mind a dozen times since lunch, but could not think of how to request leaving the protection of their home to become the breadwinner as a paid entertainer. There was no way in which she could propose the scenario to make it sound less ridiculous. Charles, like most of their former friends, felt that the lives of an entertainer and their patron should never intertwine. As members of society, the Prescotts would attend concerts and partake in any manner of theatre in Kingston, but while the players were esteemed for their artistry and capacity to amuse, the actors may as well have occupied a room at Miss Kitty's Club.

Singing as a member of society to your particular social circle allowed for the pleasures of congenial entertainment without the taboo of compensation. While a single positive performance could keep one in their collective good favour, Abigail never felt the need to act like Becky Sharp; she sang for the joy of it and hoped Charles would view her employment as a means to restore the comforts they had barely known in years.

"What do you mean by travelling across country to earn a few dollars? I will not have you degrade yourself in that way," he said, unable to consider any benefit to the plan.

"Would it not be a greater disgrace to survive on offal and oats or suffer the misery of a constant chill because we cannot burn more than a few logs per day? How can you deny me the chance to bring income into our home?"

"I will not have it. I shall find work in town to supplement us."

"Tobias is considering the collieries in Lethbridge. The Winters are almost happy that old age is upon them since there is barely enough mail to keep them afloat. There is nothing here, Charles; we must do something."

"Perhaps I could travel to Blythe and find work there. It is a better option than you working, surely."

Through his annoyance, Charles admired Abigail's figure as she walked toward the window; he watched as the highlights on her delicate features dimmed as the clouds drifted before the moon. It had been months since he had spent more than a few minutes alone with her, and now that he was faced with several days without her, he was unsure of how to cope.

"After what I will pay Tobias for his escort, and what it will cost to board Winnie, I should bring home about three dollars. Can you tell me how much we are currently earning, Charles?" she asked with a rare sternness.

"You know as well as I that we have no income," he said with his eyes downcast. Abigail took his hand and led him to the single cot he had moved into the office for his bed. She sat him down and took his hands as she tried to calm him with her voice.

"Allow me to do this for you, Charles. Allow me to help our family."

"Who will manage things here while you are gone?"

Abigail considered the empty rooms around them but refrained from imbuing her response with mockery.

"We will only be gone three days. I will make up a big batch of biscuits." Abigail waited as he sat in silence for a moment of contemplation.

"You do sing beautifully," he said, smiling. Abigail felt a connection with him in those moments that had been absent for months. It was difficult to find pleasure in each other when all that surrounded them evoked their misfortune. She wrapped her arms around him as he sat, and shared with him a tender kiss. As he felt the comfort of her arms, he understood that the benefit of the plan far outweighed his isolation.

"If Tobias accompanies you, it will be fine," he conceded. "Worries about money have certainly caused distress between us, and for that I am sorry. Perhaps all areas of our life will improve when your return."

"Oh thank you, Charles. You will see. This will give us more breathing room and a bit of our lives back. We will leave for my trial on Thursday, and if all goes well, perhaps they will have me back for a longer engagement. This could set us up for the whole of winter."

"Then you must go," Charles said as a frown again returned to his face. He could withstand her absence for a few days but had no idea how he would handle an extended engagement. As he looked at her and forced a smile, he knew there was no other option. "I shall think of you often, my dear."

Chapter Thirteen

The carriage pulled up in front of The Regent Hotel just after midday on Friday. Tobias climbed down from the driver's seat to help the ladies offload their small trunk.

"I'll take Winnie to the livery, and meet up with you in a little while."

The Regent was a three-story sandstone structure that stood as the most refined of the emerging town's buildings. The patrons of the hotel were dressed in a manner Abigail expected from society, and she hoped that her garments would not prove too outdated. As the ladies entered the bustling lobby, their eyes were immediately drawn to the chandelier and the tiny colourful lights it cast onto the walls and ceiling around it. The front hall opened to a large drawing room with a cherry wood piano in the corner. The man behind the instrument touched the keys softly and filled the space with gentle harmonies.

"Good day, we are here to see Mr. Smythe," Abigail said to the front desk clerk.

"I am Mr. Smythe. How may I help you?"

"I am Abigail Prescott. I am here for a singing engagement," she said as she fidgeted with the frayed end of her cape. The demeanour of the hotel manager changed in that instant and his over-solicitous gestures took her aback.

"Of course! Mrs. Prescott! I say! You are lovelier than I could have imagined. We have been anxious for your arrival. Come, we will get you settled in."

Abigail was uncomfortable with Mr. Smythe's flattery, particularly since she was shrouded in a thin layer of dust from a full day's travel. She hoped he would be professional during her stay for she had not the energy to fend off his advances.

"What time is my trial tonight, sir?" she asked as he gathered a key from a small cabinet of hooks on the back wall.

"We must first let you rest. You can then meet with your accompanist, Mr. Murphy, to go over your selections. He is as eager to hear you sing as I am. If you require practice or need to warm up you may do so at that time," he said, as he pointed to a porter to have their trunk taken upstairs. "You will perform at ten o'clock, after the dinner service."

The apartment was spacious enough for the ladies to room comfortably, while Tobias took a bed at the men's boarding house down the street. Abigail and Emma moved about the room languidly, expending what little energy they had left to unpack their clothes and lay out the selections of sheet music they brought along.

"I hope one run-through is enough," Abigail said as she shuffled through the stack of parchment and arranged them in performance order. "In all honesty, I was expecting you to be my accompanist."

"I believe it worked out in your favour. He plays beautifully. Are you nervous at all?"

"I never seem to get nervous before a performance. I suppose I must like the attention," she said as she pulled her finest dress out of the trunk. She shook the fabric gently and held it out in front of her. Emma examined the dress with her wide eyes, seeing pieces of their former life in the apricot taffeta and lace. She wondered how many claps and bravos those puffed sleeves had heard, and remembered instantly the last time she had seen her mother in the gown.

"You wore this the night of the Charlotte recitals," Emma said as she let the finely beaded fabric pass through her fingers.

"How on earth can you remember that?" Abigail asked, wondering how many small details of Kingston life her daughter recalled.

"You sang in the grand hall that night. Everyone stared as though you were the only one in the room."

Abigail smiled fondly at the memory and thought of how darling Emma had looked in her knee-length dress with the ruffled petticoat. She would sway and twirl to the music, whether or not she had a partner. On occasion, she would dance with boys from school, but she was too young and left Kingston before she was given a proper debut.

"I am sorry that you never had the chance to be out much in society. I suppose you missed out on a great deal in that regard," Abigail said as she sat beside Emma on the bed.

"Don't worry yourself, Mama. I have never once regretted moving to Bowlea. To be immersed in nature and its serenity is something I am thankful for. I crave the quiet now."

"There is certainly no comparison to the hubbub of Kingston, what with the clatter of carriages or the blowhorns of the steamers. I only wish there were more opportunities for you to be out in society. It seems doubtful that you will ever meet a suitor in Bowlea."

"There is always Tobias," Emma said with a flirtatious wink.

"Tobias?" Abigail returned with a tinge of shock in her voice. "He is the right age, surely, but I thought you viewed him more as a brother than a mate."

"The feelings between us have grown so gradually, its no wonder the changes to our bond escaped your notice. The more time I spend in his company, the more I realize that our souls are matched. Who else would sit by the brooks with me for hours and watch the water bubble over the rocks, or run through the grasses along the lakeshore to watch the warblers scatter? He is a fine man, Mama. I'm in little hurry to marry, but hope to entertain a proposal soon."

Abigail held her daughter's hand and gave it a gentle squeeze. As she glanced down at her delicate fingers, she wondered at what kind of ring Tobias could afford, and the working class future their vow would entail. She was at a loss for what to say and considered what advice her own mother could have proffered before her marriage to Charles. She wondered what kind of life the young couple would have in a town that was barely breathing and if they would be compelled to leave.

"He is kind and gentle," Abigail began, "but with strong virtue and will. His passions match your own, that is clear, but I ask you to consider the struggle of trying to start a family in a town with so few prospects. If our business was thriving, I have no doubt father would hire on Tobias permanent and pay him a fair wage. As it stands, you must consider that your only option may be to move away from Bowlea."

"I would never leave you, Mama," Emma said as she squeezed her mother's hand in return. "Tobias and I have spoken about such things often. We worry about the future, but we know that whatever the circumstance, we want to share that future together. Consider your own relationship or that of a great number of other young ladies. They risk everything to follow love and the hope of a life filled with joy and happiness. You can no more fault me for wanting that than grandfather could have faulted you or Papa. We will face our challenges together and, god willing, have the good fortune to remain nearby our little town and beloved family. Do not fret, Mama. I understand the risk in following my heart."

With Emma left resting in their room, Abigail wandered down to the main hall to introduce herself to the pianist.

"How do you do, Mrs. Prescott? James Murphy," he said as he extended his hand.

"Pleased to meet you, Mr. Murphy. I heard you playing earlier when we first arrived. You are a wonderful talent," she said as he ushered her closer to the instrument.

"I appreciate the compliment. The venue is a far cry from the concert halls back home, but folks in these parts seem to appreciate the entertainment more," he said, as he regained his seat.

"Here are my selections," she said as she handed him the wrinkled sheets and took her place along the mahogany curve of the piano.

"These are rather simple. Are you sure you would not prefer something else? I can play most anything," he said, as he thumbed through the collection of basic folk songs.

"No, thank you. These are the songs I enjoy singing," she said, feeling slightly worried that the tunes would prove too plain for the society crowd.

"I quite like them myself," he said with a smile. "Do you need any rehearsal?"

"My daughter and I ran through all of the songs just last night. I trust you are far more accomplished at the piano than she, and I want to preserve my voice for the performance. If you would be so kind as to play through each piece, I will count to myself to ensure our timing is on. There are nine songs in total."

"Yes, of course. We would not want to tire you. Are these in performance order?"

Abigail smiled as she gave him a nod. She planned to start off with a slow ballad and end with *A Rose's Thorn*, for she felt the final high notes were the ideal conclusion to an evening of song. She tapped her foot and counted along as Mr. Murphy elegantly played each simple selection. She closed her eyes and imagined her voice lilting above each successive note.

After a short nap, Emma returned downstairs to find Tobias. He was occupying a bench in the lobby and had spent the better part of an hour observing the patrons milling about the grand entrance.

"Life would be so different if we had this many guests at The Prescott," she said when she met him.

"That would be an awful lot of work, Em. How about half as much?"

"Better still, how about a quarter? Plenty to afford everything we need, with time enough for leisure."

"I like your plan better," he said with a smile.

"Come let us join Mama," she said as she pulled his hand gently and urged him to follow.

They took the pair of seats nearest the stage so as to fully appreciate the efforts of both musicians. The song was nearly complete, and Emma watched as her mother's hand gently thumped her thigh to the gentle rhythm of the bass line.

"Excellent," Abigail said as Mr. Murphy tapped out the final few notes. A smattering of applause could be heard from the lobby, and Abigail's confidence grew at their appreciation of even the most modest of melodies. She was very much looking forward to the evening's performance.

"Until tonight, then," Mr. Murphy said as he extended a hand for her to shake.

"Yes, thank you. I shall be down just before ten o'clock."

"Oh, Mama, his style is delightful!" Emma said as she and Tobias scurried to her side. "So much better than I can play. You will sound very well together."

"I can't wait to hear you sing tonight, ma'am."

"Thank you, Toby. It is a great comfort to have you both with me."

"Beg pardon, ma'am, but would it be alright if I leave you two for a while? I'd like to explore the town a bit. I'll be back in plenty of time to see you tonight," he said, itching to leave.

"Yes, of course you want to look around. In fact, Emma and I may do the same," she said as her daughter nodded in agreement.

"I'll meet up with you later," he said as he dashed through the lobby.

"Where do you suppose he could be off to in such a hurry?" Abigail asked with a playful nudge to Emma's side.

"I am not sure, but I doubt it's to look at ribbons or petticoats," she said as they moved out to the courtyard. "Look! There are some shops down that way." She tugged her mother's arm as she did whenever she spotted a candy shop in Kingston.

"We must ensure we do not lose our way."

"The Regent is the tallest building on the avenue, Mama, so there is little chance of that."

The road pulsed with activity as the late afternoon crowds moved on to their evening engagements. As they ambled down the avenue, Abigail was reminded of the Saturday outings they would take down Princess Street in Kingston before visiting the Grand Theatre for an evening of opera. They would dress in their finest garments, and stop for tea and pastries before the show. Abigail was well-known and liked in society, and those occasions were a missed facet of her former life.

"Isn't she lovely?" Emma said discreetly, as a young woman no older than sixteen walked in their direction. She was dressed in the latest fashion with a high lace collar, large puffed sleeves and a wide-brimmed hat tilted by heavy piles of silk flowers, feathers and ribbon.

"She reminds me of you," Abigail said as the young lady passed. Emma laughed aloud at her mother's remark and was quick to point out the great difference in their style of dress.

"I suppose in my mind I still see you as that little girl in lavender lace." She paused in front of a shop window. "I often think of you as you were in Kingston."

"I see all of us that way, especially Papa. He hardly seems like the same person."

"Your father has endured a great deal in his life, as we all have. Just as he begins to feel settled, he is uprooted and forced to re-establish his life. When he came from Halifax in his youth, he had nothing. He struggled for many years to make a place for himself and prove he was worthy of success. It is as though he is again that child with all the burden of an uncertain future before him."

"I hope he does not view his property in Bowlea as a burden," Emma said loudly as they continued down the avenue and tried to maintain their conversation over the roar of the carts.

"I believe he is in fear of losing everything. It is difficult to be hopeful in times of desperation."

"Perhaps that duty must now fall on you. You have the means to alleviate some of that fear, have you not?"

"I hope so. One can hardly predict how patrons will react to an elegant entertainment, never mind the folksongs of a tired amateur."

"Then we must make you look the part," Emma said, stopping in front of the flower shop.

"The entire point is to earn money, not spend it, my love."

"A quarter-dollar spent on some fresh flowers and ribbon will be well worth the expense."

Abigail stood in front of the long mirror and quietly examined her own reflection. Her eyes moved from the coral shoes on her feet, up the train of her embellished peach skirt to the high pile of deep auburn curls upon her head. Emma had twisted and pinned her mother's natural curls into a variety of plaits and knots and interlaced the strands with wisps of violets and baby's breath.

"You look splendid, Mama. There will be no averted glances when you enter the room."

"You have worked some magic, Emma. I cannot remember the last time I felt so pretty," she said, as she tugged on the fabric of her long ivory gloves.

"You look pretty in any style of costume you wear, even your work dress. Are you ready to go down?"

"I am actually more nervous than I expected," she said, as they exited the suite.

"You will have both Tobias and I in the wings," Emma said, as she gave her mother a kiss on the cheek. "Good luck."

Abigail stood at the top of the stairs and took a deep breath before she began her descent. With each step, her excitement grew, and she soon found herself at the entrance of the main hall where she was greeted by the owner.

"Mrs. Prescott, how fine you look this evening," Mr. Smythe said, as he lifted her hand to his lips for a kiss.

Abigail felt a rush of excitement as the guests began to gather in the hall. The perimeter was flanked by a number of seating areas and the chairs set up around the piano were already occupied. As the last of the guests took their seats, Mr. Smythe made his way to the front of the room.

"Ladies and gentlemen, we have an exceptional entertainment for you all tonight. A voice like you have never heard. I am pleased to introduce Ontario's songstress, Mrs. Abigail Prescott."

The crowd turned in their chairs to watch as Abigail made her slow walk to the piano. There was a hum amongst the patrons as they admired her beauty and simple grace. She kicked the heavy beading of her dress in front of her as she walked, and spun around to position herself next to Mr. Murphy at the piano. Emma sat with Tobias in a rear seating area and admired how demure her mother was in her address of the crowd, meeting them only with a subtle smile and slight nod of her head.

From the moment Abigail uttered the first lyric, the crowd was enraptured with her rare talent. The notes filled the air with a longing for a simpler life; each phrase was imbued with tender emotion. The audience was silent and seemed to hold their collective breaths as Mr. Murphy pounded out the coda. She raised her arms as she released the final notes, and produced a clarity of sound few in the room had ever heard. As she took a breath and opened her eyes, the crowd erupted into cheers and applause. Bravos were heard from all corners of the hall as they rose to their feet to offer their praise.

"Your mother is wonderful," Tobias said to Emma, struggling with a description that felt too simple for such a vibrant performance.

She looked on as her mother stood motionless in the midst of overt adulation. Abigail was but one song into her performance and was taken aback by their immediate support. She bowed her head graciously and motioned for Mr. Murphy to begin the next tune. As she sang, a longing for the life she left behind took over her thoughts. She marvelled at her own complacency, and how she could have left so much of what defined her back in Kingston. With each note, she felt a renewed sense of purpose and was joyous to be exposed to that world again.

Abigail's nine songs took the better part of half an hour to perform. Each tune melded into a blurred cycle of gentle piano and thunderous applause, and she wished she had prepared more selections to please the audience. Calls for an encore could not be refused, and so Mr. Murphy made her a swift proposition.

"Let's give them one more, shall we?"

"We have nothing rehearsed."

"Then we must sing your favourite. There must be a song that you know by heart and can perform without rehearsal. As I said, I can play most anything."

Abigail looked out at the crowd and spied her daughter. She recalled the song she would sing each morning upon waking in Kingston, and how Emma would hum along as she was held in her arms. It reminded her of the gardens and woodlands her own mother would describe when sharing stories of her young life in Surrey. Abigail had changed the lyrics to reflect the Canadian gardens they had at Shelby House and to fill her daughter with wonder and hope of all that lay beyond those stone walls.

"Well then, *English Country Garden*, if you please," she said with a wink.

Mr. Murphy nary missed a beat and began to softly tap down on the keys. The gentle melody lulled the crowd, who instantly fell calm and returned to their seats.

How many gentle flowers grow in a Kingston country garden?
I'll tell you now, of some that I know, and those I miss I hope you'll pardon.
Daffodils, hearts-ease and flocks, meadow sweet and lilies, stocks,
Gentle lupins and tall hollyhocks,
Roses, fox-gloves, snowdrops, forget-me-knots in a Kingston country garden.

How many insects find their home in a Kingston country garden?
I'll tell you now of some that I know, and those I miss, I hope you'll pardon.
Dragonflies, moths and bees, spiders falling from the trees,
Butterflies sway in the mild, gentle breeze.
There are hedgehogs that roam and little garden gnomes in a Kingston country garden.

How many song-birds make their nest in a Kingston country garden?
I'll tell you now of some that I know, and those I miss, I hope you'll pardon.
Babbling, coo-cooing doves, robins and the warbling thrush,
Blue birds, lark, finch and nightingale.
We all smile in the spring when the birds all start to sing in a Kingston country garden.[2]

---

[2] Adapted lyrics from *English Country Garden*. Traditional folksong. Author unknown. Published 1859.

When she finished the song, the audience again cheered but followed their ovation with a hurried dash to meet her. Dozens of guests rushed the piano, and Mr. Murphy moved in before her to buffer the throng. She could not help but laugh as she looked towards where Emma and Tobias stood, giving them a roll of her eyes at the absurdity of her reception.

"You could sing opera, ma'am, truly," said one of the young ladies.

"You must have been in hiding! How is it possible we have never heard of you?" said a gentleman in the back. Abigail could hardly answer one question before being asked another.

"Madam Prescott will be performing again tomorrow evening. Please feel welcome to join us for another engagement," Mr. Smythe said as he ushered her away from the crowd and led her to a small office adjacent the lobby. Emma and Tobias followed closely behind and accompanied her inside.

"Splendid, my dear. Truly sublime," Mr. Smythe said as he motioned for the group to be seated.

"Thank you, that is very kind," Abigail said as a blush rose to her cheeks. "It was rather a good reception, was it not?"

"It was wonderful, Mama."

"I have seen all I need to, my dear. What a draw you will be indeed. I could charge a dollar per ticket. 'Alberta's Songbird Performing Nightly!'"

"Nightly! My apologies, Mr. Smythe, but that cannot be," she interjected. "My husband will be expecting my help at home. I thought, perhaps, a few shows per month."

"I am willing to pay ten dollars for six shows per week, including room and board for you and your children. I have in mind that you will drum up a great deal of business for me, Mrs. Prescott."

"I thank you for your generous offer, Mr. Smythe, but I must return home to my husband and his business. I cannot stay on for a fixed engagement," she said, as she felt Emma tightly grip her trembling hand.

"Mr. Smythe," Emma said, "might my mother be able to perform for just a few months? Say until September? Surely the coming months are your busiest."

"Yes, certainly. I will take however much time you can spare, for your talent is not to be missed." Mr. Smythe boasted a broad smile and was unable to hide the gleeful tone that the prospect of several hundred dollars per week in revenue brought to his voice. "I shall put you on the payroll starting tomorrow, then?"

Abigail fell silent for a moment as she considered how she would decide without Charles' deliberation or consent. She understood that the severity of their situation warranted the lack of consultation, but she felt that being away from Charles for any great length of time could further harm their relationship, particularly just as things were starting to mend. She looked over to her daughter, whose wide eyes and subtle nod encouraged her to think only of the money and to accept the offer without another moment's pause.

"Thank you, sir. I shall start tomorrow night."

Chapter Fourteen

May 6th, 1902

Dearest Charles,

Life in Red Deer is vastly different than Bowlea, although there are many elements of this hotel that remind me very much of Kingston. I have just completed my twentieth performance, and the reception and praise grow stronger each night. Tobias has managed to find day work at a smithy. He is not so eager to learn more about a trade but is happy to earn some money. I have given him a stipend of a dollar per week for his escort, and a have allotted myself a half dollar to help brighten the dull hours between shows.

The rooms provided for us are very comfortable, and Mr. Smythe has informed me that both you and Emma are welcome to visit, but only under the condition that your stay will be complimentary. I have been asked to perform at the town's Founder's Day celebrations on May 31st. I have developed quite a positive reputation since my arrival, and it would please me a great deal if both of you would attend.

I miss you more than I was able to express in our last days together, Charles, and take comfort in the bond and intimacy we were able to share before I departed. Please understand that it is only the benefit of helping our family that makes our time apart worthwhile. You are in my thoughts both night and day and I look forward to when we will meet again.

With love, Abigail.

Charles put down the letter and counted out the twenty-five dollars enclosed with it. The money was a minor consolation for the endless hours spent without his wife. Most days, he was overcome with loneliness, and even though he shared his daughter's company, their household duties and his cold disposition were enough to limit conversations between them to a few short minutes per day. His chores consisted of hauling and splitting dry timbers for the fire, tending the garden and ensuring a steady supply of hot water for Emma's work. He mucked the barn and swept what little dirt had accumulated on the guestroom floors. When he was not occupied with helping keep the hotel at its best, he spent his time alone on the porch watching the western hills and waiting for his next party to arrive.

It had been nearly a month since Emma returned from Red Deer and the hotel had seen only three guests pass through its doors. The first was a doctor who ambled along the back roads in search of patients who were unable to travel to one of the larger towns. He was accustomed to sleeping in his converted carriage, but the lure of a hot meal and comfortable bed saw him stay on for three nights in total. His next patrons were a young couple with a baby in tow who had travelled east from Red Deer to settle their claim of Dominion land. They were exhausted and worn, and he saw so much of himself in their idealism. When the young man inquired as to the prosperity of the region, Charles could not muster the truth and offered only: "It's a pleasant land," as a response. The last guests were a father and son who stayed only one night, and whom Charles felt obliged to house for free. They were travelling from Lethbridge in search of work, but their lame horse had made the journey intolerably slow. They had been forced to leave their carriage in a muddy grove and continue on horseback, able to transport only what they could carry. For the remainder of their trip, Emma packed them a satchel of soft potato bread, black currant preserves and butter.

When the father and son pushed on, Charles wondered how he and his family could have been so fortunate. Their own journey from Kingston was long and uncomfortable, but at that time they had never experienced hunger or poverty. He wondered why, with even less money than he had brought, others would venture to that part of the country. He lamented their foolishness but could think of no way to articulate a warning. Some settlers had fared remarkably well, and others lived in modest comfort. He did not see the point in offering caution when he knew so little of their intentions or circumstance.

Emma had occupied herself during those long weeks by attempting to master her mother's recipe for scones and seeing to the overall management of the household. The trickle of guests bred laziness, and so she took it upon herself to place advertisements in the regional papers; she wanted desperately to ease the relentless boredom. When her father arrived back from the post office that morning, she hoped he had some news.

"I received a letter from your mother today, petty, and some money as well," Charles said as he entered the kitchen. "She has asked that we join her in Red Deer for the Founder's Day festivities."

"But what about the hotel? Summer is nearly here. Would it be wise to close for any length of time?"

"It will only be for a few days. With the money your mother sent we can afford a coach, and will not risk damaging the carriage if we encounter thick mud."

"When shall we leave?"

"I hope to head out next Thursday and return that Sunday. Have you anything to wear that would be suitable for such an occasion? I suspect there will be a great number of influential people there." It had been several years since Charles had been amongst society and would not pass up the opportunity to drum up potential business.

"All I have are house dresses, but I'm sure I can find something amongst Mama's things." Unlike her father, Emma had little chance to expose herself in society, save for Abigail's first two performances earlier that spring. Her neighbours in Bowlea were a working-class folk, and their modesty better suited her sensibilities.

"Very good, that will do."

After supper that evening, Emma retreated to her mother's room and within her tall, ash wardrobe found a small collection of formal gowns. Charles had been unable to afford much in the way of fashion since their migration and was only ever able to provide them with the most basic garments. Abigail never wore her gowns, and Emma had long since outgrown her formal dresses. Within the wardrobe hung dresses more extravagant than she had ever worn, and she was eager to feel its weight against her skin. She carefully sifted through the rack and examined the fabric, embroidery and fine beading on each one.

A lavender dress was the last on the rod, tucked in behind a heavy wool overcoat. She removed it from its hanger and laid it on the bed. As she traced her fingers over the indigo ribbon and ivory lace, she recalled the last night her mother had worn it. Music had filled Wilborne Hall, and she had watched as her mother floated through each dance in her father's embrace. She remembered how they laughed and smiled without a care on their minds. But as Emma reminisced about that special night, sadness crept into her heart; she struggled to remember the last time she had witnessed such a tender moment between them.

Red Deer was but a village when compared to Kingston, but when Charles arrived with Emma just before the noon hour, he felt instantly energized by the commotion. He had not left Bowlea in more than four years, and it was not until he was surrounded by countless new faces that he acknowledged his longing for social interaction. As the stagecoach arrived in front of The Regent, he immediately took notice of the building's fine construction. He looked up at the pattern of windows and wondered on which of the three stories his wife resided. As he observed the carousel of guests enter and exit through the heavy hardwood doors, he felt they would not have been out of place in the elite Alwington district back home.

"Welcome to The Regent, sir," Mr. Smythe said as Charles and Emma approached the front desk. "Have you a reservation?"

"We are here to see my wife, Mrs. Prescott."

Emma straightened her posture and gave the owner a friendly grin when she caught his eye, sure that he would recognize her from the month before.

"Yes, of course. She mentioned you would join us for tonight's show. John, could you please let Mrs. Prescott know her family has arrived," he said to the porter.

"It is a pleasure to see you again, Mr. Smythe," Emma said, extending her hand to shake his.

"Miss Prescott! My apologies for not recognizing you sooner. I see so many faces that it is sometimes difficult to notice even the most familiar." He took her hand and led her to the main hall while Charles followed closely behind.

The room was arranged differently than when Emma was there last, and she was impressed by the number of chairs they were able to squish into the space. Instead of numerous groupings of tables and chairs, the room was now configured like a concert hall, with rows of single chairs staggered to afford each guest a view of The Regent's star performer. Emma was weary and chose a seat at the front, while Charles paced in the aisle beside her in an effort to quell his anticipation.

"It is fortunate you've arrived so early, Mr. Prescott. You have the whole afternoon to explore our little town before tonight's celebration. She will be just a moment."

"I wonder what time her performance will be?" Charles asked after Mr. Smythe excused himself and returned to the front desk.

"I understand she performs in the evenings after dinner. I presume tonight will no different." Emma glanced up and saw her mother at the top of the stairs. "Papa, over there!" Charles scanned each step of the staircase until he met Abigail's gaze. He felt his heart fill with joy at the sight of her. She stood with a demure confidence and presented herself with the same reserved grace as the woman he forever altered the day they boarded the train to Calgary. Although it had only been seven weeks since he last saw her, he was as reliant on her as she was on him, and he felt a great loss in her absence.

Abigail stood at the top of the stairs for a moment as she spied Charles down below. The view put in her in mind of their wedding day and her decent down the shallow oak staircase at The Charlotte. There he stood with a playful smirk, once again anxious to be alone with her. She tilted her head demurely and descended the stairs under Tobias' guidance. In Red Deer, as in Kingston, she was the envy of all who saw her; not because of wealth or connections, but rather talent and beauty.

"Oh, my dears, how I have missed you," she said, as she embraced her family. The warmth Charles felt as he leaned in closer and held her tight was an intimacy he had craved since well before her departure.

"It has been too long already, Abby. I wish it were fall already."

"As do I," she said as she kissed him tenderly on the lips. "Tobias and I are making do the best we can, but the fleeting friendships and instant acquaintances hold nothing to spending time with you both."

"How are you, Toby?" Emma asked as she looped her arm through the space her mother had relinquished and walked with him to the drawing room.

"I want to tell you how much I've missed you, but no words seem to match how I feel. There were so many things I took for granted in Bowlea, and spending time with you every day was one of them."

"Did you know, until you went away we had seen each other nearly every day since I was twelve," she said with a laugh as they followed her parents to the seating area near the fireplace. "I've missed you more than I ever could have imagined. Even with you away, I still sprint down to the lake each day after chores. I have no choice but to chase the geese since there is no one else to swim with."

"The work in the smithy is so hot, Emma, that I've dreamt every single day of swimming with you. As soon as I get back home, I'm going to run straight for the lake and jump in like a cannonball off the north bank."

As Charles was seated and began to feel the radiant heat of the flames, he noticed that Abigail was garnering a great deal of attention from the hotel patrons. Nods of hats and salutations were met with friendliness on her part, and it seemed to Charles that she was quite accustomed to the attention.

"You seem to be adjusting to the society quite well," he said as she took the seat beside him.

"Yes, I forgot how much I enjoy being amongst this level of society. I seem to be quite at home."

"I would think you would be eager to get back to our home, particularly at this time of year. The lake is certainly missing your attention," he said with a smile.

"I do miss it a great deal, but I will be home before long. You will hardly notice my absence once the summer travellers start to come through."

Charles downcast his eyes, for he doubted they would host more than a few guests the entire season.

"We will manage. Tobias, how goes your time here?" he asked in an attempt to redirect the conversation.

"I'm thankful for the bit of money, sir, but this is not the life I am used to. My place is in the country working the land and helping in the hotel. The heat inside the smithy is so bad that I can hardly think most days. It's nothing to working in the fresh winds that blow through Bowlea. I'll be happy to go back when the season's over," he said, turning to Emma with a smile.

"Red Deer seems much busier this time around," Emma said, returning his flirtation with a smile of her own. "Folks must be in town just for the occasion."

"We have certainly seen a great many more guests over the last few days," Abigail said as she took Charles' hand. She suddenly felt discomfort being the centre of attention around him, and well understood the immodesty of her occupation. "My audience is sometimes so large that there is no option but for them to stand, and yet, I fear nothing will compare to the crowd this evening. I hope my nerves do not sabotage me."

"Fear not, my dear, you will be splendid. Will your performance be here?" Charles asked.

"No, it is down at The Alexandra, the oldest hotel in town. Mr. Smythe's colleague has offered me five dollars to be the main attraction. It seems the general manager, Mr. Davis, is quite an admirer of my voice," she said in an attempt to reassure herself with prior praise. "You both must be famished. Come, let us have luncheon."

"Would you mind, Mama, if Tobias and I sat in the courtyard?"

"The Club Café has sandwiches, and we would be just right outside," Tobias said, hopeful that he could secure at least a few minutes alone with his dear friend.

"It will give you both a chance to catch up," Emma said without waiting for approval, as she nudged Tobias from his seat and hurried towards the exit.

Abigail and Charles smiled at one another when they realized they would have until the evening's show to enjoy each other's company. They retreated back to her room without a single thought about dining.

"Spring in Bowlea is not the same without you, Toby," Emma said as they wandered through the gardens and up to the tract of C. & E. line that ran behind the hotel. "The swans have returned, you know. They look as fat as ever."

"And the hares?"

"Mostly back to brown. There is one that lazes about near Ashcroft Brook who still has a tuft of white on his rump. It will never change back if it never sees the light of day," Emma said with her melodic giggle.

"I think about the brook all the time. Sometimes, remembering how it felt to splash around in that cold water with you is all that gets me through the day. I can hardly describe the heat, Em. It's like that summer when all the wildflowers drooped under the weight of their blooms, and it felt like we were choking. After chores, we ran to the brook as fast as we could, but it barely helped. Now, imagine that heat twice over, but within a space so small you can barely grab a breath, and when you do it's filled with smoke and soot."

"Mama is giving you a stipend from her earnings, is she not? Surely you don't have to endure such conditions."

"She pays more than your father, plus I get room and board. I don't like the smithy, but I can't just sit around with nothing to do all day. I need to be of use."

"Perhaps you could find employment in a shop or at the livery. Surely there are more opportunities here than the blacksmith's."

"There are so many men on the lookout for the same jobs. Whatever work I can find is a chance to sock away money. If I can tough it out, I should have a fair sum when I return in the fall."

"What are you saving up for? You are not planning to leave Bowlea, are you?" she asked as the thought of his leaving caused her voice to quiver. Tobias took her hand and stroked it gently.

"I could never leave Bowlea, Emma. I could never leave you. Being away has made me realize how much I need you in my life."

As the pair stood and watched the afternoon traffic pass by, each wondered how they would bear the next season apart. Although Tobias had been working hard to further himself beyond mere survival since his father died, he did not carry with him the good fortune of business prospects or connections that men like Emma's father were afforded.

"I've done pretty well for myself since I came to Red Deer. With the pay from your mum and my wage from the smithy, I have managed to save close to ten dollars," he said with unabashed pride. He had earned more in the last month than he had in the previous six back home.

"What a positive start!" she said as she set aside propriety and gave him a jubilant embrace.

"I plan to have at least fifty by the end of summer." He reached into his tattered vest pocket and retrieved a scarlet handkerchief turned crimson by soot. "I was going to wait until I got back, but as soon as I saw you, I wanted you to have it right away."

Emma held her breath as he unbundled the piece of cloth, curious as to the secret hidden within. She thought, perhaps, he had made a small token for her out of a twisted horse nail or rivet. Instead, he presented a thin pewter ring adorned with a simple pattern of filigree. There were no inset stones and the price paid was less than a week's wages.

"Tobias, how lovely! Surely there is no occasion to warrant such a gift, especially considering how hard you must work for each day's pay."

"I needed to give you this promise. Our future is together, and I will work hard every day to be a good man for you. I hope to have a family," he said as he struggled to restrain tears forming in the corners of his eyes.

She took his hands and held them to stop their trembling. He gently placed the ring upon her finger.

"I spoke of my wishes with your mum. It was a very long talk," he said as they shared a laugh.

"And she was receptive?"

"She said I've been welcome in your family since the day we met, and that she was glad we would now be bound by marriage."

"And Papa? Has he given his consent?"

"I spoke to him before we came to Red Deer, and he gave me his blessing. He warned me of marrying too young, and I agreed. We aren't ready to go out on our own."

"Surely you do not mean to leave Bowlea. I would not bear it, Toby. That is our home."

"I would never even think to leave, Emma. Steady work would be nice, but I will make do well enough so we can all be together. I also spoke to your father about moving rooms. Seeing as how Laura's likely never coming back and Mr. Prescott doesn't seem inclined to hire anyone on, I thought it made sense to move into the housekeeper's suite. When we're ready to marry, there would be plenty of space for us and our family. We can all stay together."

Emma felt enthralled at the prospect of her engagement and future marriage. She wished she could stay in Red Deer or stop the show immediately and have Tobias join her again in Bowlea. But she knew that for the sake of their future, she must hold him close in her heart while being miles away. Patience was her payment for a family.

"Could you help me with this, my love," she said, as she removed the string of costume beads from the vanity drawer. "It adds something to the occasion, does it not?"

Charles stood behind his wife, feeling her energy as he moved in closer to affix the necklace with the loop and hook. His hands grazed the contours of her neck and shoulders as he smiled at her reflection in the mirror.

"This is an occasion I will think of often. It feels like home holding you close, being with you." He placed a gentle kiss on her neck. He watched as she pinched her cheeks in intervals in order to achieve a rosy complexion. "You are so lovely, my dear. This is how I envision you in my mind's eye. Not elbows deep in dishwater. I never wanted that for you."

"Charles," she said as she turned to face him. "I have always been the same person on the inside. We have been forced to make allowances, particularly in the way we present ourselves, but we are all very much the same as we ever were. One does not lose who they are simply due to a change of society."

Charles could not help but snicker at the lie, for they both knew that anyone who rode west on the transcontinental rail was never the same again.

"I thought this would be our lot, a place like this. Perhaps I was naive and took Edwin's advice with too much optimism. I knew the work would be hard, but I never once imagined a scenario where you would earn the lion's share of our income. I am not proud, Abigail, and I am exceedingly thankful for your help. But thankfulness does not negate my disappointment."

"Things may not have turned out exactly as planned, but you must not allow your feelings to veer in a negative direction. We have property, a home, a business and each other. Those are the things that matter. And as for the hotel, Mr. Smythe has promised to recommend it to any guests heading in that direction and I've seen a few of the advertisements that

Emma has placed. You will see, Charles. Just because things are hardly turning out as planned, does not mean they are not turning out at all. Do you not enjoy your freedom here?"

He offered a forced smile to Abigail, unsure of how to respond to a sentiment so contrary to his own. Since his arrival in the district, he had felt shackled. He had left the refuge of dependence to feel the full burden of responsibility.

"We are adventurers," she said with a grin. "Now, if you will be so kind as to help me with my gown."

Charles stood motionless in the middle of the room as his wife stirred about him with mounting confidence. In her final quip, he knew that her support was unwavering; he had never felt more in love.

Spring, 1882

Chapter Fifteen

The butterflies fluttered with relentless vigour in the stomachs of Abigail and Josephine. The steam engine chugged as it began its slow departure from the station in Cobourg. The previous day of travel overflowed with sights neither girl had experienced before, save for a few recollections from Josephine Delacourte who had travelled from Montréal to Kingston eight years prior.

"How long will it be until we arrive in Toronto, Father?" Abigail asked with her nose pressed up against the window. The heat from her breath fogged the thin plate, and when she grazed her finger against the glass, she left behind a shaky question mark.

"It should only take another five hours or so. The Grand Trunk is one of the fastest lines on the continent," Mr. Wallace said, proudly. He had been one of the early investors in that branch and relished any opportunity for its promotion.

"Do not worry yourself, Abby. We will be dining late and dancing at Rossin House in no time," Josephine said with her unabashed exuberance.

Miss Delacourte was only a year older, but under pressure from her mother, she had been tossed into society three years before. At only seventeen, she had already procured four marriage proposals and two ivory barrettes. However, none of the gentlemen met her mother's strict criteria of money, property and lineage.

"I beg you not to fill each other's heads with nonsense," Mr. Wallace said as the echoes of chatter and constant giggles filled their private cabin.

"Yes, sir," Josephine said with a smirk as she downcast her eyes in feigned guilt. "Although Mama did say this was the perfect chance for both of us to be exposed to broader society."

"The main objective of this trip is to further your education," he said curtly to the shallow groans of the two young ladies. Sensing their disappointment, he changed his tone to be more congenial. "But I have no doubt that you will further your acquaintances as well." As the train skirted the edge of Lake Ontario, Mr. Wallace smiled at his daughter who returned with a shy smile.

The scenery passed by in a flicker; the girls' eyes darted quickly back and forth so as not to miss a single view. The train wound its way deliberately through Port Union, continuing through the dense forests of southern Ontario. An early spring on the eastern continent had long since melted the deep furrows of snow, and the slender branches of elm showed the change of season through their tender jade buds.

"Are you much acquainted with Mrs. Cunningham, sir?" Josephine asked as they were seated in the dining car for luncheon.

"We have met on many occasions, as I conduct business with her husband. She has shown herself to be a kind and jovial sort. I pray that you all get on. Three months is a long time to spend in adversarial company."

"She is not an old lady, is she?" Josephine asked, playfully using her smile to offset the vulgarity of her remark.

"Josephine, hush," Abigail quickly interjected. But Mr. Wallace simply smiled and chuckled.

"Do you think me so cruel as to set you with an old maid for the season? Mrs. Cunningham is a few years younger than your mother with no children of her own. She is well respected in society, and I hope she will be a positive influence for you both."

"I have heard there is not a day in the week when she is not invited to one party or another. Her calendar is so full up with teas and suppers that she is forced to turn down even her closest friends," Abigail whispered as her father returned to his day-old edition of *The Daily Globe.*

"She sounds fantastic," Josephine sighed.

"Yes, she surely does."

Expanses of foliage receded as stone, brick and timber rose out of the ground, branchless trees setting roots in the dynamic city. The train meandered through the port lands as Toronto's Union Station came into view. The girls' difficulty in restraining their excitement resulted in a series of tiny squeals that defied years of ingrained decorum. The bells of St. Andrew's church rang four times as the train halted on the edge of the main platform, and Abigail marvelled at how quickly they could relocate from their sleepy mercantile town to a booming city.

The crowd occupied nearly every available space on the marble platform. Mr. Wallace had made this journey dozens of times and was not at all startled by the mass of people. He marched swiftly as he led his companions through the concourse, but their attentions were directed elsewhere, for they ambled behind and gawked as the latest fashion plates walked by.

"Her hair! Did you see the sheen on her curls?" Josephine cried as she spun around to see the next beauty.

"The heels on her boots! I would surely topple over," Abigail said as she clung to her friend's arm for fear of losing her.

"I will have to wire Mama. I must have one of those," Josephine said as she pointed to a tall lilac hat burdened with yards of ivory ribbon and navy ostrich plumes.

"And I one of those," Abigail said as she pointed to a finely groomed poodle and laughed.

"Rosedale, if you please, driver. The corner of Avondale Road," Mr. Wallace said as the group boarded the cab. The snap of the leather reigns signalled the horses to move, and with a sharp jolt forwards the carriage left the terminus behind.

"Josephine, look there," Abigail whispered as she discreetly pointed to a gathering of young men carousing by the doors of a social club. The ladies' furtive giggles were met with a glare and stern words from Mr. Wallace who encouraged them to maintain decorum in their banter.

The carriage wound its way through the streets of Toronto, a city on the cusp of modernity. Black smoke rose from the laneway to their right as hot tar was poured and manipulated by labourers and heavy steam-powered machinery. The bumpy road on which they travelled would soon run smooth, but the eventual promise of a comfortable ride did little to offset the odour.

"What is that smell, father?" Abigail asked as she covered her nose with a gloved hand.

"That is the smell of a growing city, my dear. With growth comes opportunity."

The rows of commercial buildings along Yonge Street transitioned into manicured parklands with many of the private gardens inhabiting just as much acreage. To Abigail, the houses were castles, rising up through pages of land as they did in her favourite novels. To Josephine, however, they represented the ideal: a rich husband and lifelong stability.

"The homes are so grand, Father," Abigail said, jostling with Josephine for the best view out the window.

"The families of Rosedale do very well, indeed. With such a new, young country, there are many ways for a man to earn his fortune. The city is brimming with possibilities."

"Are there possibilities for young ladies as well?" Abigail asked.

"Marriage, of course," Josephine interjected before Mr. Wallace had a chance to respond.

"That cannot be the only option, Jo."

"I must agree with Josephine," Mr. Wallace said. "A stable lad and healthy children offer your greatest chance at happiness."

Abigail leaned back on the padded bench and sighed. The carriage slowed its pace as it approached the gate of Rosehurst Manor. The house stood at the crest of a small hill, lending it even more prominence than its size automatically commanded. The wrought iron gate was adorned with tall golden finials; vines of iron wound their way through the bars and bloomed with rose-coloured brass at the ends. The gardens were crafted in the English tradition, and the cobblestone cart path was flanked by white oaks. The manor's footman lifted the latch and pushed the heavy iron gate open to allow the carriage to pass through.

Mrs. Cunningham peered through the drawing room window as the carriage approached; she moved quickly to greet the party as they arrived.

"Henry, they are here," she said as she moved past her husband and pressed firmly on his shoulder.

"Yes, yes. Benji is well known for his promptness," he muttered as he stood and brushed the biscuit crumbs from his waistcoat.

The Cunninghams' second footman swung the heavy doors wide to reveal the trio of guests.

"We could set our clocks by your timekeeping, my boy," Mr. Cunningham said as he slapped Mr. Wallace's back.

"You may thank the train for that, Henry. Good day, Lydia. You are looking well," he said as he brought her delicate hand to his lips.

As Abigail moved out from behind her father, the lady's tender scent delighted her senses. She had read about French perfumes in *The Young Ladies' Journal* and wondered if Mrs. Cunningham was truly intoxicating up close.

"How do you do, Benji?" Mrs. Cunningham asked gracefully as she situated herself before the two young ladies. "We have been so looking forward to seeing you all."

"May I introduce my daughter Abigail and her dear friend Josephine," he said, nodding for them to come forward.

"Good day, madam," they sang out in unison as they each dipped into a low curtsy.

"I was just telling my husband how much I have been looking forward to your visit. Please, do come in."

The master staircase rose three stories and branched off to the chambers on each floor. The second level housed the guestrooms, and the darkness of the corridor was broken only by a flushed, pale glow emanating from the library. As they proceeded, Abigail slowed her pace and leaned over the bannister for a better view. The doors were ajar and in the centre of the room stood a large mahogany piano.

"Hurry along, Abigail," Mr. Wallace said as he urged her to hasten her ascent. With a hurried pace, she returned to Josephine's side.

"Did you see their piano? It is as large as the carriage we travelled in," she whispered.

"Just imagine the parties they have around it," Josephine returned.

"Here we are, ladies. I have arranged for you both to be situated here. Take some time to settle yourselves. I will call back in an hour," Mrs. Cunningham said as she turned to continue her escort of Mr. Wallace. "Benji, you are just down the hall."

The young ladies entered the room behind their trunks, which were placed at the foot of each canopy bed. As they stood in the middle of the spacious guestroom, their eyes travelled from the small sitting area along the wide bank of windows, up along the gold filigree wallpaper to the thick ash beams which rose high and stretched the entire length of the ceiling.

"This bedchamber is larger than our drawing room," Josephine said.

"I would wager it is larger than our entire first floor," Abigail said as she plopped down on the chaise lounge and kicked up her pointed toes.

"Garçon, tell the Cunninghams I will be down shortly. I must count my diamonds before we dine," she said with her nose raised so high her head fell back.

"And then, of course, there are the emeralds and rubies," Josephine said as she took a seat next to Abigail. "In fact, there are so many jewels that we may not have time for supper at all."

Mr. Wallace could hear their giggles echo down the hall and smiled at the prospect of his daughter enjoying herself.

"Did you see what she was wearing?" Josephine asked, lifting the lid of her trunk.

"Her afternoon dress is more elegant than anything I own," she said as she sifted through layers of carefully packed garments. "My gowns are so plain in comparison."

"I would imagine most of her pieces are silk."

"Even Mr. Cunningham was dressed finer than I have ever seen Father. How can we be expected to fit in amongst these people?" she said, laying her frocks on the bed.

"Perhaps we are not meant to fit in. We are from Kingston, after all; that alone should afford us some level of understanding."

A knock came as expected a short time later. In the doorway stood Mrs. Cunningham dressed for supper. The young ladies were unable to speak as they gaped at the stunning vision of their hostess. Her blonde hair was plaited and wound tightly against her head with curls cascading around the nape of her neck. Although it had been years since Abigail played with toys, she was instantly reminded of her favourite porcelain doll.

"You both look charming," Mrs. Cunningham said as she saw herself into their room. Josephine was transfixed on the six-strand collar of pearls which seemed to hold the lady's head even higher than her social rank warranted; Abigail could not help but admire the intricate lace of her bodice. "You both must be fraught with excitement to spend an evening amongst strangers."

"Are there to be many guests this evening, madam?" Josephine asked.

"My dear friend's son, Charles Prescott, is in town for the season. He will be our only other guest. His mother has long since passed, and I take it upon myself to make sure he is well taken care of whenever he is in town. I ensure he is well fed and has a comfortable respite whenever he may need. He has travelled east quite extensively and should be a great source of conversation," she said, turning to lead the young ladies to the drawing room.

Josephine rolled her eyes at Abigail who well understood the prospect of listening to a visitor's travel stories for the whole of an evening; it would not be the first time either girl had been trapped by a droning monologue.

The drawing room was lively, and the party's voices echoed through the broad halls; the sound of collective pleasure taunted those absent to join in at once. The ladies followed their hostess as close to her skirt as lost puppies. Abigail could hear the voice of her father already engaged in conversation. She peered out from behind Mrs. Cunningham and caught sight of him with a young man. When the fellow turned to meet her gaze, she held her breath and crept back out of view.

"My dears, at last. We have been waiting," Mr. Wallace said. "Mr. Prescott, allow me to introduce my daughter, Miss Abigail Wallace, and her companion Miss Josephine Delacourte."

The young man stood tall and thin, not yet comfortable with his growing stature. He was dressed appropriately for dinner, but not so fine as to be mistaken for one of the family. His chest puffed out slightly as he bolstered his courage and tried to remain steady before the young Misses.

"Good evening, Mr. Prescott. How do you do?" Josephine asked as she flashed a smile and thrust her hand forward for a kiss. He met her bold introduction with politeness which enticed a further emergence of her coquetry, but his attention was drawn away by Abigail's delicate beauty.

"Hello," Abigail said with a gentle smile. She was met with a broad grin from the twenty-year-old, who wasted little time in furthering their acquaintance.

"How do you do, Miss Wallace? I hope that your journey was not too uncomfortable."

"It was pleasant, thank you. I suspect I may have enjoyed it more than I should have. You see, this was my first journey by rail."

"Never been on a train? But how can that be?"

"Supper is to be served in the small dining room this evening," Mrs. Cunningham said, interrupting the budding dialogue between them. "Charles, come. I have saved you a seat next to Abigail."

Josephine watched as Charles asked for Abigail's arm and led her into the dining room. He pulled out her chair and bowed slightly as she was seated. When the whole of the party was in their seats, Mrs. Cunningham rose her glass of chardonnay and addressed the group.

"I would like to welcome you all to Toronto, and into our home. Spring has always been my favourite season and it brings me such pleasure to be surrounded by old friends and new. I trust you will enjoy your stay with us. If there is anything we can do to make your visit more comfortable, do let us know. Enjoy your supper." As the last of Mrs. Cunningham's words echoed through the large room, their hum mingled with the conversations rising from around the table.

"I understand you arrived from Kingston, Miss Wallace. That is one area of the country I have not yet seen," Charles said, shifting slightly in his seat to address her directly. "You must have lived there your whole life if you have never been on a train before. You must never have left it."

"It is not as though I am a recluse, Mr. Prescott," Abigail said with a smile. "I have been on excursions to the parkland outside of town, and some day trips along the St. Lawrence, but we always took the democrat."

"But your father, is he not an investor? I would have assumed you had travelled extensively by train."

"There is nothing more dull than travelling for business, so I avoid it at all costs."

"Is that not why you are here now?" he asked in a hushed tone while giving her a playful smirk.

"When I was young it felt as though my father's whole life was spent in brokerages and lending houses. He often took me with him, which was certainly a bore for a young girl. But when he spoke fondly of his friendship with the Cunninghams, I could not wait to meet them, even if business was the main reason for our visit." She smiled demurely as she pushed bits of cucumber salad around her plate.

"I have travelled extensively, Mr. Prescott," Josephine said in an attempt to divert his attention towards her. "But my experiences have been mostly in Europe. Have you travelled to the continent yourself?" she asked as she peered around Abigail's petite frame for a better view of the young suitor.

"I have not yet had that pleasure," Charles said with a dismissive air as he returned his focus to Abigail. "I confess I have little desire to travel to Europe. It seems so old and stodgy compared to the boundless unexplored regions of our own country. Look at the north or the west. Certainly, there is more to see than some dusty old city in France or Spain."

"From what I have read about the west, it seems a wild and ferocious place."

"Perhaps, but imagine the exhilaration of placing your foot on a piece of land that has never been trodden upon before, except by huge wild bears or buffalo."

"Or massive wild cats with fangs as big as your head," Abigail said as her eyes grew wide and she placed down her fork to turn her delicate hands into claws. In light of her good-natured humour, Charles believed that she well understood the potential of their young country.

"What is it you do for employment at present, Mr. Prescott?" Josephine asked, changing her previous pleasantries into a more direct line of questioning.

"I have just begun an apprenticeship at a small hotel here in town. I hope to learn the business. I have a long way to go, that is certain, but Mr. Cunningham assured me that the prospects for hoteliers are good in any city."

"A hotelier? That seems a fair prospect," Josephine said enthusiastically. Abigail kicked her shin under the table, for she preferred to proceed with the conversation unassisted.

"At which hotel do you work, Mr. Prescott?" Abigail continued.

"At The Red Lion Inn on Yonge. It is quite a respectable hotel, and puts me in the path of many influential people."

"It must be fascinating to encounter new people every day. Do you hope to settle in Toronto?"

"Yes, for the time being. With no family of my own, I tend to rely on the kindness of my mother's old friends for contacts and business opportunities."

"And Apple Charlotte," Abigail said as she took a large bite of her dessert and grinned at Charles. Josephine sighed as she watched their interaction; she wanted to be swept off her feet like the damsels in the romantic novels she was so fond of, but Charles' interest could not be drawn away from her friend.

As they each finished supper with a dainty scoop of citrus ice, the conversation meandered from Charles' upbringing in Halifax to his travels down through New York and Boston to stay with one relation after another following the death of his parents. As Abigail became increasingly engaged in the conversation, Josephine became increasingly distracted.

"Do famous guests ever visit your hotel, Mr. Prescott? Harry Rich, perhaps?" Josephine asked when the party returned to the drawing room.

"Yes, I suppose. I never pay much mind as all of our guests receive the same level of attention and respect," he said, focusing on Abigail. Her eyes twinkled as he spoke, and the fluttering in her stomach increased as the geniality of his character became more apparent.

Josephine crossed her arms and slumped back in her chair at his answer, for he would not be revealing any salacious gossip that evening.

As Abigail and Charles chatted, Mrs. Cunningham noticed the separation growing between the two young ladies. She rose from her seat on the room's head chaise and walked to where the outcast was seated. Josephine looked up at her hostess when she extended her hand towards her.

"Come along, my dear. I suspect you may be interested in my opinions on the finer details of Toronto society."

"Oh thank you, Madam," Josephine said, as she leapt from her seat without another thought and left her companions behind.

"Your friend is an interesting sort. I hope she enjoys her time in town," Charles said.

"Josephine holds gossip, status and material possessions above most other things; but she seems well pleased enough."

"How does that differ from you?"

"I hold family above all things, although that is a dwindling resource as only me and Father remain. Josephine seems to think that her beauty and coquetry will lead her into the life she desires, but I am far more ambivalent. I strive to experience as much joy as possible, but in the formation of my future, I prefer to rely on fate." Abigail felt the intimacy with Charles increase as they spoke. Although they had only known each other since just before dinner, it felt as though they had been friends for ages.

"What is it you do to bring you joy, then?"

"I love to sing. I have been singing since before my mother died. She would take me to see this silly old man named Maestro Shields. I remember the first time I went to his studio for a lesson. He sat down at the piano and played the most beautiful music. He told me that with enough practice I could play like him."

"You play the piano, too?"

"Oh, by no means. During my lessons, I would stare down at my fingers and try to will them into playing. They would clink and fumble and make horrible sounds. Maestro thought it best to focus on voice."

"I should very much like to hear you sing, Miss Wallace," Charles said, discreetly brushing the top of her hand with his fingertips. Mrs. Cunningham overheard the exchange and moved in quickly to interject.

"Did I hear you say that you sing, my dear?" she asked as she stood behind Abigail and placed a gloved hand on her shoulder. "Benjamin, you never spoke of Abigail's talents."

"Have I not?" Mr. Wallace said as he smiled at his daughter. "She is a wonderful little chickadee."

"Would you do us the honour of a song, Abigail? Come, let us move to the library," she said, gesturing in the direction of the stairs. "My husband shall accompany you."

"I have only sung for my parents and my instructor, madam," she whispered as she looked up at her hostess. "I have not performed much in society." Charles watched as her porcelain skin began to flush at the impending certainty of her performance.

"You will do well, Abigail," he said with a kind smile.

"I cannot," she said, pleading with her eyes to stay in the parlour.

"Which tune would you care to sing, Miss Wallace?" Mr. Cunningham said when the party moved upstairs. He took his seat at the piano and handed Abigail a leather-bound portfolio of music. She placed it atop the piano and caught her trembling reflection in the polished surface of the instrument. She closed her eyes and squeezed them tight for fear of weeping.

"How about *Song of Night*? I wager you know that one by heart," Mr. Cunningham said, sensing her trepidation. He pulled the sheet music from the stack and handed it to her. Abigail looked at the crisp vellum sheet, and sighed deeply, for she recognized the song straight away.

"Thank you, sir, that will do very well."

She glanced at her father, who smiled with anticipation, and then looked intently at Charles as the music began to play. Her nervousness subsided as she sang the meandering melody, and each fear was erased by each note that was played. Through each graceful phrase, she grew more confident and surrendered herself to song. The party watched intently as her voice increased in power and volume as Mr. Cunningham pounded out the crescendo. As she sang out the final verse, she felt the piano's chords hold her up as her knees fell weak.

"Well done, Abby!" Mr. Wallace said with a rapturous applause as he relished the pride of her accomplishment.

"Splendid, my dear," Mrs. Cunningham said, rushing forth to commend her.

A wide smile grew on Josephine's face, and she gave Abigail a nod of approval. She had watched her friend's grace and poise amplify during the performance and felt certain that the positive reception would impact her friend long after the evening's final glass of sherry.

"Sing us another, Miss Wallace," Charles said. "I am sure we can all agree that there would be no finer amusement." He had seen many young ladies perform in society, whether in the homes of his parents' wealthy friends or during the many balls and social events hosted at The Red Lion; but as he watched Abigail's performance, he could not help but notice the differences between the entertainers. The society ladies sang with immodesty and pageantry, and manipulated audience reception for their own selfish benefit. As Abigail began her next tune, he noticed that there was nothing false in her intentions, but rather, a sincere love of song.

The party demanded song after song from the young performer, and their endless encores continued well past midnight. Abigail was pained by the tenderness in her throat, and Mr. Cunningham understood when she requested an end to the recital.

"We offered them quite a show, did we not?" he asked as the party approached the piano.

"Yes, I believe we did."

"Splendid, my dear! I have not heard anyone of your abilities since we left the continent. Simply wonderful," Mrs. Cunningham said.

"Thank you, madam. I am rather surprised myself."

"You are an undeniable talent. I only wish it was still afternoon so you could sing for longer."

"I thank you, but I must retire. This evening has been exciting, but I am quite taxed."

"Yes, of course, my dear. We will not keep you. It is time for all of us to bid goodnight."

Charles hurried to the front of the group and slid into the space beside Abigail, eager for a few words before the party dispersed.

"That was wonderful, Miss Wallace," he said in an attempt to break through her modesty. "I should think your voice is the happiest sound my ears have heard. I hope this occasion is often repeated."

"Thank you, Mr. Prescott, you are very kind," she said, as she was tapped on the arm by Josephine who wished to hasten their retreat.

"One moment, Jo," she said, turning back to receive Charles' hand.

"I was not expecting anything to come from this evening. I have been invited here so many times as a member of the party, forced to be outgoing and amiable with whomever the Cunninghams hosted. But with you everything was easy."

"I never expected to meet you," she said, first looking into his eyes then dropping her gaze to the simple beadwork of her handbag. "I hope we meet again during our stay."

"I pray that I see you many more times," Charles said as he took a step closer, drawn in by her engaging energy.

In that moment, Josephine's impatience overtook her, and she hurried to pull her friend away from Charles, leading her in the direction of the stairs.

"Come, you shall meet another time," Josephine said as she rushed her along.

"Goodnight, Mr. Prescott," Abigail said as she looked back at him.

"Goodnight, sweet songbird."

Chapter Sixteen

Time passed quickly with the season, and the frequent teas, suppers and luncheons shared among the group had seen the seed of intimacy between Charles and Abigail blossom. Hours were spent in each others' company, and Abigail would have felt neglectful of Josephine had she not been introduced to a wealthy banking family and their youngest son within weeks of their arrival.

"I believe Francis is going to ask me to be his wife, Abby," Josephine said just days before their visit was to end. Abigail looked up from the washbasin and saw her friend's cheerful reflection in the mirror.

"His wife? But you are just sixteen," she said, allowing the cool water to drip off her chin so as not to miss a single moment of her explanation.

"Perhaps, but we both know I am expected to accept as soon as a suitable offer is presented. How can I refuse?" she asked as she unbuttoned her Basque bodice and moved towards Abigail for help.

"Surely your mama does not expect you to marry a man you do not love, especially after so short an acquaintance," Abigail said as the loosening laces seemed to deflate Josephine's aspirations.

"Marriage to a man of wealth and good family is rarely a wrong decision; we will be settled and have a family of our own before I am twenty. It is ideal, Abigail. I know it must seem strange to you, having been raised by your father. Your mother would have approved, I am certain. Mama said she was as smart as she was beautiful, and there is little chance that she would have made an alliance with your father had she not seen the promise of comfort that his wealth and connections would afford. It is not uncommon for a young lady in my position to seek out the same in a partner. Even Mrs. Cunningham agrees that it is quite in keeping with propriety."

She watched as Josephine progressed through the motions of preparing for sleep. Each movement was imbued with boastfulness and self-importance; she had the same conceited smugness of many of their other friends, but Abigail paid little mind because they were so close.

"And you, Abby? Is there a proposal in your future?" Josephine asked in jest, knowing full well she had little intention of marrying so young. She wanted a life like her mother, who had travelled for years before she met her father and had indulged her passions long before children entered her life. Abigail shrugged, in an effort to dissuade her teasing.

"All I can hope for is to leave Toronto on good terms and pray that I meet him again."

Charles had been staying in staff quarters at The Red Lion, but under Mrs. Cunningham's persuasion, took up residence in Rosehurst for the duration of Abigail's stay. Mrs. Cunningham had made the same offer to him some years prior, but a relentless ambition and need for autonomy in his affairs had allowed him some freedom outside of the direct support of his adopted family.

He lay in bed that evening and contemplated how he would approach Mr. Wallace to ask for Abigail's hand. His own hands were empty, and all he could offer was the promise of his devotion and the desire to define his success by the assurance of Abigail's comfort and security. He stared at the lamplight flickering across the walls and ruminated over every possible outcome of that conversation.

"What if he refuses? What if he refuses and tosses us off without a dowry? What if he accepts and she refuses?" The questions swirled in his mind like the filigreed teardrops embossed in the copper ceiling tiles above his bed. His acquaintance with Mr. Wallace had grown in tandem with his relationship with Abigail, and Charles was fond of him. They shared a passion for travel, and an upbringing on the shores of the Atlantic. Charles could imagine any number of reasons why he would refuse, for he had little money and no family; true love was his only recourse.

Charles awoke the next morning cold and weary; his anticipation had allowed for only a few hours sleep, and he had kicked his blanket to the floor. Once his face was freshened with a splash of water, he began his morning routine by warming his feet with his thin woollen socks. He wanted to be at his best when he met with Abigail's father, and so took a swish of Watkin's Peppermint Rinse and combed his hair neatly into place with a dollop of wax. His suit was a gift from Mrs. Cunningham for his eighteenth birthday. He brushed the fabric with a soft ox horn brush to freshen the tweed. He planned to keep his arms in a gentlemanly fold, so as not to reveal the frayed edges of his cuffs.

As he opened his door to the hall, his anvil feet clung to the parquet floor. No matter the force behind it, he could not will himself to trod forward. As he stood in his door's threshold, he wondered how so many other young men had faced that same rite of passage with their own future fathers-in-law. Charles wanted to catch Mr. Wallace before he went down for breakfast to avoid the suspicion of requesting his audience away from the group, and so took a deep breath and stepped out into the hallway. He walked softly on the balls of his feet, quietly passing the rooms of the Cunninghams and his intended. He arrived at the entrance to Mr. Wallace's room and paced back and forth for a long while before the door opened without any provocation.

"Good morning, Mr. Wallace. I trust you slept well," Charles said as he approached the occupant and thrust his clammy hand into his.

"Oh! Good morning, lad. I presumed it was you hovering outside my door this last quarter hour," he said with a grin as he released his hand from the tight grip to loosen his cravat and smooth the creases of his waistcoat. Charles looked at him sheepishly.

"Forgive me, sir, I meant to speak with you alone. I have something I wish to discuss. It regards Abigail."

"Does it so? Why then, let us find somewhere to talk."

Mr. Wallace turned and led the way down the stairs. As Charles followed, he ran through the script in his mind one last time. His anxiety brimmed to the surface until the warmth of the dawn's rays through the library windows began to calm him.

"Shut the door and take a seat, my boy."

Mr. Wallace thought it appropriate to occupy one of the seats next to the large terrestrial globe to somehow provide Charles with the comfort of knowing that within a few minutes, his feet would again be planted firmly on the ground.

"How do you do today, sir?" Charles asked shyly as he made himself more comfortable in the chair.

"I am still fine, Charles. You seem a bit green, however," he said with a chuckle. With that laugh, Charles knew that Mr. Wallace was well aware of their impending topic of conversation. Anyone who had witnessed the interactions between the young couple these past months had noticed their mutual affection.

"I am rather new to all of this," he stammered.

"Oh, this is only your first proposal, then? In that case, I shall give you some leeway."

"Thank you, sir."

"Just breathe, lad. It is really only a matter of who you are choosing to spend the rest of your life with."

"I choose Abigail, sir," he said as his pursed lips widened into a broad smile.

"Well, that is a start. Why have you chosen my daughter? Why not Josephine, perhaps? She comes from a family far more prosperous than ours."

"With respect, sir, I do not love Josephine. I love Abigail."

"How can you be certain?"

"Do you recall the day of the Smithfield luncheon, down in High Park near Grenadier Pond?" he asked. Mr. Wallace nodded in agreement. "That was the first time we had more than a few minutes on our own to explore our mutual interests and passions. We share a love of books, and nature and family. We both lost parents at a very young age, and that too strengthens our bond. We discovered that we both long for the connection that only a family of our own and a lifetime of memories will bring. It was in those hours that my heart opened. I knew that I wanted her in my life forever."

"You are willing to move to Kingston, then?" Mr. Wallace responded, seemingly more concerned with logistics than Charles' sentiment.

"Kingston? To be honest, sir, I had not thought that far ahead."

"Before I give my consent, there are certain details of this union that you must consider. I will not have my daughter living in town; she is too young, and I will not abide being so far removed from her. You must also secure employment, and by that, I mean an apprenticeship with prospects for a career. All she brings with her is a modest dowry of three hundred dollars and my father's gold watch. I suggest that you offer your hand before we depart with the understanding that you are not to wed until those conditions are met."

Charles' demeanour degraded from hopeful to dejected as he considered the stipulation of his career. He was only now just starting on his current path and was unsure of his future prospects.

"Do not forget that you have friends in me and the Cunninghams. We have connections and may be able to find you something more suitable for the long term." Mr. Wallace looked at him kindly, and Charles returned with an encouraged smile. "I like you, young man. I want to see you and Abigail happy. Although she has not said anything to me directly, I can tell by her looks that she loves you as well. I have not seen a young lady so smitten since my own wife some twenty years ago. I trust you will do well by her." Mr. Wallace stood and extended his hand to the seated young man. "I give you my consent, Mr. Prescott. Now, choose your moment wisely for it is one she will never forget."

On the final day before the party was to catch the train bound for Kingston, Mrs. Cunningham arranged for luncheon to be served near the pond in her rear gardens. As summer approached, the days had grown longer but the midday temperature was not yet overbearing. The foliage within the manor's grounds had evolved from tiny sprouts to lush leaves and flowers which grew in splendour with each passing day. Throughout her stay, Abigail had made a point of spending as much time outside as possible, for she had only a small patio with mismatched pots of violets and geraniums to look forward to back home.

When Charles would join her after work or on his free days, they would walk the perimeter of the pond and admire the waterfowl along the banks. On one occasion she was able to convince him to wade knee-deep into the pool which was quite a feat for a man whose near-drowning had kept him out of the water since boyhood. That afternoon, Mr. Wallace had instructed the party to give the young couple time alone to bid a proper farewell. Charles spread a blanket on the velvet grass near the marsh where the family of beavers had made their home. It was Abigail's favourite spot in the gardens, for if they waited patiently, the large rodents would emerge and slap their tails on the water before them.

"Do you think they will come out today, Charles?" Abigail asked as she took a seat on the blanket beside him and sheltered herself from the sun with her crepe parasol.

"I hope so. It would be a shame not to say goodbye."

The ivory clouds drifted in lazy plumes above them, tufts of buttercream casting patchwork shadows on the hills and trees surrounding.

"I am thankful that we have the chance to say goodbye. I feared you would be occupied at the inn and miss our last day together." Abigail looked at Charles and cocked her head to the side. She tried to ascertain if the sun was reflecting the colour of the grass or if he was indeed that shade of green.

"Is anything the matter, Charles? Are you unwell?" she asked, placing her hand atop his. She could feel his body trembling through her light touch and grew worried as she searched his eyes for a clue. "You are shivering. Let us retire back to the house and take some peppermint tea."

"No, no, I am quite well," he said as his voice quavered. "Please forgive me, Miss Wallace. I have something of great importance that I wish to say, but I fear my nerves are undermining my efforts."

Abigail opened her satchel and withdrew a piece of pale blue cloth. She had chosen the fabric and embroidered the bunches of violets in each corner herself. She had meant to give him the handkerchief before they parted as a token of their perfect spring.

"Dear Charles," she said with a dab of the cloth on his forehead. "You must calm yourself. I understand my departure is upsetting; I have lost control of my own emotions several times today. I hardly know how I gathered the strength to face you, knowing that it could be the last time we met." Abigail swallowed hard and looked down at her lap. "I do not know how I will bear not seeing you tomorrow."

As Charles sat paralyzed by his admiration for her, he could not help but reminisce about his most cherished memories of their time together. He smiled bashfully and worked to gather his breath as he recalled the same flutter in his heart as when they toured High Park by carriage throughout the season; Mrs. Cunningham's escort proffered just enough preoccupation for the young couple to steal flirtatious glances or the occasional light touch on the back of their hands. Abigail was relieved to see his smile as the pallor in his face receded. It was the same coy grin he would give her before each dance at Government House or before he was to disclose another detail from his youth.

"Do you wish to see me again, Miss Wallace?"

"Yes, of course. I have grown to care for you a great deal." Abigail folded the handkerchief into a small square and held it out before him. "I wish I had more to give you."

"Our time together is the greatest gift of my life. I know we have only been acquainted a short time, but in these few months, I felt I have grown as close to you as family. When you speak of your mother and the bond you shared, I cannot help but feel envy. She was in your life for thirteen years; the cholera left me an orphan when I was only four. It has been a struggle since then to feel a sense of place, of belonging; perhaps that is why I have travelled so much."

"I hope you understand that my past was not entirely ideal. After mother passed I hardly ever saw father. He spent most of his time aboard trains and freighters. Business was always his excuse, but I suspect he could not bear to see me or have any reminders of her at all. That is behind us now, of course, but I understand what it means to feel alone."

Charles took Abigail's hands and felt the warmth of her kindness as she combined a gentle squeeze with a smile.

"If we spend our lives together," Charles said, "we shall never again feel the ache of loneliness."

Abigail felt her muscles weaken at Charles' declaration. She was thankful they were not currently involved in their daily stroll along the cobbled path from the manor, for she most certainly would have stumbled. She had told Charles of her feelings so many times in her mind, but could never muster the courage to articulate them aloud; she could hardly believe that he felt a similar kinship.

"Abigail, I have spoken with your father."

She felt a surge of excitement move to the bottom of her stomach; she quickly released her hands from Charles' grip and held them in her lap to keep them from shaking. She resisted the urge to look back at the patio to see if Josephine and Mrs. Cunningham were watching.

"What did you speak of?"

"Your father has made me aware of some connections he has in Kingston. I may be able to complete my apprenticeship there."

"Charles, that is splendid news! That will most certainly allow us to see each other."

"I hope that will allow us to marry," Charles said, as he mustered the courage to offer his hand with conviction.

"You wish to marry me?"

"I have thought about sharing my life with you since that first night in the library. I know we are young, but our youth will allow us to enjoy the full extent of our lives together."

Abigail was filled with a joy that she could not suppress. Tears of delight filled her eyes, and she blotted her cheeks with the back of her gloved hand.

"I am very much obliged, Mr. Prescott."

They both laughed at the formality of her response, and Charles was particularly grateful for the levity. With that affirmation, he sprang to his feet and raised Abigail up to stand beside him. He wrapped his arms around her waist and drew her in for a close embrace.

"I can hardly bear to think of my departure tomorrow," Abigail said. "I wish with all my heart that you could be on the train with us."

"In good time, my dear. I would not expect it to take long for us to be reunited."

The group on the patio had furtively watched the young couple's exchange for the better part of an hour. As soon as she observed their embrace, Mrs. Cunningham began her descent towards the pond. Mr.

Wallace tried in vain to prevent his friend's interference, but both she and Josephine had quickly convinced him that immediate congratulations were in order.

"Is everything settled between you?" Josephine asked as she rushed ahead of their mistress.

"Josephine, hush," Mrs. Cunningham scolded. "Miss Wallace, might you have any news that you wish to relate?"

Spring, 1902

Chapter Seventeen

It took several minutes for the applause to subside. Abigail relished the warmth of the spotlight on her face and the energy that pulsed forth from the crowd. As she stood, she made eye contact with her benefactor who gestured for her to join him at the rear of the hall. Although her family had left just two days prior, she already missed them greatly; her sole motivation for desiring their presence at that moment, however, was to avoid the obligation of meeting another of Mr. Smythe's associates. She obliged her patrons with a shallow curtsey and moved towards the hotel owner as he patrolled the group of tables reserved for only the wealthiest of guests.

"Dear Abigail, how splendid your performance was this evening," he said with an over-solicitous smile. "But then, you haven't hit a false note since you arrived."

Abigail met his compliments with modesty, and as she averted her gaze in a show of decorum, she caught sight of a handsome fellow at the table beside them.

"Good evening," said the gentleman when he noticed her attentions.

"Mrs. Prescott, allow me to introduce Mr. Baxter Carlisle," Mr. Smythe said.

"How do you do," she said as she extended her hand to receive his. His palm was rough and calloused, which surprised her considering the elegance of his attire.

"With such talent, I wonder why you chose the frontier?" Mr. Carlisle asked.

"Because Mr. Smythe invited me, I suppose," she said with expert deflection, for each evening she was subjected to rampant flattery and advances from all manner of guests. She was eager to shed the notoriety that came with her employ, for even her leisure time was subject to approval and judgement. Each moment away from Bowlea was part of her performance.

"Our stage needed you, my dear," Mr. Smythe interjected. "I knew within seconds that you were a treasure." His attention was diverted by an argument over cards, and he hurriedly excused himself to settle the drawing room row.

"Would you care to join me, madam?" Mr. Carlisle asked as Abigail stood tall on the tips of her toes to observe the ruckus. "I imagine a drink would do you well after such a lengthy performance."

"Thank you, Mr. Carlisle, but I tend to avoid spirits. I find them harsh on my voice." Abigail remained standing as a bottle of whiskey, and two glasses were brought to the table. As he uncorked the bottle and poured himself three fingers, she imagined Charles in his study swirling a glass of brandy after a trying day at The Danbury. She knew better than to object, for there were no funds for such luxuries in Bowlea. "But then," she continued, "how can I refuse such kindness?"

"I am glad to have you join me. Anyone who would travel on their own to be an entertainer on the frontier must have stories to tell," he said as he leaned back and smoothed his short beard with the palm of his hand.

Abigail could not help but notice the cut of his hair and the crispness of his white, starched collar. There was not a burr on his tweed, and his moustache was neatly trimmed and waxed. His attention to dress reminded her of Charles; he always appeared at his best with the expectation that each person he met was a potential customer.

"I assure you, my history would seem quite wholesome to you."

"That would be a welcome change from the conversations I have had since leaving Toronto."

"I am from that part of the country myself. Kingston."

"We are neighbours, then. Did you travel often to town?"

"Not so often. I was there only once, although it was for the whole of the season."

"And how did you find it?"

"It was lovely. The gardens, especially."

"Come now, surely that cannot be the depth of your recollection."

"You seem intent on prying stories from me, Mr. Carlisle," she said with a teasing cadence to her voice.

There was something in her companion's manner that enticed her towards a further acquaintance. Although Tobias was a reliable escort, his topics of conversation fell within the narrow scope of Emma, Bowlea, and their homestead. To the hotel staff, she was merely an entertainer and fell into obscurity with the rest of them after each show. The guests, whose interest in her never seemed to wane, were left with only brief, superficial interludes when she scurried back to her room at night's end. With only a few hours of work to occupy each day, she well understood his craving for conversation.

"If we are to shed boundaries by sharing a drink, surely you can call me by my given name."

"So informal? I have known Mr. Smythe for months now, and would not know his name to call it," she said with a gentle smile.

"He is called Reginald."

"And you are called Baxter." She took a sip of her liberal glass of whiskey and felt the burn of the liquor sting her lips. "I am Abigail."

He followed her lead but downed his portion in a single gulp. He wiped the tiny droplets from his moustache as the effects of the sharp liquor twinged his eyes and made their colour appear even more blue.

"I have no reason to pry into your personal history, Abigail, and only ask as a reminder of what I have left behind. It has been several months since I have been home, and I see little opportunity for me to return anytime soon. I suppose homesickness happens to the best of us. I feel a sort of kinship with the people I meet along the way and cannot help but ask them of their history, of their experiences. I have my own motivations for being in this part of the country, and I am curious about theirs."

"Are they willing to share with you?" she asked, unsure if she was prepared to do the same.

"In some cases, yes. In my business, I interact with workers and all manner of folk every day. One cannot help being captivated by their stories; how they came to be in the district, and if they would encourage others to experience this part of the country. You are obviously a well-mannered woman and precisely the status of clientele we hope to entice."

Abigail smiled and wondered if he would be as persistent in his interview if he knew she had spent the better part of the day sewing a hole in her dress by hand.

"This may sound strange, and you may think me a fool," Baxter said as he refilled their tumblers, "but I feel we may have met before. It would hardly be a surprise considering the proximity of our social circles back home."

Abigail paused for a moment and looked at her companion. She studied the details of his face with a squinting eye. Baxter grabbed his ebony pipe and restocked the chamber with tobacco as she continued her study. As her gaze settled on his sculpted moustache she let out a faint gasp.

"I believe I do recall seeing you once, although we were never formally introduced."

"It must have been a grand affair if circumstances did not permit us to meet."

"Might I ask, did you happen to pass through Calgary several years ago with a large entourage?"

"I travel through Calgary frequently, and am rarely without my porters," he said, as the smoke from his pipe rose up around him.

"I think you may have seen me when you were checking in to a hotel. The name of it escapes me, but I am sure it was you."

Baxter eyed her in return as he tried to place her, and leaned back in his chair as he let out a baritone laugh.

"Yes, indeed! I do remember you. I seem to recall an unfortunate encounter with a chambermaid."

Abigail smiled at the gleeful twinkle in his eyes. She was at once surprised and flattered that he remembered her from an encounter so brief they had not even spoken.

"Yes, that was me. The whole scene was rather embarrassing. Sometimes I think it would be better for me not to move at all for fear of disaster. Even worse, I suppose, is the fact that I have always considered myself graceful."

"I presume you were in town for an engagement?"

"We were just passing through. I was having breakfast with my daughter that morning. She will be happy to know that you were as amused by my stumble as she was."

"She is not here in town with you, then?"

"No, she is of age now and stays on at our little homestead while I am away."

"That is quite a different environment than the one in which you came of age, I am sure."

"We left Kingston when she was just twelve, so she has had little exposure to formal society. In many ways, I am grateful; she is rarely idle and has fostered her mind instead of the superficiality of society relationships. She has her father to keep her company while I am away, and more than enough chores to occupy her time."

Baxter let out a shallow grunt and drew a languid breath from his pipe. Red Deer was tamer than many towns in the district, but like other young settlements, it grew with the ferocity of weeds while its inhabitants sought success and a firm placement of their roots. With the town's rapid expansion came the turbulence of uncertainty and a harshness that challenged even the toughest men. He admired the tenacity of the woman before him but wondered what circumstances had compelled her to leave her family behind.

"Since you travel without your husband, I must assume he is much occupied with business."

"He is one of many men who have sought opportunity in this place."

"And how goes that venture?"

Abigail fell silent as Charles' morose demeanour flashed in her mind. As she thought of the state of his business, she could not help but envision him waiting for hours on the front porch nursing a cold cup of tea.

"He does what he can with the resources available," she said with a nondescript answer that revealed little of the torment of the previous four years. "He sought independence in business and has certainly succeeded in that regard."

"That entrepreneurial spirit is something you share, then."

"I am paid for each performance, to be sure, but it is the craft that brings me the most pleasure. The money is merely a happy consequence."

Baxter smiled at her disclosure, unaware that the true motive for her present engagement was quite the reverse. She had gone to great lengths over those lonely months at The Regent to project an image of success and propriety and thought better of making a man of his wealth aware of her family's destitution.

"I have always been drawn to music," Abigail continued. "I remember my first opera at the Grand, being enchanted by the orchestra and the voice of Miss Emma Albani. Through their music, I felt every triumph as keenly as each sorrow. Their mastery of craft gave me such respect for them as artists. Each note is forever etched in my memory."

"Well then, surely we cannot offend The Regent's artists by forgoing a dance. Can I persuade you to move from your chair just this once to risk disaster with a waltz?"

The small house band that Mr. Smythe had assembled would not have been out of place in one of the finer hotels in Kingston. As Baxter led Abigail into the centre of the dancefloor, she could instantly feel eyes upon her. With an equal number of people focused on Baxter, she wondered if he was more pleased with being the centre of attention than he admitted.

"You seem to have many admirers, Mr. Carlisle. Are you a frequent guest of The Regent?" she asked as she moved in closer to her partner and rested her thumb and forefinger on the back of his shoulder.

He gripped her hand with a gentleness she thought in charming paradox to his commanding persona. As the music played, he led her through dozens of other couples who were navigating the complexities of the Viennese waltz. As he twirled and spun her through each movement, her thoughts drifted to the dances she would share with her father. Baxter wore the same heavy tweed, and if she were to close her eyes and notice only his piney aftershave and the fabric beneath her fingertips, she would have sworn she was being paraded through a swarm of suitors at a Queen's College luncheon.

He pulled her closer and drew in a shallow breath of the faint almond scent of her hair. He resisted the temptation to kiss the soft auburn curls on her forehead or to brush her porcelain cheek with the backs of his fingers. She looked up into his smiling eyes as she floated above the floorboards and giggled softly with each languid turn. The momentum of each step drew her head down to rest on his chest; it was not until she felt the rough fabric against her chin that she opened her eyes and quickly drew back.

"I am sorry," she said hastily as she pushed herself away from Baxter, whose brawny arms now hung limply beside him.

"Mrs. Prescott, what is it?"

"A breath of air. I must take a breath of air," she muttered quietly as she removed herself from his company. Baxter felt awkward, as the episode in no way escaped the notice of the other dancers. He smiled nervously and gave a nod of his head as he walked off the dancefloor alone.

Abigail hurried as she skipped down the back steps and out to the courtyard. She glanced back to see if her companion had followed and was relieved when she believed he had not. The wrought iron bench opposite the stone fountain was the closest seat available, and the trickling water replaced the beat of the music inside and helped drown out the confusion of her thoughts. It also helped to disguise the footsteps that approached behind her.

"Mrs. Prescott," Baxter said as he took notice of her delicate frame against the rough stonework around them. She hesitated before speaking and did not turn around, for she hoped his hand would once again occupy the spot at her waist. When she did not respond, he continued his purposeful steps around the bench until he stood before her.

"You are blocking my view, Mr. Carlisle," she said as her eyes remained fixed on the bubbling water.

"I see that I have offended you somehow, madam. I fear that years amongst the unrefined has left rough edges on my manners." He was uncomfortable with the feeling of looking down upon her and asked cautiously for a place beside her.

Abigail scooted her bottom along the bench to leave room for Baxter, unconsciously giving the seat a few quick taps like she did when she requested Emma to join her. As Baxter smoothed his moustache with a practiced spread of thumb and forefinger, Abigail let out a sigh before responding.

"It is I who have offended. It is understandable that one would expect the role of a female entertainer to include an obligation to continue her arts off the stage. I can see from your dress and your occupation that you are a man of wealth. Perhaps tonight you presumed you were the highest bidder of something you mistakenly thought was for sale. I say this to ensure no ambiguity in the situation. Before signing my contract with Mr. Smythe, I made it explicitly clear that those services would not be part of the agreement."

One might expect Abigail's supposition to anger the refined sensibilities of Mr. Carlisle. However, because of the air of the ridiculous surrounding her statement and the matter-of-fact way in which she denounced him, he could not help but chuckle.

"Am I to understand that you are not open for business?" he asked in jest, hoping to produce a smile.

"I am sorry if Mr. Smythe gave you any indication that I was…open," she stuttered, as her gaze remained fixed on the fountain's moonlit cascade of water.

"Well then, do you know of anyone who might be available?"

"Certainly not!" she scolded as she turned in her seat to face him.

His sheepish grin and playful gaze brought forth an uncomfortable laugh from Abigail.

"I am sorry, Mr. Carlisle. Since I began this engagement, I have spent most evenings trying to make it back to my room without being propositioned. Sadly, it is a consequence of life on the stage."

While Abigail attempted to utter those words in a pleasant tone, Baxter was struck by the underlying shame that shone through. He could hear a tremble in her voice and wondered if the pain it expressed went deeper than mere embarrassment.

"I am sorry, Mrs. Prescott, but you greatly misunderstand my intentions. I am married with a wife back home in Toronto."

"If you are married then why in heaven's name did you ask me to drink with you? That is the standard method used to approach the ladies upstairs."

"One might ask why you accepted."

Abigail was stung by the sharp words of her companion, and instinctively sunk her chin down to her chest in a sort of penance; she was not in the habit of drinking or dancing with strange men.

"Mr. Smythe is a great friend of mine," Baxter said in a conciliatory tone. "We are in business together on a large barracks in Winnipeg. I always stay here when I am passing through town. Tonight was the first time I have seen you perform. It has been more than six months since I last stayed, and Smythe was keen for us to meet."

Abigail felt ashamed for having accused Mr. Carlisle of an act that seemed now to contradict his character.

"Might I ask," she began with caution, "what brings you here now and without your family?"

Baxter shifted in his seat at the awkwardness of the query and wondered how best to broach the subject. The only way he was able to bear life without his wife was to bury her memory deep in his mind and try not to speak of her to others.

"Madeline never liked the frontier. I brought her out with me many years ago when I worked surveying the route for the Pacific. She had always been a Moodie fan, thrilled by stories of the rugged wildlands. But, sadly, living day-to-day in that environment was more than she could bear."

"You live apart, then?"

"It is for the best. She has her occupations and friends to keep her entertained, and I have the pull of business and success keeping me here. I cannot have both at once."

"So you choose your work," Abigail said as she shook her head. "When I first noticed you I thought you looked a great deal like my father. I see now that you may have much more in common."

The air around them cooled as the minutes passed, and as Abigail tightened the thin shawl around her shoulders, Baxter suggested they take their discussion to the drawing room and settle in next to the large fire.

"I hope you understand that it was not only my business that brought me here, nor is it the only reason I stay. You see, I cannot seem to separate myself from the majesty of Alberta or the people I encounter on my travels. It is impossible to regret the opportunities I have been given."

"I can see how you would feel fortunate, indeed. In my settlement, there is little opportunity to meet new people at all."

"And not of the society you are accustomed, I imagine. It must have been quite an adjustment for you," he said as he tilted his head back and took a long, slow draw of his pipe.

"In some respects, it was. When I consider my situation here in Red Deer, I am grateful. And yet, there are certain memories of life in Kingston that I prefer to leave behind," she said with a broad smile. "I cannot help but recall touring the city with my father in my youth. As he conducted business on the wharfs and in the shipyards, I felt as out of place as the fish pulled from the Saint Lawrence."

"Come now; I would think the smells alone would entice you to return at your first opportunity."

Abigail felt a shiver travel up her spine to the nape of her neck and she fumbled to adjust the shawl around her shoulders. The warmth of the drawing room was starting to make her more comfortable, but still, she extended her hands towards the fire to hasten the process. She tried not to notice how the firelight made him appear even more handsome and was careful not to make him aware of her admiration. She would blame the sudden blush of her cheeks on the affects of the fire.

"When we decided to come out here, I thought I would miss the people the most. I realize now that my acquaintances proved to be little more than strangers. It was not long before I realized how little in common I had with them. I enjoyed the interactions of society, of course, but I see now that they were all superficial. My only true friend from that life is my dear Josephine. She often writes to relate gossip and tales of life back in

Kingston, but from here it all sounds so unreal. I wonder if they are truly as contented as they appear to be."

"Were you as contented as you appeared to be?"

Abigail looked at him for a moment as she pondered her response. She wondered at his own life and the simultaneous courage and cowardice it must have taken for him to abandon society and family life to think only of his own contentment.

"My husband's pursuit of success in business has been his main motivation is all aspects of his life. As a businessman I am sure you understand the monopoly that those priorities have on one's time. I often felt alone in that big house, and alone in raising our daughter."

"But Smythe tells me that you were quite the star in Ontario. Surely you could not have been lonely."

Abigail thought of the countless times she awoke to find Charles already gone, and the nights she would retire without so much as a kiss goodnight because his quest for occupational perfection had kept his side of the bed cold long after she had gone to sleep.

"I dismissed my feelings, for the most part. It is not so difficult when your mind is occupied elsewhere. It felt as though my whole life was consumed with hosting and appearing at engagements. Projecting success is not merely attending parties and wearing the finest things; it is about making connections and promoting oneself. Some are born into that life, and so come about it naturally. Others are thrust into it and find themselves forced to dedicate their time to social conformity. I do not believe I ever quite succeeded in that regard."

"You are far too unique to fit in amongst any society. Believe me when I say that anyone who has met you is better for the encounter. Just look at how many people you affect with your voice."

Abigail was flattered that he would recognize her individuality but was uncomfortable with what she perceived to be a continuation of his earlier flirtation. She was enjoying his company and wished to prolong their dialogue, but felt it necessary to focus the conversation on the most innocuous of his statements.

"That may well be, but there is a vast difference between singing for people you are acquainted with and singing for strangers. Strangers are far more accepting."

"Yes, I could see the benefit of anonymity," he said.

"They could hold me in judgement, and I would be none the wiser."

"The same could be said for their praise, although I imagine they give that up far more readily."

"A bit too readily for my taste. Most of the time I feel like I am either hiding or trying to escape," she said with a chuckle that concealed her hatred of the notoriety. "With each arrival of the train, a calmness comes over me. I cherish those hours of obscurity before I give my next performance. I can wander through town and look at the shops, and guests will only know me as a fellow visitor. There is a freedom in exploring all that is modern without having to explain why you wish things would stay as they are."

"The world is forever evolving. You cannot expect things to stay the same."

"Expecting things to stay the same and hoping they will not change are different matters. Kingston is steeped in tradition and industry while Red Deer is raw and rough and new. I understand that Kingston has had decades to evolve, so I never knew otherwise or had the opportunity to experience it in its natural state. Red Deer is so young that I cannot help but long for the natural and unspoiled way it was just a short time ago. When we first arrived in Calgary, I was in awe. Although the mountains were in the distance, I felt as though I could capture their energy if I just extended my arms towards them."

"I had similar feelings when I first saw the ocean. When I was a boy, my parents took me aboard a steamer to see our relations in St. John's. We travelled for days through the choppy waters of the Saint Lawrence, flanked on either side by wide tracts of land. I spent a great deal of my youth on the shores of Lake Ontario, but nothing could prepare me for the open waters beyond the gulf. The boat would slap down on the water as it was tossed like a child's toy between the massive swells. The power of the wind and waves made me feel as though I could do anything in this world. That is one of the reasons I have decided to make my permanent home near a lake. I find the water very soothing, and a much-needed respite from a stressful business like mine. After this final project, I hope to retire from this role and move into simple management. With all of the travel and the task of handling rowdy work crews, it seems I have little time left to enjoy my surroundings. As I head into my forty-fifth year, it seems fitting to focus more on myself."

"It will be nice for you to feel settled," Abigail said. She thought of her current situation living in a posh hotel and longed for the modest pleasures of her home.

"Indeed. I have worked extremely hard to obtain this position, and I hope I am not overcome by a sense of idleness."

"How can that be? You will have the opportunity to enjoy the lands for what they are. How fortunate for you to have the chance to connect with yourself and your place within nature. And since it will not be so rugged, perhaps then your wife will join you again."

Baxter smiled and withheld any response, for he was unsure of how to articulate the fact that his wife was further removed from his life than he had acknowledged. He moved swiftly to divert the conversation.

"Am I to understand that you live near the mountains, then?" he asked.

She was careful not to reveal to him the exact location of where she lived. Although they had now spent a few hours together, the full extent of his character was as yet unknown. Still, she wished that she could speak to him like a trusted friend, relaying without inhibition the feelings that she had been relegated to express only to the hens and gophers around their property. Propriety and integrity had prevented her from ever speaking ill of Charles to Emma or from gossiping about her family life with any of the older women who inhabited Bowlea. Letters to Josephine were regular, of course, with correspondence being exchanged several times per year. For the most part, the content was condescending, with Josephine remarking on Abigail's strength and sense of adventure while lamenting the formality of the season and the tired obligations of her society life. Despite their flaws, each letter was hand sealed with scarlet wax and contained a crisp five dollar note. Abigail never informed Charles of this addition to their coffers, and whether from denial or ignorance, he never seemed to wonder why they never wanted for tea or sugar.

"No, I live in a meadow. Near a lake."

She smiled and turned her gaze towards the fire. As she watched the flames lick lazily up the sides of the stone chimney, she felt compelled to let down her guard. In the hours that followed, she spoke of the loneliness of being in a strange town and how being surrounded by a transient society prevented her from forming any real attachments. She admitted that although feelings of loneliness often consumed her, even while in the company of loved ones, she also craved solitude; she longed to float above the lake water, aloft on the tip of a reed like the black birds with the red wings, disturbed only by the brush of a breeze against her feathers. They laughed at the dull conversations she would have with Mrs. Winters about the state of the roads, and how she would pray for inclement weather just to have something more diverting to talk about.

Baxter revealed only minute details about himself, but Abigail believed that to be more a result of modesty than a desire to conceal. He described his time with the Canadian Pacific and the prospect of someday owning his own rail line. He spoke fervently of his love of the country and his desire to expose the district to as many newcomers as possible; he admitted to the guilt formed by the drastic changes to the landscape, as well as his desire to keep it unexplored and accessible only to those who would promise not to change it.

"So, how large is this lake of yours?" he asked as the last of the embers lost their glow, and the radiance of the dawn replaced the firelight's tawny hues.

"Not so large as Lake Ontario, but large enough that it frames the view from my window and forms a pool of jewels with each sunset."

"It sounds quite magical."

"I spend as much of my free time out there as I can. Even in the winter we sled down the embankment and slide out onto the lake."

"I used to skate on the lake as a boy," he said with a smile that reflected the fond memory. "I always wondered what happened to the fish beneath the icy cap of water. When the relentless, biting cold would cause the water to freeze so rapidly, I would wonder if the shift from liquid to solid felt like infinite shards of glass against their flesh."

"I suppose they find the warmest place they can and call for their family and fellow fish to join them. They must huddle together to keep warm and survive."

"If a bear can hibernate, why not a trout?" Baxter said as they both shared a laugh and Abigail smiled at his subtle sense of humour.

As the conversation ambled towards six o'clock, Abigail was forced to excuse herself; the many hours of discussion had made her hoarse, and she needed to ensure her voice was prepared for the evening's performance. She and Baxter moved from their solace and approached the bar.

"Good morning, Dieter. Might I have a cup of tea with honey, please? I seem to have a sore throat this morning," she said to the young man who was preparing the dining room for the breakfast service.

"A sore throat on our songbird? We can't have that, can we? I'll fetch it right away, Miss Abigail."

Baxter moved beside Abigail and leaned his elbow on the mahogany counter.

"I must tell you how refreshing it was to speak with you tonight, Abigail. Travelling with wagons full of coarse mouths and bawdy tales can leave a fellow wanting for more cordial conversation."

"Yes, this evening was certainly unexpected. I usually head to bed straight away after a few obligatory handshakes."

"I trust that you felt no obligation in spending time with me tonight," Baxter said coyly. He felt uneasy at having made her feel uncomfortable earlier that evening; in that moment, however, he felt as close to her as anyone he had encountered since leaving Toronto.

Abigail gently placed her hand atop Baxter's as it rested on the bar.

"Will I see you this evening?" she asked.

"You will not, I'm afraid. I had a few legal matters to attend to yesterday, but my schedule dictates that we must push on after breakfast."

"Today? You will hardly have time to sleep at all."

"I would not have slept, regardless. After such a conversation, I wager it will be some time before I am able to think of anything else."

"It was lovely to have met you." She winced at the aloofness of her remark but was uncertain of what else to say. It would be improper for her to relate how much she shared his enjoyment of their dialogue, and how she wondered how she had survived that strange town thus far without his companionship.

"Perhaps we shall cross paths again. From what Smythe tells me, he may want to have you on permanent."

"My, that would be a consideration. I can hardly stand being away from my home and family for even these short months. If I stayed any longer than agreed to, I am quite certain my heart would break."

"Well then, perhaps you will return for a special engagement. I hope there is something that will draw you back and allow us to meet again. Goodbye, Mrs. Prescott."

"Goodbye, Mr. Carlisle."

Baxter picked his bowler hat off the rack and toyed with it between his hands as he stood before her. He wished that he did not have to leave, but understood why fate made it so. As he turned and walked away, he felt himself yearning for the newness and excitement he felt as he learned each new thing about her. He well understood the affects of loneliness and was grateful for at least one night of friendship that was not attached to a commercial agenda. He placed the hat upon his head and bandied up the stairs two at a time; Abigail watched and waited for him to turn back and look at her once more.

"Your tea, Mrs. Prescott," Dieter said as he placed the hot beverage before her. It was enough of an interruption that by the time Abigail looked back up towards the stairs, Mr. Carlisle was gone.

* * *

Abigail was thankful for the lack of accountabilities that came with her current employ. She had but one role and no commitment to be anywhere other than the concave side of the piano each evening at half-past ten. This lack of rigorous occupation usually brought with it severe idleness and scores of repetitive trips to the same dozen shops around the hotel. Although she had hours enough to lay down to bed that morning, like Baxter, she would not get a single wink of shut-eye.

As she settled back into her room, she was inclined to write a letter to Josephine but had not even the slightest notion of what to say. She took a sheet of the hotel stationary from the side drawer and laid it upon the desk. She smoothed her hand over the crisp sheet and wondered what she could write so as to elicit commiseration from her friend while discreetly communicating a fondness for a man who was not only not her husband but someone she had known for only seven hours and would likely never see again. As she stared at the paper before her, she could not escape memories of her season in Toronto and how it felt the first time she encountered a gentleman who shared similar interests. She laid her fountain pen down, leaned back in the cushioned chair and closed her eyes.

Looking back on all that had initially drawn her to Charles, Abigail felt guilty that she had allowed herself to be attracted to a man who was not her husband. She pondered the sacrifices Charles had made throughout his life and career to give their family a good life. But as she reflected, she could not shake thoughts of Baxter's own sacrifices and the toll the distance from his family had placed upon him. She considered her time in Red Deer to be both a necessity and a burden; she understood the financial obligation of her employment but lamented the miles of hills and woods that separated her from her home. She will speak modestly of her experiences when asked about her time at The Regent and will hold close to her heart the self-content and accomplishment she felt after leaving the stage each night. She will neither speak of the nights she laboured for sleep upon a pillow dampened by tears as she longed to have Charles' warmth beside her, nor the memory of Mr. Carlisle and the kinship that came to her when she was most in need. Unwittingly, he brought forth a reminder of why she was truly there and for whom she was performing.

Chapter Eighteen

Charles sat up in his seat and craned his neck forward as a large plume of dust began to rise behind the hill in the distance. He watched in confusion as the cloud grew to a size that far exceeded what could be created by a simple stage and four. Abigail and Tobias were expected to arrive that day, but the coach usually did not make its stop until quarter past three. He thought perhaps they had left earlier than expected, for Abigail had written the week prior to inform him of her decision to leave Red Deer before her engagement was complete; the distance between them was more than she could bear.

Charles had been diligent in the allocation of every cent Abigail sent him, careful to spend only on necessities. He had allocated enough to cover coal and lamp oil for the remainder of the year with enough funds remaining to keep them well-fed through the harshest season. He was pleased that her venture had offered their family a greater sense of security, but he never believed that the separation from his wife was truly worth it.

He shaded his eyes as he scanned the horizon and squinted as he tried to ascertain the type of vehicle through the dust. A brisk wind pushed the particles high in the air, clearing the path as four black horses crested the mound with a large covered wagon in tow. His heart began to race at the prospect of potential guests, but his excitement was short-lived; as the wagon descended down the hill, another peaked over the crest and followed the leader on its descent. Charles watched as wagon after wagon rolled towards Bowlea.

"Surely they cannot be stopping here," he said aloud to himself. He counted eight wagons in total and wondered what had brought this large party to such a remote part of the district.

Emma was occupied with laundry that afternoon and reached down to grab a bundle of bedsheet. She unfurled it in the air before her, careful not to let it touch the tops of the tall grass. She watched as the moist fabric cracked against the air and captured pockets of wind between its folds. The sun shone through the spray of water as she shook the sheet, and the tiny fragments of coolness kissed her hot skin. She breathed in the fresh scent as she whipped the sheet up to fold over the clothesline and secured the top corners with wooden pegs.

"Emma, come around and look at this," Charles called out to his daughter.

She swiftly skipped up the back steps and around the porch to meet him at the front. She gasped when she caught sight of the wagons on their approach.

"My goodness! Who do you suppose they are?"

"I am not sure," Charles said as his gaze remained fixed on the procession.

"Perhaps they have come to settle here?"

"That seems unlikely, for what is there for anyone in this place? I am more concerned about whether they are just passing through or intend to stay on, even just for the night. Are we prepared to house more than a dozen men?"

"We have little choice but to manage, Papa," she said as the carriages entered the township and she hurried to swing the front doors wide to welcome them.

Charles stood proudly with his hands tucked into his waistcoat pockets. He breathed deeply to steady himself as the first of the wagons halted in front of the hotel. From the front seat of the first wagon came a man some years older than Charles and similarly refined. His dress was elegant, yet functional, and Emma marvelled at how clean he had managed to keep his attire despite his recent journey. As he approached the pair, his friendliness was revealed by his kind smile and tip of his hat.

"How do you do, sir?" Charles asked as he extended his hand in welcome.

"Good day. We are from the Northern Pacific Rail. I believe you are expecting us."

Charles stood in bewilderment as the gentleman spoke, for the only telegram he had received recently was from Abigail. His confusion was a conflation of being left unprepared for the caravan's arrival and the revelation of the purpose of their business.

"Please accept my apologies, sir. I have received no notice of your arrival. I beg your pardon, but did you say you are from the railway?"

"Indeed. You know, I should know better than to rely on the wire in these remote parts. A letter would have been more appropriate."

"Never mind that now, for you are here and we are more than happy to have you," Charles said as he led the gentleman into the hotel's lobby.

He could hardly contain his enthusiasm, as a quick review of the caravan informed him that he would soon be generating more revenue through one booking than he had in the year thus far.

"How many rooms are you in need of, sir?"

"We have fifteen men in total, but four of them will stand watch over the wagons until morning. When the rest of the supplies arrive from Red Deer tomorrow, we will be reduced to eight. The men will set up camp at the worksite, and only myself and the foremen will stay on."

"You are in luck. Our last occupants pushed on yesterday." Charles gave a subtle wink to Emma who appreciated his motivations for telling their new tenant a falsehood. Although it had been a few weeks since their last guest, she understood the art of portraying a successful image. She saw her father grease his hair and iron his trousers every morning in anticipation of business. Each day at dawn he would sweep the wooden planks of the verandah and set out the bi-fold sign with the confidence of a hotelier whose rooms were already at capacity.

As Charles pulled his heavy ledger from its place on the shelf underneath the counter, the guest took a moment to rest by leaning against the counter. Emma noted his fatigue and approached him.

"May we offer you some refreshments?" she asked, knowing full well that there was little more than cold porridge and day-old biscuits at the ready.

"Thank you kindly, miss, but for now I think we are all in need of a bit of sleep. A simple supper in our rooms will do us fine." He was impressed that she exhibited genuine concern for his welfare; when he smiled reassuringly, she returned the gesture. She had little opportunity in Bowlea to interact with men of his station and was intrigued by the way in which he carried himself.

"May I have your name for the register, please?" Charles asked as he dipped the nib of his pen in the inkwell.

"Baxter Carlisle, superintendent of the western branch of the N.P.R."

"Pleased to make your acquaintance, Mr. Carlisle. Charles Prescott, owner and general manager. Allow me to introduce my daughter, Emma."

"How do you do?" Baxter asked. Although he was affable, their introduction was little more than rote formality to a man whose days were often occupied by endless interactions with strangers.

"If you would be so kind as to follow me into the drawing room," Charles said, "we will see to your luggage. You see, you have caught us on our own this morning."

"Is that so? Very well," Baxter said. He turned and walked back outside to where his men had gathered to stretch muscles long made weary by miles of rugged terrain.

As his potential source of income moved out to the porch, Charles was overcome with the realization that his lack of suitable staff would cause him to lose out on a great deal of money. Sensing her father's panic, Emma rushed forward and followed Baxter outside.

"Wait!" she cried.

"You are responsible for your trunks today, lads. This young lady will direct you to your rooms," he said with a measured authority that instantly snapped the crew to attention. They unstrapped the tarpaulins from the first wagon and unloaded the men's personal effects with the precision of a military regiment.

Emma stood in awe as the men worked with speed and efficiency around her. Her distraction did not escape Charles' notice, but as the hotel was currently vacant, he was able to determine the room allocations without her assistance.

"First in gets room eleven then work your way back to the stairs. Show Mr. Carlisle to room twelve," he said to Emma as the first of the men entered the lobby. He handed her a small notepad and pencil and instructed her to obtain the names of each man and their corresponding room number for the registry.

As each of the workers was settled, Charles began to ruminate over the figures. Once the men's board was accounted for, he would net nearly ten dollars for the first night alone. Within the span of an hour, his demeanour had transformed from melancholy to optimistic; he wished he could move the brass hands of his pocket watch forward to allow Abigail to walk through the door at once, for she would see that his venture was not a complete failure after all.

"Here you are, sir," Emma said as she ushered Baxter into the large corner room that overlooked the lake. "We are very pleased to have you stay with us. If there is anything you need, please let us know. Supper will be brought to your rooms promptly at seven."

"Thank you, miss. You are very kind," he said with a smile as she closed the door behind her.

He removed his hat and ulster coat and set them on the chair in the corner. He raised his arms high above his head, clasping his hands together and feeling the deep stretch run down his spine. He looked out the window to the lake below and scanned the perimeter to the far north side. The camp would be set up in the meadow beyond the hill, and with tools and supplies arriving in the next day or two, he planned to break ground within the week. Although business was his passion, he also had a kinship with the land and was exceedingly sad whenever his pursuits marred the unspoiled wilderness. Tomorrow he would photograph the area to obtain evidence of the splendour of the valley before the tracks of modernity changed the landscape forever.

The stagecoach from Red Deer was right on schedule, which was a surprise considering the large divot that had cracked the rear wheel and resulted in a delay of nearly two hours. The dry terrain on the road from the stopping house and the swiftness of the team had allowed them to make up time enough to arrive in Bowlea just after three.

Travelling all day in the heat of late spring had left both Abigail and Tobias tired and worn. The enticement of the cool water of Bowlea Lake came second only to the warm familial embrace that awaited them just over the hill. As Abigail fantasized about jumping into the water to soothe her sore muscles, her companion called out as soon as the hotel came into view.

"Look there, Mrs. Prescott!" he said as he pointed to their home in the distance. Through the open window, Abigail could see the stark white canopies of the wagons surrounding the property, appearing to have sprung from the ground like mushrooms overnight. As the coach crawled closer to their destination, she could see a figure moving about the stables and leading a pair of horses to the portion of the pasture that was fenced in. As evidenced by the ease with which he handled the ponies, she could tell that it was someone other than Charles; she wondered if he had turned to livery services as a means to earn more income.

Their arrival at the hotel a short time later went unnoticed, and it was not until Abigail positioned herself before the front desk that Charles even knew they were there.

"Charles, what is going on here? Are we now in the business of boarding horses?" she asked as he and Emma buzzed around them.

"Guests, Abby! We have guests!"

"Guests?"

"They arrived a few hours ago. Now that the men are settled into their rooms the real work begins. Thank goodness we have you both to help now. We would have been lost if they had arrived a week earlier. I am ashamed to admit that I was unprepared for a full house, particularly with no notice."

"A full house? How can that be?" Abigail asked as she set down her bag and took off her hat and travelling coat.

"The details are still rather unclear as there was a bit of confusion when they arrived. Several of the men, at least, will be staying on for a while."

"How long do you expect that to be?" Abigail's heart thumped with the same thunderous beat that Charles had when he first saw the wagons approach.

"Several days, perhaps longer. We have enough supplies to prepare supper, but we will need to procure goods for the rest of the week. Tobias, come with me. Abigail, my dear, Emma is in need of help in the kitchen."

Tobias followed Charles' lead with the obedience of a terrier. He had assisted with the small details of the hotel before, but there were never more than one or two guests in residence at a time. The wagons had been secured by the labourers who stood at post with their rifles at their sides, working to ensure that the goods brought over from Red Deer would not be stolen. Tobias understood the need for security in places like Fort McLeod or Fort Whoop-Up but was greatly amused that the men would seek protection from the gophers and grouse of Bowlea.

The handcart that Tobias retrieved from beside the stables was unsteady and heavy, but he was happy now to move about in the open air with not a whiff of soot or smoke to burn his lungs. He hurried his pace to follow behind Charles who had already ascended the steps of Mr. Winters' Goods and Grocery by the time he caught up.

"Good afternoon, Charles. Hello, Toby. What can I do for you today?" Mr. Winters said as he moved the crate of canned beans out of the aisle to allow them to pass.

"Sorry to disturb, Louis, but we are here on a matter of great importance. We are in need of five dozen eggs, ten pounds of flour, a half-pound of yeast, a quarter-pound of baking powder, five pounds of coffee, two pounds of sugar, three gallons of buttermilk, five pounds of butter and whatever ham you have on hand," Charles said as he read directly from the list that Emma had drafted.

"My word, Charles. Is it your intention to clear out my shop?"

"We need the goods straight away, Louis," Charles said as the impatience strained his voice. "How are you for carrots, cabbage and onions?"

"I presume you mean to feed the wagoners who arrived today. We wondered if they were just passing through. Come along, let's see what we can do."

Mr. Winters tried to work efficiently to complete the order, but his pace was slowed by distraction.

"So, who are those men?" he asked as he portioned the sugar into a small linen sack.

"We know very little as they came without warning and retired to their quarters straight away. One fellow mentioned that they were from the Northern Pacific Rail. I do not wish to speculate, but that can only mean good things. I trust this will provide a good business for several of us in town," Charles said as he passed the sack of sugar to Tobias.

"Perhaps they mean to finish the extension. Heavens that must be it!" Mr. Winters said.

"I will keep you abreast of any details that are forthcoming. This may, indeed, turn out to be quite a blessing. In the morning I will provide a list of things we will need for the rest of the week. We will be by in the afternoon to pick up the order."

"Certainly, Charles. Yes, this is good news indeed."

As they moved the cart back to the hotel, Tobias could not help but chuckle to himself over Mr. Winters' enthusiasm.

"I wonder how long it will take for the whole village to know your guests are from the rail?"

"Well, Mrs. Winters has likely been informed by now, so I would not expect it to be long."

Chapter Nineteen

Abigail moved through the kitchen with an efficiency that satisfied her need to be useful again. As she mixed the large batch of dough, she could feel the muscles in her shoulder begin to ache. She rolled the mass onto the large wooden table and watched as it gave way slightly when she imprinted the surface with the pad her thumb. She found comfort in the familiarity of the process as she floured the surface of the table and began to roll out the first batch of biscuits. After they were cut with the flour-dusted end of a tin can, she arranged them evenly on the baking tray and placed them in the oven. She knew that timing was everything; if she hurried there would be time enough to prepare another batch before the others were switched off the tray to cool.

"Mama, I cannot tell you how happy I am to see you. You have arrived at just the right time. It seems as though our fortunes are changing," Emma said with unrestrained cheer as she set out eleven enamelled trays on every available surface in the kitchen.

"I was so anxious to get home after seeing you in Red Deer. But I must say, I never expected to come back to this."

"We never expected it either. Truth be told, I believe their arrival came as quite a shock to Papa."

"Well, when business has only ever been a trickle, it is no wonder that a flood would be overwhelming."

Emma arranged each of the supper trays in the same way: two fresh biscuits spread thick with butter, a cup of hot molasses beans, and a few hearty slices of ham. In the corner stood a tall glass of salted buttermilk and a cup of tea, while tucked in beneath the linen napkin was a pair of Abigail's sweet oat cookies. Although the ladies were in a hurry to set the trays and deliver them before the promised supper hour, they had taken a few minutes to cut enough wild daisies to fill each of the tiny vases with a spray of sunshine.

As the platters were chock full and could only be carried one at a time, the women moved like clock gears, ticking up the stairs as the other went down; their gentle raps on each successive door were met by weary-eyed travellers with open palms and grateful grunts.

The final room to be disturbed was that of the superintendent, and Abigail moved swiftly to discharge the remaining fare. She rested the tray on her hip and knocked on the door. Muffled steps could be heard on the other side of the partition, each heavy foot punctuated by a groaning of the floorboards. As the door swung open he came into view. Gone was the towering, dominant figure presented to Emma and Charles earlier in the day. Standing in the doorway was a weary, worn man who had spent the last several hours in a deep sleep.

"Hello there," he said, still blurry-eyed from his nap.

"Baxter?" she said with a gasp as she nearly dropped the food before her.

"Abigail!" he said as his shock mirrored hers.

"Mr. Carlisle," she stammered, "whatever are you doing here?"

"I have just arrived to begin work on our new project. Here, allow me to help you with that," he said as he removed his supper from her hands and placed it on the bedside table.

"I do not understand," she said as she tried to steady her hands by grasping them tight against her apron front. "How on earth did you discover where I live? There were few people in Red Deer with whom I trusted that information."

"It is a happy accident, I assure you. If you recall, we spoke at length about my work and how it has taken me all over the country, particularly in the Alberta district."

"Yes, of course, I remember. I am sorry, Mr. Carlisle, but this seems to be a rather convenient coincidence." Abigail backed slowly out of the room as he tried to explain. She did not want her husband to discover that she held an acquaintance with a man of his wealth, status and power. Charles would certainly question her if it was discovered that they had known each other outside of Kingston society.

"Abigail," he said as he extended his hand and moved towards her.

"Mrs. Prescott," she said in correction as the reminder of her married name instantly registered for him. He realized at once that he should have recognized the name of the hotel owner when he first arrived.

"Mrs. Prescott, please understand that there is no ulterior motive. I am merely a businessman working to extend the rail line in this part of the country."

"You mean the rail line will be completed, at last?" Abigail asked as her apprehension at his presence was replaced by a sense of joy that the hotel would finally become profitable.

"I will be staying on for the duration of the project, although some of that time may be spent in camp. There are others who will join me, of course, but unlike today there will be ample notice of their comings and goings." He watched as the astonishment on her face receded, and the blush returned to her cheeks.

"Please accept my apologies, Mr. Carlisle. I was alarmed when I first saw you, but I must admit that your presence here is a great comfort. The absence of the rail line has had a rather unfortunate affect on our business, but it seems that our luck is finally turning around."

He gave her an abbreviated smile as Emma's calls for her mother to return downstairs interrupted them.

"If would you hand me that small basin, my daughter will bring you some hot water to wash with before bed," she said, hesitant to enter the room and retrieve it herself.

"Thank you kindly. You know, it is always a challenge to move on to a new place, but I feel it will be made a great deal easier with you nearby."

Abigail was unsure of how to respond to his flattery other than to offer a gentle smile before turning to walk back down the hall.

The evening drew to a close earlier than the Prescott women were used to, for they were due in the kitchen no later than four o'clock the following morning. Once the supper trays were collected, Abigail and Emma bid each other goodnight and retired to their rooms as the evening sky transitioned from maroon to sapphire, and the last sliver of sun was replaced by the light of the rising moon.

In their first moments alone since she arrived home, Abigail wanted nothing more than to feel Charles' embrace and reassurance that all would be well. Instead, both were swayed by distraction and a realization that their working lives would soon be much different than either had felt before.

"It is so good to have you home, Abby. I've scarcely had a chance to speak with you."

"It is good to be home, Charles. I was not expecting a scene like this, I can assure you. How would you have managed if we did not come home today?" she asked with a smile, as she pulled back the heavy quilt and slid between the cool bed sheets.

"I suppose the simple answer is that we would have struggled a great deal. Even now that you are here, there are still a great many things to do in the morning."

"Do you suppose they will stay long?"

"I have a feeling they will stay on for some time. Even if they are here just to survey, it will take some weeks to accomplish. I doubt they will start laying track until the spring, but that is just a supposition for I do not know their business at all."

"Perhaps this good fortune is a sign of things to come."

Charles pulled Abigail in close and embraced her tenderly. He reached for her hand and could instantly feel the scratch of her dry, chapped skin.

"Tomorrow when I am at the Winters', I will post an advert for a part-time chambermaid and laundress. I will have to keep you on in the kitchen, but I do not believe we could find anyone with superior skills."

"I appreciate the sentiment, dear, but surely we cannot afford it. Not yet."

"We can. I will post it tomorrow. What is the benefit of income, if we do not have the energy left at the end of the day to enjoy it?"

As the couple shared an intimacy, Baxter lay awake in the room directly above, with his eyes transfixed on a small grass spider in the corner of the windowsill. He watched as the shadow of its web grew as it spun, its trap becoming more powerful with each passing second. His window was slightly ajar, and he could hear the muted buzz of a field fly as it encircled the room. With the occasional pass by his head, he felt compelled to give it a swat but was half-hearted in his attempts so as not to cause it harm.

He rose from his bed and ambled to where his sport coat hung and removed a thin linen handkerchief from the top breast pocket. He approached the web with a delicacy that its architecture demanded, and grasped the spider gently in the cloth. With his other hand, he pushed the window open and shook the spider from his grip to tumble into the tall grasses below. Although its repeated collisions into the thin glazed panes would indicate a great desire to leave the confines of the room, in the brief moment when the window was open, the fly did not escape.

Chapter Twenty

Baxter was plagued by a fitful night's sleep and spent most of the night perplexed by the serendipity of meeting Abigail again. Although he was in awe of the circumstance, he knew there was no other choice for his business but to continue forward as intended. He had procured little more than two hours sleep but still rose before dawn to ensure there was ample daylight for his resources to build their encampment.

Charles awoke at the same hour, as was his custom even when the hotel had no occupants; he was taught by Mr. Danbury about the early bird and continued with the practice even when the worms were scarce. A knock came on the door just as he was budgeting the week's income against the expense of the men's board; his delay in responding elicited another rap, to which he responded at once.

"Come in," he said without lifting his eyes from his work.

"Have you a moment, Mr. Prescott?"

Charles looked up in surprise when he heard the question asked in a baritone voice, for he expected the interruption to come from his wife or daughter.

"Mr. Carlisle, this is a pleasant surprise," he said affably as he stood and began to shuffle the papers before him. "Do sit down. I trust you slept well?"

"I always sleep well after a long day's travel. Last night was no exception."

"Well then, I am glad to hear it. What can I do for you this morning?"

"The crew is expected to make camp today, and once the supplies arrive, we hope to break ground by the end of the week."

"So soon? I would have expected that a great deal of planning would be required before you set to laying track."

"Typically, yes. But the land has already been surveyed, and our building plans have been drafted. All that remains is to give the lads the go-ahead, and we are on our way."

"I spend a good deal of time watching the activities of our town, and I do not believe I have seen any men from the rail before. Perhaps I was occupied elsewhere and did not notice."

"It would have been before your time, surely. I had the privilege of staying here once before when Olesky was the owner."

"Is that so? And how did you find his hospitality?"

"Congenial, but the purpose of my visit caused some animosity. When I informed him that construction had been delayed indefinitely, he was rather distraught. When I offered to purchase his business and property, he refused. It was a decision I believe he regretted almost instantly."

"Yes, I believe he faced foreclosure."

"When I discovered the hotel was once again on the market, I contacted Mr. Pedersen at once. But, alas, you beat me to it."

"I was fortunate to secure this property very quickly."

"And at a reduced rate," Baxter said as he leaned back in his chair.

Having worked in the hospitality industry for the better part of twenty years, Charles had encountered guests of all sorts. He was well familiar with men like Mr. Carlisle who succeeded by financing their way out of complications.

"It was within our means, and we were grateful to secure it."

"Of course. It is a fine stopping house, to be sure. But consider, once the line is completed and the station and hotel are built, you may find it difficult to do business here."

He watched with pity as the look on Charles' face changed from hopeful to dejected with a single revelation. He had not considered that a hotel would be built in tandem with the train station. Baxter knew that suffering was always parallel to success but could not disregard the possibility of a lower-class existence for someone as spirited and lovely as Abigail.

"We have been here four years, and have managed thus far," Charles said defiantly, while Baxter resisted his inclination to ask him how his success had enticed his wife to work as an entertainer outside of the home. He decided, instead, to offer him more money than he could refuse.

"I am prepared to offer you three hundred dollars, Mr. Prescott. Certainly, that is a fair return on your investment and will allow you and your family to return home."

Charles responded without hesitation.

"I thank you for your offer, Mr. Carlisle, but this is our home. I am confident there will be more than enough business for the both of us."

"But surely you can see that two hotels…"

"You are very generous, but I must return to my work. I ask that you maintain your discretion about our conversation. I would not wish to upset my wife and daughter."

Baxter resisted the temptation to shake his head, for he did not want to reveal any outward befuddlement at the motivations behind Charles' decision.

"If you could do the same as it regards my hotel, I would be very much obliged. It tends to cause unnecessary resistance with the townsfolk when they are aware of the details before completion."

"You have my word."

"You have a lovely family here, sir. I respect your decision. Good day."

"Good day."

As the door shut, the tie around Charles' neck tightened, and he rushed to the window to call on the cool morning air to revive him. An unbuttoning of his top collar offered fleeting relief, for even after a few deep breaths he was still acutely focused on Baxter's disclosure. He had felt a similar sense of panic when he first learned of Mr. Danbury's decision to leave him stranded, but he had learned early in life that it was always best to follow one's intuition. He also learned that even when faced with destitution, it is a man's obligation to carry on with dignity and self-respect. It would be impossible for him to return to Kingston without the judgement and mockery of his friends, and even with Mr. Carlisle's generous offer, it was not enough to relocate and elevate his family back to their former status. They would be no better off financially if they relocated to another area of the district, and would be relinquishing a home they had grown to love.

Chapter Twenty-One

The house was roused by the smell of fresh baking and strong coffee. Abigail had arranged the tables in the dining hall to accommodate the men and set each place carefully with the breakfast china. Heavy steps were heard clambering down from the second floor, and the thunderous trampling did not cease until every guest was seated. Concurrent conversations took place around the table, and it was difficult for the ladies to decipher the dialogues.

Abigail watched with awe as the labourers' meanderings halted immediately upon the arrival of Mr. Carlisle. They quieted themselves to such an extent that the only sound to be heard was the scraping of chair legs against the birch plank floor as the superintendent took his seat.

"Good morning, Mr. Carlisle. I trust you slept well," Abigail said as she poured him the first cup of coffee. Her hands trembled slightly as she set down his cup, and she hoped no one noticed her uneasiness around him.

"Yes, thank you. I believe I will have little trouble finding rest here. I must say that the chorus of birds outside my window woke me well before dawn. I would have been grateful for a bit more sleep, but I find their song quite charming."

"We are very fortunate to be surrounded by such beautiful wilderness."

They smiled kindly at each other as Abigail pondered his peculiar existence. She did not know where he found the resolve to awake in a new place nearly every day, and without the benefit of familial support. Baxter, in turn, watched as Abigail's movements turned from nervous to graceful as she worked her way around the dining room. He followed her with his gaze as she poured cups of coffee for each of his staff and set down several steaming baskets of biscuits in the centre of the table. He could not help but wonder at the circumstances that found such a refined woman working in such an unforgiving environment.

The hours after Baxter's arrival saw the Prescott ladies work harder than they ever had before. Abigail served and cleared while Emma cooked, ensuring that the men had enough biscuits, porridge and eggs to sustain them until the setting sun called them back for supper. The tending of the guest rooms and laundry had taken their toll, and although Emma moved through her duties energetically, Abigail merely mimicked her daughter's endurance and speed, often taking a moment's rest when she was left unaccompanied.

"Could you help me move these to the porch, Mama?" Emma asked as she began to haul heavy hampers down from the guest rooms into the kitchen. As Abigail rose from her momentary respite, she felt her joints creak. The wicker baskets overflowed with soiled linens and bed sheets, and as she clunked through the chore, she could not help but think of

Baxter's wife and the life he had left behind in Toronto. She wondered at Mrs. Carlisle's taste and the arrangement of her décor. She imagined a refined lady who could buy macarons from Pierre's on Yonge or purchase a fine gown at Murray's without a single thought as to their expense. She thought of the laundry room that must have sat in the rear of their home, where girls of Emma's age were paid well to ensure their mistress never felt the burden of labour.

As she hung the sheets over the clothesline, she heard footsteps on the porch behind her. She turned on her heels expecting to see Charles but was instead greeted by Baxter amidst the smoke of his day's first cigar.

"Is there not a girl who can do that for you?" he asked, as he watched her struggle under the weight of the heavy cloth.

"No," she said with a bemused grin. "Just me and my daughter. We have rarely been so busy as to need more than that."

"We are hiring a new girl, as a matter of fact," Charles said as he moved from the shed towards the kitchen with arms full of firewood. Although he resented Baxter's query, he could not chastise him, for it was his business alone that facilitated the expenditure.

"That will take some of the burden off, certainly," Baxter said as Emma brought out another two baskets and quickly returned to the guest quarters to collect the remaining linens.

"I wish I could help you with those," he said as he moved into a willow chair seat near the clothesline.

"I doubt very much that your help would be acceptable to my husband; he is quite steadfast in his application of etiquette. I am rather surprised that he has been so lenient with our conversations. Staff from the back of the house engaging with guests is quite improper."

"Surely, anyone as pretty as you should be front of the house."

Abigail dipped her fingertips in the soapy water and flicked them at Baxter who smiled broadly as the cool droplets kissed his cheek.

"Will you stay in Bowlea for the whole of construction?"

"I doubt I will travel much at all. When a man oversees a project of this scale, it is unwise to leave the job site. The men are capable of completing their work, but without a guiding hand, they can lack motivation."

"Have you any idea how long you will be with us?"

"We expect to work through the winter and into next spring."

Abigail stood in stunned silence beside the dripping linens, her arms limp at her side. She could hardly fathom the promise of Baxter's assertion and wondered how long he and his men would reside at The Prescott.

"Speaking of motivation, I must heed my own advice and push on to the worksite. Do not work too hard today, Abigail. The boys will be fine with yesterday's bedsheets."

The sun's ascent beyond the hills cast wild rose ripples on the surface of the lake, and as Abigail clipped the last peg on the clothesline, she offered Baxter good tidings for the workday ahead. He held back a moment when she returned inside and savoured the last few drags of his cigar. Although the view from the Prescott property was incomparable, he could not shake the image of Abigail with a dampened hem and rolled-up sleeves, with a grey kerchief wrapped tightly around her brow. He was determined to house his men there as long as he could to afford Charles his additional staff.

He snubbed the tip of his cigar on the sole of his polished boot and placed the stub in its silver case. He walked around the building to where the wagons were hitched and directed the men to harness the ponies. After his mount was saddled, he led the group up through the meadow to the worksite.

Abigail hurriedly moved through the kitchen, pushed through the draped partition into the lobby and positioned herself behind the front desk.

"Could you excuse us, Tobias. I must have a word with my husband."

"Yes ma'am," he said, as he exchanged places with her and moved to the kitchen.

"What is it, Abby?"

"I have just spoken with Mr. Carlisle. He and his party will be here at until next spring at the least."

"Are you certain?" he asked, finally lifting his gaze from his paperwork to meet his wife's eyes.

"He told me so himself just a moment ago."

"Strange that he would tell you his plans before informing me."

"Why? Do we have other bookings to consider?"

Charles smirked and gave her hand a gentle squeeze.

"Are you quite certain he said spring?"

"Absolutely."

"Construction projects rarely end on course, you know. Their work may even extend through next summer or fall."

"Even if only a few of them intend to stay on, we should see a profit at the end of each week, should we not?"

"Yes, particularly if they require board. We may receive other guests as a result of the line as well. As soon as word gets out that our little town is successful, it is sure to increase in population. Business has no choice but to flourish."

"It will have been a long time in coming, and with much effort," Abigail said as she massaged her fiery finger joints.

"I realize this has been a trying time for you, my dear, but I hope you realize it has not been easy for me either." Charles moved in closer and brought the volume of his voice down. "You do agree that this is the most positive event that has happened to us since our arrival, do you not?"

"Yes, of course. I am just tired. None of us have been accustomed to this level of occupation."

"I am sorry, Abby. You should not be expected to take on so much of the burden yourself. I will post an advert in Winters' store this afternoon when Tobias and I pick up our order. I can spare him in the interim if he can be of use to you."

Abigail felt the tension in her back release and a wave of relief wash over her.

"I am grateful for your decision, Charles, but there is no need to take Tobias away from his duties. Emma and I have a handle on things."

"This booking will involve a great deal of hard work, my dear, but the completion of the rail has the potential to keep us employed for the rest of our lives."

"Do you truly think it will have such an impact?"

"From what I overheard this morning, they are set to begin construction on the train station. Once there is a fixed destination in Bowlea, the town will grow in size before your eyes. Do you not see how that will drive visitors to the area?"

"Yes, of course. I had not considered that."

"And as Bowlea grows larger, so too will our business. The Northern Pacific brings no other cargo but prosperity."

"I have no doubt Mr. Carlisle has brought with him a great many things. One can hardly think of how to thank him."

The following evening, the lamps in the hallway were dimmed as the labourers retired for the night. Baxter was instructing one of his men on the duties of his morning shift when he heard a chorus of laughter at the other end of the hallway. He bid his foreman good night and strode towards the merriment. The hoots grew louder as he approached the open door's glow, and when he found himself at the threshold, he knew only a hearty greeting could interrupt their celebration.

"Good evening, gentlemen."

"Mr. Carlisle," Charles said confidently as he rose to his feet to greet his guest. "We are sorry to disturb you this evening, but it could not be helped."

"Not at all. It does one good to relax after a long day's work."

"You are welcome to join us," Tobias said as he motioned to the empty chair near the stove.

"Please do, sir. We are having something of a celebration," Charles said as he returned to his seat and poured his guest a glass from his only bottle of brandy.

"Is that so? What you are celebrating?"

"This young man has proposed to my daughter, and she has accepted. I could not be happier."

Charles raised his glass and prompted the others to follow suit.

"Welcome to our family, young man."

"May the wind be always at your back," Baxter said as he tapped the crystal gently against the rim of Tobias' glass. Once the brandy passed his lips, he retrieved from his breast pocket a slim cigarillo for each of them. "When do you plan to marry?"

"Emma wants to marry in August," Tobias said.

"Do you plan to join a rail crew or head down to the collieries after your wedding?"

"We plan to stay on here in Bowlea. Mr. Prescott has started teaching me some of the business, and I think I could enjoy the work a lot."

"Running a hotel is not an easy task. It takes a great deal of organization and discipline. Your focus rests entirely on ensuring the pleasure of others."

"Well, sir, I know that staying in Bowlea is very important to both of us."

"You are a very fortunate young man. I fell in love with a young lady very much like your Emma. There is nothing like the love of a woman, and it is meant to be cherished."

"And where is your beautiful lady, Mr. Carlisle?" Charles asked as he thumbed a small box of matches.

"I do not see her anymore. The wilderness proved to be too harsh. She is happier where she is."

"And is that not the goal of every marriage? To make the wife happy?" Charles asked with a chuckle.

"You must remember that, Tobias," Baxter said with a forced smile. "I believe there may even be a pamphlet on it."

As Charles laughed and puffed his cigarillo, Baxter wondered if he and Abigail shared many laughs together. He imagined her to be a source of great comfort and congeniality.

"I envy your happiness, Mr. Prescott. You have a fine family."

"Thank you, Mr. Carlisle. Everything I do is for them."

Chapter Twenty-Two

The weeks passed quickly and the days' light shortened as swiftly as the trees' leaves lost their vibrancy. Baxter and three of his foremen had stayed on at The Prescott while the rest of his crew moved to the camp. Their white canvas tents spotted the meadow like the plump bodies of the swans who had already departed for their southern destinations.

The laundress duties had been allocated to Charlotte Bauer, the daughter of a pig farmer with a small plot of land three miles west. Like other early settlers in the region, Mr. Bauer was well acquainted with hardship. Although his family's quality of life had improved since Charles began placing regular orders, they were not so successful as to refuse an offer of employment.

The morning sky was melancholy, and the tall reeds around the hotel stooped limply as evidence of the previous night's thrashing of hail and strong gales. The landscape mirrored Charles' emotions, for no matter how many guests he accounted for each night, his business was still clouded by uncertainty. He was keenly aware that Baxter's residence was temporary; without the tenancy of his team, his meagre savings would face steady depletion. During his tenure at The Danbury, he had earned a reputation for meticulous attention to detail and a steadfast dedication to his guests' wishes. Although they were no less important to the success of his business, his current duties were substantively different. No longer did he task himself with such refinements as locating a faultless bunch of peonies or hand-selecting the perfect blend of tea to suit a guest's tastes. He now spent much of his time mucking the soiled hay in the stables and fencing off the cabbage patch to keep the rabbits from his family's main source of food.

"Good morning, sir. Ready to face the day?" Tobias asked cheerfully as he approached the chicken coop.

Charles offered his son-in-law little more than a low grunt before moving past him to take up the pail of feed. Within days of Baxter's arrival, large caravans of goods began to move through town, and although Charles was grateful to let a few rooms each week, he had grown weary of interacting with guests. Although he was attentive and offered pleasant solicitudes, he kept his interactions to a minimum for fear of appearing disingenuous. He treasured the time before daybreak when he could interact with his animals and monitor the progress of his garden; their success was under his control.

After the chores and daily accounting and were complete, Charles no longer sat on the front porch waiting for guests. Instead, he took his chipped china cup and pot of coffee to the back yard where he would sit in his wicker chair until each drop was drunk. In his solitude, he would watch the procession of goods travel the newly-formed roadway up to the worksite. Wagons were heaped high with ballast or neatly stacked with oak ties, while rails arrived on flat-bed carts; he marvelled from afar as the horses strained to haul the steel lifeline.

As Abigail worked to prepare each of their daily meals, she would watch Charles through the blurred panes of the kitchen window. His preference for not interacting much with guests was disconcerting to her, for she had always known him to be affable and welcoming, particularly to patrons of elevated means. His recent preference for isolation had bled into his relationships, and his family felt the brunt of his disengagement. Abigail was not initially alarmed, for he was prone to a melancholia that she attributed to the marked disconnect from their previous lives. As of late, however, his manner was unusually severe; he had again taken to sleeping in his office and preferred to take his meals upstairs.

As tea time approached, Abigail realized he had not yet eaten that day and so fashioned a small plate of scones with butter and honey in the hope that their sweetness would improve his spirits.

Charles could hear the rustle of dry grass as someone approached from behind, yet his gaze did not move from the activity across the lake. As the intruder grew closer, the tension in his neck muscles increased. When he felt the weight of a hand upon his shoulder, he winced slightly and pulled away.

"How long have you been out here?"

"I hardly know," he mumbled as his eyes reminded fixed on the worksite.

Abigail felt that a light kiss on his forehead was worth risking further rejection, and so touched her lips softly to his skin.

"I have made your favourite," she said as she placed her offering on the overturned basket beside him.

As he dropped his eyes to the cinnamon surface of the raisin scones, his stomach released an audible growl. He had not eaten since the previous day's breakfast and had not realized the extent of his hunger.

"Thank you," he said with a faint smile.

With that small inkling of appreciation, Abigail felt the sting from his initial recoil begin to fade. She returned his smile and again placed a soft hand on his shoulder.

"I am in awe of how the landscape has changed in such a short period," she said. "I have little concept of how long it takes to erect a structure like a train station, but in my eyes, it is all happening very quickly."

"It usually takes a while to see any sort of progress, but I wager the men on this job have built the same type of station many times along the railway's route. Their operations are likely well-established and efficient."

"The Bowlea station seems rather large, does it not? Perhaps we are to be some sort of terminus or transfer point? I cannot imagine there would be a need for such a large building in this part of the district."

As Charles listened to her remarks, he marvelled at her naivety. He understood that her ignorance was in keeping with the other townsfolk who looked on the building as nothing more than a station. He wondered how they could not see the building for what it was, but when he considered that a train station was often a town's largest structure he could not blame them. There was no way to respond to her remark other than to corroborate her assumptions and honour Baxter's wishes.

"I have been tempted to ask that question myself, but Mr. Carlisle has not been very forthcoming with the details surrounding his work. I thought it imprudent to inquire."

"I suppose that is for the best. I would imagine he has every person in town asking about the progress of his project. It is little wonder why he keeps the details to himself."

The preparations for the evening meal were nearly finished when the N.P.R. crew funnelled into the dining room at a quarter to seven. Charles welcomed them half-heartedly until each one of them was seated, then excused himself to take supper in his study. Baxter found it unusual that he would not join his family for their evening meal and could see a longing in Abigail's looks when Charles returned upstairs.

"How do you do this evening, Mrs. Prescott?" one of the foremen asked as Abigail set a basket of rolls on the table before him.

"I am very well, Mr. Shae, thank you. I am in no place to complain about my workday in the company of anyone who works on the rail. I doubt I have seen any man work as hard."

"The labourers toil, indeed," Baxter interjected, "but I would not give that same consideration to Shae. His is a foreman, after all."

As the party laughed heartily at their leader's remark, Abigail offered a smile. The warmth of her emotion was felt readily by Baxter, who was pleased to be on the receiving end of the first happy look he had seen from her in days. As she watched the men engage in hearty banter and relax with a spirit that was at once jovial and fatigued, she could not recall when she had last seen Charles laugh without inhibition or project a happiness that he truly felt within.

"I read in the newspaper this morning that there have been accounts of star showers across the district," Baxter said as the men finished the last sips of their coffee and wiped crumbs of wild berry cake from their shirts.

"What is that?" Emma said as she helped her mother in the clearing of the dinner wares.

"Perhaps there is a circus coming to town," Abigail said with a wink.

"The stars are not under the big top, but rather high in the heavens. This *Herald* is a few days old, but it states that the showers often appear for a week or more. From what I understand, they are best viewed when the sky is kettle-black. We will have to stay up much later than usual if we hope to see them."

"Thank you, but we have to make an early start to the day. We would not want to see you go hungry," Abigail said.

"Nonsense," Baxter returned. "There are a handful of rolls here. Do you have more in the kitchen?"

"There is another trayful."

"And is there butter and some of your delicious berry preserves?"

"Yes, those are always on hand."

"That and a few cups of coffee would do us fine. The writer at *The Herald* insists this is a sight we would be regretful to miss."

"Come now, Mama. It sounds delightful."

"It does sound rather special. Let me call on your father. It sounds like an event not to be missed by any of us."

Abigail set her armful of dishes down in the kitchen and made her way upstairs. She wanted so much to share in nature's entertainment with Charles, but as she neared his chamber, she became certain of his response even before her knuckles rapped his office door.

"What is it?"

Abigail could hear a twinge of annoyance in his voice, and she wanted in that moment to turn on her heels and run swiftly back downstairs. Instead, she breathed deeply and grasped the brass handle of the door; its coldness sent a shiver of pins through to her bones that was mirrored by the reception she received when she turned the knob and entered.

"Might I have a word, my love?" Abigail said as she cautiously approached his desk. His chair had been positioned to face the window, and he had turned the lamps down as low as he could without snuffing the flame. He did not turn when she spoke.

"Charles, Mr. Carlisle has made an interesting proposal for us to experience this evening. There is to be a star shower tonight, and he thought it would be the perfect chance for us all to experience nature's splendour together. Everyone present tonight will share in that moment. It would please me a great deal if you were there."

"I was just about to retire. The hog feeds early, and Connie needs a milking before breakfast."

"Certainly, but…" she said before interrupting herself with a long breath of silence. She wanted to wrap her arms around him and smatter kisses on the spot on his neck that made his heart flip. She wanted to tell him that dozens of stars could fall in the sky, but the marvel would mean nothing if he was not sitting on the grass beside her.

"Will you not join us?" she asked as she moved closer to where he sat. Charles could feel her energy as she approached, and was compelled to turn and face her. He was prevented only by eyes swollen red and damp with tears.

"I am tired, my dear. By all means, enjoy yourselves."

The night sky burned in shades of violet and crimson as the last glow of light was diffused by a thin veil of clouds. The early fall evening was unseasonably warm, and Emma and Charlotte had laid out a mosaic of burlap sacks to sit upon. Each of the gentlemen brought a stool down from his room to place around the cobblestone fire pit. Tobias lit a good-sized fire, but it was barely needed in such a climate. He placed a thick log on the burning timber and took his place on the grass next to Emma. He lay on his back and stretched out long to get a direct view of the light show. Baxter moved the second wicker chair from the porch to set beside its partner and motioned for Abigail to take the seat closest the fire.

"How long does it take for them to appear?" she asked as the party scattered around them and chattered in gleeful anticipation.

"They are always there," Baxter said. "It is just that sometimes we are fortunate enough to see them."

"But why now, why today?"

"Perhaps the universe knew we were in dire need of an entertainment?"

"Entertainment or enlightenment?" Abigail asked as she embraced herself firmly, and wrapped her thick knit shawl more tightly around her shoulders. As she struggled to warm herself, she recalled past evenings when she and Charles would sit by the fire to listen to the frogs and crickets. He would always keep her warm with a kiss and his arm about her shoulder. She extended her hands towards the fire and felt a deep shiver.

"It is a shame that your husband could not join us this evening," Baxter said in a low, cautious tone.

"He is not himself tonight."

"It has been difficult to ignore the distance growing between you. I see it in all of the towns I travel through. Families like yours who have struggled a great deal, but who have such strong wills that they push through no matter what faces them. Determination is admirable, but the constancy of uncertainty is a grindstone to one's ambition. You and your family have been fortunate. Imagine how it was twenty-five years ago when the land was so thick with trees you could barely see the sunlight. Men lured by the promise of cheap land and quick money, who did not realize the tragic sacrifice it would take to clear that land and make it profitable. Your family was fortunate to have avoided that torment."

"If it was as harsh as you describe, it is little wonder your wife returned to the comforts of home. I have had that same thought myself more times than I wish to say. But there is a duty, I suppose, to work with my husband and support him in these efforts. It has not been easy, but there are moments when it feels like there is nowhere else I would rather be."

"And the other moments?" Baxter asked, sensing that she was withholding her true feelings.

"I cannot imagine what it has been like for him. Life in Kingston was constant. He worked hard, came home in good spirits and enjoyed his time with us. We wanted for nothing and were able to navigate life without the girders of worry. There were, of course, long hours put in at The Danbury, but we did not realize our good fortune until it was gone. I believe Charles places a good deal of blame upon himself for the trials we have faced."

"Surely he must understand that there is no way to control one's fate."

"He is acutely aware of that fact. He is forced to live with the reality that each of his decisions have led us to this point."

"Look there! A shooting star!" Emma cried as she leapt up and pointed to the sky.

Abigail followed Emma's extended finger to the heavens but saw only the tail's final twinkle before it disappeared into the dark.

"Did you make a wish, my love?" she asked as Emma sat back down and snuggled in close to Tobias.

"I have everything I could possibly ask for," she called out as she fell into her husband's arms with a series of giggles. Abigail sat back and admired the couple's joy.

"I can hardly believe she is married. She has the same playful spirit she had as a child, and now she is excepting her own. There were so many nights during our first years here that I would lay with her and comfort her with promises of our future. I always spoke with hope rather than any feelings grounded in reality. I could not allow her to believe otherwise even though prosperity felt impossible."

"Nothing is impossible if you have will and determination."

"Is that all it takes? I thought, surely, that wealth would factor into the equation."

"That is only a means. I know plenty of men with bursting billfolds who know nothing of hard work or adversity. There is a great deal of character built through ingenuity and sacrifice."

"Then we must be amongst the most charming folks you have encountered yet."

"As a matter of fact, I find you all quite ordinary," he said with a wide grin.

"Is that so?"

"Where is the scandal? Where is the intrigue?"

"We were quite disgraced a few years ago when our cow Connie broke free and ran wild through town. When Tobias finally captured her, she had broken a window to the old schoolhouse. We were censured for the better part of an afternoon."

Baxter titled his head back and laughed at her sweetness. Through their conversations, he had grown to see her as the most captivating woman of his acquaintance. As she leaned closer to the flames, he marvelled at the softness of her beauty and the way in which her fine features were illuminated by the firelight.

"You may be the most beautiful thing I have ever seen," Baxter uttered through a whisper, unable to suppress his admiration for her any longer.

"Mr. Carlisle, you embarrass me with your flattery," Abigail said as her disposition turned from playful to uncomfortable more quickly than the shooting stars streaked across the sky. "As we are both married, it is hardly appropriate for you to say such things."

"As each day passes, I regret that we never had the opportunity to meet when you were in Toronto. I am certain I would have knelt down on my knees and proposed to you the instant I saw you."

"Baxter, please. The others will hear you. I beg you to keep these thoughts to yourself, for they do nothing but embarrass us both," she said as she began to rise from her seat to take a place beside Emma on the ground. Baxter clasped her hand and urged her to stay.

"Is tonight not about wishes and telling your secret desires out in the open in the hopes they come true? Can you blame me for how I feel? Do you know how hard it is to watch you wake before dawn and work until sunset each day? Do you understand how it torments me to have you stand before me in service? My only recourse has been to slip silver dollars under my supper plate and pray that they somehow improve your life. Have you never wondered why we stay on here when we have tents and cots aplenty in camp? It is for the simple reason that I am determined to do what I can to better your situation. If we had met in another time, you would have not wanted for anything. Any desire would have been yours."

Although the words he spoke were wholly inappropriate and Abigail feared his flirtation would be discovered by her daughter who sat less than ten feet away, she could not help but crave his attention. She had barely felt the touch of her husband's hand in weeks, and as Baxter touched hers, she felt the same course of energy tickle her spine as when she had stood with Charles on the emerald knolls of Rosehurst Estate.

"Look there," Baxter whispered as a streak of light pierced the flesh of the dark plum sky. He squeezed her hand tightly and looked overhead to await another. A second star shot through a similar path as if chasing the one that had passed before it. "Quick, Abigail, make a wish."

Despite her companion's ardent statements and the connection they shared in that moment, when she closed her eyes tight she thought only of Charles. She wished that he would awake in the morning joyful and full of life, sweeping her into his arms and kissing her tenderly. She wished the front doors would spring open with guests clamouring for a chance to stay at the famed Prescott Hotel. She wished for a safe birth for her daughter and grandchild, and a family income so secure that the whole household would be taken care of long after the newborn was grown and with child of her own. As she felt the weight of Baxter's hand on hers, she wished for a swift reunion for him and his wife, and a happy life for them together. When she opened her eyes, she could see Baxter's face brightened by the starlight.

"What did you wish for?" he asked.

"The same things that everyone wishes for. And what was your wish?"

"The same as yours, evidently."

Abigail laughed at his wit and thought how fortunate his wife was to have a husband in good humour.

"That means that you wished for your family to be well and safe and to remain forever close by. Will your wife be joining you once you are settled?"

Baxter released her hand and lowered his gaze to focus on the enflamed embers in the pit.

"I would rather not speak of that right now."

Abigail reached out and touched his chin to gently raise it from his chest.

"Come, turn your eyes to the sky."

Charles watched from his widow as Abigail sat back in her chair. As Baxter leaned towards her, Charles thought he was spying one of the spotted falcons as it encircled above a tiny field mouse; he half-expected

Baxter to swoop down and pierce her torso with his talons. He saw Baxter as a lonely man in need of affection, with enough money to presume that he could entice anyone into an indiscretion. As Charles was about to turn away from the window and prepare for sleep, he saw a string of pearls flash across the sky. His only wish was to forever feel the love of his family.

Spring, 1903

Chapter Twenty-Three

Charles' disposition had improved little since fall, but the constancy of the rentals offered a welcomed elevation to his finances. Although Baxter and the foremen had moved into a cabin on the worksite, the residence of visiting branch executives each month was a positive return for Charles, who spent each week's profit on equal parts family and business. Abigail and Emma were given an allowance to purchase goods for the new baby, Gail, and he set aside funds for enough fabric to yield a few new garments for each of them. Over Christmas, he had sold out the hotel for nearly two weeks when a group of N.P.R. investors were unable to leave after a blizzard dropped an impassable amount of snow. When their invoice was paid in full, he purchased two sheep and a goat for his own inventory and bought a young calf as a late addition to Emma's dowry.

The fierce storms of winter continued well into spring, and weeks of April sleet had usurped the traditional showers. The poor weather was indeed a burden for Baxter, who had spent the previous nine months navigating the extremes of late summer heat, deep winter cold and early spring floods. The most constant period was January when he could transport goods by sleigh over the windrows, but the furrowed snow had long since melted, and the roads were again dry enough to resume the expedient transport of supplies.

Although Charles still spent a good portion of every afternoon watching Baxter's business evolve, his primary interest was no longer the caravan of goods; he was now enthralled by the sheer size of the materials being used for the building's construction. It had taken nearly a month for the hard clay and sand to be excavated, and the recess for the foundation had left a pile of dirt beside it that was not out of place with the hills surrounding Bowlea. Within days of the foundation being poured, the building's masonry began to arrive. When Charles inquired as to the materials used, Baxter simply replied: "the finest limestone in the district." Each brick was as heavy as a steam engine's wheel and required hoisting with a mechanical winch. He admired the ingenuity used in the building's construction, yet when the sun rose high and cast a shadow that swallowed the lake, he knew The Prescott would struggle. He briefly considered planting crops on his pasturelands in order to tarnish the view for Baxter's guests, but he could not bring himself to mar the land he and his family had grown to cherish.

The days had become much warmer, and the most eager of the wildflowers had long since blossomed forth with their periwinkle sprouts and rosehip buds. It was Abigail's favourite time of the season and she was ashamed to admit that she often delegated chores to Emma so she could swim in the late afternoons when the sun had warmed the lake to a tolerable temperature. On the days when baby Gail would fall asleep for a solid two hours, Charlotte watched after her while Emma raced her mother to the shore like she did as a child. Abigail always reached the stony beach first and never quite knew if it was by her own volition or her daughter's affection.

Baxter had left The Prescott some weeks before, but he was still a tenant of Abigail's thoughts. She would often stare across the water as she hung out the wash and remember the times he had offered a hand. He would wait until she was unaccompanied so he could save her from the exertion of hauling pails of water or baskets of damp sheets. He would carry armfuls of logs to the corral in the kitchen just to save her skin from splinters. She felt his absence greatly; she well knew the pain of detachment and often wondered how he tolerated the physical separation from his wife. He never betrayed his feelings, but moments of distraction during their conversations spoke to the displacement of his thoughts and his affection for someone Abigail hoped to one day meet. Although she suspected that he found comfort in his isolation, she was not aware of a single person who preferred life without the company of a loved one.

Although there remained a marked separation between Abigail and Charles, she was bolstered by their familiarity and the fact that they were in each other's company at some point each day. While their emotional closeness had somewhat faded, she felt fortunate to have even modest indicators of his love. For Christmas, he had presented her with sheet music of Bach's *Minuet in G*, the same tune they had danced to at their wedding. When Emma would play the piece for them in the drawing room, they had danced as close as lovers. Abigail could hear the pace of his heartbeat increase when she rested her head on his chest, leaving little doubt of his tenderness for her.

On the day that Charles and Tobias headed out to Mr. Bauer's farm to procure feed for the summer, Abigail thought it was the perfect time to visit the new mercantile to see what types of goods were in store. With no guests at present, she determined that the ladies of the house deserved a day without work; the chores were not so burdensome that they could not be put off until the next day. Charlotte made up a batch of sweet honey flapjacks and wrapped them in a cloth to take to an admirer from the rail crew. Emma used the time to rest and was thankful that Gail was also in need of a nap.

Abigail stepped down from the front porch and strolled towards the shop. The lane heading south from the hotel had grown from a simple dirt road into a proper main street. The buildings that ran along either side had lingered within the perpetual flux of vacancy and occupation since the town's founding. Only a handful now stood empty, and there was little doubt that they would soon be occupied. News of the rail's expansion had spread like a brushfire when the lightening bolt of opportunity struck Bowlea on the day of Baxter's arrival. Each of the towns on the eastern branch of the line saw a resurgence of interest and investment and their development swiftly amplified. Every twenty-five miles a tiny settlement sprouted into a village, while the resilient old villages germinated into towns.

A new pastor had arrived just before Easter after hearing that many of the railmen were progressively moving farther away from God's word the closer they got to Edmonton. He occupied the church only on Sundays, for during weekday mornings, the building acted as a schoolhouse for the new settlers' children. Abigail was thankful that baby Gail would have the chance to form bonds with children of her own age, and would not have to bear the uprooting her mother had.

The function of the businesses in Bowlea matched its young age, and there was little in the way of luxuries or entertainments. There was no tailor or milliner for there was no society to impress; there were no saloons or taverns, for very few could afford to drink. The establishments worked mainly to foster the expansion of settlement. A hardware store with rough-sawn planks, hand-struck nails and hammers was one of several businesses that seemed to rise from the ground like the morning mist only to settle into the dawn as though they had always been there.

As Abigail continued past the livery, the stench of horses was replaced by the aroma of fresh baking. When Mrs. Winters sent word to her granddaughter that prospects were improving in Bowlea, the young lady responded by moving with her husband to open a mercantile and tea house in the Coupland's old spot. As Abigail approached the window of Tammy's Place, she could see a lattice-topped pie filled with apples and raisins. It reminded her of the tarts her mother used to order when they would take tea at the Café Simcoe in Kingston. As she looked down at the plain fabric of her dress and greyed gloves, she thought about the hours of preparation required to be seen both in the company of her mother and amongst her friends in society. The fine selections of teas and pastries were an audience of their own, and her mother would never have dreamed of insulting them by being simply attired. Although Abigail wanted to stop and sample a slice right away, she thought it best to complete the errand of finding Charles a gift first so she could savour the treat and reminisce about her mother without distraction.

The mercantile was a vast deal better appointed for the needs of the townsfolk than Mr. Winters' simple grocery, for he had kept his stock minimal in keeping with the modest demand. It had been a few weeks since Abigail had visited the new shop, and she was amazed by the diversity of inventory they had procured in such a short period of time. She wondered if there were any goods on the shelves sufficient to show Charles the depth of her affection.

"Is that a new brocade, Amos?" she asked as she approached the counter and eyed the neatly stacked bolts of fabric and ribbon. "It is quite lovely."

"Yes, ma'am. A good, sturdy fabric with a nice bit of colour. It would do for a lot of different garments," the shop owner said as he pulled the bolt from its place on the shelf and rolled out a few feet on the counter before her. She fingered the tight stitching of the embroidered vines and gave the fabric a sharp tug to test its weight and body.

"I believe this will do very well. One yard, if you please. That should be enough fabric for a waistcoat, should it not?"

"Mr. Prescott is not a big man, so a yard will do you fine. You'll need a few buttons, too."

As he gathered the notions and ran his shears through the fabric, Abigail smiled with bemusement as she considered her rudimentary sewing skills. Although there were never enough funds to provide her family with ready-made pieces, she was thankful that Emma adopted the craft in her youth, and had worked her skills to perfection. She knew her daughter would correct any of her more obvious mistakes in order to provide the most perfect gift for Charles.

"Is there anything else I can get for you today, Mrs. Prescott?"

"Let me see."

She wandered to the other end of the counter where rows of thick russet bottles were stacked to the ceiling upon thick birch shelves. Although there was not yet a saloon or bar in town, she realized there must have been strong demand from the railmen to keep such a varied stock of liquor.

"My, with so many varieties, I hardly know which one to choose."

"Perhaps you should have joined us once in a while for cards and whisky. I am certain you would have developed a taste for it."

She knew the voice well and turned to see the broad figure of Baxter moving in close beside her at the counter.

"You have come to replenish your own stock, I presume," she said, teasingly. "There is little refinement of taste required when you order one of each."

"Perhaps you should drink an extra finger, madam, to tone down that sass."

"I have been rather moderate, as of late, but I always have a bit in reserve just for you."

"Well then, I am very much obliged," Baxter said with a chuckle. He scanned the wall of spirits and pointed to a bulbous bottle on the middle shelf.

"That one there should do you well. Smooth, with just a nip of spice."

"Yes, alright. How much is that one, Amos?"

"This here is three dollars, ma'am."

"Three dollars!" she exclaimed. "Perhaps I shall get a few sticks of rock candy instead."

"Allow me to get it for you, Abigail. You deserve much more for putting up with me and my men all those months."

"No, I could not possibly. It is meant to be a gift for Charles, and he would never condone such an extravagant purchase."

As Baxter looked into her eyes, he withheld any sign of dismay that her family would consider such a modest expenditure an extravagance. He pointed to a cream-labelled bottle on the bottom shelf.

"How much is that rye there?" he asked.

"Six bits."

"That is more reasonable, surely."

"It is not the finest liquor, but it will do," she said with a kind smile. "You will have to stop by and join us for a drink one evening. I have no doubt that Charles misses your company and conversation. His mood has soured since your departure."

Baxter understood that he was likely the reason for the alteration in her husband's disposition, but for reasons far more dire than an empty seat at the card table.

"I may have to take you up on that. With things progressing so quickly, I have had little opportunity for social calls."

"There is no time like the present, as they say. Charles is not due back until this afternoon, and I had planned on taking tea next door. Would you care to join me?"

The room next door was small and quaint, even by Bowlea standards. The diminutive space held five tables with seating enough for twelve and was decorated simply with grey linen curtains and green tartan table runners. There was one other couple, seated by the window, who paid the pair little mind for they had not been residents of Bowlea long enough to know any of their history.

"I cannot wait to try their raisin pie. That and a strong cup of black tea will set me up for the rest of the day," Abigail said as the pair scanned the short menu scrawled on the slate board above the register.

"The gingered spice cake sounds like it would go well with a glass of fresh milk. The camp cook does a fine job of the basics, but he offers little more than that. When my supper tray is delivered each evening, I find myself searching under the napkin for your little oat cookies. There is a moment of sadness in both my heart and stomach when there are none to be found."

"You are very sweet."

"Not as sweet as you. Or your cookies."

"I wager that a professional's treats would be far superior to my own," she said as the blush that Baxter typically incited returned to her cheeks.

"Well then, there is only one way to settle this. We must order one of everything on the menu to maintain objectivity."

"Come now, Baxter, there is really no need. I accept your flattery willingly," she said with a smile.

"That is all I could ask for. I hope the men did not disturb your swim yesterday," he said as he pulled out a chair for her. "It is impossible to deny them a chance to cool off at the end of the day."

"Not at all. My wrinkled skin told me it was time to retire long before they jumped in. The water is only superficially warm, you know, and any time my limbs dipped below the surface I wondered if the fish had yet come out of hibernation."

Baxter smiled and cast his eyes towards the tin spoon he twiddled with his fingers. He wondered how much of their first conversation she remembered, for he replayed every detail of that night with such frequency that each time they met, it felt as though it had taken place just the night before.

"In all honesty," she continued, "I did rather prefer it when the lake felt like mine alone. Even with only a handful of fellows, it seems overcrowded. I do hope the rail line does not alter things too much. We have waited all this time for business to increase, but now that prosperity is upon us, I cannot help but feel a bit selfish. Is it too much to desire both serenity and enough business to be successful? Things have been the same for so long it is difficult to welcome change."

"Change is natural, but it is rarely easy to face alone. You are blessed to have your family with you to bear the strain. The crew and I are fortunate that it does not so intensely impact our personal lives. We tend to focus on the return on investment and the accomplishment of construction. Our feelings of triumph will only increase when we finish the hotel."

Baxter felt a sharp pain behind his eye in the exact moment of his accidental disclosure. He and Abigail had grown to view each other as confidants, and he did not realize what he had said until after the words passed his lips.

"The hotel? What sort of plans do you have for our little business?" she asked, jokingly.

In the panic of the moment, Baxter was unprepared for how to conceal the secret he had laid bare. The truth, or his best version of it, spilled forth in earnest.

"Not your hotel, Abigail, but mine. Surely you have seen the building on the opposite side of the lake. We have been making quite a bit of headway over the last few months. It is to be a grand hotel attracting the finest society from the east."

Although Baxter gave up the information without ceremony, he was not cruel. His words were tainted with an apologetic lilt, and he felt the burden of secrecy fall from his shoulders as he spoke. He was relieved to have an increased openness with Abigail, but the fact that her husband already knew of his intentions would remain the gentlemen's secret alone.

"Does Charles know of this?" she asked in a low whisper as her thoughts immediately went to her husband and the reality that he likely had no indication of the building's true purpose.

"Of that, I am uncertain, though I never told him myself. Bowlea is being modelled after the luxury rail properties in the east. When this land was surveyed several years before your arrival, it was determined that the sublimity of the lake and expansive pastures would make an ideal destination for wealthy travellers. It took several years to iron out the details, but we are well underway," he said, as he scraped the last crumbs of spice cake from his plate in an effort to dissuade his guilt with a few more bits of sweetness.

Abigail sat in silence as she allowed the details of Baxter's revelation to process. A couple of railmen entered the tea shop and tipped their hats at Baxter before approaching the counter. As they decided on which sweet tea cakes to take back to camp, she wondered if they were aware of their contributions to the demise of her family.

"You must not tell him, Baxter, I beg of you. Let us keep this only between us. Charles has worked so hard to make his hotel profitable. The irregularity of business has taken quite a toll, and his good spirits are just starting to return. He fully believes that success will come to him once the rail line is complete. Please refrain from telling him your secret. Promise me."

The walk back to the hotel was less than two hundred yards; Abigail had neither the strength to refuse Baxter's offer of escort nor the capacity to walk the distance without his arm to steady her. With his other hand, he held the lead of his horse who trembled with the urge to again gallop across the fields. Abigail's body echoed the animal's quiver, for the knowledge of her family's destitution and unlikely recovery was too much to bear. She was unsure of what to say as they walked and Baxter neglected his part in the conversation, for he was certain he had already said enough.

As they approached the hotel, Abigail could see Charles sweeping the porch planks, as was his custom each time the Red Deer coach passed through town. Fearing that he would notice her arm wound through Baxter's, she instead gripped the handle of her basket tightly with both hands, making sure to cover the liquor with the brown-papered piece of fabric.

Baxter understood why she pulled away, but in the few minutes they spent strolling from the tea house, he imagined they were a proper couple walking along the promenade at Hanlan's Point in Toronto. His escort there would not have been merely for stability, but rather to make it known to all passersby that she had chosen him above all others.

"It was lovely to see you again, Abigail," he said while they were still out of Charles' earshot. "With construction now in full swing, I do not imagine I will have time for social visits until after the first snowfall."

Abigail did not know how to respond, for her visits with Baxter were usually fun, informal and welcome; their encounter left her wishing he had stayed on his side of the lake.

"I expect us to be very busy as well," she said as she tried to force a smile through her tight lips. The effort only worked to make her grimace more obvious.

"Come now; all will be well."

"Yes. I am sure all will be well for you, indeed."

"Why, Baxter! It has surely been a long while," Charles said when he caught sight of him and laid aside the broom to give him a friendly handshake. "I have no doubt that the worksite has kept you very busy as of late."

Baxter smiled and shook his hand firmly while relaying details of the challenges he had faced with the supply chain and his relief that the waters of Ashcroft Brook had finally receded. As the men engaged in the banter of business, Abigail could not help but notice the ease with which both men spoke. Baxter expertly wove the fabric of his business dealings without relaying the slightest detail of the building's true purpose. Meanwhile, Charles maintained an optimism that Abigail attributed to his discovery of Baxter's swift progress and the onslaught of business that was sure to follow for the whole of the town. She watched them interact and noted the muted scope of their banter. Absent from their dialogue was the overt solicitation that often occurred between entrepreneurs, with each hoping to secure reverie and fodder for their respective egos. Instead, there was a measured cordiality that she attributed to Baxter's willingness to uphold his promise to her.

As the gentlemen bid their farewells and Baxter mounted his ride to return to camp, Abigail had no way of knowing that Charles' reserve hid a deep-seeded resentment towards both the N.P.R. and Baxter that was further solidified with each slab of sandstone laid.

The aromas of the evening meal worked to coax each family member to find a seat around the kitchen table. Although business had been steady in recent weeks, they were fortunate that night to dine and converse without the interruption of guests.

"Mr. Bauer's place was chock full of people buying hay and alfalfa. There were three wagons ahead of us in line," Tobias said as he took the baby from Emma's arms to bump her gently on his knee. "That must be a sign of things to come, don't you think Mr. Prescott?"

"Indeed. It is encouraging to see such hope. It puts me in mind of our first weeks here. And things have not turned out so poorly, have they?"

Charles looked around the table at his family. As he watched Emma and Tobias tickle and tease their chubby little daughter, he thought of the first months of his own daughter's life and how much joy she had brought to their new family. He remembered often hoping that baby Emma would raise a fuss so he, too, could be soothed by Abigail's sweet lullabies.

"I see you are both weary from your trip today. Is it not the ideal time to take a drink in your study? It would be the perfect end to a long day."

"That would be splendid, but I am afraid I spent the last of our spirits on the McCoys last month. It was the only way I could contend at bridge at all."

Abigail rose from her seat and opened a small cabinet in the sideboard. She retrieved the bottle and presented it to Charles, proudly displaying the liquor's front label.

"You have been working so hard lately, and our luck seems to be improving. I thought you would not object to a little indulgence." She placed the bottle into his hands and watched as his features softened further into a bleary-eyed smile.

"This is quite unexpected."

"With everything we have been through, there has been one constant: your faith that you will one day be successful. When I spoke to Mr. Carlisle today, he said that he expects the line to be completed within a year. We have already seen improvements in your business, and it can only increase from here."

Abigail spouted the words as though she were a broker trying to convince a client that their investment was sound. Charles listened to her promote his venture with more vigour than he had allowed himself to feel in months. Her optimism was infectious, and he knew of no way to contradict her sentiments. His only option was to move forward as though nothing was amiss.

"After the baby is put to bed, would you care to join me for a drink, young man?"

"Yes, sir, that would be just fine," Tobias replied with a grin as broad as his daughter's.

"Toby, let us get her ready now. Her eyes are heavy," Emma urged as she lifted Gail from his arms and moved through to their quarters.

The firelight from the hearth cast a glow about the kitchen and brightened Abigail's hair with the amber hues of a sunrise. Charles wondered if he had ever before seen her so lovely. The softness of her features reminded him of a time when the lamplight blurred their figures amongst the pale linens and pillows of their marriage bed, a place he had left cold since before the new year.

"Thank you for the gift, my dear. It was very kind of you," he said with his eyes cast down at the bottle's label.

"It is you who are kind. You have provided us with all that surrounds us, and through so much adversity, you have kept us well. I wish I could give you more."

"The constancy of your support is thanks enough, Abby," Charles said as he took her hand and placed it in his. "You spoke of the constancy of my faith in the business, but you failed to mention the constancy of my melancholy. I can hardly imagine how difficult this adventure would have been without you. When I saw the settlers lined up at Bauer's this afternoon, I had a strong feeling that Bowlea is going to flourish. You will see. Our business will grow with the town and be more profitable than we ever imagined.

"When I look at what our family has accomplished," he continued, "I am exceedingly proud. We have all worked to make this business a success, and our achievement will be a cornerstone of prosperity for the rest of the town. You know, as we drove the carriage back into town today, it looked different than it did when we left this morning. It felt larger, more alive. Perhaps the façade of failure has been replaced with faith."

Abigail hardly knew how to respond to Charles' unexpected optimism, and so simply smiled and tightened her grip of his hand.

"When we arrived back home, and I saw that you were out, I thought it wonderful that you made time to enjoy what we have of society. As Bowlea grows, think of how wonderful it will be to again have friends of the same mind and pursuits."

As she thought of her current friendships, her mind went instantly to Baxter; she imagined he was sitting in his cabin at that very moment counting his stacks of silver and twenty dollar notes.

"You and I are of the same mind, are we not?" she asked.

"I fear my mind has been so occupied with business that I have neglected to maintain our friendship, let alone our marriage. There is nothing to do but plead for your forgiveness."

"Sweet Charles, there is nothing to forgive. It is a selfless act to surrender yourself to your business for the benefit of your family. It may feel like it has weakened our relationship, but I can assure you, it is quite the opposite."

In that moment, Charles did not think of Baxter, The Prescott or the fate of their respective ventures. He thought only of making his wife happy, and never again allowing her to feel the burden of his sadness.

"Will you join me tonight, my love?" she asked as the firelight danced in her eyes. "I should very much like you there beside me."

"From this night on, there is nowhere else I will be."

When Charles and Tobias retired upstairs a short time later, Abigail was left alone with her thoughts for the first time since Baxter's revelation. She understood what he was set to gain from a lack of disclosure to Charles, but did not understand why he withheld his true intentions from the rest of the town. His secrecy had prevented the spread of gossip and denied them any forewarning of the N.P.R.'s master plan.

"Is everything all right, Mama?" Emma asked as the door snapped closed behind Abigail who hurried down through the moonlit field towards the lake. She did not reply to her daughter's query but instead maintained a steady march toward the water's western edge. Emma called out for Charlotte to mind Gail and then hastily followed her mother to her favourite seat atop the old fallen log.

"Whatever is the matter? Is it Papa?" Emma asked as she took a place beside her. In that instant, Abigail felt defeated. She clasped her hands at her breast and sunk into Emma's embrace, relishing the soft comfort of her daughter's arms.

"We are ruined," she whispered with no force behind the words.

"Ruined? How can that be? We have done good business lately, and more bookings are expected tomorrow. Calm yourself, Mama, I beg of you."

Abigail pulled away slightly so as to read her daughter's face when she learned the news.

"It is not a rail station that Mr. Carlisle's men are building."

"If not a rail station, then what?"

"A hotel."

"A hotel?" Emma asked as she felt a strong pang in the pit of her stomach.

"I spoke with Mr. Carlisle this afternoon, and he informed me that what we all believed to be a rail station is meant to be a fine hotel."

"Surely there is no need for a large hotel in Bowlea. We are a fraction of the size and rarely have enough guests to fund our supply of fuel and lamp oil. Does Papa know of this?" Emma asked as her mother's shivers sent chills through her own flesh.

"He has not even the slightest inclination. Mr. Carlisle does not think it prudent to inform him of his intentions."

"Then we must tell him ourselves."

Abigail looked back at the hotel as she struggled to maintain her composure. She imagined Charles in his study with Tobias, laughing and cajoling as they plotted a future based on false expectations.

"My intuition tells me that it will be easier for your father to bear if he does not know. With more N.P.R. executives expected next week, it will be impossible for him to endure daily service to the men responsible for putting him out of business." Abigail paused for a moment and took a few deep breaths." As tempting as it may be to discuss the matter with Tobias, I ask that you keep this news between us. It will take more than a few days to determine our best course of action."

"Are you certain it is wise to keep this from him?"

"I fear that is our only option."

Spring, 1904

Chapter Twenty-Four

On the first morning of the Founder's Day festivities, the Prescotts' carriage pulled up in front of Red Deer Town Hall just after ten o'clock. When the letter arrived from Mr. Smythe in the last week of May asking Abigail to again sing at the annual celebration, Charles urged her to accept the three-week engagement. When The Regent's proprietor offered the family room and board for the duration of the weekend, he spoke to Mr. Wells at the Bowlea livery and rented a pony to help Winnie pull the carriage to Red Deer and back.

A large crowd surrounded the pavilion that stood in the middle of town square. The politicians' speeches were underway by the time the trio checked in and set out to find Abigail. Mr. Smythe ushered the family to their seats as soon as he spied them and informed them that Abigail was unable to greet them, for she was engaged in vocal preparations behind the stage.

A member of the town council took the stage and Charles could barely hear his words over the hurrahs from the crowd. As the gentleman proudly declared himself to be instrumental in the success of the Palliser expedition some fifty years prior, Charles wondered if he or any of the black-suited men seated to his right had a stake in the development of Bowlea. When he saw Baxter's face amongst the bearded men, he presumed they must.

Abigail was struggling to calm her nerves, as this was her largest audience to date. The instrument tuning of the Firemen's Band was loud enough to drown out her vocal preparations, while the thick velvet curtain did well to obscure her. Her performance piece was one of Charles' favourites, a melodic tune she had first sung on the cobbled terrace of Mrs. Cunningham's back garden. She had selected it during their courtship because it spoke to the thrill and newness of adventure and the compromises that must be made in the pursuit of love. She chose to perform it for Founder's Day because all who had gathered in the square that afternoon had endured the flux of settlement, and their familial bonds were forever altered by the experience.

Baxter was obliged to occupy a seat amongst the wealthy investors of Carlisle Smythe Holdings, who were in turn flanked by stakeholders of the Northern Pacific Rail. Every man around him had a stake in the success of Red Deer and had watched the seed of opportunity grow from a simple crossing point on the old Calgary-Edmonton Trail into a thriving town alongside the Calgary-Edmonton Railway. As he considered their money and influence, he wondered if new routes would branch out from the Bowlea station as new businesses took hold, or if settlers would still meander like dead leaves in the wind.

From where he was seated, Baxter had a clear view of Abigail. She was swaying slightly on her heels to catch the sunlight in the beading of her dress; the radiance of her smile matched the splendour of the tiny rainbows that were cast upon the backdrop. Baxter glanced over to where the

Prescotts were seated; when he noticed their distraction, he rose from his seat to personally offer her his well-wishes.

"Bottom's up!" he said after slinking through the crowd to join her behind the stage. She was startled by his sudden appearance, for she was doing everything in her power to distract herself from her impending obligation, and was struggling to control her nerves.

"I believe you mean 'break a leg'," she said as she turned to face him. "'Bottom's up' is reserved for toasts, is it not?"

Baxter smiled and unfastened the top button of his frock coat. From the inside pocket, he retrieved a tiny round flask, large enough for only a few swigs.

"I believe I was right the first time. Besides, is today not an occasion to celebrate?" He moved in close beside her so as to obstruct any view of impropriety at taking a drink of whisky from a flask at midday.

"What are you doing? Baxter, I couldn't possibly," she said as she pushed his hand away and motioned for him to conceal the liquor.

"Come now; I find it highly unlikely that you never took at least a bit of a drink before your performances at The Regent. Would you not prefer to settle the trembling of your hands?"

"A tipple of cordial is hardly the same as whisky," she said as she looked around at the musicians and other performers behind the stage. "I suppose one sip will not hurt."

Baxter watched as Abigail put the cool, engraved silver to her lips. The pained look on her face and short gasp of breath were tell-tale signs of the liquor's efficacy. As the butterflies in her stomach lost the strength in their wings, she was thankful to be bolstered by the potion. She walked along the stage behind the curtain and slightly parted the fabric, careful not to reveal her delicate costume before her cue.

"I was not expecting such a crowd." She eyed the dozen rows of citizens sitting in the courtyard and the many more who stood around them. She closed the peephole she had created and instantly felt the unease return to her stomach with a churning thud.

"Do not worry yourself, Abigail. During the only instance I ever saw you perform, you never faltered. If you were anxious on that occasion, you hid it so well that no one could have suspected anything but confidence."

"You are very kind to say so, Baxter, but my audiences were never this large or influential."

"Perhaps determined focus is the wrong approach," Baxter said with a kind smile.

"And you mean to offer a distraction?" she asked as he reached out and took her hand.

Through her clammy fingers, Baxter could feel her whole body tremble. He wanted nothing more than to sweep her into his arms to comfort her and assuage her fears.

"I have been rather impatient since I arrived yesterday. I have been waiting to speak with you alone. I can't help but think of the moments we spent together down at by the lake. The construction is very tedious and tiresome. Every moment I spend with you seems to send me back to the camp refreshed and ready to tackle my tasks anew."

"I enjoy our time together as well," she said as the rose tones returned to her cheeks. She was to be the first performer of the afternoon and could hear that Mr. Smythe was nearing the end of his speech.

"I would like to meet you again. Somewhere without distraction."

"Charles has something planned with the family this evening, or I would ask you to join us."

"No, I mean to ask if…" Baxter paused when he heard his name mentioned by his partner, who had asked the investors to stand to be recognized for their contributions to the development of Red Deer.

"I must return to my seat. I will leave a note for you at the front desk in the morning. Please consider meeting me," he said as he rushed from behind the stage to clumsily weave through the throng of investors until he reached his chair. Charles observed him with curiosity, wondering what business he had behind stage; as one of The Regent's many partners in attendance, Charles figured he must be involved in the event's organization.

"Ah, there he is," Mr. Smythe said as his colleague appeared. "Mr. Baxter Carlisle. A man of vision and loyalty who not only sees this district for its beauty and possibilities but who is building the infrastructure to show the people of this country what the central district has to offer."

Baxter took a bow and offered a tip of his hat to the audience. As Mr. Smythe spoke of the sacrifices Baxter had made to help him build the finest hotels in Red Deer, Calgary and Fort Macleod, Abigail could not help but smile at the generosity he had shown her own family; he had even revealed himself to be responsible for Mr. Smythe's recent offer of employment.

When her name was announced, Abigail stood motionless as the wooden platform creaked beneath her feet. As the curtain parted, she stepped forward and instantly surmised that she was about to perform for most of the town. The rows of people extended out from the stage, and through the park to the low avenues surrounding the square.

A silence fell over the crowd as she lifted her peach gown at the knee and dipped into a shallow curtsey. Through the enchantment of her voice, she captivated the audience, transforming lyrics into sentiments that resonated with each of them. She sang of the tandem of success and failure and the sanguinity that lingered on even through devastating degradation.

She sang to the young men like Tobias who had to forge on after seeing their families taken by the land; she sang to the young women like Emma who brought new souls into the world to carry on the ambitions of their settler kin. She sang to men like Charles who sacrificed all of their being to do right by their loved ones.

As the final notes passed her lips, the townsfolk rang out with cheers and hurrahs that pounded through the depths of her heart. Although she was pleased with the reception of her simple tune, she knew the song's sweetness would only temporarily dull the edges of their communal adversity.

Chapter Twenty-Five

It was not uncommon for Abigail to receive notes and cards from guests who had seen her perform. Although she did nothing to solicit the admiration of the gentlemen in the audience, she welcomed their gestures as a reminder of her loved ones back in Bowlea.

"Good day, Amy. Are there any messages for me this morning?" Abigail asked in the kind manner that the hotel's postmistress had come to expect from her. During her initial engagement at The Regent, her routine saw her pick up her cards in the early morning to review them over tea and biscuits. She was curious about the note left by Baxter, but she had waited until her family returned home, and did not inquire at the front desk until she knew that they were well into their long journey home.

"You have several cards, ma'am," the young clerk said as she reached around to the pigeon-holed wall behind her. "Someone even left you a Victrola record. Oh, how I've wished for a Victrola. That is not to say anyone fancies me enough to buy me a record, but I can wish all the same."

As the young lady nattered on, Abigail set the bundle of notes on the counter and picked up the record. Resting the bottom edge gently in the palm of her hand, she reached between the two folds of brown paper and slid out the slick black disk. She held the platter carefully at the edges and tilted it slightly to reflect the lamplight off its ridged surface.

"*Can't You See I'm Lonely,*" by Ada Jones was stamped on the dark yellow label. Abigail carefully placed the record back into its sleeve and read the accompanying card.

My sweet Abigail,

I have never been more proud of you than during those brief moments yesterday when I heard you sing. Although you were there to perform for the many, it felt as though you only sang for me. It pained me to leave this morning as it pains me every time we are apart for more than a few hours. This recording conveys how I am feeling now and how I will continue to feel until we again share the same space and the memories within it.

With all the love in my heart,

Charles

As Abigail folded the note and placed it back in its envelope, her eyes swelled with tears. There were two weeks remaining until the end of her engagement, and although she was surrounded by admirers during each performance, they continued on their journeys before she could feel the impact of their friendship. Returning to her hotel room alone each night was a painful reminder of the lonesome months she spent without Charles' intimacy; having been so close to him the night before made the plains between them feel more distant than the three thousand miles of land beneath the transcontinental line.

Abigail dabbed the corner of her eye with the tip of her little finger. As she looked up from the card gripped tightly in her hand, she was faced with the eager eyes of the clerk who did not hesitate to inquire about her admirer.

"Someone special?" Amy asked as her eyes grew wide and focused on the filigreed illustration on the record's cover.

Abigail obliged her with a shy smile and put the disk under her arm. She gathered the remaining notes from the counter to read them in private, particularly eager to read the note from Baxter.

A chill swept through her room as she entered; she had left the window ajar so as to hear the chorus of chickadees from within the branches of the courtyard spruce. A part of her felt compelled to stoke the fire with the stack of cards from her unknown admirers, but she instead took a stick of seasoned wood from the corral and placed it in the stove. As it burned, the log popped and cracked as the moisture within struggled to escape. She retrieved Baxter's note and sat down on the chaise. The paper was thick and refined, a far cry from Charles' cheap penny stock and although the envelope was beautiful, she was far less concerned with tearing the embossed flowers than discovering its contents. The mere contemplation of reading it was considered an act of impropriety, and as she removed the crisp note from the torn envelope, her stomach rolled like prairie thunderclouds as it had before her performance in the town square. Instead of Baxter being the remedy, however, he was now the cause.

Dearest Abigail,

I am travelling by train this morning to the mountains in Banff. I ask tenderly for you to join me there. I have arranged for you to have your own room and to be registered as my cousin, Miss Abigail Delaney.

I have spoken to Mr. Smythe, and he has obliged to provide alternate entertainment while you are gone. I will pay your wage to ensure you have your weekly sum to take home to your family.

I understand this may seem like a rash proposal, but with my duties expanding in Bowlea, I feel this may be our only opportunity to be together. I ask this as a man eager to gain a further intimacy with you with a freedom that our encounters in Bowlea have never allowed. I have no agenda or expectations of our time together other than to hope for your companionship.

Do you recall when you first saw the misty peaks in the distance when you arrived in Calgary? You said it felt as though you could touch them if you only reached out your hand. Imagine yourself in the middle of a valley, with masses of stone towering so high that you can barely see the tops for the clouds; glacier lakes of such intense green, they would rival your eyes. Allow me to share this enchanting place with you.

A train departs Wednesday morning at half past six, and I hope you will be aboard. There will be a ticket waiting for you at will call.

Baxter

Abigail allowed the letter to fold back on itself and squeezed the crease tightly between her thumb and forefinger.

"How dare he write such a letter," she thought as his proposition caused her to pace about the room. Other than his understanding of the need to be discreet, the remaining ink scrawled across that crisp ivory page spoke only to indulgence, lack of decorum and infidelity. She could hardly believe that he had so little regard for his wife that he would make such arrangements. Although she appreciated his recent kindness to both her and her family, she had no desire to act on feelings of kinship and a closeness initially built on mutual loneliness. She knew he could not possibly expect a response. A telegraph would raise suspicion as both of them were well-known to the front desk staff, and she had no intention of betraying Charles by responding with a letter. When Baxter wrote that he would wait for her, she presumed he did not mean for the whole of the summer; he would return to Bowlea cloaked in a disappointment brought about by his own poor judgement.

Abigail could not help but feel conflicted as she set down the note and paced about her room. Baxter's kindness towards her and her family had never wavered, and she believed that his business' impact on The Prescott was strictly incidental. Abigail's father often touted the ideals of Adam Smith, and she well understood the concept of a free market society. If their hotels had been built in a more populous area, little consideration would have been given to the burden of competition.

As she resumed her seat for a moment of reflection, she tried in vain to expel his offer from her mind. Although she knew instantly that she would not meet him, she could not ignore their mutual attraction. In many respects, she thought him handsome and had considered his wife fortunate to have such a man; conversely, she wondered why he would not soothe his loneliness by sending for Madeline instead. While they had sometimes engaged in light banter and mild flirtation, she never believed it veered far from wholesome.

Mr. Smythe had put a gramophone in her room, most likely at Charles' request; she retrieved the platter and placed it on the turntable. She wound the ornate cast iron handle a full twenty times before dropping the needle gently atop the thin ridges of wax. As she stood over the disk and watched the ornate label spin like the thoughts of Baxter and Charles in her mind, she marvelled at Miss Ada Lloyd's ability to lament the complexities of her love life while relishing them all the same.

Chapter Twenty-Six

Baxter disembarked the Port Moody Express at Banff's train station just past nine o'clock. The platform was bustling with travellers anxious to marvel at the great castle and its place amongst the snow-tipped peaks. He had no porters in tow that morning and carried with him only a cross-body satchel and a small leather suitcase. Having sat on the train since it departed Calgary two hours prior, he felt compelled to walk up the winding slope to the hotel; the tiredness of his mind, however, heeded the call for a carriage.

"Might you fetch me a cab, young man?" he asked the footman who was occupied in offloading the last of the passenger luggage.

"Where are you heading, sir?"

"Up to The Banff Springs."

"Well, then there's no need for a cab. The omnibus goes right up Spray Avenue and only costs a quarter."

The omnibus bounced and jostled as it meandered over the rocky trail and up the steady grade towards the hotel. Baxter watched as the ladies tightly gripped the arms of the gentlemen who accompanied them, and soon realized he was the only person on board without a partner. As they drove through the valley and approached the building, Baxter spied the turrets breaking through the canopy of dense pines. Theirs was only one in a steady stream of vehicles, and as they rounded the final bend, the full splendour of the magnificent hotel came into view.

The Tudor-style wood structure towered over four stories, with gables peering out at intervals along the roof line. The building seemed out of place when compared to the rough log and stone cabins that populated the townsite, but Baxter felt it had adapted well to its place on the bluff above the Bow and Spray rivers. If one eliminated the monstrous mountains from the background, The Banff Springs would not have been out of place amongst the fine manors of Europe. Although the building was the inspiration for his own venture, Baxter knew there was no way to replicate the "Jewel in the Canadian Pacific Crown" that he had helped survey some twenty years prior.

Although it had been years since Baxter passed through the main entrance, Mr. Schlosser recognized him at once. The general manager temporarily deferred his duties to an assistant and hurried over to greet him.

"Why Mr. Carlisle! What a delight it is to see you," he said with a thick German accent that reminded Baxter that he was standing within a true alpine manor.

"Hans, old boy, great to see you. I see the mountains still have their hold upon you after all this time."

"I thought nothing could compare to the lush valleys and mountains of my Alps, but these peaks have enchanted me," he said with a laugh as Baxter heartily shook his hand.

"Are you still braving the wilds and climbing on Sundays?"

"Age, I'm afraid, has crept up on me. I have relegated myself to the occasional trek up Tunnel mountain, although that hardly qualifies as climbing."

"I wired yesterday with a request for two rooms," Baxter said as he followed Hans to the front desk. "I understand that you are coming up on the high season, so I hope it is not too much of a bother."

"Not at all, Mr. Carlisle. We would find room for you even if we were full to the rafters."

Baxter chuckled at the affability of his friend, who had been the manager of The Banff Springs since it opened. The manor was of an opposing style to what was currently under construction in Bowlea, but it possessed the target clientele.

"My cousin, Miss Delaney is expected to arrive on the one-thirty. I thought perhaps she sent a telegram ahead of her."

"I have nothing yet, but I will send a porter up with it as soon as it comes through."

Hans led the way through the busy lobby and up the stairs to his room. Baxter would have graciously found his own way, for he knew the building by heart; but Hans insisted on ensuring that he had no further requests before leaving him to unpack and get settled. As he stood at the door and turned to bid him good day, Hans could not help but notice the look of melancholy on Baxter's face.

"I wanted to offer my condolences for your dear Madeline, sir," he said with caution. "I offer them far too late, I know, but she is in my thoughts all the same."

"That is very kind of you, Hans," Baxter said, unprepared for a resurgence of feelings that he had worked hard to repress.

"I suppose you have come to pay your respects. I find myself in the graveyard from time to time visiting those who have died on the peaks. I always make sure to say a prayer for her."

In his anticipation of meeting Abigail for the weekend, Baxter had neglected to acknowledge that his wife would also have a presence there. Each morning, he thought about her briefly and then buried the memory so he could somehow bear to face the day without her. He offered Hans a terse smile.

"Will we see you in the dining room this evening?"

"Yes. Book a table for two, if you will."

"Certainly, sir. I believe the Beef Wellington is à la carte this evening. It truly is a pleasure to have you back with us, Mr. Carlisle. Good day."

"Thank you, Hans. Good day."

The silence surrounding Baxter was overwhelming. His suite overlooked the gardens and thoroughfare, and as he watched the procession of couples enter the building, he yearned for the sweet melody of Abigail's voice. He had no doubt she had received his letter but also understood that the need for discretion could have prevented her from engaging his correspondence. Although he ardently hoped she would join him there, he was also acutely aware of her potential refusal.

During the train ride from Calgary, he had considered the possibility of a residency in Banff without Abigail by his side. He would take his meals in his room, spend the afternoons in the garden and catch the train from Vancouver at the end of the week. He would venture to the hot springs each morning and bathe until the anguish of being alone left his weary heart. If she refused his offer, he considered that he may not even leave his room, and would instead shut the drapes tightly to block out the reality of Abigail existing in the world without him. With all of his time and energy focused on a negative outcome, he had not considered their itinerary if she did choose to join him.

As he awaited word of her arrival, he settled himself into the high-backed chair he had moved from across the room to set nearer the window. Although Abigail would not arrive for a few hours, he wanted to procure a vantage point that would allow him to see her first and afford him a few moments to calm his nerves before they met. He picked at the plate of potato hash that sat on the breakfast tray and resisted the urge to pull at the chain of his pocket watch for the sixth time that hour. He wanted for occupation but was cautious not to engage in any activity that would take him away from his perch. His eyelids grew heavy as he skimmed through *The Herald*, which was of little surprise since he had slept barely an hour the night before.

He leaned his head back and allowed his thoughts to drift into daydream. He imagined Abigail in her previous life and was curious if she had been as conformable in society as she was in nature. He wondered how she would have fared at his side on the frontier and if she would have felt at home within the wild and unforgiving terrain. He wanted to travel west on the Pacific and share the experience of riding the rails with her. He wished to see the excitement on her face when their railcar skirted the roaring cauldron at Hell's Gate. He wanted to see her first sight of the ocean and snickered as he pondered whether the pleading barks of the harbour seals would convince her to abandon prairie for sea.

A loud knock broke Baxter out of his reverie. He sprung from his seat and proceeded to the chamber's door when he realized he had lost track of the hour. The brass knob felt cool in his hands, and the resulting shiver worked to heighten his anxiety. He opened the door to find a porter holding a small manila envelope.

"Sorry to disturb, Mr. Carlisle, but there is a message for you."

Baxter took the letter and tipped the young man a fifty-cent piece before stepping back into his room and shuttering the door. As he examined the exterior of the envelope, he was overcome with apprehension. Although his recent encounter with Abigail made him feel certain of their mutual fondness, at the present moment, he was unsure. If the message merely stated that she was grateful for his offer but unable to attend on such short notice, he would take a deep breath and call on Hans to book a tea service in the parlour for later that afternoon. If the message, instead, relayed her disgust at the suggestion of such a rendezvous, he would take a nap and request a bottle of burgundy with his room-service Wellington.

He tore the envelope and removed the note.

Dear Mr. Carlisle,

A party is heading to Lake Louise tomorrow morning to view the waters and hike to the glacier's base. We will stop to take tea at the chalet. We would be pleased if you and Miss Delaney would accompany us. The carriage will depart from the front entrance tomorrow at 9:00 a.m. to board the train at 10:00 a.m. We will return on the evening train with enough time to rest and dress for dinner.

Hans

"How is it possible the note is not from Abigail?" he thought as he crumpled the letter into a tight ball. He checked the time and saw that the hands had ticked past two. He considered for a moment that the train had been delayed, but as he moved to the window, he could see the stream of carriages offloading guests as the empty omnibus bounded down the hill to await the evening traffic. He scanned the gravel road that led to the roundabout, trying to pick her out from amongst the gaggle of guests. The exercise was futile, however, for the patrons appeared too small, and the ladies' faces were obscured by the fashion for wide-brimmed hats.

He retrieved his sack coat from the back of the chair and moved down to the lobby. As he descended the stairs and entered the front hall, he was impressed by the number of new guests. At least twenty couples had arrived with him on the morning train, and another dozen were queued to check in. Baxter searched the room's perimeter with his eyes, hoping to notice Abigail's radiance from within the bustling crowd.

"Ah, Mr. Carlisle. Coming down to partake in the afternoon amusements, I see," Hans said as he observed Baxter's disorientation within a setting he was intimately familiar with. "Or perhaps you have come to confirm your inclusion in tomorrow's journey."

"I am sorry to say it is neither," he said as he abandoned his search and rested his elbow on the front desk counter. "I have come to inquire about my cousin, as she was expected to arrive on the afternoon train. Has she checked in yet?"

Hans looked down at the leather-bound ledger and noted the lack of signature beside her name.

"She has not, sir. Are you certain she was to arrive this afternoon? Perhaps you noted the incorrect date, and she will arrive tomorrow."

"You know I am more diligent than that, Hans," Baxter said with a kind smile. He understood in that moment that he had to do what he could to quell suspicion. "My aunt has not been well as of late. I wager Miss Delaney has stayed behind to care for her."

"Would you care to send a telegram? Perhaps send your condolences?"

"I thank you, but no. They live in a rather remote area, so there is no need."

"Well then, since you appear to be without a companion for the duration of your stay, there is no excuse for you not to join us tomorrow. We have several friends at the chalet who would be beside themselves to see you."

"Thank you, but I shall return to Calgary tomorrow."

"That would certainly be a shame. Surely you could manage one more day. You could at least take in a tour of the falls. I have a carriage that makes several trips each day."

Baxter was silent as he recalled the last time he had seen the Bow Falls. He had stood before the rushing water with Madeline who was unable to hide her captivation of the bright white water. He had finally found a place in the wildlands that she felt an affinity for.

"Say, have you heard anything of Eagle Claw? It would do me good to speak with him."

"He travels to the townsite once a week or so, but still spends most of his days downstream from the falls. With just a net and spear he is still the best fisherman in the valley, by far."

"Have you rods and tackle?"

"If they will entice you to stay on longer, I will deliver them to your driver myself."

"Splendid, Hans, thank you."

The spray from the falls coated Baxter with a thin layer of dew. The water barreled over the jagged outcroppings with such ferocity that he could tell it had been a long and snowy winter. There would be no brook trout in that much whitewater, and Eagle Claw would not waste the precious hours before midday so close to the falls; he would instead be found at the confluence of the Spray River.

Baxter slung the leather strap of the willow creel over his head, so the basket rested comfortably on his hip. With fly rod in one hand and walking stick in the other, he trekked the bank along a well-trod trail used for centuries by both the Nakota and the large game they hunted. The trail meandered along the edge and through the densely packed evergreens as the hollow beat of woodpeckers striking out their code led him to the sandbar on the northern bank.

The sun had risen past the fangs of Mount Rundle, illuminating the figure of Eagle Claw against the bright jade foliage. He did not see Baxter approaching, but with the intuition of his namesake, he was intensely aware that he was not alone. He scanned the river's banks for a lynx or coyote that may have wandered down to feed alongside him. It was not until he shaded the sun from his eyes and looked further downstream that he noticed the human shape. It was rare for tourists to traverse that far past the falls, so he carefully watched as the warbled figure intruded upon his solitude.

"Hau!" Baxter called as he approached. He removed his hat and smiled, hoping that his former guide would recognize him through years of hard travel and thick whiskers.

"Roaming Elk? It cannot be," Eagle Claw said as he released his reed net and let it fall atop the stones at the river's edge. "I never thought I would see you again. After Maddie, you drifted as seeds on the wind." He gave Baxter a firm handshake and consoling grip of his shoulder.

"I hardly know how I found myself back here, old friend," Baxter said as they hiked back to where Eagle Claw had left his gear.

"You have heard my song, Roaming Elk. Each night I sing with the coyote for those we have lost and those they have left behind."

Baxter followed Eagle Claw up to where his small shanty stood, a remnant of the modest shelters built to house surveyors from the Canadian Pacific. The elder had usurped the dilapidated cabin from a family of squirrels who had taken up residence once the workers abandoned it. Always the wanderer, it took the effects of old age to keep Eagle Claw from joining his tribe at Montana's border. With both his family and the buffalo expelled from the parklands, his only refuge from the aggressive easterners was the thick underbrush of forest.

The elder Nakotan navigated the steep embankment with the finesse of a mountain goat, while Baxter's agility was wanting. He was patient as he watched Baxter climb and offered him a gentle ribbing for his efforts.

"You hike like a lame otter. Where is the strong elk I once knew?"

Eagle Claw stamped the mud off his boots and kicked the shack's door jam with his toe to release the grip of any remaining pebbles. The small wood structure was only a single room and measured a mere eighty square feet. A blush grew under Baxter's whiskers at the realization that his temporary suite at The Banff Springs was larger than his friend's permanent home. While it was enough room for one man to live in relative comfort, it was a tight fit for two; it was fortunate that they enjoyed each other's company for there was no option but to be intimate in those close quarters.

The scent of jack pine filled the shanty, both from the walls surrounding them and the seasoned logs that Eagle Claw periodically placed in the small iron stove. The lodgepoles were hung with spears and traps, and a small stack of furs lay on the bench by the door. While most men trapped river otter, beaver and hare, Eagle Claw preferred the chase and used his experience to hunt lynx, wolf and coyote. He would journey the few miles to the townsite's modest post to exchange for coffee, sugar and pork. He had been introduced to smoked ham as a hikers' guide in Kananaskis and was more than willing to trade a week's work for a haunch.

"Come, be warm," he said as he removed another stack of fur from the room's only chair and motioned for Baxter to be seated near the fire. He took his place on the edge of his narrow cot and retrieved his pipe and tobacco from a small buckskin pouch.

"What brings you to these lands, Roaming Elk? The train is done. All the men left when you did. I thought you went home."

"The train through Banff is complete, that is true. But the web of tracks are expanding all over the district, from Fort Whoop-Up all the way to Edmonton and beyond."

"That will bring you much work, but it does not tell me why you are here."

Baxter sat for a moment and thought about what had brought him to Banff. He came with the intent of spending time with one woman but would leave in mourning of another.

"I suppose I wanted time away to think, to reconnect with a part of myself that I left behind long ago. Self-reflection is difficult here, though. I feel so small in these surroundings that it is hard to feel important at all."

"You were important to Maddie," Eagle Claw said as he poured him a cup of weak coffee.

"None of that seems to matter anymore," Baxter said as the reminder of his failings caused his voice to crack. He fell quiet as he stared at his wavering reflection in the tin cup, an image as distorted as his thoughts.

"I see you have not set aside the blame you put on yourself."

"How can I possibly when I was to act as her protector, and even against her objections I still brought her out here and put her in harm's way."

"She was your wife. It was her duty to follow where you led. She knew your life and your work and where it would take you both."

"But the blame is still mine."

Eagle Claw sat and watched as his head sunk lower; he could feel the pain that Baxter had held captive for the past twenty years. He knew him as a confident man who once knew nothing but freedom, but in that moment, he saw nothing but shame.

"See those traps there?" Eagle Claw said as he pointed to a wall of steel traps and sinew snares. "I go out each day and lay traps to catch game to eat, to live. Sometimes when I check the traps, I find a hare snared by his back leg. I watch him fight to get free."

"Do you release him?"

"He frees himself. The cuts and tears, the blood and pain last long after he breaks free. But even that small creature knows that the sting is better than being trapped."

Spring, 1905

Chapter Twenty-Seven

The hotel rose up from the prairie like a beautiful weed, its white sandstone façade gleaming in the morning sun. Abigail stood at her favourite spot on the lakeshore and felt the buildings oppression, even from a distance. There was to be a celebration that evening for The Carlisle's grand opening; Baxter and his staff had spent the last month furnishing the interior, stocking the pantries and wine cellars, and setting instruments in the ballroom in preparation for their first guests. Abigail had been steadfastly avoiding him, and if they by chance crossed paths in town, she still struggled to meet his gaze. The manner between them had been altered since their encounter in Red Deer the previous spring and evasion was the only way she could think to cope with his unwanted advances.

For many in the community, the hotel's opening was a cause for great joy. Through her conversations with the townsfolk, Abigail discovered that their understanding of the project was limited, and they merely hoped the station would bring additional income. As far as she was aware, Emma and

Tobias were the only folks other than the rail crew who knew the building's true purpose. She was explicit when she told Emma not to relay details of Baxter's business to Tobias, but she also understood the burden of secrecy and the intimacy of bedtime conversations.

As the sun continued its ascent, she stood on the banks of the south shore and raised her arms to the sky. She was warmed by the sun on her face, and as the birds continued their morning melodies, she felt compelled to join in. Although the birdsong was uplifting and optimistic, Abigail reverted to a folk song from her youth. As she sang the old colliery tune, she made it clear that she took no pleasure in the day's celebration.

The cruel melody drifted through the window of the master bedchamber. As Charles listened to the melancholy tune, he was dismayed that his wife's voice possessed little of the joy of the previous spring. The moments they spent together in Red Deer were amongst his most cherished memories, and he did not understand the alteration of her mood. Her demeanour was pleasant, but there was a preoccupation that overshadowed her usual affection; he wondered if the structure across the lake was to blame. He moved to the window and opened it wide. Abigail's song perfectly accompanied the tenor of his own emotions.

There were no guests in his hotel at present, a fact that Charles found at once distressing and of little surprise. Makeshift residences had appeared in the vacant spaces throughout town, with shop owners and tradesmen hoping to turn a profit in any manner that presented itself. He could not compete with offers for two-bit cots in rooms with ten others and the promise of an easy rest after a night of indulgence; he thought it prudent to close his doors for the evening so his family could partake in the festivities. It would also allow Charlotte time to view her husband's masonry work on the new station.

"Good day, sir," Tobias said, as Charles emerged from the kitchen with a cup of coffee in one hand and a small plateful of honey rolls in the other.

"Good morning, lad. I trust you both slept well?"

"Yes, sir, very well. Now that Gail is sleeping through the night, I feel me and Emma are in better spirits."

"I am glad to hear it."

With a nod and brief smile, Charles brushed past him and returned to his office without another word.

"I think your father is feeling in a bad way today, Emmy," Tobias said as he joined his wife and daughter at the kitchen table. "Maybe this party is just what he needs."

"I am quite certain it will take more than that," she said as she scooped a bit of currant jam onto a scone and urged Gail to take another mouthful. "I cannot account for his disposition, but I will say that he seems to grow more despondent the closer it gets to the opening ceremony. I cannot help but suspect that he knows more than we thought."

"I didn't say a word," Tobias said instantaneously, raising his hands to his chest in a plea of innocence.

"Of course not, Toby," she said as Gail squished the scone between her fingers and squealed with glee. "But when you consider how much time he spent in the company of Mr. Carlisle and his men, surely he must know something."

"Who must know what? Of what are you speaking, my love?" Abigail asked as she returned from outside and took her place at the table.

"Mr. Prescott, ma'am," Tobias said, averting his eyes.

"What must he know? That the building the railmen have toiled over for the last three years is actually a hotel? No, I believe Mr. Carlisle has hidden his true objective quite expertly."

"Then how would you account for his temperament?" Emma asked quietly, ashamed that she was questioning her father's behaviour.

Abigail subtly dismissed the question, for she did not want to give her family any indication that she was mindful of Charles' worsening manner. She had surmised that his withdrawal was a consequence of her friendship with Baxter and that he was acutely aware of the relationship.

"None of us enjoy the winters here and the months of cold and darkness that accompany it. Lengthening days and nature's signs of spring will certainly improve his state of mind."

* * *

The ceremony was to begin after tea with music and dancing reserved for the evening. Abigail did not care to change clothes for the event and wished that her threadbare dress and soiled apron would suffice. But with the rest of the town in their finery, as well as Charles' place as a special guest, she prepared her most elegant afternoon dress of periwinkle and cream. Emma had already dressed and taken baby Gail to stay with Mrs. Winters, whose gout forbade her from venturing far from home. Tobias was plainly attired and was busy readying the carriage for the short trip up the hill and around the lake.

Charles stood in his brocade waistcoat, white shirt and high collar and stared at his reflection as he tightened his cravat. Today he would play the part of the affluent hotel owner and would do his best to hold his head high whenever he was in Mr. Carlisle's view.

"You look very fine, my dear," Abigail said, as she moved beside him to take up her portion of the looking glass.

"As do you, Abby." As he stood in silence and watched his wife's ritual, he recalled occupying the same position beside her at her vanity in Kingston. Her reflection had altered, but even through skin aged by sun and wind, she still radiated with remarkable beauty. Charles, conversely, possessed dark eye circles enough to betray that he was no longer a member of the privileged class.

"I must admit, I am rather grateful for the opportunity to enjoy a full day of leisure," he said as he moved to the wardrobe to retrieve his grey woollen lounge coat.

"I believe we all are. Is it not amusing that we hope and pray for a full house, but are relieved when our rooms are empty?"

Abigail joined him at the wardrobe to retrieve a finely knit shawl Emma had given her the previous winter. Charles draped it over her shoulders and fastened the ends at her heart with a swallow-shaped brooch. He affixed the black and white enamel piece with its head pointed towards the sky and placed his hands on her shoulders.

"The physical exertion required to tend to a few guests is nothing to the mental exertion of worrying if they will arrive at all."

"We must hope, then, that the station brings guests to our door with the regularity of each passing train," she said as her eyes double-checked the freshly buffed scuff marks on her shoes.

The carriage bounced and shifted as Winnie trotted up the dirt road towards the celebration. Deep grooves were cut into the ground where hundreds of horses and wagons had irrevocably altered the landscape in much the same way as The Carlisle would forever alter the lives of the community. As they drew nearer, the structure grew larger until the breadth of it overtook their entire view. The Prescotts' perspective from their side of the lake was such that it provided little concept of its actual size until the whole of the crew, most of the town and a score of investors were gathered under its shade.

The citizens of Bowlea had assembled beside the structure more swiftly than the spring run-off in the Ashcroft Brook. Baxter watched from his office on the upper floor as the carriages parked in succession and the crowds pooled at the base of the front terrace. The pilgrimage of lower classes brought immense pleasure to the investors who had travelled from Calgary, Winnipeg and Toronto; as they contemplated the assured increase to their respective wealth, they took their places on the granite steps to await their leader. Meanwhile, the swarm of onlookers buzzed as they anticipated the nectar of fortune that rail line would bring.

"I never thought it would be finished," one man said.

"No sir, not these ten or twelve years," Mr. Winters added.

A hush came over the crowd as the large hardwood doors opened and the figure of Baxter Carlisle appeared. The townsfolk looked up at their benefactor in astonishment and halted their breath until he spoke.

"Ladies and gentlemen, townspeople of Bowlea. I would like to welcome you to our grand opening festivities. I would also like to take this opportunity to thank our investors whose resources have allowed us to push through the unrelenting cold of winter to finish ahead of schedule."

The crowd erupted into cheers and hurrahs; Baxter stood before them revelling in their admiration and applause. Their positive reception helped reassure him that his accomplishment would be a source of security and prosperity for the region. He reached into the inner pocket of his coat and retrieved what appeared to be a large, heavy nail.

"I would like to take a moment to bestow upon the Prescott family this railway spike as a token of thanks for welcoming us into their boarding house. They made it as comfortable for us as a home, and we shall never forget their kindness. Please join me in acknowledging Mr. Charles Prescott and his family."

The community turned their attention towards the family like wild daisies turning their heads towards the sun. Their appreciation made

Charles uneasy, for it felt as though they were celebrating his insolvency. As he looked over the faces of his friends and acquaintances, he was pleased that they would soon see an improvement in their quality of life. Abigail and Emma flanked him on either side and clapped so heartily that both were left with stinging palms. As he considered their future and wellbeing, he was overcome with sadness; he believed that while the other folks of Bowlea would prosper, his family would merely survive. Baxter's promotion to the rest of the town left him unaffected, and as they clung to each phrase he uttered, Charles looked up to the sky. He wondered how long it would take the vultures to begin their unceasing circles overhead.

"As you know," Baxter continued, "a project was undertaken some twelve years ago to bring the rail to this small community. Surveyors came, and promises of development were made. I am told that a great many people who staked their claim on that promise left Bowlea when it seemed that no progress would be made at all. Five years ago, my partners and I purchased this extension and saw the great possibilities for Bowlea as a transfer point to Red Deer, Edmonton and points beyond. As we continued our survey, we believed Bowlea could be a destination in and of itself. If you look behind you at the lake below, you can see the gift that God has left us. We would like to share this gift with the world. After years of careful planning and construction, we are ready to open our doors. May I present to you The Carlisle Hotel and West Central Station."

Gasps and confusion arose from the gallery as a man to his left pulled a thick rope cord to release the canvas tarpaulin that covered the chiselled lettering above the entrance.

"A hotel?" one of the men gasped.

"We ain't hear nothin' 'bout no hotel," said another.

"You withheld the truth from us, Mr. Carlisle," said Mr. Winters, whose disapproval was shared with many of the townsfolk.

"Charles, this must come as a shock," Abigail said in a whisper as she grasped his hand tightly and motioned to Emma and Tobias to return to the carriage. "Let us go. We can discuss this news at home."

"We are here now, let us hear what Mr. Carlisle has to say," he said, not budging from his place and maintaining a gruff countenance to ensure his prior knowledge of the revelation was well concealed.

"The truth was not withheld for any reason other than to allow us to work without questions or interruptions. This project, you see, is for the betterment of all of us. Mr. Winters, will you not be appreciative of increased mail traffic and increased sales in your grocery? And Mr. Harrow, we will require meats and eggs and fresh milk daily; that will surely mean an increase in your business, will it not? You can all be assured that I will be looking to the community for staff and goods before I source from elsewhere. I have placed advertisements in the rail station for a number of positions, all of which require staffing immediately. Now, if you will follow me, we have refreshments in the main hall." As Baxter turned and entered the hotel, it occurred to Abigail that although he had addressed the crowd's concerns, he had made no apologies.

As Charles followed his family through the threshold, the sheer size of the hotel overwhelmed him. Although he had watched carriages ferry goods to the worksite for months, he could not have imagined the splendour they were creating within those walls. As the beads of sweat began to form at the base of his spine, he looked around the room with panicked glances, seeking out the entrance with a desperate need to flee. As the procession of folks continued through to the hall, he could do little but join in on their admiration of the parquet hardwoods underfoot, the ornate tapestries in the staircases, and the rich oils that depicted the sweeping prairies that each guest would flock to see.

Abigail steadied herself on Charles' arm as the crowd moved through the corridor and into the train station. She could feel his body begin to tremble as Baxter took his place on the platform and turned to address them all.

"The first train will arrive from Calgary a week from tomorrow. On the community board, you will find postings for the available positions. You may apply to me with your interests and credentials."

As the group began to gather near the notice board, Emma pulled Tobias by the hand and snaked through to the front.

"Wait, wait! Where's the fire?" Tobias asked as more than one elbow found its way to his ribs.

"Perhaps there is work for us, Toby? I would so much like to stay in Bowlea," said Emma as her eyes swiftly scanned each advertisement. Although there were rumours of new collieries opening in Bellevue and Edmonton, Emma could not think of leaving her parents, or a home she had grown to dearly love. Tobias knew there was little money to be made at The Prescott, and even the extra work at Mr. Winters' was not enough to give him peace of mind. The uncertainty of their future caused more sleepless nights than baby Gail's colic, and while Tobias had no desire to separate his wife from her family, the welfare of his household was his chief concern.

"Look here, Emmy. They have their own livery!" Tobias declared. "I should talk to Mr. Carlisle right away."

As the crowd jostled to get sight of the postings, Baxter moved to the corner and motioned to Charles and Abigail to join him.

"Mr. Carlisle is calling us over, my love. I doubt either of us want to be the sheep to his wolf today. Come, let us return home. You have made an appearance, and there is no shame in going back to your own affairs. He cannot expect all business to cease on account of his celebration."

“He is no wolf, my dear. He is merely an opportunist,” Charles said, as he took her hand and walked towards Baxter.

“I wanted to thank you again, Mr. Prescott, for all you have done for us,” Baxter said as he extended his hand in conciliation. “We would not have been able to complete the job so swiftly without your kindness and hospitality.”

“You are quite welcome, sir,” Charles said with a studied affability that concealed his despondency. “While we had no hand in the actual construction, I am pleased to think that we helped all the same.”

“Indeed you have. As a thank you to you both, I would like to offer you a place in my hotel for the evening. The master suite is the finest in my establishment and includes a view of the lake. It would be a great honour to have you stay.”

“Thank you, but we did not bring our bedclothes,” Charles said as soon as the words passed Baxter’s lips.

“Perhaps your daughter and son-in-law could return to the hotel to gather your things. They would be welcome to stay on as well.”

“Thank you, Mr. Carlisle, but we would not wish to inconvenience you on such an important occasion,” Abigail said in Charles’ stead when she sensed his discomfort at the proposal.

“I should have invited you to stay to begin with. It was a poor showing on my part not to include you in tonight’s engagement. The investors have heard nothing but good things and would be pleased to have you. I will not accept your refusal. Come, let me show you the room.”

Charles’ feet clung to the polished hardwood like blocks of iron, and it took all of the strength he had to chug forward and follow Baxter’s lead. The room was situated on the third floor, and its position on the corner offered a panoramic view of the lake and settlement below. From his vantage point, Charles could see his property in the distance, with only the great expanse of water separating the two hotels.

"I am confident you will find everything you need here," Baxter said with a satisfied air.

"Yes, you certainly have fine rooms here, Mr. Carlisle. Any guest would be delighted to spend a night in such comfort," Charles said.

"You are very kind. I must return downstairs. The party for the townsfolk with continue until five o'clock and the investor's gala will commence at seven. I look forward to seeing you both there."

"Thank you, Mr. Carlisle. We will join in shortly," Abigail said as he handed her the room key and left their quarters.

As Charles peered out over the lake to its southern shore, his hotel seemed to ripple upon the bank like a mirage. Its appearance was so inconsequential that Charles felt as though he could reach out and pluck it from its foundation, place it in his breast pocket and conceal the effects of his poor decisions from everyone.

"Come, Charles, let us return downstairs," Abigail said as she moved in close and placed an arm about his waist. "Emma and Toby will be wondering."

He struggled to acknowledge his wife's request as the heaviness in his feet remained.

"You go on ahead, my dear. I shall head back home and retrieve our evening attire and bedclothes. Is there any particular dress you would like me to bring?"

In that moment, Abigail found the light streaming through the large windows excessive; she wished they were in their own drawing room where the dim light would have done well to conceal her worry. As she reached out and squeezed his hand, Charles could not recall a time when her skin was so pale; he thought its pallor was perhaps enhanced by the room's dark hardwoods. Although she feigned a smile and acted as though nothing was amiss, he could sense the absence of her usual cheerfulness. In her eyes was nothing of the gleeful young lady he courted, nor was there any inkling of her love for their life as it was now. As embers began to singe the innards of his belly, he felt certain that she shared his despair.

"Why not select the gown you would most like to see me in tonight?"

Charles looked at her and smiled as he remembered how often they would prepare for society events in Kingston.

"Do you remember how we used to dress together before dining at The Charlotte? I would wait until you were ready for your pearls just so I could kiss you right here," he said, caressing the spot under her ear.

"I think of those moments often. Just the two of us without distraction. If we must attend dinner, let us dress together. I no longer have my pearls, but I would welcome your kiss all the same."

A peach blush washed over her face as Charles took her head in his hands and kissed her softly. She was surprised at the marked change in his countenance and was pleased that he was able to remain upbeat considering the day's revelations. While her spirits were improved, Charles' face grew more sallow; he concealed his expression by embracing her tenderly and tilting his head to breathe in the comforting scent of her hair. As he placed a kiss atop her hand, he ushered her out the door and escorted her to rejoin Emma and Tobias in the main hall.

"Would you like to stay the night?" Emma asked as Tobias filled his plate with date squares and egg salad sandwiches.

"I would like to spend the night at home with you and Gail. Could we stay for dinner, though?" he asked as he picked up a butter tart and stuffed it in his mouth.

Emma giggled and agreed that a fine supper uninterrupted by shrieking refusals to eat would be most welcome.

"Why don't you go along with your father and pick up your evening clothes?"

"There is no need, Mama. These clothes are as nice as any we have at home, and besides, Tobias owes me a dance."

"Very well," Abigail said. "If you hurry back, Charles, we will have time to dress before cocktails."

Charles watched as his daughter and her young husband dashed into the midst of the other swirling couples on the dance floor. Emma knew the waltz from her fumbling attempts to perfect the simpler arrangements of Strauss' work but had only ever danced in practice with her mother. This version of the song worked well to entertain all manner of folk, as formality and technique were not required. Still, Tobias took her hand in his and led her to the far corner of the hall, for he was shy in admitting his ignorance of the steps. Emma was patient and kind and tried to teach him as they danced. He was tense and awkward, and her laughter when he tread on her toes was endearing to anyone fortunate enough to see it.

Charles left Abigail's side and moved to where the pair were doubled over in laughter. He separated them with a quick tap on Tobias' shoulder and then took his daughter's hand. He placed a hand on the small of her back and took a leading step forward.

"I never realized you were a such a good dancer, Papa," she said as he took her through the languid turns of the song's first bars.

"You appear to be similarly accomplished. Your mother has taught you well."

Charles moved through the dance with a practiced elegance that had not been employed since the last Kensington Ball he attended in Kingston.

As he led her through each movement, he was reminded of the long hours he spent with Mrs. Cunningham working to impress Abigail with his delicate steps.

"I must apologize to you, petty," he said as he slowed the pace to make it easier to converse.

"Whatever for?"

"You were never allowed a proper debut. The young men would have lined up all the way down Queen Street for a dance with you."

"I would never have done well in society, Papa. I always preferred the company of you and mother."

"You have been fortunate to have Tobias' friendship too. There is no pretention there."

"He is all I could have hoped for."

Charles looked over to Abigail, who smiled as she tried to teach Tobias the basic steps of the dance.

"There looks to be a great many opportunities on the job board. You know you are welcome to take any that are of interest to you. You must remember that the most important thing is the welfare of your child. It pains me to say so, but you will be able to earn more here than I am able to pay. Tobias would do well to get on as a bellman or porter. He is capable and has a good way with people."

"Even though we may find employment elsewhere, I hope you know that we will be there to support you and Mama. The Prescott is our home, and I could not dream of leaving. We will stay on as long as we are welcome."

"Then you shall stay forever."

The music stopped as the pair took their final steps, and Charles dipped Emma into their final pose. As she again stood straight, she laughed heartily and took her father in a warm embrace.

"Thank you, Papa. I will expect another dance after supper."

She kissed him on the cheek and weaved between the couples who milled about and waited for the next dance. As she rejoined Tobias and Abigail, Charles remained fixed in his spot near the centre of the room. The faint sound of his family's laughter harmonized with the string quartet, and he could barely see them through the twirling twosomes. As he caught short glimpses of his daughter speaking with Tobias, he was overcome with grief; it pained him greatly to know that she would never be a guest at The Carlisle, and would only ever be in service to the people who stayed there.

Baxter's office was adjacent to the front desk; as Charles moved through the lobby towards the entrance, he noticed his host slip away for a moment's respite. He quickened his pace and approached the open door, unconcerned that he was interrupting one of the few moments of privacy the gentleman had experienced all day.

"Excuse me, Mr. Carlisle. Might I have a word?" Charles asked after a quick rap on the door's threshold.

"Mr. Prescott, you seem to be right on time. I was just coming to refill my cigar case," Baxter said as he pointed to one of the padded chairs in the centre of the room. "Come, join me."

"I can see why you would be anxious for a rest. It is certainly quite the occasion," Charles said as he entered the room and took a seat. He looked up at the ornate filigree that bordered the ceiling and the emerald green vines that papered the walls. "I suspect that my entire first floor could fit into your office."

"I daresay I should not show you my master chamber."

Baxter's attempt at wit was lost on Charles, who offered little more than a few blinks in return.

"You seem to have done very well for yourself, Mr. Carlisle," he said as Baxter struck a match and puffed his cigar to ignition.

"My success did not come without sacrifice, I can assure you." Baxter held out his cigar case and insisted that Charles join him.

"You must feel gratified that your endeavours have seen a positive return. I understand that this is but one of your properties."

"It is all relative, Mr. Prescott. You have the good fortune to have your family around you, and a dear wife with whom to share your life."

"And you have the good fortune to have fortune."

"Money can buy a great many things, but it cannot buy the intimacy of relationships or the loyalty of family. It is hard to know who to trust in this business. That is why I feel so privileged to have met you and your family. I have never once doubted your intentions. You run a fair business and operate your life with honour and pride. I admire your resolve a great deal."

Charles took a long, slow drag from the finest cigar ever to touch his lips and wondered how a man of Baxter's status could hold him in esteem.

"You mentioned that the first train from Calgary is to arrive next week."

"Yes, the first of the luxury cars. With a new set of visitors set to arrive weekly, we should be at near-capacity for most of the summer."

"Will their porters require lodging?"

"Our staff quarters are well-appointed, and they will be staying downstairs during their masters' stay." Baxter could sense that his response was not welcome to Charles, who he believed to be anticipating lodgers of his own.

"I would not fret, Mr. Prescott," he continued. "The first few trains will be luxury cars, but it is only a matter of time before transport trains arrive with settlers and their families. We are going to be at the forefront of expanding this region. It will be a very exciting time for your little town."

As he spoke, feelings of rage percolated within Charles; he could hardly believe that Baxter would dare placate him with forecasts of future business.

"Do you recall the offer you made to me when you first came to Bowlea, Mr. Carlisle? You said that the south side of the lake was very fine, and the location of my hotel provided the ideal vantage point."

"Yes, I recall."

"Since you can see the infinite potential of our little town, perhaps you would again be interested in purchasing my hotel?"

"You mean to offer your business?" Baxter asked, immediately concerned about Abigail's welfare. "How can you possibly consider selling now that the rail line is open? Surely you must see the possibilities!" He winced at his own salesmanship, but could not imagine his life in Bowlea without Abigail's presence. He assumed that Charles would take whatever sum he earned from The Prescott's sale and return to Kingston.

"When I refused your offer of purchase, I was foolhardy. I thought the train would come through and solve all of our problems. Instead, all it has done is magnify them. We cannot subsist on a few bookings per week."

"Is it not premature to judge the extension's success? We are only just beginning."

"I have every belief that the line will be successful, and for that, you must be very proud. But when you consider the clientele and differences in our establishments, the outcome is clear. Be honest when you tell me who would want to stay in a simple brick boarding house with a mere dozen rooms when they could stay here?"

"Having stayed in your rooms myself, I can say that you take pride in your work, and pride in your family. There is a warmth and friendliness there that cannot be bought with hired staff."

"Because we cannot afford any."

Baxter shifted in his seat and reached for his glass of brandy.

"I understand your position, but I cannot purchase your property. We have already built and no longer have a need for that land."

Charles snuffed out his cigar and rose from his seat.

"I am sorry for having taken up your time, especially today. I will not keep you from your celebration any longer."

"Perhaps we can work out a loan or some other way to make your life more comfortable," Baxter said as he considered Abigail's future. "The young lad is familiar with the workings of your hotel, is he not?"

"Tobias has stood over my shoulder and watched me for years, but I maintain the ledgers myself. He helps mainly with the livestock and gardens."

"If he has seen the inner workings of a boarding house, the rest is easy enough to teach. I have a proposal for you, Mr. Prescott. I have placed an advertisement in *The Herald* for an assistant manager. What would you say to coming on board? I could offer you a steady salary, and I know from your work ethic and attention to detail that you are just the sort of person I need at my side."

As Baxter droned on through the terms of his offer, Charles was overcome with the sensation of thousands of embroidery needles pricking the tips of his fingers and toes. The bookshelves on either side began to spin as the ceiling overhead drooped as if laying its full weight upon his shoulders. He had a similar reaction upon hearing the news of his mother's death; since the tingling in that instance had preceded a fainting spell, he interrupted Baxter's monologue without hesitation.

"Thank you, Mr. Carlisle. I have known you to be generous, and you have reaffirmed it with your kind offer. That being said, I must decline. As an entrepreneur yourself, you know doubt understand my reasoning. I bid you good day, and good luck."

Once Charles departed, Baxter skirted the edges of the crowd that still occupied the main hall. He spied Abigail in conversation with her daughter and did not wish to disturb them; he moved instead to take up his place amongst his investors on the opposite side of the room. He wondered what the ladies could be discussing, and doubted he would have anything to contribute to their conversation.

"You should see the number of positions there are, Mama," Emma said as Tobias joined them at one of the small tables that bordered the dance floor. "The wages are more than fair."

"There will no doubt be many folks who find themselves working for Mr. Carlisle," Abigail said as she watched the members of the crew and community enjoying the music.

"One can hardly fault them when it means a better quality of life," Emma said. Her mother cast a reproving glance that cautioned her to be less expressive in her gratitude towards the hotel's owner.

"Come on, Emmy. I think I've got this sorted out," Tobias said as he pulled her hand and led her into the dance.

Abigail smiled as Tobias moved through the crowd and scuttled his bottom out towards the other dancers in order to create more space. His steps were slow, yet confident, and Emma beamed as she gave her mother a quick look of thanks. As she watched the young couple dance as though there were no cares in the world, her thoughts were with Charles. She was grateful for a moment of solitude to consider her surroundings and the impact of such opulent competition.

As the investors around Baxter discussed the residency of several hundred guests over the course of the summer, his thoughts were elsewhere. The moment he spied Abigail alone, he sprang from his seat and hurried to request a seat beside her.

"I daresay, this is a far sight nicer than The Regent," she said as she admired the large paintings of prairie birds hung along the hall's perimeter.

"This is my favourite of our properties. I wished I owned it outright, but there is an option in my contract to buy in five years if we prove successful."

"I have no doubt you will be. You know, although I knew this building's true purpose all these months, I could never have imagined the interior. The craftsmanship is quite remarkable."

"You were the inspiration for this room. It is called the Songbird Ballroom. I never paid much attention to music until we met, but hearing your gift has made me appreciate all of nature's melodies."

"I am honoured, Baxter, thank you. I imagine there will be many fine balls in this room. It is decorated so beautifully."

"Will you be gracing us with one of your lovely tunes this evening, Mrs. Prescott?" Mr. Smythe said as he interrupted the pair and took Abigail's hand for a kiss.

"Tonight is all about Mr. Carlisle, and I would do nothing to distract from that."

"Just your presence here is distraction enough," Baxter said with a playful wink.

"It is a shame that your wife was not able to attend," Abigail said as she worked to dismiss his flattery. "Is this not your crowning achievement?"

"Sadly, Madeline left us before she could see any of our properties,"

Mr. Smythe said with a low shake of his head.

"Surely as railmen, you could set her up with a ticket."

"A ticket?" he asked confusedly. "Heaven is not one of the stops on the Northern Pacific's route, I'm afraid."

"Come now, Reggie. I can see Bennett is looking for you. You would not want to miss a chance at promotion," Baxter said as he grabbed his partner's arm and steered him in the direction of the investor.

"I thought your wife was in Toronto?" Abigail asked in a state of confusion. "I have not misunderstood. I heard it from your own lips. She could not handle the wildlands and so detached from you to return home. Is that not what I heard? Is that not what you said?"

"Please understand, Abigail. I never intended to tell you a falsehood."

"And yet you told it all the same." She could feel the colour rise in her cheeks. Instead of the usual cause of her flush being Baxter's flirtations, she was now affected by anger and betrayal. "Excuse me. I must take some air."

She weaved through the crowd, making her way to the large front terrace. Baxter followed, navigating through the calls of congratulations and slaps on the back to catch up to his friend.

"Abigail, wait!"

The terrace was not as crowded as it was inside, for as the sun dipped below the hills, the music's change of tempo called many folks to return inside for a dance while others headed back down the hill towards home. The few people who remained to watch the kaleidoscope upon the lake's surface took no notice of Baxter as he hurried to where Abigail stood against the carved stone railing. Her drawn face and sloped shoulders signalled him to approach with caution for fear of upsetting her further.

"You are rather adept at telling lies, Mr. Carlisle. I see now why you are so keen to form acquaintances with strangers. No one who knew you would put any faith in your word at all. And why should they?"

"Abigail, please allow me to explain," he said as he encroached further to stand beside her. Her usual energy, which was enough to entice him to pine for her from across the lake, was now warning him to maintain his distance.

"I have no desire to listen to anything you have to say unless it is the absolute truth. I now wonder if that is something you are even capable of."

"Madeline did have an aversion to the wilderness. That is the truth. She was never fully comfortable accompanying me on my surveyance, but because of the deep love we felt for each other, she accompanied me, regardless. For three years she worked with the other wives to take care of us and the camp. Things were so different then. During the early contracts with the Pacific, it was quite literally man against nature. All but one of the crew brought their wives along. Without our Indian guides, we would have had no idea how to navigate the wildlands; but were it not for our wives, we would not have had the strength to continue. They supported the crew in whatever way they could."

"When did she leave the party and return back home?" Abigail asked with unwavering anger as her gaze remained fixed on her home across the lake. As Baxter formulated his excuse, she could think only of Charles; in the whole of their relationship, she could not think of a time when he had told such a hurtful and deliberate lie.

"She did not return home," he said as his head drooped lower. "We were just north of Roger's Pass, and part of the crew tasked with surveying the route for a bridge that was to pass over an offshoot of the Columbia River. Our guides had warned us of the danger of hungry bears in the early spring. They warned us to maintain a safe distance from the elk, particularly when they were rutting or calving. They warned us of the wolves that were so vicious they would eat the weakest of their own cubs.

"The terrain in that part of the country was rough and unstable. We travelled on horseback with pack mules, and did not have the option to sleep above ground in a carriage or covered wagon." Baxter paused for a moment when his voice began to crack. She turned to face him when his pain could no longer be concealed. Against her better judgement, she grasped his hand, and with a gentle squeeze, urged him to continue.

"We had set up camp that day on the plateau above the river's banks. Maddie had not been feeling well all day and was having a fitful night's sleep. I shared her unrest until I finally dozed off. I am not sure of the hour. My exhaustion was so great, and my sleep so deep that I did not notice her get up and leave the tent."

"Why would she leave?"

"That is a question I have asked myself a thousand times, and one I will never have an answer to. It was not until I heard her screams over the growl of the wolves that I finally awoke. By the time I got to her," he said, pausing when the constriction in his throat became too tight. He closed his eyes and drew a shallow breath. "It was too late."

Abigail released his hand and stood motionless as her mouth gaped at his revelation. Although he spared her the gruesome intricacies of what occurred upon the pitch dark riverbank that night, and the sight he beheld at camp the morning after, she felt the tragedy would not be out of place in one of Emma's N.W.M.P. adventure serials. She felt the bite of tears in her eyes and wiped them away as he continued.

"When I told you that Madeline was alive and well back in Toronto, it was not you I was lying to, but myself. It has become my custom when travelling to tell strangers that she was back home and we would reunite when I was more established. It was easier to avoid the awkwardness of explaining her absence and the pain of reliving her death. That night at The Regent was the first time you and I had met. It was easy for me to tell you that lie because, quite frankly, I never thought I would see you again."

Abigail turned back towards the lake. Although Charles' disposition was often taciturn, she was thankful she was still able to spend time each day in his company and each night in his arms. She could not fathom being forced to exist without him.

"When we met again," he continued, "I was so pleased because you reminded me very much of the life I lost, of what was left behind. You embodied the life I could have had if only…"

"But we have spoken of her many times, even after I was no longer a stranger," she said angrily. "I thought you trusted me enough to be forthright."

"What was I to say? How would I even have broached the subject? As our intimacy and friendship grew, I could think of no occasion to reveal such news."

"You are fortunate, then, to have been spared the discomfort by Mr. Smythe's indiscretion."

"If I am to be perfectly honest with you, as I should have been from the first moments of our acquaintance, it is likely I would never have spoken the truth about her. In a way, never speaking of her death makes it less real. In my heart, she is alive and well and waiting for me."

The light from the large lanterns along the edge of the terrace helped to conceal the tears that had formed in the corners of his eyes. As Abigail turned to face him, her feelings were so contrary that she did not know how to react. A part of her wanted to yell and scream and pound his chest as punishment for being a distrustful brute. Another wanted to hold him tight and soothe him with a gentle sway to let him know he was not alone in the world. A soft utterance of, "I am sorry for your loss," was all she could manage.

Chapter Twenty-Eight

Winnie ambled towards The Prescott with no design at all on getting there quickly. In normal circumstances, Charles would have given a sharp snap of the reins to her rump, but he was in no hurry to arrive back home or to return to the party. The bustle from the celebration drowned out the sound of the rising night, and the crickets and frogs were only noticeable once the carriage had rounded the east bend and began its final descent towards town. Each of the horse's steps echoed the throbbing behind Charles' eyes, and even the cool sweep of air from the lake could not calm his racing thoughts.

As the carriage crawled closer to The Prescott, he could not help but notice that it appeared miniature, even when it was close enough to encompass the whole of his view. A rough-and-tumble barn flanked the left side, and the rear was occupied by wash basins and clotheslines. There was a well-trod path to the lake with old tree stumps and boulders as the only seats along the shore. There was no marble or limestone, and upon the greyed wooden planks of the verandah stood only a few wicker chairs and Charles' favourite ash rocker. Small windows stood at intervals along the second floor, and the only enticement to enter was a sign, chipped and worn, that Charles had painted himself.

The mental exhaustion of the previous three hours had left Charles with barely enough energy to dismount the carriage and tie Winnie to the hitching post. The sensation of spinning had not yet ceased, but his surroundings had certainly altered. The fine decor of Baxter's office was replaced by simple country furnishings, which appeared even more plain without fine oils or tapestries to enhance them. The front desk felt as diminutive as a school pew, and the sums written in his ledger were equally slight. The bare wooden floorboards creaked under his weight as he moved through the kitchen and into his bedchamber. Their room at The Carlisle was embarrassingly large, and as Charles looked about his master suite, he wondered how they had ever found comfort in such close quarters.

He stood before his wardrobe and selected the only garment he owned that was appropriate for such an occasion – his bridegroom suit. He laid it atop the bed and brushed the wool gently to revive the tired fabric. For Abigail, he chose the pretty peach gown she wore for her Founder's Day performance, gently laying it beside his suit and smoothing down the folds of the fabric with the palm of his hand. He knelt down and retrieved their good shoes from an old potato sack under the bed.

As he set the shoes on the floor under their respective outfits, he was overcome with emotion. He grasped onto the side of the bed and fell into deep sobs. He shivered as he wept and tried to understand how he could have had such poor judgement on so many occasions. While his decision to move to Bowlea was made in haste, he did not feel it was ill-informed.

He had made inquiries to friends and colleagues about prospects in the west, and they seemed viable. He had taken a risk and reaped little reward save for the torment of having ruined the lives of his wife and daughter.

With all of the strength he could muster, Charles gripped the quilt tightly and pulled himself onto the bed to sit next to the gown. Its beaded fabric was blurred by his free-flowing tears; he reached into his breast pocket for the handkerchief from Abigail. Presented to him in the garden of Mrs. Cunningham's estate, the token represented a promise of their future. In that moment, he felt it signified the shortcomings of his past. With the threadbare cloth, he wiped the tears from his eyes and cheeks and tried to collect himself. He held his breath as he pushed down through his legs and regained an unsteady standing position.

Even through sniffles and the pounding in his head, Charles could feel a steady polka beat bounce across the lake from The Carlisle. As he heard the music's call, he was drawn into the kitchen, through the lobby and up the stairs to his office. He swung the door wide and walked towards the small chest that sat under his desk. In the years preceding Emma's sixteenth birthday, Abigail had spent each Sunday evening crafting wares to fill her hope chest. Charles had been unable to afford one of the fine cedar chests that were suitable for young ladies coming of age, so he made her a rough sawn version from old barn board instead. When she saw his simple craftsmanship and the effort he took to delicately paint the top and sides with vines and wild pink roses, she urged him to make one for himself. She felt it unfair for the token of hope to be reserved only for her. Instead of a trousseau, the miniature version he fashioned for himself contained his secret supply of cheap brandy and a two-dollar pistol from Sears-Roebuck.

Charles reached into the box and pulled out the bottle, smoothing over the peeled paper label with his thumb.

Live the Good Life. Bull's Brandy. Medicine Hat, Alberta. 1903.

As he read the faded words, he unscrewed the top. The warm liquor stung his tongue and he felt a burning in his chest as it moved down to the pit of his belly. The sensation of pain was a welcome relief, and he took another large swig to temper his misery. After another few nips, he set the bottle down and retrieved a small bundle of canvas from the barnboard chest. He pulled down the lead latch of his office window and pushed the pane outwards, swinging it open until it bumped the exterior wall.

The revolver felt heavy, and the simple steel mechanics of the piece rattled in his grip. As he closed his eyes and cocked the hammer, he was tortured by the thought that his family would be elated when they discovered that they no longer had to yield to his will. He placed the gun's barrel against his temple.

"My dears, Abigail, Emma," he sobbed with a forced breath. "This will be my final failure."

***

"What is keeping father? We would like to head home and need the wagon," Emma said through winded breaths as she and Tobias surrendered their place on the dancefloor to rejoin Abigail at their table. "Mrs. Winters will want to get to bed soon."

"He should be arriving any moment, my love. Perhaps he is having trouble with my choice of gowns."

"Still, he has been gone for nearly two hours. Surely there is nothing that could delay him for so long."

"Perhaps he has received some new guests, as he was hoping. I would not fret, my love."

"If that is the case, how will we get back to town?"

"Pardon the interruption, but is there something wrong?" Baxter asked as he cautiously approached them. "I have not seen Mr. Prescott for a while now."

"We have been expecting him," Abigail said, straining to conceal her lingering displeasure towards him. "He appears to be taking his time."

"If it would be more convenient for you to stay another time, I would be happy to return you to Bowlea. If we leave straight away, I will be back in time for supper."

"You are very kind, Mr. Carlisle, but we would never dream of removing you from your own party. Surely you have a man who could be spared?"

"Nonsense. I should be very glad to be relieved of my duties."

"Where is the wagon?" Abigail asked as Baxter's carriage approached The Prescott.

"Whoa!" Baxter cried as he pulled back the reins and stopped in front of the hotel.

"There!" Emma said, pointing to Winnie wandering down the lane with reins dragging in the dirt behind her.

"She must have wrangled free," Abigail said as her furtive glances around town made it clear that unexpected guests were not the cause of Charles' delay.

"I'll fetch her," Tobias said as he hopped down from the carriage.

"After she is tied, could you stop by Mrs. Winters? I'll prepare Gail's bed," Emma said. With a smile and quick nod, he sprinted towards the wayward horse.

A dim light emanated through the windows on the main floor, and an even fainter glow painted the upstairs windows. Abigail was drawn into the hotel by a curiosity that usurped any consideration for those with her. As she ascended the steps with Emma close behind, she forgot that her escort was even there.

"Would you like me to wait? Perhaps you both can join us after all," Baxter said as Abigail turned the cold iron handle and pushed the door open.

"Yes, perhaps. I will check and see what is keeping Charles. It will take me but a moment to prepare a bag."

"Thank you for a lovely evening, Mr. Carlisle," Emma said with a broad smile that signalled her approval. "Were it not for my daughter, I would have danced all night. You may wait inside if you like."

"Thank you, but I would prefer to take in the evening air."

Abigail stepped into the lobby and immediately called out for Charles. The fires had been out since morning, and the cold air instantly enveloped her and sunk through her skin.

"Charles?" Abigail called. She waited a moment and called out again.

"Where is he, Mama?" Emma asked as she followed her into the kitchen. The candle on the counter near the sink was still lit, with the flame gasping for fuel as it burned down to the sconce. The door to their master chamber was ajar, and the lamplight cast a welcoming path onto the kitchen floor. Abigail called Charles' name as she approached. With Emma at her side, she entered the room and was confused when she discovered it empty. Instead of Charles, she found their evening clothes.

"See, Mama, he is just laying things out and preparing your bags. I wager he forgot something upstairs or had a matter to attend to before going back to the party."

"Yes, that could be," Abigail said confusedly as she stared down at the bed. Her dress was laid out carefully, with her mother's brooch festooned on the shoulder. Abigail received it after her death and was told it would bring her love and happiness for the rest of her life. As she fingered the silver, she was touched by his sentiment to include it. She then noticed the handkerchief in the breast pocket. She reached forward and removed it, allowing it to blossom in her hand like the flowers that adorned it. As she ran her fingers over the violets she had lovingly stitched for him, she noticed the peculiar way in which the clothes were arranged; the delicate lace of her dress' sleeve was wrapped around the arm of Charles' suit.

"Charles?" Abigail called out as she lifted her head and shouted through the ceiling.

"Come, Mama. Surely he is occupied and not paying attention. You know how he gets when he is looking over his figures."

Abigail hurried to the stairs and began her ascent with Emma following behind. She had hollered for him to come to supper many times before and knew it was not for lack of hearing that he did not respond. She understood that the events of the day were overwhelming for him, and was not surprised that he would take a few minutes to collect his thoughts before returning to The Carlisle.

The acrid smell of burnt gunpowder hung in the air and stung Abigail's nose as she rounded the corner into the hall. The wind whipped up from the lake and banged the open window hard against the shutter. She entered the room with Emma's hand gripped tightly in hers; her eyes fixed immediately on the open box under the window and the flickering lamp beside it. As she moved nearer to it, the light glinted off the gunmetal as it lay next to Charles' limp body.

Abigail rushed to his side and dropped to her knees. The fabric of her dress began to absorb blood from the pool around him. She could barely breathe as she hunched over his body, but she was still able to elicit a scream. Tobias heard the cries as he placed Winnie in her corral, and rushed towards Baxter who extinguished his cigar and hurried to the source of the shriek.

"Emma!" Tobias called out as feelings of panic constricted his throat. "Emma, where are you?"

"Toby, please hurry! It's Father!"

Through symphonic wails and cries, the young lad scaled the stairs as fast as he could, pushing the gentleman aside as he bumbled forth in rescue. As he entered the office, he was wholly unprepared for the sight before him. Even when his father had been gored to death, he was spared such a sight, for the dirt had absorbed most of the blood.

"It must have been a bandit!" Tobias cried, rushing to Emma's side to console her as she held her mother.

"No, Toby. There was no bandit," Emma sobbed. "The shot came from own hand."

Baxter froze and braced himself on the door's threshold the moment he saw Abigail's face. In her arms lay the lifeless body of her husband; she could not speak for the uncontrollable sobs which overtook her. Baxter shuddered as he beheld the scene, and resisted his instinct to rush to her side. She caught sight of him through her swollen eyes and gripped Charles closer to her breast.

"Look what you have done!" she screamed. "This is all your doing!" Her stare was cold and pierced Baxter with the force of a bullet.

"Calm yourself, Mama. Now is not the time to make accusations," Emma said as Tobias held her tightly.

"Not the time?" Abigail raged as she laid Charles back down on the ruby-stained floorboards and returned to her feet. She was visibly trembling and unable to contain her sorrow. "What better time than when the blood is still warm on my hands. Has the blood on yours cooled yet, Mr. Carlisle?"

"I had nothing at all to do with this. Abigail, you must see that I had nothing whatever to do with it."

"How much did he have to suffer for you to be satisfied? If only Charles had known your true intentions, this could have been prevented," Abigail sobbed. Emma held her tight across the shoulders to keep her from falling.

"He did know," Baxter said, distressed that he was forced to reveal a betrayal of her trust for the second time that evening. "I told him within days of my arrival. I withheld nothing. I only asked that he remain silent on my business dealings so we could build quickly and in peace. I meant nothing but goodwill. Even today, I offered him a position as one of my managers."

"You mean to tell me he knew of it all along? And you had the gall to offer him work? Your arrogance is astounding. Can you not imagine the pain he would have suffered in helping your hotel succeed while his was left to rot?"

"That is quite enough, Mama," Emma said with a measured scold. "Let us send for a doctor."

"A doctor when he lay dead at my feet? No, bring him the reverend. He will do well for Mr. Carlisle as well."

Chapter Twenty-Nine

Tobias moved about the upper floor as quickly as he could, removing the sheets from a number of guest beds in order to help contain the blood. He laid out a patchwork quilt in the centre of the office and squatted down behind the body. As he reached under the pits of Charles' arms to hoist him, he nearly fainted at the sight of his missing quadrant of skull. For a slight man, Charles' body was heavy, and although Tobias could not imagine asking his wife to move the corpse of her dead father, he wished there was someone to give him help. He lay the rigid body in the centre of the quilt and tucked the edges in tightly around him. He covered Charles' head and face with a linen pillowcase.

Emma placed her mother's arm about her neck and raised her from her knees. Numbness had taken over the lower part of Abigail's body, which did well to moderate the pain that trembled through her. As the pair moved out of the office and down the stairs, it was only their reliance on each other that allowed them to reach the main floor. Emma walked Abigail to the kitchen and sat her down at the table. She was unsure of what to say, but knew it did not matter; even if she spoke, her mother would not hear her. Abigail stared forward and gently rocked herself, hunching over to protect what was left of her heart.

Dishware clanked as Emma flitted about the room and tried to assemble the makings of a cup of tea. She was desperate for occupation; ensuring her mother's welfare had left her little chance to acknowledge her father's death. She stopped milling about when she caught sight of her mother examining the thick layer of drying blood on her hands and forearms. Emma looked down at her own painted fingers and shuddered at the sight. She inspected the skirt of her dress and was astonished to find only the smallest of spatters along the hemline.

"Come along, Mama. Let us wash up," she said as she took Abigail's hand and led her outside to the small bathhouse. She sat her down to rest on the stool beside the tin tub.

"I will light the lamp if you would take care to remove your clothes. I will place them all in the fire."

"Never mind the lamp," Abigail muttered as she fumbled with the ribbon at her neck and made the stuck knot even tighter. Emma reached out and took the satin strand in her hand. She picked the bump with her nail and loosened it enough to pull the long end through to untie it.

"There we are. Carry on. I will fetch the hot water for the basin."

Abigail reached down and grasped her daughter's hand as she turned back towards the kitchen.

"The reverend will arrive shortly," she said in a low, morose tone. "I will need two or three towels, at least. And a face cloth."

"Yes, Mama. Straight away."

Emma lit the fire and prepared the kettle with a speed that highlighted how welcome the tasks were for her state of mind. As she waited for the pot to squeal, she wandered into her parent's bedchamber to retrieve fresh clothing for her mother. When she entered the room and saw her father's shoes, she could no longer suppress her grief.

"Why did you do this, Papa?" she said aloud as she sobbed into her hands. "Why would you do such a thing? You cannot be gone. You cannot."

She steadied herself on the back of her father's dressing chair and shuddered as she failed to catch her breath. Her nerves were soothed when the scent of wild rose drifted through the open window. She was reminded of the flowers they would pick near Ashcroft Brook, and his request to always handpick the petals for her mother himself.

The wail of the kettle matched the pitch of Abigail's first cries and tore through Emma with a vicious bite. She rushed to the stove to remove the pot from the fire only to reach out and grab the scorching handle without a mitt. The sharp sting of pain that pulsed through her palm was matched only by the throbbing in her head. She could not envision her life without him.

Abigail sat on the stool and watched as the prison bar shadows from the bathhouse planks gripped her unclothed body. Her skin twinged with each gasp of air that passed through the slats.

"Here you are, Mama. Good and hot," Emma said as the numbness affecting her mother crept into her own limbs, and she struggled with the cumbersome kettle. She poured the water into the basin to mix with the cool well water and tested the temperature with her fingertips. She added castile soap and a twig of rosemary and swished the facecloth around until it frothed. She gave the cloth a gentle squeeze before holding it out for her mother to take. Abigail stared forward and gave no indication that she was even aware of Emma's presence in the room.

"They will be here soon, Mama," she urged while taking her mother's hand and gently leading her to stand before the basin. "Here, I will help you."

Emma wiped the blood from her mother's skin in long, swift strokes. She was methodical in her movements and paused only to rinse the crimson cloth, believing that speed would somehow lessen her mother's grief at having held her dead husband in her arms just minutes before.

"How could he have done such a thing?" Abigail cried as she placed her hands on either side of the basin's edge and began to tremble. "We have faced hard times before, but…"

Emma wrapped her mother's shivering body in a blanket and led her into her bedchamber. She tried to calm her by rubbing her upper back in small circles like she did whenever Gail was distraught.

"It is not for anyone to understand, Mama. Those who commit such an act do so for reasons of their own. Those left behind can only wonder."

Emma's energy was bolstered when she, at last, saw her mother emerge from her room with a countenance of calm resignation; she no longer wept or trembled and walked towards the fire with the singular purpose of warming herself.

While boiling kettles of water to prepare Tobias' bath, Emma made a pot of Abigail's favourite tea. She set the tray in the dining room to prevent any sight of Tobias before he was able to remove his soiled clothes and wash.

"Would you like some sugar?" she asked her mother as she watched the thin stream of cream swirl into the tawny tonic.

"Do you remember the first morning after we arrived here?" Abigail asked as she observed every detail of the room through swollen eyes. Her voice was steady and measured, yet hoarse from the previous hour's sobs. She relented into distraction easily because she knew that the most respected members of the community were about to witness the outcome of an act so grievous that she had already expelled the image of it from her mind.

"You were enchanted by every nook of this house," she continued. "You endlessly questioned us about the previous owners, and even when we had nothing to reveal, you imagined the best for them and whatever venture they pursued."

Abigail ambled towards the small collection of books they brought with them from Kingston and clicked her fingers along the spines of each one. She stopped at Emma's copy of *Audubon's Birds* and pulled the heavy volume from the shelf and into her arms.

"This volume weighs as much as you did when you were born," she said as she laid it on the table with a gentle thud.

"I have not looked at this in years. Isn't it funny how something so treasured can be so easily forgotten?" Emma asked as they sat down with the book between them. "Papa used to sit with me nearly every night to learn about a new bird together."

"Which was his favourite?"

"He was fond of the bluebird. I always loved it for its bright blue feathers and tiny little beak. I never asked why he was so taken by it."

Abigail's drawn face cracked into a slight smile as she pushed the book closer to Emma.

"Might you find it for me?"

Emma leafed through the book that she knew by heart and stopped at the plate of the bluebird with its cobalt plumage and pretty peach shoulders. As Abigail observed its outstretched wings and swooping action, she suspected it was its itinerant nature that Charles most admired.

"Do you suppose the new owners will wonder about us when we are gone?" Abigail asked as she closed the book and ran her hand over the cover.

Emma reached for her mother's hand and clasped her cold fingers firmly.

"They will do as anyone would. They will think of the welfare of their own family and move forward with hope."

Chapter Thirty

Baxter's face was as pale as the lifeless body he had seen on the floor of The Prescott just moments before. He fought the urge to whip his ponies to a steady gallop, for although he was anxious to ease Abigail's pain in any way he could, he could not imagine how to confront the reverend and doctor with such desperate news. His carriage jostled along the moonlit road and had difficulty maintaining its course; he had neglected to light the headlamps and were it not for the impediment to his journey, he would have been satisfied to spend the rest of the night in darkness. There would be no light on the prairie until dawn, and he felt there would be no light in the Prescott home for many years to come.

As he rounded the bend of Bowlea Lake and made the final ascent, he could not discharge from his mind the image of Abigail's skirt streaking through the crimson pool like a pendulum at her feet; it swayed as though it sought equilibrium and a return to the normalcy that was so suddenly lost. The stains blossomed like poppies and brought to mind the colour of

Madeline's night gown when he had knelt beside her drawn body and fought to revive her.

The notion of suicide was not foreign to Baxter, who once managed a railman who jumped from a trestle over an unfortunate night of poker and the loss of his life savings. It pained him that many on his crew cast the blame his way, for although he had swiftly denied the young man's request for an advance in pay, he had no knowledge of the extent of his debts or desperation. Now that the blame for a man's death was again at his feet, he could not escape his belief that he was solely responsible for it.

Baxter pulled up in front of The Carlisle and was about to step off the carriage when he heard a coyote's howl. Eagle Claw's song rang in his ears, but as he looked back towards The Prescott, he thought only of those left behind.

"We wondered at your whereabouts, sir," one of the stewards said upon his arrival. "You may not even have time for a change of clothes, as supper has already begun. Mr. Smythe thought it best to proceed without you."

"I need to speak with the Reverend Kerr and Dr. Benson, Alan. I will be in my office. See to it that they join me at once," he said as he hurried up the front steps.

"You wish for me to interrupt their supper, sir?"

"At once."

"Yes, sir. Right away," Alan said as he moved quickly into the dining hall.

Baxter's office was as cold and damp as the shame that shrouded his flesh and made his limbs tremble. He drew air in short, quick spurts, and forced his eyelids closed in an effort to steady the beating of his heart enough so he could take a full breath. As he waited for the gentlemen to arrive, he wondered if Charles had left anything for his family, or if he was counting on the kindness of the community to help see them through. A rap on the door caused him to jump and thwarted his efforts to regain calm.

"Yes."

Alan escorted the reverend and doctor into the room. Baxter squinted as he tried to focus on the blurry trio. Dr. Benson was alarmed by the pallor of his complexion and hurried over to his desk.

"Baxter! Are you unwell? Here, you must take a rest," the doctor said as he moved his new patient to the window chaise.

"Whatever is the matter, Mr. Carlisle?" Reverend Kerr asked as his voice strained with concern.

"Gentlemen, please sit down," Baxter said as he found his seat and took a moment for a drink of water.

"I apologize for taking you away from your supper," he stammered. "There has been an accident."

"An accident?" Reverend Kerr repeated.

"Are there injuries?" Dr. Benson asked as Baxter looked up from his folded hands and eyed them directly.

"It involves Mr. Prescott. He left earlier this evening to gather some things for an overnight stay. But," he paused. He took a deep breath to steady himself. "But it appears he chose to end his own life."

Reverend Kerr's mouth gaped open and in his attempt to speak all he could do was gasp.

"Whatever do you mean, Baxter?" Dr. Benson said, barely able to articulate what the reverend could not.

"He left his family here to enjoy the party and headed home. When he did not return, I offered to take the Prescotts back. None of us had in mind that his suicide was the cause of his delay, but when we came upon him in his study, the extent of his plan became clear." Baxter's stoic disposition was suddenly betrayed by emotion, and as he prepared to utter the final details of the situation, he closed his eyes to will the tears back in place. "He shot himself in the head."

"Lord have mercy," the reverend said as he downcast his eyes and instantly clasped his hands together in prayer.

"And what of Mrs. Prescott? Mrs. Boychuk?" Dr. Benson asked.

"I am sure Emma is tending to her mother's comfort and care. I doubt she has had much time to process what happened. Abigail is quite inconsolable."

"They are alone in the house of with the body?" Reverend Kerr asked.

"Mr. Boychuk is with them, but I feel it is imperative that you both go there as soon as possible."

"You mean for us to go on our own?" Reverend Kerr asked. "Surely it would be best if you came along."

"I have abandoned my guests long enough this evening, but the ladies are expecting you. Tobias can assist with the body."

"Did Mr. Prescott leave a note or anything behind? Does anyone know why he would do such a thing?" Dr. Benson asked.

"He seemed contented enough, though I did not know him well," Baxter said.

"If you take the lead, Benson, I will follow behind in my carriage. The ladies will be disappointed not to stay for the dance," Reverend Kerr said.

"They will understand as soon as they learn the gravity of the situation," Dr. Benson replied as he rose to his feet.

"I will provide carriages for your wives, who are welcome to stay until the very last dance. In consideration of Mrs. Prescott, I would appreciate if you both kept the details of this tragedy to a minimum. The news will spread soon enough."

"Yes, of course," Dr. Benson said. "You may be assured of our discretion."

"Ma'am," Tobias said softly as he entered the dining room with the two gentlemen treading cautiously behind. "The doctor and reverend are here."

Through weary eyes, Abigail searched their faces for a clue as to why Charles was no longer alive. In the doctor, she saw a genuine desire to ensure her welfare, while in the reverend she saw both shock and dismay for the grievous sin. She was cautious not to speak, for she feared her words would swiftly devolve into wails; Emma was obliged to respond on her behalf.

"Thank you for coming so quickly. Mr. Carlisle has told you of our situation," Emma said, struggling to find the right words to describe an event that would be so harshly judged by the community.

"Mrs. Prescott, Mrs. Boychuk, how hard this must be for you," the reverend said as he shuffled forward and offered a hand to each of them.

"Reverend Kerr?" Abigail asked with a softened voice and direct gaze that splintered through his skin. "Is it natural in times such as these to trust God's will?"

"One cannot rationalize such a sin. Even though he died by his own hand…" He struggled to articulate the gravity of the sin and finished his statement as he would a prayer, with folded hands and downcast eyes.

"Come now; you have both suffered a great shock. We need not speak of that now," Dr. Benson interjected. "The matter of most importance is Charles. May we see him?"

Emma rose from her seat with the intention of leading the party upstairs, but a cool hand on her forearm drew her back and allowed her mother to assume the position. Abigail moved through the lobby and up the stairs with rigid movements and an unblinking glare which caused the fellows to feel both apprehension and alarm. They followed her into the office and released a collective gasp at the sight of the dead body on the floor. Dr. Benson kneeled down next to the swaddled package and placed the back of his hand on Charles' yellowed brow.

"There is little doubt he is dead, doctor," Abigail said. "It is now the reverend's turn."

Chapter Thirty-One

The trains' schedules had been fixed for the past three months, with runs passing through both north and south each Wednesday and Saturday. While the steady stream of visitors offered Baxter an early assurance of success, it did little to assuage his feelings of shame and regret. Although he was contented by interactions with guests and staff, he most often longed for the intimacy and familiarity of Abigail's friendship. He knew their relationship would be slow to mend, and so made little effort to initiate contact.

A chance encounter with Emma near the café one day had prompted Baxter to offer her employment, but her hearty refusal further indicated that the bonds he once shared with the Prescott family were severely fractured. He would have offered Tobias work in his livery but thought better than to entice the only male remaining in the home to earn his living at The Carlisle.

As he waited in his office for his tea to arrive, he wondered at the state of the Prescott family's affairs and what measures they were taking to survive their new situation. From his side of the lake, nothing looked amiss other than the constant darkness within the second-floor study. The light used to shine in that window from dusk until the plover's first call at dawn. Baxter thought little of it at the time, attributing the canary glow to forgetfulness or an inability for the patriarch to sleep. Now that he allowed his own lamps to burn well into the night, he believed Charles' thoughts were most certainly consumed by worry for his family's welfare.

"Here you are, sir," the maid said as she placed the tea tray on his writing desk.

"Thank you, Julia," he said, unable to remove his eyes from the view across the lake.

"Will there be anything else, sir?"

"There is one thing. Have you happened to hear any news of the Prescotts?"

"It's such a sad tale, isn't it? I haven't heard much, sir, but my cousin used to be their chambermaid. She was let go right after…" She stopped her thought short and took a step back towards the door as if reacting to an imaginary boundary.

"Have you heard anything of the family? Are they hosting guests?"

"Charlotte only said that her mistress spent most of the day in her room, and when she did come out you could tell she'd been crying. When I heard that, I didn't think it would be right to ask any more questions. I don't know anything about their hotel, but if they were busy, they would have likely kept her on."

"Yes, quite right. Thank you, Julia, that will be all."

"Mrs. Sheffield made sure to include your favourite oat cookies. They should cheer your mood some."

As the latch clicked shut behind her, Baxter squinted his eyes in an attempt to make out Abigail's figure from amongst the shadows milling about the back porch. The time of day implied that the ladies were occupied with laundry. He sat back and remembered how beautiful she looked, even with a soiled apron and the damp curls that clung to her hairline. Even at her most humble, Baxter saw Abigail as an elegant entertainer who imbued each activity with grace and feeling.

In that moment, Baxter sat up in a start, dripping milky droplets of tea onto the breast of his vest. He had spent a good deal of time considering how best to take away the suffering of his dear friend and her family, and even considered giving her an annuity. He suspected that such an offer would be as readily refused as if he had offered her a position as a hotel laundress. As he took another sip from his fine china cup, he thought of an offer that was not only appropriate but difficult to decline.

Chapter Thirty-Two

The keys jangled in Abigail's apron pocket with the same hopeful melody as when they had hung from the belt loop of Charles' trousers. She had used the keys on the guest room doors, and followed the same ritual of inspection in each: lift under the mats and mattress, check under the bed, look under the washbasin in search of any tokens that may have been left behind. She rifled through the drawers with the pretense of searching for money but was instead searching for answers.

"Have you found anything?" Emma asked as she soothed baby Gail's colicky cries by stirring her midday porridge with one hand while cradling her bottom with the other.

"No, and I am starting to lose faith that I will."

Abigail sauntered over to the biscuit dough and plopped the sticky wad onto the floured countertop. Emma watched as her mother rolled out the delicate pastry with far more force than was required to yield a toothsome product. With each turn and pat, she saw the tension in her shoulders release. Abigail put her love and care into each meal she prepared and cooked as though Charles would still be there to wipe the crumbs from his moustache, and sop up the remnant bits of gravy with his last buttered biscuit. Emma stared at her mother's hands as she twisted the mason jar's lid through the spongy dough and tore each delicate round from the sheet. She laid them one-by-one on the tray and brushed them with egg wash to prepare them for intense heat and a reemergence as something completely new.

As Emma watched the thin coating of egg drip into small puddles around each piece, she was suddenly reminded of the bloody pools surrounding her father's dead body. When she closed her eyes to clear the image from her thoughts, she realized there may never be an appropriate time to speak of his suicide. The wind kicked up and thrust the back screen door open and cracked it hard against the exterior wall. The gunshot bang startled the women and caused baby Gail to whimper. Abigail hurried to secure the door before any black flies trespassed into the kitchen.

"What about Papa's office?"

"I have already looked, my love."

"But you have not set foot in the room since that night."

Abigail smeared a thin layer of bacon grease on the second baking tray and lifted a sticky round from the counter. She carefully laid it in the corner of the tray and followed with each successive circle until the sheet was full.

"When your father was removed from his office, I felt there were rooms enough elsewhere in this place never to have to enter that one again. But when it became my business to know the state of his affairs, I faced my fear of again entering his space. It was not until I opened each box, crate and safe that I became soberly aware of all that was absent."

"He left nothing behind?"

"I found a twenty-dollar note tucked into an envelope at the back of his ledger, and a tin with a few dollar bills and coins."

Emma set the baby in the high chair and removed the porridge pot from the fire. She portioned out a small dish for Gail, sweetening her serving with only a thin ribbon of molasses.

"Surely there is a will?" she asked as she moved to the oven and removed the tray of cooked biscuits.

"I have searched every place I can think of." Abigail took her place beside the baby and began to scoop small spoonfuls of the gruel into her tiny pink mouth. "The only options remaining are to pry up the floorboards or start digging holes in the dirt under the verandah."

***

Abigail had sent a letter to Josephine shortly after Charles' death. Although she was eloquent in relaying the torment of uncertainty surrounding her family's future, she neglected to reveal the most shocking detail. Despite her best efforts, she could not conjure the words nor force a spell upon her pen to make it write the truth; she was fortunate that decorum negated the need for a detailed account. Her friend responded with kindness, but her contrition was apparent; she was ashamed to have encouraged their resettlement so keenly. She lessened her guilt by atoning in the only manner she knew how. Although Josephine's was the sole letter she had received from Kingston, Abigail continued her thrice-weekly pilgrimage to Mrs. Winters' with the hope of receiving another ten-dollar note.

"Good afternoon, Mrs. Winters," Abigail said as the flat ting of the door's bell signalled her arrival. Despite the vast difference in their ages,

Mrs. Winters always held a caring regard for her well being, as evidenced by her kind enthusiasm.

"It looks like a bit of good news has come your way," she said as she reached into the mail cubby reserved for C. Prescott and retrieved a letter from its place. "It looks to be a letter from Mr. Carlisle. After all he has done for the people of Bowlea, you must feel honoured to be singled out."

"He is generous, indeed," Abigail said without the corresponding emotion behind it.

"I have heard talk that some of the young rail men plan to find work in the Edmonton collieries."

"Is that so?" she asked distractedly as she looked over the flourishes of Baxter's elegant hand.

"I hope Tobias doesn't have such notions. We would miss him far too much if he went away. We don't seem to get up to Edmonton at all."

"I have heard no such thing. He means to help run the hotel and raise his family in Bowlea. He is close to all of us, Doris. We will not let him go so far away."

"You best carry on with your letter, then. It always gives a boost of spirit when you discover someone is thinking of you." Mrs. Winters' eyes glinted with a gentle smile as she parted the thin cotton curtain and returned to her kitchen.

Abigail's brow furrowed as she examined the embossed "B.C." on the black wax seal and as she walked across the lane to the schoolyard, she wondered at the letter's contents.

"Would he offer an apology? Would he demand one from me?" she wondered as she took a seat on a stump under the flickering shade of a poplar tree.

She took a deep breath and cracked the seal.

Dear Mrs. Prescott,

I hope this letter finds you well. I understand the nature of your current circumstances and their effects on your finances, and so wish to offer you an opportunity.

Your skills in voice and the emotion with which you sing are unlike anything I have heard. I believe my guests will agree. I wish to offer you an engagement three times per week on the stage at The Carlisle. The performance times I have in mind are Fridays and Saturdays after supper and Sunday after tea.

The wage is on par with what you received from Mr. Smythe. I hope that will entice you to join the Carlisle family. I look forward to your reply.

B. Carlisle, Esq.

Abigail laid the letter in her lap and gently shook her head. He had written of the emotion she expressed through song, but his words showed nothing of the passion he had displayed in the only other piece of correspondence between them. Reading over his sentiments again, she wondered if he truly wanted her to perform or if he was merely seeking out a way to initiate contact.

When she returned home a short time later, she hurried over to the dusty stack of sheet music that sat atop the piano and leafed through until she found her favourite piece.

"Can you come to the piano, my love?" Abigail called out.

"What is it, Mama?" Emma asked as she hastened to join her. "I was just putting Gail down."

Abigail spread open the parchment leaf and laid it on the piano's rack as Emma stood at the bench. "Can you play this for me?"

"You mean for me to play a song? I have hardly played a note since Gail was born."

Abigail rocked back and forth on her heels like Emma had done as a child whenever she was bursting to reveal a secret.

"I received a letter today. I have been offered an engagement."

"From Mr. Smythe? How wonderful!" Emma said as she bounded forth to embrace her.

"It was not from Mr. Smythe, my love," Abigail said as she pulled away sheepishly. "It was from Mr. Carlisle."

"Mr. Carlisle?"

An uneasiness washed over Emma as she heard his name spoken for the first time since he had shared in the discovery of a most unforgettable incident. She had banished her good opinion of him to the furthest corner of her mind and thought of him only to consider the brutal circumstances of his own death, as though the cruel thoughts would somehow resurrect her father.

Abigail was far less certain where the blame should lay and spent many a night tossing and turning through each witnesses' version of the truth. Although it was only natural to lay part of the blame upon herself, she could not escape her conclusion that the fault lay chiefly with Charles.

"I have thought a great deal about something you said the night of your father's death. You said no one was to blame but him." Abigail set down the music and motioned for Emma to make room for her on the bench.

"I was shocked and upset, Mama. I was not in my right mind. How dare I lay the blame at his feet when Mr. Carlisle is so clearly at fault?"

"But your father knew of Mr. Carlisle's intentions all along."

"Then why did he not say so?"

"You may well ask the same question of us. People have different motivations for withholding the truth. We felt we were protecting him and saw little fault in our concealment. Perhaps Papa was reticent because he knew the true impact of Mr. Carlisle's business; it was not real if he did not acknowledge it."

"And what of Mr. Carlisle's motivation? You would think a businessman would solicit his venture at any opportunity. Why was he so secretive?"

Abigail paused for a moment as she felt a cold dew begin to form on the crest of her brow. She clenched her fists until her fingernails pinched her palms. She took a slow, deep breath to quell the emptiness in the well of her stomach.

"I believe he was protecting me."

"Protecting you? Whatever for?" Emma asked confusedly as she stood up from her seat and took a few steps back. Although she had witnessed their mutual fondness, she had never presumed an indiscretion between them.

"Mr. Carlisle and I were acquainted before he arrived in Bowlea," Abigail said, attempting to maintain Emma's steady gaze.

"Is he from Kingston?"

"Toronto. But our paths crossed during my residency at The Regent. We were introduced by Mr. Smythe and soon found we had a great deal in common."

Without playing a note, Abigail's fingers grazed the piano's keys as she recalled the melody that had played during their first and only dance.

"You must have known the torment I felt when your father was so often cold and distant. He never wilfully caused me harm, but it was no less hurtful and isolating. Days without conversation, weeks without contact, the feeling of being completely alone even when he stood right beside me."

"And then you met Mr. Carlisle."

"He happened to be there when I most needed someone. You must trust me when I say there was no impropriety. We danced, we talked, we laughed. My cheeks had not felt a genuine smile in months."

"If it was just talking, how did he happen to end up in Bowlea?"

"That was mere happenstance. I do not feel the need to explain beyond the fact that we formed a bond. When his letter arrived today, I thought perhaps he was seeking to rekindle our kinship. Instead, he means to offer me employment."

Emma turned away from her mother and walked over to where the family portraits hung on the opposite wall. Each image showed her family at a different stage in their former lives; a delicate oil commissioned by Mr. Danbury hung beside a series of tintype photographs taken at the fiftieth anniversary of his hotel. Her parents looked youthful, and she was still just a girl. Although they each wore a wide smile, their happiness was frozen in time.

"What has he offered?"

"Three performances per week at a rate of five dollars per show."

"Fifteen dollars per week?"

"You can see now that I cannot refuse. You and Tobias are capable of running things during those few hours away. I doubt we will ever have so many guests that you will notice my absence."

As Emma paced about the drawing room and contemplated the offer, she could not escape the memory of her father's words.

"Do you remember Papa saying that a man never fully knew his worth until he was left with nothing?"

"I recall him saying that a time or two," she said with a smirk.

"What better way to demonstrate your worth than to respond to Mr. Carlisle with an offer of your own?"

Chapter Thirty-Three

Abigail sent a note to request a meeting with Baxter as soon as her proposal was determined. Tobias escorted her to The Carlisle and set to occupy himself with a tour of the stables until he was needed for the return trip. Abigail stood on the terrace a moment to collect herself before adjusting the wide brim of her hat and walking confidently into the lobby. The train from Regina was due to pass through in less than an hour, and the grand entrance throbbed with energy; the outgoing guests prepared to board the train for Edmonton while hotel staff prepared to welcome the newcomers. Baxter's office door was shut, obliging Abigail to inquire at the front desk.

"Just give the door a good rap, madam," the clerk said. "He is expecting you."

She stood before the carved mahogany doors and waited for her heartbeat to steady its pace. Her anxiety felt no different than when she stood centre stage before a performance. The sound of her knock was muffled by the orchestra of footsteps resonating through the hall, and she wondered if a more forceful thump was in order. She stared down at the brass handles and held her breath as she waited for them to turn. The engraved initial of his surname swivelled counter-clockwise until it formed a "U", and in one smooth motion, the door opened wide.

Abigail invoked her training in the arts of elegance and poise, standing with her head held high and careful not to betray any sign of timidity. As Baxter came into view, she found herself unable to prevent the corners of her mouth from turning upwards.

"Mrs. Prescott, how do you do?" he asked as her pleasant expression worked to disarm him. Her eyes were soft and kind, and the tension in his back eased as her attitude signalled her amenability to his proposal and a gratefulness for the sorely needed source of income.

"Good day, Mr. Carlisle. I am quite well, thank you," she said, unaccustomed to such formality between them.

"Well then, I am glad to hear it. Come, take a seat."

Baxter's anxiety at their meeting dissipated further as the faint aroma of almonds seduced him as she moved before him to take the chair opposite his desk. He struggled to find words to begin the conversation and so made an offer of refreshment before his awkward segue.

"I have not yet had the opportunity to share my condolences with you. I am so sorry for your loss and for what you were forced to experience that night. While I cannot exactly compare the circumstances, please appreciate that I know the feelings that come with a sudden and shocking loss."

Abigail pursed her lips as she recalled Baxter's account of discovering Madeline's mauled body.

"It has been difficult, indeed," she said with a guarded tone that informed Baxter to consider her emotions and change the subject.

"You have no doubt had time to consider my offer," he said, taking his cue and removing a cigar from his silver case.

"I have. I must admit, it was a quite a surprise."

"I do not suppose to know your present situation, but I thought an extra income would be beneficial to you."

"I have known you to be kind and generous, if not entirely truthful," she said in a manner that caused Baxter to drop his gaze to the flakes of singed tobacco scattered beside the crystal ashtray.

"I do not blame you for feeling angry."

"I did feel anger, for a time. A feeling so deep inside of me that I could see no colour but red. Every memory was painted with the same hue, as though nothing could scrub them clean. I am embarrassed by how much I let those feelings consume me. It was nearly the end of spring before I could leave my bedroom."

"I had no idea," Baxter said as he looked up and met her gaze. He expected to see eyes welled with tears, but instead saw only her shy calmness and the twinkle that came to her eyes when she was bemused.

"You are not the only one who can keep a secret."

"The first news I heard of you was so desperate. I could not stand it. I knew I had to offer my support to you at once."

"Things were never so desperate that we could not manage. Necessity forced me to find creative solutions for our situation. Your offer presented me with one such remedy and had nothing whatever to do with stretching breakfast oats or washing linens without soap. It did, however, bring to mind the one matter that was of most concern to Charles."

"Which was?"

"The need for self-reliance."

"What do you have in mind?"

"As I see it, there is little hope of my property being successful as a boarding house. If one considers maintenance and staffing costs, coupled with the lack of lower-class visitors, there is no way for me to compete with your hotel."

"It would be difficult, indeed."

"If we were to clear out the dining room, there would be ample space to fit the piano and seating area. In the evenings after supper, your drivers would ferry guests to our stage where I would perform an assortment of songs. I would charge five dollars per person of which you would receive half. With such an arrangement, you would earn far more than if my shows were merely included in the price of their rooms."

"And you would maintain your independence."

Baxter sat in silence for a moment as he contemplated her proposition. As he twisted the thick hairs on his chin, he looked at her and smiled. He had known her to be strong-willed and determined and could not hide his pride for her innovative spirit.

"Not all employers are bad, Abigail," he said with a chuckle. "I believe I treat all of my staff with a certain level of fairness."

"I have no doubt that you would be a kind and just employer, but those are my terms and what I am prepared to offer."

"If we position it as a sort of day adventure, we could arrange for the carriages to take the parties for a tour around the lake, with your performance as the final destination."

"I could be ready by Saturday, I am sure of it," she said as her smile grew like a song's crescendo. She put her hand forward to secure the deal, but Baxter hesitated and extended his own just slightly out of reach.

"I have heard your terms, and am willing to accept the offer."

"Thank you, Baxter. I feel certain this arrangement will benefit us both."

"There is just one condition."

"Only one?"

"You must allow us to share experiences again as friends. This place means nothing if I can not marvel at its beauty with you. Our ventures will feel mundane if we cannot enjoy the eccentricities of the guests together."

"Such as the old woman in the lobby who hides behind layers of lace while her little spaniel nips at her heels?"

"Who spends more on one night of cards than most of my staff earn in six months."

The crow's feet grew around his eyes and put Abigail in mind of their first encounter at The Regent. As the pair shared in a laugh, she thought of the comfort it would bring her to again have him in her life. She took his hand and shook it firmly.

"I am amenable to those terms, Mr. Carlisle."

"Very good, Mrs. Prescott. My accountant will draft the contract and have it delivered to you in the morning."

Abigail left his office and walked around to the stables with a certainty and haste that intrigued Tobias as she approached.

"What did he say, ma'am?" he asked as she climbed aboard the carriage.

"Everything that needed to be said."

"Are you to work for Mr. Carlisle?"

"No, Toby. I am to work for myself."

Chapter Thirty-Four

The papers were delivered to Abigail the following afternoon; she reviewed the contract as Baxter's courier waited in the drawing room and signed without hesitation. With only five days until the launch of their new venture, there was no time to delay. It had been over a year since Abigail had performed, and even longer since Emma had practiced the piano. The dining tables were disassembled and moved into a storage room at the back of the house. The piano was rolled through the lobby and positioned at the back of the dining room which, despite its previous purpose, was steadily taking the shape of a proper society hall. The dressing and desk chairs were carried down from the guestrooms and any available seating from the Prescotts' personal quarters were arranged in rows of six down the full length of the room. Tobias affixed the drawing room drapes to the back wall with instructions from Abigail to overlay them with the sheers from her bedchamber; the effect offered a rose-coloured backdrop against which the ladies would perform. The cleaning and rearrangement of the main floor took less time than expected, allowing them three full days in which to rehearse. Abigail and Emma had discussed which of the songs to feature for opening night, but could not come to a consensus.

"Should you not perform your most difficult numbers on the first night, Mama? Do you not want them to leave here in awe of your talents?"

Emma sat down at the piano, and Abigail took her place beside it, smoothing her hand over the instrument's dark oak cabinet.

"I want to impress them, but I also want to ensure that all of the songs are properly rehearsed."

"Surely you can sing them all from memory."

"Yes, but what of your accompaniment?"

"I have played this instrument since I was a child and I will play through the numbness and pain until each one of these pieces is executed perfectly. You need not worry. I will not take anything away from the beauty of your voice. I feel confident, Mama."

Abigail met her daughter's eyes and marvelled at the countless times she had been obliged to lean on her for support. Emma had grown into a smart, sensible woman, and Abigail wondered how she would have navigated both the frontier and Charles' death without her.

"Do you remember when I used to sing to the birds at Shelby House?" Abigail asked, sifting through the stack of music. "You would plead with me to sing all day long."

"So many memories from that time have faded, but the sound of your voice remains. I always hoped to sing like you, but I never had the talent."

"You have many other accomplishments, my love. When we first arrived here, I thought it held so much promise, but I could not shake the feeling that we were dissected from our home. You have helped see me through so much, and have made this feel as much of a home as what we left behind in Kingston. Gail watches you and listens to you, and I know you will be as impactful to her life as you have been to mine."

As Emma ruminated on their special bond, she suddenly gasped and pulled the stack of music from her mother's hands.

"I know just the song, Mama. Why did I know think of it before? It will be perfection itself."

As Emma handed her the piece, Abigail scanned the title and smiled.

"*Sweet Thoughts of Home*."

Working to ensure that each of them had ample time to practice, Abigail left her daughter to rehearse on her own; the outbuildings would permit her to sing while allowing the baby to nap undisturbed. She shuttered the slatted stable door behind her and marched through the thick layer of straw covering the ground until she was standing directly in the middle of the small barn. She cleared her throat and began a shallow warm up, allowing her voice to steadily relax. As the notes rang out, tiny chirps and the flapping of wings drew her attention to the rafters where dozens of tiny finches huddled in the warm spaces of the hayloft. As her throat warmed, her tone and volume increased, and the barn birds began to sing along as they fluttered from beam to beam. She was amused by their accompaniment and continued to practice through their melodic interference.

When the weather was warm enough, the windows to Baxter's office were almost always open. With the amount of coal used to keep the hotel comfortable, he longed for the fresh prairie air. As he sat in his office that afternoon, he could hear Abigail's voice as it careened off the lake. He knew of no other songstress who could so move him with a simple melody and turn of phrase.

"Excuse me, sir, may I have a moment?" asked one of his bellmen who stood at the open door.

"Yes, Martin. What is it?"

"We are getting a number of inquiries about the music coming from town. The guests want to know who it is."

"Is that so? Their timing could not be better. Tell anyone interested to gather in the lobby. I have an announcement to make."

"Yes, sir, right away," Martin said as he tipped his hat and hurried away.

Baxter made his entrance shortly thereafter, moving through the crowd to situate himself behind the front desk. His expectations for an audience were exceeded tenfold as it appeared he was about to address the majority of his guests.

"Ladies and gentlemen. Thank you for gathering on such short notice. I understand there have been a number of inquiries regarding the melodies coming from across the lake. In celebration of Sunday's solstice, I will be hosting an entertainment this Saturday evening. Never have you heard a voice so sublime. After supper, our carriages will transport you on a tour of the lake, followed by a show at The Prescott."

"But who is she?" A young man called out over the hum of questions rising from the crowd.

"All shall be revealed on Saturday. Tickets will be available to purchase from this very desk tomorrow morning. Good day."

"Will any of the townsfolk get to see her?" a chambermaid asked as Baxter snaked back towards his sanctuary.

"Anyone with the fee in hand will be welcomed to the show. You may be standing room only, though, as this event is meant mainly for guests."

"How much is a ticket?"

"Five dollars a head."

"Five dollars! Heaven forbid! How can anyone afford five dollars for a show?"

"We have set the fee based upon who we expect to attend."

"I guess I'll have to settle for listening to the wind."

Chapter Thirty-Five

"What about this one?" Emma said with her head buried in the wardrobe as she sifted behind her father's old suits to retrieve her mother's peach dress. "You looked so lovely in this on Founder's Day."

Abigail stepped back a few paces to distance herself from the garment. Emma floated the dress into the air with a swoop of her arm; Abigail watched as it fluttered in delicate waves onto the surface of the quilt, falling into the last position she had seen it.

"It is by far the most exquisite dress you have."

"Yes," she muttered. "I will need some time on my own to decide, my love. It will give you time to try on my lavender gown."

As Emma closed the door behind her, Abigail remained standing at the foot of the bed. The light from the window was caught in the patterned prism of beads that extended from the delicate clusters along the hemline, feathering upwards to the bodice. She approached it carefully, touching it with her eyes before she had the strength to caress it with her fingertips. As she stepped closer, she was overcome with the memory of the day Charles took his life. The way her dress was positioned forced her to imagine Charles' suit as it had laid beside it, and its present place in Bowlea Cemetery.

"You once told me that you felt most at home with a hotel full of strangers," she said aloud as she studied the part of the sleeve where his own had wrapped around it. "We expect a full house tonight, but it will forever feel empty without you here."

Abigail stood at her window and watched the procession of carriages begin their descent towards town. One of the auburn curls from the pile atop her head had escaped and cascaded over her shoulder; she twisted it nervously around her finger as she watched the carriage headlamps bob against the black hills like lightning bugs.

"The first of the guests are just arriving, Mama," Emma said with a soft rap on the door frame. "Tobias will take their payment, and I will seat them. Once everyone is settled, I will come fetch you."

"That will do fine. Thank you, my love."

She turned to face the small mirror which hung above her vanity. The last month had taken more of a toll on her than she had realized, and the pocked black marks and tiny cracks of the glass could not hide the lines and age spots of her reflection. She was no longer the young idealist who willing accompanied a blindly ambitious man to Alberta's frontier. She was now charged with ensuring her family's survival and the legacy of her husband's namesake.

The noise from the dining room began to rise up through the halls. As the drone intensified, Abigail knew that any anxiety was wasted, for nothing would compare to the tension of performing at Red Deer's town hall. She took a deep breath and turned towards the door when she heard the summoning knock.

"Please tell me you are here to offer a tipple of whiskey," she said with a smile as Baxter leaned against the door frame. He brought forward his hand from behind his back, and produced not his flask, but a delicate wildflower corsage adorned with a pewter clasp.

"I thought it would add a sense of occasion if I were to escort and introduce you."

She moved in closer and allowed him to pin the ornament to her dress, just above her heart.

"Shall we?" he said, extending his bent elbow in her direction.

"Just a moment," she said, hesitating to take his arm. "I would very much like to thank you, Mr. Carlisle. I was never under the illusion that my voice would bring me anything but a few dollars and some minor praise, but when singing came to produce the lion's share of our income, a shadow was cast on Charles' failings. I am grateful that the residence of you and your crew allowed him to feel some degree of success."

"I am ashamed to admit that we stayed on longer than intended," he said as he felt the warmth rise in his cheeks. "It was my way of thanking you."

"Whatever for? I did little beyond what was included in your board unless you count a few extra cookies now and then."

"Your modesty does you credit, but you must know how our acquaintance has affected me. Before you entered my life, I was unsure if I would ever know intimacy again. I was joyless and empty, and I did not yet know how to find pleasure in a life without Maddie. It was not until I observed the joy you took in your surroundings, that I understood that intimacy could take many forms. I never paid much mind to the sound of rustling leaves or the call of the frogs from deep within the duckweed. I had never before felt the embrace of a sunrise or the kiss from a shooting star. You have fostered my relationship with mother nature. She has taken me into her bosom and made me feel at home at last."

She took Baxter's hand and gave it a firm squeeze. He could feel her energy pulse through his palm, matching the pace of his own heartbeat. He held her hand as they walked through the kitchen to the converted parlour, and laced it through is arm when decorum dictated that his duty as escort usurp his role as friend.

The audience was silenced at their first sight of Abigail. They craned their necks and turned in their seats as she walked down the centre aisle towards the makeshift stage.

"Good evening, and thank you all for coming. I trust your short journey was comfortable," Baxter said to cheers and chuckles from the crowd. "Never have I met with more kind and hospitable folks than the Prescotts. Beside me stands a remarkable talent with a remarkable spirit. She brings joy and comfort to all who know her and enchants all who are fortunate to hear her. Allow me to present Alberta's songstress, Mrs. Abigail Prescott."

Summer, 1905

Chapter Thirty-Six

Abigail opened the window of her bedchamber wide, allowing the morning breeze off the lake to rush over her skin and leave goose pimples in its wake. The rest of the house was still asleep, and she knew it would not be long before Gail's hungry cries would deny the household any additional rest. As she looked out to the other side of the lake, she could see the terrace lights dim as the lamps were snuffed. She wondered if Baxter's night had been as restless as hers.

The tobacco tin was stored under her bed overnight, as she had thought better of spoiling the evening by entering Charles' study to place it securely in the safe. She crouched down on her knees and felt for the jagged fabric of the canvas sack she had placed it in, digging to the farthest point of the corner to retrieve it. The container felt much heavier than when it held Charles' supply of tobacco, but when she opened the lid, the smell of its original purpose was imbued into each of the five dollar notes.

Every one of the sixty chairs had been occupied, and as she looked at her half of the night's take, she wondered if Charles had earned a hundred and fifty dollars in the whole of their residency in Bowlea. She counted off five dollars each for Emma and Tobias, guaranteeing them more income than they could earn most anywhere else. She carefully folded another of the bills and placed it in her old silk satchel as a promise for Gail's future dowry. The rest of the money she returned to the tin, knowing that the surplus would do well to make the main floor as welcoming to guests as The Carlisle. She was unsure if she would again welcome boarders, and was content with the thought of her husband's spirit being the only upstairs tenant.

Abigail knew the rest of the house would not be asleep for long and so rose with the stealth of a grassland pika and made her way out to the back steps with nary a sound. The morning dewdrops clung to the tall grasses and dampened her skirt as she marched towards the lake. The path was overgrown and neglected and not nearly as well-trod as it should have been by that time of year. As she stood on the shore, the water clapped against the rocks, enticing her to greet the day with a song.

As she began to sing, the small shorebirds around her fluttered up from the labyrinth of reeds and extended their wings to fly. Their tiny silhouettes dotted the honey sky. As she sang she floated to the clouds, a songbird among them.

About the Author

Lindsay Shayne is a writer from Edmonton, Alberta, Canada. She has her Bachelor of Arts in English and Creative Writing, and a Masters of Archival Studies. Born in the River City, she has travelled and worked extensively throughout Alberta and formed a bond with its nature, history, hotels and rails. Her family, the Toanes, were early settlers in central Alberta, and the inspiration for *Seven Springs*. She enjoys singing, walking the trestles in Mill Creek ravine, and riding the steam engine at Fort Edmonton Park.

Made in the USA
Columbia, SC
19 January 2018